Lily Herne ██████████ ██████ rwich,
UK, and ca██████████████████████████████ e. Her
interests include chainsaws, steampunk and cake. You can
follow her on Twitter at @Herne13 or friend her on Facebook

'H██████████
is slowly being ████████ ████████ ████ story lies in the lives
of the teen exiles, told with meticulous detail...Worthy to be ranked
among the likes of *Twilight* and *The Hunger Games*.'

The Times (South Africa)

'I don't know how to express how completely besotted I am with this
series . . . I've not adored a book so much for a long, long time. Go
buy yourself a copy – that's an order! In fact, write to me and I'll send
you a copy . . . my life seems to have become a mission to make sure
the world has read this book. It's worth the time and money – really,
honestly, truly.'

Guardian

'Fantastic! Teen-fighting zombie-fun. *The Hunger Games* meets *The
Walking Dead!*'

Lauren Beukes, author of *The Shining Girls*

'Enjoyably fresh pacey prose packed with cliff-hangers, and an
ensemble of diverse and likeable characters...political satire via a
pop-culture plot.'

SFX

'An emotional rollercoaster ride, sad, terrifying, funny and thought-
provoking all in one. The writing is fast-paced, easy to read and
engaging.'

Reader's Society of South Africa

Also by Lily Herne

Deadlands
Death of a Saint

THE ARMY OF THE LOST

LILY HERNE

Much-in-Little

Constable & Robinson Ltd.
55–56 Russell Square
London WC1B 4HP
www.constablerobinson.com

First published by Penguin Books (South Africa) (Pty) Ltd, 2013

First published in the UK by Much-in-Little,
an imprint of Constable & Robinson Ltd., 2014

A copy of the British Library Cataloguing in
Publication Data is available from the British Library

ISBN: 978-1-47211-194-4 (paperback)
ISBN: 978-1-47211-202-6 (ebook)

Part One
Welcome To Jozi

Tommy

Tommy hangs back while Mooki, Jess and the other newbies swarm out of the kombi and whoop their way towards the townhouse complex across the street. He waits until they've chucked their crowbars and shopping bags over the spiked metal gate, then heads in the opposite direction.

It's his fourth day out in the suburbs, and he's determined that this time he's going to come back with *something*. He rambles along the cracked pavement, pausing every so often to peer through the long-defunct electric fencing. The chances of spotting an unlocked security gate are slim – he's learnt from bitter experience that most of the houses will be locked up tighter than bank vaults – and the crowbar and skeleton keys in his bag are useless against tungsten burglar bars and reinforced glass.

He finally decides on a small single-storey cottage with crumbling stucco walls that's set back from the street. It's flanked by sprawling Tuscan wannabe-mansions, and Tommy reckons that it was probably the shabbiest residence in the area even before the dead took over Jozi. But that doesn't mean that breaking in is going to be a piece of cake. Even from here he can tell that its burglar bars are made of good-quality metal, and the porch's overhang has protected the front door from water and sun damage.

Relieved that Mooki and the others aren't around to see him, Tommy struggles over the fence, the baggy sweatshirt he always wears to mask his gut riding up. He lands clumsily in an overgrown garden buzzing with insects, the path smothered in moss and creepers. A garden gnome grins cheekily at him from its perch on the top step, and, remembering one of the tips he heard at runner camp, Tommy pushes it over with his foot, disturbing a nest of baby scorpions. There's a glint of metal in the circle of dust where the gnome sat – a key. *Score!* Barely able to believe his luck, he picks it up and wipes it on his jeans.

The lock is stiff but after Tommy's fiddled for a couple of minutes the door creaks open. Taking a deep breath, Tommy slips inside. 'Hello?' he finds himself saying, as if he expects an answer. He stills his breathing, listening for any sign that one of the dead might be trapped inside. There's the scratch and scrabble of mice or rats in the ceiling, but that's it. He's heard horror stories from experienced runners about opening bathroom or closet doors only to find a walking corpse rushing out like a rotting jack-in-the-box. He doesn't know how he'd react if he saw one right up close. He'd almost puked when the kombi pulled out of the parking lot on their first day of training. Even Mooki had been stunned into silence at the hideous sight of the surging sea of decaying bodies lurching around Sandtown's high walls, everyone fighting not to gag as the overpowering musty stench of the dead invaded the vehicle. It is one thing to hear their constant moaning – it's provided the soundtrack to eleven years of his life, after all –

4

but quite another to come face to face with the reality of empty eyeholes and decomposing flesh.

Using the gnome to prop the door open – it's gloomy inside; the ivy growing over the windows blocks out most of the natural light – he creeps further into the hallway, his feet clunking over the dusty wooden floor. The house stinks of rot and rodent pee, but the ceilings are high, so the odour isn't overwhelming. He peers into the first room that leads off the corridor, a lounge dominated by a huge flatscreen television and heavy wooden furniture. A flash of movement in a shadowy corner next to a cabinet catches his eye, and his heart leaps into his throat. Steeling himself to run, he inches forward. Oh, *gross*. One of the armchairs is alive with baby rats. He backs out, deciding to try the kitchen across the hall instead.

His old supervisor was always going on about how kitchens are usually the best bet for sourcing high-quality merchandise, but this one doesn't look too promising. There are two plates still smeared with the calcified remains of old food on the table in the centre of the room, along with a bottle of tomato sauce that's crawling with black mould. The chairs lie on their backs, as if they were pushed back in a hurry, and the sink is piled with dishes. His foot knocks against something – a dog's bowl, the name Teddy painted on the side. Goosebumps crawl up his arms. Tommy reckons that every house, every room, every shop probably tells its own story about the panicky minutes after the dead swarmed through the city, stories that he would prefer not to think about. He fights a powerful urge to flee out into the sunlight; he's come this far, he can't allow himself to get spooked.

Trying not to look too closely at the faded photographs still stuck to the kitchen cupboards (most seem to be of a dark-haired girl wearing thick black make-up and cradling a white terrier in her arms) he roots through the cupboard under the sink, ignoring the cockroaches that gush out onto the kitchen floor. He pulls out a bottle of bleach, a tub of caustic soda and a can of WD-40, one of the items on the list of most prized items. *Score again!*

Deciding to leave the lounge and its rat infestation till last, he wanders into the smaller of the two bedrooms. Its walls are painted dark purple, so it's even gloomier in here. The bed is covered in a moth-eaten duvet, spiderwebs loop from the light fixtures and the chest of drawers is littered with dried make-up tubes. There's a creepy poster of a skinny cavorting fellow on the wall above the bed, a wildly grinning pumpkin where its head should be, and Tommy wonders what sort of person would want to wake up with that staring back at her.

Simo, Tommy's handler, has ordered more plastic Transformers for his collection, but there are no toys in sight. There's a craze for iPods at the moment – the handlers like to fashion them into necklaces and tie them onto their clothing – so he rummages through the drawers just in case, feeling weird as he roots through bras and underwear. He grabs several pairs of stripy socks, then scans the small bookcase next to the bed, even though the last thing Simo wants is reading matter. Most of the paperbacks fall apart in his hands, their pages fragile lace – the moths and silverfish have done their worst – but on the bottom shelf he pulls out a comic book protected by a thick plastic cover. *The Ballad of Halo Jones*. Awesome. He takes it out into the hallway where the light is better, carefully removes it from its covering and flicks through it. If he gets the rest of his shopping done quick sticks he'll have time to read it before he's due back at the kombi.

Tommy's been so lost in *Halo Jones* that Mooki and Jess are almost on him before he notices them. For the last half-hour he's been chilling out on the front porch, enjoying the shade, and it's only when Mooki sing-songs, 'Hey, Piggy Piggy, guess who?' that he's snapped back to reality.

Stomach sinking like a stone, Tommy quickly shoves the comic book up under his sweatshirt to hide it, but it's too late to stash the rest of his haul.

'Check it out, Jess,' Mooki sneers, effortlessly vaulting over the gate, Jess close behind him. 'Little Piggy's found himself his own little sty.'

Jess giggles and flicks her glossy, straightened hair over her shoulder. Tommy may be sick with dread, but he doesn't miss the way her too-short T-shirt rides up, exposing her flat, brown stomach. He's got a bit of a crush on Jess, even though she can be a total bitch, but he's wary of Mooki. Mooki's as mean as a dog with a sore tooth.

'What do you want, Mooki?' Tommy says, fighting to keep the wobble out of his voice.

'"What do you want, Mooki?"' Mooki scoffs. 'What do you think, Piggy? What you got in the bag?'

'Not much. Just crap really,' Tommy says, knowing that even someone as dumb as Mooki will see right through him. He decides to try to diffuse the situation. 'How about you guys?' he asks, keeping his voice light. 'Get some good stuff?' He glances at Jess, willing her to help him out, but she's examining her nails, a cruel smile on her lips.

'Duh,' Mooki waves his empty bag in Tommy's face. 'Does it look like we got anything? Whole complex is locked up tight, and anyway, looked like there were JoJos inside.'

'It's *jujus*, dumb-ass,' Tommy says before he can stop himself. He's heard Mooki trying to use runner slang before, as if he's a swaggering old-timer instead of a newbie, and he always screws it up.

'What you say?' Mooki says, his tiny eyes flashing with malice.

'Nothing,' Tommy sighs, hating himself for being such a coward.

Mooki reaches behind Tommy's back and grabs the bulging rucksack. Tommy makes a half-hearted attempt to snatch it back, but he knows it's futile. He's no match for Mooki's bulk – Mooki's always bragging about how he's been able to get served in the shebeens since he was twelve. Mooki tips the bag upside down, and the tins and bottles clatter down the porch step. 'What's this crap?' Mooki says, kicking the plastic bottle of bleach.

Tommy shrugs, trying to act cool. 'All I could get. Told you there wasn't much.'

'Pathetic.' Mooki grins at Jess. 'Help yourself, Jessie.'

She curls her nose up at the tinned beans Tommy unearthed on his second swing through the kitchen, but picks out the WD-40 and the socks, as well as the antibacterial handwash, the toothbrushes and the hand cream he discovered in a bathroom cabinet. She squirts a glob of cream over her palms and wipes it slowly over her fingers, glancing slyly at Mooki as she does so. Mooki helps himself to the rest – the tinned goods, a Woolworths shirt still in its packaging that was in the wardrobe in the main bedroom, an old *You* magazine and a sealed tin of paraffin.

Tommy tells himself that they can take what they want – he can always go back inside the house and restock – but when Mooki picks up the half-full bottle of Pantene shampoo he feels his anxiety turn to anger. He was saving that for Olivia, looking forward to seeing her face when he pulled it out of his bag. He won't be able to replace it; it's the only bottle in the house.

He stands up and tries to grab it out of Mooki's hand. 'Give that back!'

Mooki smirks, holds it up out of his reach, tips the container upside down and squeezes. It makes a farting sound as the last drop finds its way out of the bottle. 'Oh look, Jess, sounds like Piggy's pooped his panties.'

Jess squeals with laughter, acting as if this is the wittiest thing she's ever heard, but Tommy only has eyes for Mooki. Maybe it's because he's been reading about a couple of hardass girls who don't take any crap, maybe it's because he doesn't want to look like a weakling in front of Jess, but before he really knows what he's doing Tommy shoves his palms against Mooki's chest.

Mooki stumbles back, the surprise in his eyes instantly flicking into spite. 'You're going to be sorry, you fat *pig!*'

Big mistake. Tommy makes a break for it, dodging to the left, but Mooki's too fast for him. He grabs the collar of Tommy's sweatshirt, yanks back hard, and Tommy trips over his own feet and lands heavily on his tailbone, a bolt of agony shooting up his spine and bringing tears to his eyes. He twists around onto his hands and knees and starts crawling away, knowing that he looks stupid and pathetic, but unable to stop himself. He feels Mooki's full weight landing on top of his back, squashing his stomach into the path's paving stones and winding him. 'Get off!' He wriggles and twists, but Mooki's way too heavy to shift.

'Pull his jeans off, Jess!' Mooki shouts.

Tommy struggles again, kicking his legs to make it as hard as he can for her, but the weight on his back restricts his movements, and he can only draw in shallow breaths. As the fight drains out of him Jess snakes her arms under his stomach – every inch of him mortified at the thought of her touching the spare tyre that hangs over his waistband. 'Eeeeew! He's all sweaty,' she shrieks as her fingers fumble at his belt. Then, dragging his shoes off his feet, she lugs the jeans down over his legs. Despite the paralysing humiliation, he's relieved that at least he's wearing a clean pair of boxers, but that doesn't stop the pressure from building up in his chest. He can feel the tears coming.

'Thanks, Piggy,' Mooki hisses in his ear. 'That was fun.' Then, suddenly, the weight is gone from his back and he can breathe again. He turns his head to see Jess skipping down the path, waving his jeans above her head like a flag, Mooki lumbering after her.

Tommy lets the tears roll down his cheeks, chest hitching with every sob. He stays where he is for several minutes, feeling the edge of the comic book digging into his chest, his heart thudding in his ears, the steady throb of his bruised tailbone. The sun beats down on the back of his bare legs and his insides feel like they've been scooped out and replaced with churned butter. How could he have been so stupid? He knew Mooki was planning on jumping him sooner or later and he should have been on his guard. But what he can't figure out is why Mooki decided to single him out as the runt of the litter in the first place. Tommy knows he's overweight and slow, but so's Kavish, and Kavish has specs and a lisp, which you'd think would make him even more of a target.

It's not the first time Tommy has been picked on of course – Sandtown is teeming with wannabe gangstas and tyrants – but sharp-eyed Olivia put an end to any bullying before it got too hectic. But he can't let her fight all his battles. He's fourteen now. He has to stand up for himself.

Still, at least he managed to keep the graphic novel out of Mooki's claws, and for that he's grateful.

The kombi's horn beeps out the five-minute warning. Bad enough that he has to go back home without anything to show for it, but he'd rather be pegged a runaway than return without his trousers.

Ignoring the pain at the base of his spine, Tommy retrieves the key from where he'd replaced it under the gnome and races back inside the house, bare feet sliding on the dusty floor. He heads straight for the main bedroom. Most of the clothes he'd checked out earlier were covered in black mould and stank something awful, but beggars can't be choosers. He digs through drawers, chucking garments all over the floor, ignoring the silverfish swarming over his fingers. The jeans and trousers all look way too small for him, but he finally unearths a pair of tracksuit pants with only a few holes in the knees. He shakes them out and pulls them on. They're slightly too tight over his thighs and the elastic waistband digs into his gut, but they'll have to do.

The horn beeps again. Last warning. There's no time to restock his bag.

Tommy scrambles out of the house, pausing to pick up his shoes and socks, pitches himself over the fence and hightails it towards the kombi. He's completely out of breath when he thumps up next to it, sweat dribbling down his face.

Ayanda – today's driver – peers dubiously at Tommy's bare feet. 'Where you been, man? You okay?'

Tommy nods, feeling Mooki's eyes burning into him.

Ayanda's eyes crinkle up in concern. 'You sure? What happened to your pants?'

Tommy feels a lump forming in his throat. He doesn't want to lie to Ayanda, but he knows he'll only make it worse for himself with Mooki if he squeals. 'I'm fine. Ripped my jeans on the fence as I was climbing over.'

Ayanda nods at the bag hanging limply over Tommy's shoulder. 'Didn't you find anything?'

Tommy shakes his head.

'Shame, man, Tommy. Hope you've got an understanding handler.'

Tommy doesn't want to think about Simo right now. He'll worry about that when the time comes. But in any case, it's not really Simo's reaction he's dreading. It's Olivia's. He knows she won't tell him off, but the disappointment in her eyes will slay him. He owes her his life, and this is how he repays her? By being the world's worst runner. *Awesome*. It's official. His life totally sucks.

'Nice pants, Fatty,' Mooki calls as Tommy climbs on board, and a gale of laughter follows him as he squeezes past the others. Tommy tries to catch Kavish's eye – they used to hang out in the old days – but Kavish's gaze slides away from his. Tommy doesn't blame him; he'd do the same if he were in Kavish's position.

The only empty seat is in the back, next to Jacob. No one likes to sit next to Jacob and even the supervisors treat him like he's contagious. Unlike the rest of the runners in the minibus, all of whom are newbies on probation, Jacob is an Outsider, apparently picked up from some place in the Eastern Cape. Rumour has it that Jacob's tried to flee Jozi three times and is on his last warning. No one knows how old he is or why he's been put in with the newbies, but judging by the lines around his eyes he has to be ancient – at least forty. Jacob huddles in his seat, mumbling to himself and tapping his dirty fingernails on the window. He stinks, stale sweat staining the air around him, but Tommy has to concede that he doesn't smell too sweet either – the raggedy tracksuit pants honk of mould and mildew. Tommy doesn't have a clue who Jacob's handler is, but suspects he or she is probably a low-level stallholder or trader. He can't see one of the amaKlevas – the super-rich, elite handlers – sponsoring such a high-risk runner. He has no idea why Jacob hasn't just been sent to join the honey wagon committee, the dumping ground for the Lefties who are too old, useless, mad or dangerous to run. You don't need to have your wits about you to empty Sandtown's septic tanks and dump the human waste out in the city, after all. Tommy glances at the floor and notices that Jacob's bag is full of shopping. Just great. Even a deranged runaway is a better runner than he is.

The minibus moves off, its front wheels jolting over the edge of the pavement as Ayanda executes a three-point turn. It won't take long to get back to Sandtown, worst luck. Now that the Outcasts are getting braver, and targeting the malls nearer to home, Jova's decided that for safety's sake newbie runners can only forage in the suburban warrens close to the Tri-Hotel area. Tommy almost hopes the Outcasts will strike – at least then he won't have to face Olivia's disappointment and Simo's whining.

Sitting back, Tommy tries to block out Mooki's voice. He's boasting again about how he's going to take the trials as soon as he's paid off his sponsorship, how he'll ace the test and be welcomed into the Army of the Left with open arms. Tommy hasn't told anyone – not even Olivia – that this is also his dream. He knows that the AOL's first wave is already at the army base, preparing to wage war on the dead, although Tommy isn't sure what sort of a war this will actually be. If you're a Leftie, the dead don't fight back.

The kombi nips through the streets, slowing occasionally

to manoeuvre around the rusting skeletons of long-abandoned vehicles and the occasional group of lurching dead. The anxious knot in Tommy's stomach tightens. The moans are increasing in volume – they're only minutes from home now – and he looks down at his hands so that he won't have to see the seething mass of the dead swarming around Sandtown's outskirts.

Ayanda presses the brake, pulls off the main road into a side street and beeps the horn. The reinforced gate shudders up and a couple of blues jog towards them, weapons at the ready in case any of the dead attempt to slip inside. They're given the all-clear, and the kombi slides into the dark concrete mouth of the parking lot. Flicking on the lights Ayanda guns the engine and the bus speeds through acres of empty parking garage, heading lower and lower, sweeping around the curving bends so fast that Tommy starts to feel dizzy.

Ayanda squeezes the kombi in between a honey wagon and a fuel truck and slaps the steering wheel. 'Everybody off! Catch yous tomorrow.'

Tommy gets wearily to his feet. All he wants to do is hole up in the room he shares with Olivia and baby Nomsa, lose himself again in the comic book and forget about Mooki, Jess and today's humiliation. He tries to formulate an excuse for why he's returning empty-handed, but can't come up with anything that Simo, or more importantly Simo's dad, will buy. At this rate he'll be as old as Jacob before he manages to pay off his sponsorship; his dream of joining the AOL is further out of his reach than ever.

'See you, Jacob,' he says.

Jacob peers up at him with rheumy eyes, then suddenly lunges forward and grasps Tommy's wrist.

Tommy yelps and looks around for help, but the seats

around him are empty. He doesn't want to fight back and provoke Jacob. He could well be unhinged enough to be dangerous. He decides his best course of action is politeness. 'Um ... Jacob? If you don't mind, please could you let me go?'

'Wait,' Jacob croaks. He thrusts his free hand into his bag and pulls out a yellow-and-green soccer shirt still wrapped in its plastic covering. 'Take this.'

Tommy feels his mouth hanging open stupidly. 'What? But ...'

'Take it,' Jacob says, sounding almost angry.

'Um ... Thank you.' Tommy opens his mouth to say something else – he doesn't know what – but Jacob drops his wrist and turns back to the window, humming to himself.

Tommy exits the kombi and follows the others towards the stairwell entrance. What just happened? He looks down at the shirt in his hand. Amazing. He's off the hook. It isn't a Transformer, sure, but at least he has something to show Simo and Olivia.

'Tommy!' the blue at the gate shouts, waving at him.

Tommy starts guiltily – the blues always make him feel guilty for some reason – then he recognises Molemo, who used to own the sleeping bay two curtains away from him and Olivia. Tommy hears a derisive snort of laughter – Mooki and Jess are looking over at him and pulling faces. 'Nice friends you got, Piggy,' Mooki spits at him, pushing rudely past Molemo and disappears into the stairwell.

'You doing okay, my friend?' Molemo asks, clapping him on the back.

'It's *so* good to see you too, Molemo,' Tommy says, overcompensating for Mooki's behaviour.

'Tell me, Tommy. How is Olivia doing?'

'She's good, thanks.'

Tommy suspects that Molemo's got a crush on Olivia, despite the fact that he has two wives. In fact, he's pretty sure *everyone* has a crush on Olivia, which is why he always feels uncomfortable when anyone asks him about her. It's not as if she's his actual mother – Tommy can't remember his real mom; he can't even call up the vaguest impression of her face – but Olivia's the closest thing to a parent he's ever known. He also suspects that Olivia is the reason he managed to secure such a wealthy handler in the first place. She'd insisted on accompanying him to his interview, and Simo's father, a giant of a man who's high up in the energy committee, hadn't been able to drag his eyes from her face. And since then Tommy's spied Simo's father hanging around in the corridor outside their room on a couple of occasions, and try as he might, he can't come up with a reason why a man of his standing would bother to walk all the way up to the staff quarters. He's rich enough to have a whole floor in the first third of the Hilton, after all.

'She like it in the new place?'

'Of course!' Tommy hesitates, Molemo might have secured one of the few permanent jobs in the Tri-Hotel area, but he is still stuck for life in Sandtown, whereas he and Olivia are now free of its noise and stench and over-populated corridors. Tommy doesn't want to rub his good fortune in Molemo's face. 'I mean … it's okay,' he says with a non-committal shrug.

Molemo leans closer. 'Hey, you hear?'

'Hear what?'

'Gonna be a market.'

'Today? But it's Tuesday, isn't it?'

'Ja. Special dispensation. The Army's found some more Outsiders.'

Tommy frowns. 'Seriously? I thought they weren't searching

any more? Not after what happened with the Outcasts.'

Molemo shrugs. 'Just repeating what I heard. Soon as my shift's over I'm going to head to the square, check them out.'

'You mean they're *sponsoring* them today?'

'Ja.'

'Wow. That's weird.'

'You going?'

Tommy shrugs. He knows that he should really head home as fast as possible – he doesn't want Olivia to worry – but if Molemo's right, and there is a market on today, then why shouldn't he go and check it out? It would only take a couple of hours, and he could always tell Olivia that Simo had sent him on an errand (although he loathes lying to her). The only Outsider Tommy has ever met is Jacob, and he wouldn't mind catching a glimpse of the fresh ones they've found.

Molemo steps back to give Tommy room to squeeze past him. 'Say hello to Olivia for me, nè?'

Waving goodbye to Molemo, Tommy starts to trudge up the concrete steps. Then he hesitates. Now that he's a runner he's at liberty to travel through the well-patrolled service corridors used by the handlers and their underlings, but he'll reach the square far quicker if he takes a short cut through the Archies, the lower tunnels that cut right under Sandtown. Olivia hates him using the Archies; they're notoriously dangerous, especially for a runner who may or may not be carrying goods that could be worth a fortune on the black market. The blues who patrol the Tri-Hotels' service tunnels and the main thoroughfares are scarce down there, so if he runs into any trouble he'll only have himself to blame. But now that he's got the shirt in his possession he's feeling lucky, and besides, he knows the labyrinthine tunnel network like the back of his hand. He shoves the shirt and comic book in his bag, pulls it over his shoulders and ties it across his chest so that it will be harder to snatch off his back.

Molemo is swapping gossip with one of the honey wagon crew, so it's easy for Tommy to tiptoe back down the stairs and slip past him without any fear that it will get back to Olivia. He heads deeper and deeper, feeling the hairs on his arms standing up as the temperature drops. The bored-looking blue seated on a cracked plastic chair at the bottom of the staircase shoots him a suspicious glance, but as she's there to prevent untouchables from sneaking upwards, and not the other way around, she waves him past without a word.

Stepping through the door Tommy pulls his sweatshirt up over his mouth to block out the stench of urine and mouldering concrete that rolls over him like a wave. The air down here is damp, the crumbling walls drip with green slime and he has to duck every so often to avoid being conked on the head by the kerosene lamps that hang from the curved roof, bathing everything in a sickly yellow glow. Hunched figures scurry past him, and he's forced to step over the bundles of rags that line the edges of the walkway. Family groups huddle in the gloom; wide-eyed children with dirty faces and naked torsos bob and weave between the passers-by, the offspring of the lowest of the low who can't even afford a bay in Sandtown and are forced to live in the service tunnels and old sewage pipes that stretch beneath the city.

Tommy keeps his head down, refusing to catch anyone's eye. Inyangas practicing their trade, their wares hidden in the shadows of the tunnel's recesses, screech at him to stop, but he hurries on.

'Yo! Boss! My friend, my friend!' A scabby old man grabs at his sleeve. Tommy shakes him off and increases his speed, but the old guy jogs at his side, the tops of his ripped takkies flapping like angry mouths. 'You want a runner, boss? Tell your parents I am good. Very fast. Don't eat much. Small, small appetite me. Tiny.'

'No thanks,' Tommy says, forced to slow his pace as the crowd thickens at an intersection.

'Please, boss, I'm a good Leftie. Ask anyone, they'll tell you.' The man pulls up his sleeve, showing off a seeping wound on his forearm. 'Look, boss, I got proof. Got the tattoo. Regular Leftie, me.'

Tommy hesitates and takes a closer look at the mark on the man's arm. The tattoo is clearly home-made – he must have sliced into his own skin with a razor blade, then smeared the cuts with cheap ink. It's weeping with yellow pus, and it looks more like a tree than the outline of a left hand.

Tommy realises that the guy's a faker, the first one he's ever encountered. Without saying a word he rolls up his own sleeve, showing off his legitimate tattoo. It hadn't hurt as much as he thought it would and, thanks to Olivia's insistence on covering it with plastic wrap, it had healed within days. The old man grunts and takes a step back. 'Sorry, boss, sorry. You won't do a Benni on me will you, boss? You won't tell the blues, boss?'

Tommy knows it's his duty to report this guy, but what would be the point? There's no way anyone is going to sponsor him, so there's no chance he'll put anyone in danger. Tommy can't imagine feeling so desperate to survive or leave Sandtown that he'd lie about being left-handed. Tommy's heard the horror stories, heard about the runners who had innocently set off into the city, unaware that one of their number actually wasn't what he or she claimed to be.

'I won't say anything,' Tommy says.

'Thank you, boss. Thank you. You spare me a few browns

for a cup of rooibos?' His eyes skate greedily over Tommy's bag.

'Sorry,' Tommy says, diving into the crowd before the guy can accost him again.

Drifting along with the horde, Tommy allows himself to be funnelled through one of the doorways that leads into the heart of Sandtown itself. News travels fast, and everyone seems to have decided to jack work in for the day and head to Mandela Square. Cooking smells fight with each other – curry and roasting meat and boiled samp – and he catches a whiff of the fertiliser from the open-air vegetable plots on the first floor. The air is filled with the noise of screaming babies, laughter and shouted conversations, and he spots a couple of men arguing over a plastic bottle of pineapple beer in one of the bays next to the escalators. He briefly considers heading down to the floor below and checking out his and Olivia's old bay, but decides against it. A month ago, after he passed the test, Tommy was delirious with excitement at the thought of escaping Sandtown's constant noise, odours and the ever-present spectre of disease. Their new room on the Hilton's staff level is small, sure, but it's a vast improvement on the tiny space they shared with three other families, a filthy curtain the only concession to privacy. And the Tri-Hotels has the unimaginable luxury of running water, which, after years of queuing at the pump for hours every morning, still gives him a thrill. So Tommy's surprised by the jab of nostalgia and homesickness he feels for Sandtown's hustle and bustle.

The crowd streams into another narrow stairwell, coming to a standstill as a bottleneck forms at the top. Elbows poke into Tommy's sides, the people around him chatting and laughing good-naturedly, waiting patiently for their turn. Then, suddenly, he's moving again; the mass of bodies surges forwards and he's popped like a cork out into bright sunlight.

He's never seen the square so busy – not even on Freedom Day. It's teeming with Sandtown's dentists, hawkers, stallholders, doctors, muti-sellers, sangomas, tarot readers, hairdressers, leg-waxers and musicians, all taking advantage of a bonus day to hawk their wares.

A group of sweating blues is busily keeping the handlers' area next to the auction platform free from riff-raff, and Tommy shields his eyes and glances at the Nelson Mandela statue next to them. Olivia is always going on about how the real man was a genuine hero, but when Tommy was a kid the statue had featured in most of his nightmares. He'd endured months of night terrors as it came to life and chased him through Sandtown's tunnels and aisles. He suspects it's because there's something weird about the statue's proportions – he's never been able to figure out if its arms are too short or its head is too big for its body.

Tommy pushes through the crowd and finds himself a shady spot next to a stall selling a meagre selection of second-hand books, most of their covers ripped and tattered. The bookseller, an elderly woman with skin as dark and shiny as polished boot leather, smiles at him, mistaking him for a prospective customer.

Ahead he can just about make out two elderly men who have climbed up onto the platform: probably a couple of Lefties taking the opportunity to hawk themselves and convince the crowd to sponsor them. They both start speaking at once, much of their spiel swallowed by the cries of the hawkers and the screams of fighting children. One of them, a guy so wrinkled he looks like a naartjie left out in the sun for a week, is rambling on about his year working for the energy committee, boasting about the hundreds of litres of diesel he collected for the city.

Tommy's sure he's lying. There's no way a fuel runner would ever have to sell himself in such a humiliating fashion. The other speaks way too fast in a mixture of Zulu, Afrikaans and English, but from what Tommy can make out he seems to be bragging about the time he found an intact shipment of Baby Soft toilet paper in a warehouse. Seconds later they're chased off the stage by a red-faced blue, and he loses sight of them as they're pushed into the crowd.

Tommy's starting to feel uncomfortable – the bookseller's figured out he isn't a buyer, and she's shooting irritated glances in his direction – so he decides to edge closer to the platform. He inches his way through the tightly packed bodies, cringing at the black looks thrown his way. Feeling only a twinge of guilt for using his status to get what he wants, he rolls up the sleeve on his left arm to reveal his tattoo, and the going gets easier as people melt back in reluctant respect.

He's only metres from the handlers' area when he realises his mistake.

Dammit. Simo and his father are sitting behind the velvet rope that separates the handlers' area from the rest of the square. He holds his breath, waiting for one of them to turn his head and catch him loitering, but they don't even glance at the commoners surrounding them. Fortunately, out here in the crowd of untouchables, Tommy is invisible.

The crowd parts again and an immensely fat man dressed in a white linen robe bobs towards the handlers' section, the attendants carrying his chair grunting under the strain of his weight. The man waves a white, feathered fan in front of his face, his bored expression accentuated by his hooded eyelids and downturned mouth. 'Who's that?' Tommy asks the woman next to him.

She clicks her tongue. 'Steven Coom, of course.'

Tommy whistles under his breath. The Outsiders must be something special if someone of Coom's status is attending the auction. As the head engineer of the energy committee Coom's even more powerful than Sindiwe, the Tri-Hotel's top administrator, or Jova, Commander-in-Chief of the Army of the Left. Coom's team of specialist runners is the stuff of legend – it's their job to scour the city's outskirts for the spare parts and fuel that keep the generators powered up. Only those from the very highest echelon of the AOL are chosen for this position; fuel running can be dangerous, especially now that the Outcasts are upping their game. But Tommy's heard stories about Coom – that he's capable of twisted acts of cruelty; that he's above the law; that you don't want to get on the wrong side of him. That despite his standing in society and the unprecedented luxuries and power his runners have access to, you don't actually want to be picked to be part of his team. Especially if you happen to be female.

Scattered applause ripples through the audience as Sindiwe approaches the platform. The gaudy pattern on her floor-length kaftan is so bright it hurts Tommy's eyes, and today the tresses of her long blonde wig are piled in a beehive that wobbles on top of her head. She flashes a toadying smile in the handlers' direction before acknowledging the horde below her with a curt nod. In contrast there's an ear-splitting roar as Jova steps up behind her, and Tommy cranes his neck to get a better view. Jova raises his clenched fist above his head, eliciting another barrage of deafening cheers, then pushes his glasses up his nose and looks down at his ever-present clipboard. Tommy has never spoken to Jova – doubts he'll ever get the chance – but every time he sees him he feels some kind of invisible kinship, as if he knows that they're meant to be friends. Jova's skinny, his bones as delicate as a girl's, but

23

Tommy can't imagine Jova ever allowing an idiot like Mooki to push him around. A tall guy wearing sunglasses, his arms covered in tattoos, climbs up gracefully next to him: Lucien – Jova's right-hand man.

'Welcome, good people,' Sindiwe says in her beautiful deep voice. 'Today, as you may have heard, we are to have a very special auction.' She beams down at the handlers again. 'Thanks to the good work done by the AOL' – she's forced to pause as the crowd cheers again – 'three new runners have been collected to help us fight the good fight! With time and training I am certain that they will add greatly to our ever-growing army, which will soon set us free!'

Tommy winces as the woman next to him screams joyfully in his ear. All around him people are chanting: 'Jova! Jova! Jova! Jova!'

Jova smiles modestly and waves a hand up and down as if to quieten the audience while Sindiwe stands rigidly, a fixed smile on her face. Gradually the chant dies away and finally Sindiwe opens her mouth to speak once more, but her words are cut off as the crowd roars again. Tommy's forced to stand on his tiptoes to see what's going on – everyone is straining to get a better look – and then there's a sudden hush as a group of blues hauls the Outsiders up onto the platform.

They're younger than Tommy was expecting. Not that much older than he is, in fact. A small pretty girl with a shaven head and a tall guy with long straight hair and ripped clothes are fighting the guards who are dragging them across the platform, resisting with every step. But Tommy can't drag his eyes away from the third Outsider, who towers over everyone else, a cloud of bright orange curls framing his sunburned face. He's leaning on a crutch, his head hanging down. Unlike the other two, who look like they're about to explode with fury, the ginger-haired guy looks defeated – a felled giant.

Without looking up from his clipboard, Jova raises a finger and Sindiwe scurries over to him. They share a brief whispered conversation, then Sindiwe barks an order to one of the blues holding the dark-haired guy. The blue nods, and he and his partner start manhandling the Outsider off the stage.

'Where are they taking him?' Tommy asks his neighbour.

She shrugs. 'I have no idea, my boy. Perhaps straight to the training camps.'

Impossible, Tommy thinks. Lefties always start off as runners – they have to prove their worth and trustworthiness before they're allowed to take the trials, everyone knows that. So what's so special about this guy?

Sindiwe holds up her arms for silence. 'Who will give me a hundred for the girl?'

Tommy watches the handlers carefully, sees Coom run his tongue around his lips before languidly raising a hand. One of his attendants dabs at his master's sweaty face with a handkerchief, but Coom bats him away impatiently. 'A thousand!' he calls.

There's a stunned silence, followed by a collective gasp which turns into a rumble as everyone talks among themselves. A thousand rand as a first bid is unheard of – the girl will have to work for years to pay that back. Even Jova looks up from his clipboard in surprise. And as he does Tommy sees Lucien whirl on him, shaking his head and shouting something, his words lost in the crowd's excited babbling. He prods Jova in the chest, but Jova shakes his head and shrugs. For a second, Tommy is certain that Lucien is about to hit him, but then he turns on his heel, jumps down from the platform and stalks away.

'I have a thousand!' Sindiwe says, struggling to regain her composure. 'Do I hear more?'

'No chance,' the woman next to Tommy says. 'No one would dare bid against that bastard, even if they did have the bob.'

Tommy feels a wash of pity for the girl. If the stories about Coom are true, no one deserves that fate.

But she's not going to go easily. She arches her back, twisting her body and kicking out at the two blues either side of her. The guard on her left is forced to pull her arm up behind her back to stop her lashing out at him, and the crowd laughs as she turns her head and spits in his face. As she's dragged off the platform he hears her scream: 'Ginger!' And this time the giant raises his shaggy head, blinking at the mob in front of him as if he's only just noticed it. But this revival is temporary and as the girl leaves the stage his head slumps forward once again.

Tommy feels a sharp pinch at the back of his neck and turns to see Mooki standing behind him. *Awesome.*

'What you doing here, Piggy?' Mooki asks. 'Shouldn't you be handing over all the stuff you collected today?'

'Get lost, Mooki,' Tommy says, feeling braver now that there are other people around.

Mooki wafts his hand in front of his nose. 'Smell that, Piggy?'

Tommy sighs. 'Smell what?'

'The crappy stink of the honey wagon calling you. All you're good for. Who wants a runner who's fat and slow and cries like a baby?'

'Screw you, Mooki.'

Mooki grins nastily and nods towards the red-headed guy. 'You're the one who's screwed, Piggy.'

Tommy opens his mouth to answer back, but the words stick in his throat as he sees Sindiwe bending down to shake Simo's dad's hand. Simo's grinning and jumping up and down in excitement, acting like a kid who's just been given a new toy.

'Looks like your handler just got himself an upgrade,' Mooki sneers.

Tommy's blood runs cold. He has no idea what this means for him, but whatever it is, it can't be good.

Lele

'Where are you taking me?'

I've lost count of the number of times I've asked the driver this question. I'm not expecting an answer, which is just as well, as I don't get one. He stares straight ahead, barely seems to be breathing. He's as bald as an egg, his scalp pitted with old lesions. His right ear is nothing but a hole framed by shiny scar tissue.

He swings the golf cart into another tunnel that stinks of human waste and mould. This one is as dark as the last, and as we hum along, the headlights bob over faded graffiti sprayed on the brick walls. I catch the words: 'i luv u zombimama' and 'danger gevaar oh shit'. Most of the tunnels are ancient, their curved brick walls stained and mossy; others look as if they've been recently constructed, their sides bolstered with wooden and metal struts. Every so often, One Ear's forced to manoeuvre the cart around small rockfalls and piles of crumbled brick. Part of me hopes the ceiling will fall in on us; at least then I won't have to face whatever they've got planned for me.

A blip of condensation drops onto my scalp and dribbles down my cheek. There's no way I can wipe it off: I'm trussed up like a goat, my wrists bound behind my back with cable ties that bite into my skin, my ankles similarly shackled. I've barely slept since the crash, and it would be so easy just to give up, let them do whatever they've got planned for me without putting up any resistance. The tendrils lurking in my veins have done their job and the wound in my thigh is healing, but the rest of me throbs as if I'm one big bruise – a dull pain that's radiating from deep within my chest. Besides, even if I did have the energy to lash out at One Ear, there's a pistol holstered at his hip. I may heal unnaturally fast and Hester may have taught me to handle myself in a fight, but I'm not a superhero. I'm not bulletproof.

'*Please* tell me where we're going.' It hurts to beg, but it's even worse not speaking. Because if I'm not fighting or shouting or struggling to get free, then all I've got are my thoughts, and now the disbelief and shock has worn off, they're becoming dangerous.

It's the images of Saint and Ember that are the most malignant. At least I know Ash and Ginger are alive, although I'm not sure 'alive' really describes what Ginger is now. The guy who was once able to put a positive spin on a zombie apocalypse has been reduced to a mumbling, humourless wreck. As we stood on that stage, being auctioned off like cattle or sheep, he barely seemed to be aware of what was happening. And what of Ember? Is she even alive? Lucien and his crew made sure we were restrained separately in the bus that brought us from the crash site to this hellhole, and the last time I saw her she was unconscious, lying prone on the back seat, her lips taking on a greyish hue.

And Saint ... I'd allowed Lucien to drag me away from her

after she opened her eyes. She wasn't on the bus. They'd left her behind on the tarmac as if she was nothing more than a bag of garbage, along with Bambi, Ginger's adopted hyena cub.

Why hadn't I fought harder for her? Why had I allowed myself to be carted away? I know I was anaesthetised with shock but that's no excuse. Because *she* would have fought for me. And this is the worst thought of all.

A blast of cold air chills my face and I realise my cheeks are soaked with tears.

One Ear twists his head in my direction and sighs. 'I'm taking you to Mr Coom.'

So he's not made of stone, after all. 'Who the hell is Mr Coom?' I was too busy fighting to take note of everyone around me, but I do remember a whale of a man being hoisted above the crowd. 'Please tell me he's not that fat pig wearing a dress.'

One Ear grunts. 'You don't want anyone to hear you saying things like that, girl. He's the most powerful person in the city.'

'I thought Jova was the most powerful person in Johannesburg?' As well as the most snake-like. I can't believe he used to be best friends with Ash, along with Lucien, our betrayer deluxe. What a threesome. Maybe they deserve each other – I don't recall Ash doing a whole lot to help Saint, either. 'What does this Coom want with me?'

'Just do as you're told, girl,' One Ear says. 'You'll be okay.'

'That's not an answer.'

One Ear shrugs. I need to keep him talking – it keeps the sorrow monster at bay. 'Why doesn't Coom live back in that craphole with everyone else?'

'He's got his own place.'

'Where?'

'You'll see.' Another non-answer. Not that it matters

anyway – I don't have a clue about this city's layout. From the little I've seen of it, Johannesburg isn't anywhere near as devastated as Cape Town, and the survivors we've encountered so far are holed up in a shopping mall of all places. A mall that was once high-end, judging by the open piazza, huge statues and the ornate architecture of the buildings surrounding it. The old Ginger – the Ginger before the crash – wouldn't have been able to resist cracking jokes about this. How ironic, the Mall Rats captured by survivors who live like rats in a mall. Ha ha. *Hilarious*.

'And what about my friends? Ash, Ginger and Ember? Where have they been taken?'

He snorts. 'Ash, Ginger and Ember? What sort of names are those?'

'They're nicknames.'

'Look, girl. I don't know about your friends. But if they're like you they'll be fine.'

'Like me?'

'A Leftie,' he says, with a trace of bitterness. It strikes me to check if he's a southpaw. Doesn't look like it – his gun is slung on his right-hand side. I open my mouth to put him right, explain that the reason I'm immune to Rotter attack has nothing to do with being left-handed, but my old reluctance to blurt out my secret kicks in. Only … it's no longer a secret, is it? Ash must have seen the silvery tendrils knitting up the wound in my leg and the gash below his shoulder. He didn't see what I saw: Saint waking up after the accident, her brown eyes flooding with a flat sickening darkness, but he's not stupid, he must have put two and two together. He must know what we are by now.

'Listen. I'm really scared.' I put on my best little-girl-lost voice. 'There's no chance you can just let me go, is there?'

'Why would I do that?'

'Because you're a good person. Because it's the right thing to do.' The tears are starting again. The little-girl-lost act is becoming real. 'One of my friends is badly hurt, I need to help her. I've never done anything to you. *Please*.'

'It's not going to happen.'

Anaemic light drifts out of a tunnel on our left. One Ear turns into it, swings the wheel hard over and the cart's engine whines as he powers it up a narrow tarmac slope. I'm hit with the stench of dust and diesel fumes; we've entered what looks like the basement floor of a huge gloomy parking lot. The light is poor, but I can make out the hulks of several huge vehicles lurking in the shadows. We putter up another couple of sloping roadways, and One Ear draws to a stop in front of a metal door. The light is better in here, and a familiar moaning sound echoes in the distance – Rotters.

One Ear turns to look at me. His eyes are expressionless. 'I am going to cut you free now. Are you going to give me any trouble?'

'Would you shoot me if I did?'

'Yes.'

I believe him. 'Then I won't.' At least, not yet.

One Ear pulls a bowie knife out of his boot and slices through the rope binding my wrists to the back of the seat, but doesn't remove the cable ties keeping my arms shackled behind my back. His right hand resting on the butt of the gun, he leans down and frees my ankles. He stands back and gestures for me to step out of the cart. We stare at each other in silent assessment. I'm way shorter than him, but he doesn't relax his body language, clearly doesn't assume that just because I'm a girl and half his weight that I'm harmless. He's not stupid, which is good for him, bad for me.

He grabs my upper arm and drags me over to the door. Cigarette butts litter the floor next to a rusting ticket machine. What is this place? Does the parking lot feed another mall? The gaps between the concrete pillars on the far side are boarded up so I can't see outside, and the only indication that there's any life in this dump are the muffled moans of the Rotters.

One Ear presses an intercom box stuck on the wall next to the gate. 'It's Sihle.'

A crackle of static and then a tinny voice says: 'Code?'

'Land Rover One.'

There's the screech of a latch being drawn back, and the door swings open. A blonde woman peers out at us. She's wearing combat boots and a dark blue uniform, a faded SAPS badge on her shoulder. 'Howzit, Sihle,' she says. 'This her?'

'Obviously,' One Ear snaps.

The woman flinches. 'She's to be taken straight to the lower runners' clinic.'

One Ear bristles. 'Those aren't my orders. They checked her back in Sandtown. She's clean.'

As I'm grimed with dirt and dried blood, he must mean free from disease. A woman in a grubby white coat peered into the small windowless room into which I was shoved when we were first brought to the city, but she didn't do anything other than glance at me. I swore and spat at her, and she made a hasty exit.

'It's nothing to do with me, Sihle.' She's really squirming now. 'This came straight from Mr Coom. You know what he's like. Hey, is it true she's from Cape Town?'

One Ear glares at her and sighs. 'Come on,' he says to me. He drags me past the woman, who's forced to jump back smartly, and hauls me along a featureless corridor. Still, I reckon if I manage to ditch One Ear – aka Sihle – I could take her easily.

One Ear bangs his fist on a pair of heavy wooden doors at the end of the passageway, and they're hauled open by a guard who looks to be roughly my age, his round baby face at odds with his combat boots and the automatic weapon slung over his shoulder. He nods at One Ear, looks me up and down and scrunches his nose. Who does he think he is? It's not my fault I'm filthy.

'I know I stink, okay?' I spit in his face. 'But you know what? I can have a wash, whereas you'll always be a jerk.'

The guard blinks, steps back, and One Ear makes a grunting sound that could be laugh. He pushes me through the doors, and when I see what's behind them, I almost forget I'm in deep kak here.

We've emerged into a cobblestoned street, a *fake* street, lined with quaint colour-washed houses complete with peeling plaster, their balconies spewing plastic flowers. The garish buildings around me clearly once housed shops and restaurants – several still sport menu boards and colourful signage above their doors. Pointless windows look down on twee alcoves and courtyards. Above me there's a painted blue sky, complete with fluffy clouds. It immediately makes me think of the movie *Pinocchio*, my brother Jobe's favourite film when we were small – but there's an undercurrent of rot in the air, as well as the lingering trace of old smoke. Musak wafts in the background, that same kind of plinkety-plonk I remember hearing back at the mall in Cape Town.

Aware that I'm gawping like an idiot, I allow One Ear to lead me down a boulevard flanked by a row of bogus apartments dripping plastic ivy. 'What is this place?'

'Montecasino. In the old days people used to come here for fun.' There's something about the way he says this that implies there's not much of *that* to be had these days. He gestures towards a darkened area, where rows of silent slot machines lurk behind glass. This ghost town is quite a contrast to the heaving mass of humanity I saw at that marketplace. 'And Coom has this place to himself?'

'Ja. Coom, his bodyguards, his wives and his Lefties.'

I have to keep my wits about me. Try to figure out where the exits are, just in case I get a gap and manage to ditch One Ear. The sky morphs from baby blue to black, pinprick lights glittering across it. I'm beginning to feel hemmed in, claustrophobic; the air feels heavier. A couple of headscarfed women hauling a cleaning cart shuffle out of a phony Tuscan cottage. They pause to stare at me and I'm sure I can read pity in their eyes.

One Ear pauses outside a columned building, its plate glass windows smeared with white paint and the stencilled words: 'Lower Runner Clinic'.

He bangs his fist on the door, and an elderly man with shaking hands waves us into a stark white room. He peers at me as if I'm a thing, not a person. He stinks of tobacco and his teeth are stained. He wrinkles his nose, glances at my torn jeans and then addresses One Ear as if I don't exist: 'I will need to examine her thoroughly. Ensure there are no signs of tuberculosis, cholera or smallpox. Then take a blood sample, of course.' His eyes snap back to me and he gestures towards a screen in the corner of the room. 'Get undressed.'

'Forget it.'

The doctor blinks. 'Young lady, I am under orders from Mr Coom—'

'Coom can go screw himself. And so can you. You're not sticking a needle in me, and I'm not taking off my clothes.'

One Ear's lips twitch. 'Is that really necessary?' he says to the doctor.

The doctor sighs. 'The least I must do is check for signs of cholera and TB. If Coom wants her she'll get a thorough examination later on. If he doesn't ... well,' – the doctor coughs – 'it doesn't matter, does it?'

I don't like the sound of that.

One Ear looks at me, touches the gun on his belt. 'You going to behave?'

'Whatever.'

I pretend to be cowed, allowing the doctor to listen to my chest, and coughing when he asks. I even open my mouth to allow him to press a spatula on my tongue. He's rough, pushing my head to one side to check my ears.

'Hmmm,' He says, turning to fetch a syringe. 'Chest is clear but we must take a blood sample now.'

I wait for him to get close, then slam my knee up between his legs. The doctor yelps and drops to his knees. I lunge forward, but One Ear is quick, and I don't get far. I arch my back and try to slam my heel on his toes to escape his grip, but he twists my upper arms with such force the tendons in my shoulders feel as if they're about to snap.

'Okay, okay!'

'Get her out of here,' the doctor squeaks.

One Ear drags me back into the alleyway and shoves me forwards. 'That was stupid.'

'Yeah? What would you have done in my position?'

'Girl, if I could let you go, I would. I got my own issues to think about. If you run, I *will* stop you.'

And now he knows for sure that I'm willing to fight. *Way to go, Lele*. Saint is – *was* – always on my back about being too impulsive.

But would Saint have done any different? She was a fighter too. She wouldn't dream of backing down.

We pass more empty shops made to look like ancient vil... turn into another darkened alleyway, and then One Ear pushes me through a pair of glass doors and out into fresh air. The air outside is hot and dry but I'm grateful to be out of that bizarre environment. He leads me towards a huge courtyard ringed by yet more artfully aged fake buildings, one of which appears to be a bell tower. We're heading for a palatial monstrosity on the other side of the space – it has the look of a hotel or conference centre.

A small group of men and women with eyes as blank as One Ear's and guns at their hips are loitering outside the building's glass doors. I look down at my feet, feeling myself growing hot with so many eyes checking me out. One Ear barely acknowledges them, tightens his grip on my arm and drags me through the doors and into an opulent lobby, all marbled floors and glinting chandeliers. A small woman, twentyish with clipped hair and a nervous grin, rounds a corner and skitters towards us.

'I'm sorry I'm late,' she says, out of breath. 'I thought you were assigned to the clinic first.'

'She was,' One Ear says. 'Doctor Hlope was ... indisposed.' I catch what could be a twitch of amusement in his voice.

The skittish woman tries to smile at me. 'I'm Busi. I have been assigned to take care of you.'

'What do you mean, take care of me?'

'All of Mr Coom's guests are assigned personal carers, ma'am.'

'So that's what I am? A guest?'

The woman flutters again, glances at One Ear. 'Um ... that's what you are for now, yes.'

'Then if I'm a guest I'd like to get the hell out of here.'

'Behave yourself,' One Ear barks.

'Please, ma'am,' Busi says. 'This way.' She leads us to a stairwell stuck next to an empty reception desk. There's just enough room for me and One Ear to climb up the stairs side by side. I count four flights and my calf muscles are aching by the time we reach the top. A long corridor, lined with identical doors, stretches endlessly in front of us. My feet shush over striped carpeting, the pattern making my eyes swim. Busi bustles ahead of us, pauses in front of one of the doors and slides a card into a slot above the door handle. She gestures for me and One Ear to follow her inside.

Whoa.

The room makes the Resurrectionists' luxurious quarters back in Cape Town look like an outhouse: deep white carpeting, abstract artwork and a bed that could sleep four, its pillows smothered beneath a mountain of throw cushions. Enormous picture windows take up most of one wall, displaying a view of the bell tower opposite and the courtyard below.

One Ear cuts my wrists free. I scrub my hands over my face, then roll my shoulders to ease the ache in them.

'I'll be outside the door,' One Ear says to Busi. 'Any trouble, call me.' He jabs a finger in my face. 'There's no way out of here, except through me.'

I could take Busi easily – she's barely an inch taller than I am and just as skinny – but One Ear would be a challenge even for Ash. I fleetingly consider taking Busi hostage, but there's nothing in the room I could use as a weapon unless I decide to smother her with one of the cushions on the bed. Now that the adrenaline is ebbing, exhaustion creeps up on me. Even if there was a way out of this high-class prison, I'm not sure I've got the energy to fight any more.

Busi smiles nervously. 'I have run you a bath, ma'am. The

water should still be hot. And could you tell me your size so that I can pick out some clothes for you?'

'Stop calling me, ma'am. My name's Lele.'

'Sorry … Lele. Um … after you have bathed, Mr Coom is expecting you to join him for dinner.'

'And what if I refuse?'

'I'm … I don't …' She's really floundering now, and I decide to back down. It isn't this woman's fault I'm here. It's obvious she's just a pawn, nothing like the Resurrectionist guards back in Cape Town who seemed to enjoy flaunting their power and beating the crap out of us. And I'm pretty sure One Ear isn't like that either. He's definitely a badass, but he's no sadist. He did say he'd let me go if he could, didn't he? He's just doing his job.

But history's full of people who just did their jobs, isn't it?

Busi gestures towards the only other door in the room. 'The bathroom's through there.'

I poke my head inside it. Swanky, clean, mirrors everywhere. I jump as a skinny, filthy girl glares at me through bloodshot eyes. I look worse than I imagined. The whole side of my face is crusted with dried blood.

A round bath sits in the centre of the room, curls of steam rising above it. Hot water! When was the last time I had a good wash? Must have been back when we stayed the night in that prison, run by that crazy warden, in what's it called – Bloemfontein. There was no hot water there, of course, and the soap was dried and cracked. Saint and I had giggled together, joking that we looked worse than a bunch of Rotters as we did the best we could with a couple of old rags and a bucket of cold water.

I push the memory away.

'I will leave you now,' Busi says, closing the door softly behind her.

I pull off my clothes, kick them away. Even my mom's old army boots are a sore reminder of everything I've lost. My jeans are stiff with blood – *my* blood from the gash in my leg, which is now just a slightly puffy scar.

As my body slides into the water I'm aware of every ache, every strained muscle. I grab the soap, a pink perfumed bar that would have cost the earth back in Cape Town, and start the long process of trying to get clean. The dirt of the last few days has wormed its way into my pores and I have to scrub hard to remove it, the water becoming cloudy. I lie back and let it lap over my face. Close my eyes and concentrate on the throb of pressure in my ears. I hold my breath until my lungs scream for oxygen. What would happen if I didn't raise my head? If I let the water seep into my lungs, if I …

And then I'm back, right there, at the scene of the accident. The memory is so strong I can almost smell the nostril-burning stink of spilled diesel, hear the morning's birds and insects going about their business as if it was just an ordinary day. See the half-hidden shape of Saint's body lying in that culvert where she'd been thrown when Ember lost control of the bakkie. I would give anything to go back there now. Have one more chance to change things. One more chance to put it right.

The door clicks open.

'Hello, Lele.'

I know that accent. I know that voice.

Lucien.

Electric fury whips through me and I stand up, grab the edge of the bath, spring over its lip and launch myself at him. A low keening rockets out of my throat as I lash out blindly, forgetting my training, punching him, kicking him, all I care about is making him pay. He doesn't fight back at first, but he's forced to grab my wrists as I go for his eyes. I try to twist away, can hear myself sobbing, my chest ache aching with the force of it.

His eyes drop to my body – I've been so incensed I've forgotten I'm naked. I wrestle my hands free, grab a towel and wrap it around me.

As fast as it came upon me, the anger recedes, violent grief taking its place. The tears won't stop, and I double over and try to catch my breath. Gradually, my pulse slows, the pressure in my chest eases and I'm able to look him in the eye. 'What do you want, Lucien? Come to gloat? Well done for double-crossing us. You had us all fooled.'

'I needed to see you. To explain.'

'Explain what? How much did you get for us, Lucien? I hope it was worth it.' My fists are throbbing from where I slammed them into him. *Good.*

He sighs, wipes away the blood that's trickling from his nose. 'I tried to warn you – the last thing I wanted was for you to end up here … like this.' His eyes dance over my body again – how can he even think of checking me out at a time like this?

'You just left Saint lying there!'

'We could not take her with us.'

'Why not?'

'She is a Guardian now, Lele.'

'So?'

'There are no Guardians in Jozi. If I brought her back with us, she would have been …' He struggles for the right word. 'Destroyed.'

'What do you mean "destroyed"?'

41

'What I say. When we first reached the city, Jova and I and a group of survivors – the left-handed of course – went from settlement to settlement, wiping them out.'

'How did you kill them?'

'In the same way that the dead can be destroyed.' He attempts a smile. 'If you do not have a head, then how can you exist?'

I don't return his smile. He's not off the hook. But there *is* something I do want to know. 'How did you and Jova discover that the Rotters wouldn't attack left-handed people in the first place?' Despite myself, I'm interested. When Saint put two and two together and figured out that the reason Ginger and Ember were immune to Rotter attack was because they were both southpaws, Lucien had acted as incredulous as the rest of us. But he'd known all along, had been biding his time before luring us to Joburg to sell us to the highest bidder. The anger reignites, but I do my best to dampen it. I can't lose control again. I need answers.

'I think I told you that after we left Cape Town, Jova and I stayed in a village in the Eastern Cape.' I nod, gesture for him to get on with it. 'This is where Jova noticed the phenomenon. The people there, they had initiation ceremonies where the young boys of the village would be forced to stay out at night surrounded by the dead. Jova realised that the only ones who came back alive were left-handed. Like him.'

'So why didn't you come back to Cape Town to spread the news? Tell us that we could survive without the Guardians?'

'You know why we did not, Lele. Because we were branded as criminals, as terrorists. The Resurrectionists would not have listened to us.'

'Maybe not. But *we* would have listened. The ANZ would have listened.'

He shrugs. 'We did not know that for sure. And even the Anti-Zombian League had turned against us at that point.' He sighs. 'After the explosion.'

Yeah, I think bitterly. The explosion that had blown a hole in the enclave fence, causing scores of innocent people to be infected by Rotters. And all thanks to Jova, Lucien and Ash. Terrorists who caused more damage than those they were fighting against.

'But you're not left-handed, are you, Lucien? If you die ... then you'll become just like Saint – a Guardian.'

'*Oui*. That is correct.'

'So Jova *does* know what you are?' On the journey to Johannesburg, Lucien implied that Jova was unaware of the infection – a more intricate version of the white tendrils that keeps the Rotters animated – that lives inside a select few of us. An infection planted inside us by the Guardians when we were children for reasons known only to them. An infection that heals our wounds faster than is natural and will turn us into soulless automatons if we are mortally wounded. We'll become Guardians, the very things that caused the dead to rise and civilisation to implode eleven years ago. If we die, we become the enemy.

Lucien hesitates. Is he about to lie to me? I watch him carefully. '*Non*. But he is not stupid.'

'I thought you were friends.'

'We are not as close as we were. Remember I have spent much of my time travelling through the country looking for other survivors, other people who are left-handed.' Another one of those trademark Lucien shrugs. I don't know if I believe him. 'Lele. Jova has a plan that could change everything.'

'What plan?'

'He is creating an army. He is planning to wipe out the dead once and for all. Set the city free. And then, the rest of the country.'

I blink. I don't know how I feel about this. Isn't this what I've always wanted? A world where people would be free from the tyranny of the Rotters and their puppet masters, the Guardians? 'And you're not worried that the Guardians will try and stop you?'

'Like I say, there are no more Guardians in Jozi.'

'But there are in Cape Town.'

'That is a long way away, Lele. A different world.'

And there's no way the Resurrectionists would stand by and let those they worship get their heads lopped off. But I don't want to think about Cape Town. It only reminds me what I've left behind.

Jobe.

No. I need to shove those thoughts into a basement and lock them away. I'm vulnerable enough as it is and there's nothing I can do for my brother while I'm trapped in a city over a thousand kays away.

'So why not just *ask* us to join you, Lucien?'

'Because Jozi does not work like that, Lele. It is not only Jova who has the power. There are many variables. Coom, for example. The man to whom you have been sold.' I wince at this. *Sold*.

'Tell me about him.'

'Along with Jova, who has popular support, Coom has the power behind him. He controls the fuel in the city, he handpicks the strongest Lefties who keep the city's supplies running and maintain the infrastructure. He has his own army.'

'So why didn't he buy Ash?'

'Jova wanted Ash. As a compromise he allowed Coom to take you.' Lucien frowns.

44

'Okaaaay. So you're saying I have to go out into the city to find fuel or do maintenance or whatever.' Ha. That will give me plenty of opportunities to run.

'*Non*. I am certain that he has ... other plans for you, Lele.'

'What plans?'

'Coom has many wives. All of them are left-handed. All of them are immune to Rotter attack. It is possible, Lele, that he may wish for you to join their number.'

'But I'm not left-handed, am I?'

'*Oui*. That is true. But he does not know this. It is best that he does not.'

'Excellent. So let me get this straight ... I've been sold by you and Jova' – he opens his mouth to interrupt but I talk over him – 'to a perverted tyrant who has a thing for left-handed women.'

'I am sorry, Lele.'

'What if I say thanks but no thanks?'

Lucien doesn't respond.

'Why does he need so many wives?' But there can only be one answer to that – so that he can have a crapload of children. But being left-handed isn't genetic is it? Maybe it is. What would I know?

'Coom is a superstitious man,' Lucien says. 'I think he believes that if he is surrounded by those who are left-handed then he will be safe. I am sorry. If I could have stopped Coom taking you, then I would have done so. I tried, Lele.'

Not hard enough. 'And you and Jova just let him get away with this?'

'It is the lesser of many evils. Lele, I have seen what people can do to each other. I have seen real evil—'

'Yeah, yeah, whatever, Lucien. Far as I'm concerned you and Jova are evil personified. Get to the point.'

45

'I am saying that we know what Coom is capable of. He is useful. He is contained. He is powerful, *oui*, but at the moment he serves a purpose.'

'And Ginger? Has Ginger also been sold to the army?'

'I am not certain about Ginger, but do not worry about him. He will be taken care of. Ash has already been taken to Jova's training camp.'

'Training for what? How to be an asshole? Ash won't just follow Jova blindly, Lucien.'

'Do not be so sure, Lele. Remember, they know each other from the old days. There is history between them, and Jova can be persuasive.' The compact walkie-talkie on his hip crackles and he frowns down at it. 'I must go.'

He makes for the door.

'Wait! How's Ember?' How can I not have asked him this before? What kind of a friend am I?

He sighs. 'She is not good, Lele. She is in the Sandtown Clinic – for now.'

'What do you mean, "for now"?'

He sighs. 'I must go. I will come again soon.' His eyes flick once more to my bare legs, and then he's gone.

I pace up and down the room. I need to calm down, get my thoughts in order. Freaking out isn't going to help anyone.

There's a hesitant tap on the door and Busi pokes her head into the bathroom.

'Ma'am? Lele? I have placed your clothes out on the bed. It is almost time.'

I pad into the bedroom. A short silk dress, similar to the one I wore to the dance back at Malema High a million years ago, is draped over the coverlet. Is *everything* in this place going to remind me of the past? If it is, I'll have to grow a thicker skin or just curl up in a ball and let the despair take me.

Busi averts her eyes as I drop the towel, pull on the lacy underwear she's laid out for me and drag the dress over my head. It's slightly too big, but who cares? I ignore the fancy shoes wrapped in tissue paper, and retrieve my mom's old army boots from the bathroom floor. Busi glances at them dubiously.

'Busi? Are you also a prisoner like me?'

'You're not a prisoner.'

'What am I, then?'

'You're ...' I let her search for an answer for several seconds, before deciding to put her out of her misery. If I want to get out of here, I'm going to need allies.

'Never mind. Shall we go?'

She sags with relief. 'Yes. Please.' She knocks on the door and the lock disengages.

One Ear smirks when he sees me.

'What? You never seen a girl in a dress before?'

He grunts. 'You've really got a mouth on you, you know that?'

'I've been told that before.'

Busi hides a smile with her hand, then leads the way to the stairwell. I don't even consider making a run for it – One Ear isn't far behind me.

A delicious waft of roasting meat greets me as we emerge into the lobby. I'm sick with trepidation, but my stomach grumbles and saliva floods into my mouth. One Ear hangs back as Busi ushers me towards a dining room, etched glass windows sealing it off from the rest of the lobby. I hang back and peer through the glass – before I step into the lion's den I need to know what I'm dealing with. On the far side of the room, a row of chefs is busily chopping and frying and carving and serving behind a stainless-steel counter heaped with whole roast chickens and bowls of vegetables. My stomach growls again.

The table closest to the entrance is occupied by a bunch of tough-looking guys dressed in black combat gear. Two of them are wearing sunglasses and have matchsticks poking out of their mouths as if they're about to audition for one of the cheesy action movies Ginger used to lap up.

I nudge Busi, who's fidgeting anxiously next to me. 'Who are the idiots dressed in black?'

A sigh. 'Those are Coom's head runners.'

'You don't sound like you're a fan.'

'They take advantage,' she murmurs.

I recognise that doctor I floored earlier sitting at another table, between a woman wearing full sangoma gear and a thin-faced man in an ill-fitting suit.

Busi follows my gaze. 'Coom's doctors. Coom ... he is very particular about his health. After the cholera epidemic, he is almost paranoid.'

I point towards a larger table at which six or seven women are chatting and laughing. They range in age from a few years younger than me to a couple who look like they're my stepmother's age – forty or so.

'Don't tell me, those are his wives.'

Busi nods.

And sitting alone in a darkened corner of the room, the man himself. He's even more repulsive than I remember. His chins wobble as he shovels food into his mouth and his pale skin has a slight sheen to it, like the underbelly of a slug. A massive guy with a barrel chest and arms the size of hams stands a metre or so behind him.

'Lele,' Busi says. 'You must go in now.'

'Aren't you coming with me?'

'Lower-tier staff are not permitted in here. I will see you later.'

I straighten my back and stride into the room, doing my best to radiate a confidence I don't feel. I can sense the occupants of the tables staring at me as I pass, and there's a weighty hush as I slip past the wives' table. One of the wives – an older woman with no-nonsense cropped grey hair and smooth copper skin – attempts to catch my eye. I ignore her, just as I pretend not to notice the assessing glances of the jerks dressed in black.

Coom looks up as I approach, eyes glinting in doughy flesh.

'How lovely to meet you. Lele, isn't it?' His voice is plummy, sounds as if he's speaking through a mouth full of stones. I get the impression it's not his real voice, but an affectation. I ignore his outstretched hand. 'I am Steven Coom. I hope that eventually we will become very good friends. Please, sit.'

I'm in deep crap here, but my empty belly couldn't care less. I slump down next to him, and it's all I can do not to snatch the food off his plate and shove it into my mouth.

Coom inclines his head an inch to the right, and a waiter rushes towards us. He sweeps a plate in front of me. My favourite: roast chicken and mashed potatoes swimming in gravy.

'Please,' Coom says, 'Eat.'

I don't have the strength to resist, although what I should really do is pick up the plate and tip its contents into his lap. Ignoring the cutlery, I snatch up a chicken leg, hot with grease and gravy, and bite into it. I don't even taste the first few mouthfuls.

'Why, you're starving! Why didn't you say? Busi should have brought you some refreshments earlier.'

'It's not her fault,' I say with my mouth full, not caring as flecks of food pepper the pristine tablecloth. 'I wasn't feeling hungry back then. It was only when I smelled the food.'

When the chicken leg is picked free of flesh, I grab the fork next to my plate and shovel potato into my mouth.

My stomach cramps. I've eaten too quickly and I'm starting to feel nauseous. I glug back a gulp of water, push my plate away from me and let out a long loud belch. Coom doesn't react.

'I believe you gave Doctor Hlope some trouble earlier. It seems you have a belly full of fire.'

'A belly full of fire? Do you *want* me to throw up?'

Coom chuckles as if I've just made a joke instead of dissing him.

'So. What do you want from me, Mr Coom?'

'Steven, please.'

'Okay. What do you want from me, *Steven*?'

I wonder if he knows that Lucien came to see me earlier. I'm pretty sure he must. Coom doesn't look like the type of man who misses much.

'I have a proposition to put to you, Lele.'

I push my chair back and stand up. 'Whatever it is, no thanks. Appreciate the food, but I'll be going now.'

The thug lurking behind Coom's chair steps forward.

Coom's lips twitch. 'Please, sit.' I slump back down. 'I spent rather a large amount of money securing your services, and I'm afraid that if you left, I'll be out of pocket.'

'I'm not for sale. And neither are my friends.'

'Yes … that brings me to the subject of your friends, Lele. You see, you are in a prime position to help them.'

Here we go. 'What do you mean?'

'I believe there is one in particular who needs assistance. A girl with red hair.'

'Ember!'

'Is that her name? How pretty. I believe she is in a bad way.'

'I need to see her!'

'Yes, yes. Well, we shall see what we can do about that.' He waves a hand vaguely in the direction of the wives' table. 'Thembisa's sister is disabled, an old war wound. Finds it hard to get around the city. But I have made sure that she is well cared for. Thanks to my ... arrangement with Thembisa, her sister has secured a fine posting in the Tri-Hotels area.'

'And what sort of arrangement is that?' But I know what it is. Of course I do.

'If you agree to join yourself to me' – I can't help it, I shudder – 'I will see what I can do for your friend. I have the best medical staff in the city at my disposal.'

'So what you're saying is that if I agree to become one of your wives, then my friend will get proper medical care? If I don't, then you'll just let her die?'

'Think of it as a business arrangement.'

Ugh. How can all those women bear to have this giant slug slobbering all over them? 'You're disgusting. I'd rather die than marry a fat pig like you. You can't make me do anything.'

Coom chuckles again. 'No one is here against their will, Lele. I am not going to lock you in a room and rape you.' I blink at his directness. 'You are welcome to join my runners if you prefer. But it is dirty and sometimes dangerous work, and doesn't come with the same ... perks. The choice is yours. Think on it a while. I am not a monster, Lele.'

I can't count the number of times I've heard this. From Lucien, from the Resurrectionists. Even from my stepmother. Always the same phrase, *I am not a monster*. There's no difference between Coom and the Resurrectionists who lord it over the citizens back in Cape Town.

'There were men and women like you, *monsters* like you, back in Cape Town.'

'Oh, my dear,' he says, picking up his fork and spearing a piece of broccoli. 'There have *always* been men like me.'

Jack

3 July 2010

There's nothing remarkable about the boy. He's around Jack's age, seven or eight, stick-thin, plain and bespectacled, but Jack's eyes are drawn to him again and again. He's sitting cross-legged in the dirt, a small peaceful island in the chaos of the soccer stadium, apparently unaffected by the claustrophobic press of human bodies, the reek of raw sewage and the constant sobbing, muttered prayers and shouting as people fight for space and food.

It's the thing cradled in the boy's hands that has Jack so entranced: A Nintendo Game Boy. He can't believe the boy has managed to hold onto it for so long.

Jack has been trying to work up the courage to approach him, but the boy is so immersed in his own world, his fingers jabbing frantically over the Game Boy's buttons, it feels wrong to disturb him. And … what he's doing, it's not normal, is it? Jack doesn't think he's actually mad like some of the others, the ones he's learnt to avoid at all costs. Like the woman who snatched at his clothes in the water queue, screaming her son's name in his face, as if saying it loud enough would turn Jack into the child she lost. Or the men willing to fight to the death over a stick of biltong.

Worst of all are the silent ones – the ones who rock back and forth on their haunches, their unfocused eyes as glazed and unseeing as those of stuffed animals in a museum.

But Jack isn't the only one studying the boy. A stocky teenager in a filthy Bafana T-shirt is eyeing the Game Boy for very different reasons. It's like watching a lion stalking a gazelle. As the teenager approaches, Jack opens his mouth to shout a warning, but fading into the background has kept him alive so far and he decides to keep quiet and see what happens.

'Hand it over,' the teenager says in a nasal voice. He plucks the device from the boy's grip and frowns, stabbing his finger on the buttons before tossing it into the mud. 'Broken. What a freak.'

The boy stares up at him, face devoid of any emotion. He doesn't even make a sound of protest as the teenager snatches his satchel and upends it. Three books and an empty Energade bottle topple out, landing with a squelch in the mud.

The teenager stamps on a book, pressing it into the muck. Jack isn't sure what compels him – this isn't his fight, after all – but he's on his feet and running towards them before he can change his mind.

'Hey!' Jack shouts. A couple of adults glance at him but he knows they won't step in. It won't be the first time they've seen a fight break out.

Bafana scoffs, wipes his nose with the back of his hand. 'What the hell do you want?'

Jack feels his face growing hot. He's seen how bullies

54

operate at school. Knows that they are like the stray dogs that ghost around Lavender Hill, baring their teeth at passers-by, but skulking off, their tails between their legs, the moment you growl back at them.

He shoves at the solid wall of Bafana's chest. The teenager doesn't budge an inch, laughs in Jack's face and then flips a leg behind Jack's knees and trips him up. Jack loses his balance and falls back, his hands meeting mud as he flails to catch his weight.

'Nice try, laaitie,' the teenager sniggers. Jack waits for Bafana to turn his attention back to the boy before he kicks out, catching him hard between his legs – which is what his uncle Cyrus said to do if anyone ever tried to mess with him. Bafana groans and sinks to his knees, clutching himself. 'You little bastard.' Jack feels a flush of elation – he can't believe how effective that one strike has been.

Someone tugs at his collar and he turns to see the boy, the strap of his filthy satchel leaving a dark smear across his shirt. 'Let's move!'

And then they're running, kicking up mud and sludge as they dart through the packed mass, climbing over the barricades that separate the playing field from the stands and leaping over the mounds of sleeping people that clog up the dark tunnels and walkways. Before long the thrill of just running for the hell of it has them laughing between gasping breaths.

Jack follows the boy to a heavy door with a 'Staff Only' sign. The metal is buckled and dented as if the Hulk has been using it as a punching bag. He hesitates.

'It's safe. You can trust me.' The boy smiles up at him and Jack finds himself smiling back. 'This is where the hooded ones enter when they bring the food. I've seen it.'

Jack feels the delicious thrill of knowing he's doing something forbidden. It takes them a few hard shoves before the door opens onto a cordoned-off loading zone, empty but for several crushed cardboard boxes. A strong wire fence is the only thing separating them from an ocean of the dead. They surge around the fence, blindly clawing at it.

For a moment Jack imagines the linked steel buckling. The dead pouring through. Gnarled fingernails reaching for his eyes. He shoves the thought away. If he squints, he can almost fool himself into thinking they're just overenthusiastic soccer fans. Like the ones who jostled and cheered during the fan walk just days ago, chanting anthems at the top of their lungs. Some of them foreigners who had travelled thousands of miles to South Africa to support their World Cup favourites. But the dead aren't cheering.

And ... the sad moans floating towards him are strangely almost beautiful. Nothing like the exaggerated groans of the zombies in the movies he and Sasha used to watch when mom was at work. Like a morbid choir, each voice is different and yet in harmony with the others.

Jack finds himself searching their faces, hoping against hope that he won't see any hint of his twin's mismatched eyes or his mother's glossy black hair. Deep down he doesn't believe they're dead, even though he's searched for them endlessly in the stadium. He tells himself that he would know if Sasha was dead, that he'd feel it the way you flinch and laugh if someone tries to tickle you before their hands have even touched your skin.

'Thanks, by the way.'

Jack jumps, he's almost forgotten about the boy. 'No problem.'

'What's wrong with your eyes?'

Jack squirms, waits for the boy to make a joke about his mismatched irises: one brown, one grey. 'There's nothing wrong with my eyes. They're just different colours, that's all,' he says stiffly.

The boy nods. 'They're cool. Makes you unique.'

Jack shrugs, secretly pleased. He watches as the boy carefully wipes mud off the covers of the books. Jack isn't much of a reader; he's one of the few in his class still stuck on the grade two books. His twin sister Sasha's the exact opposite, devouring anything with pages put in front of her. 'The Game Boy was broken,' he says to the boy.

'Yes.'

'But you still played it?'

'It helps me think.' He packs the books back inside his satchel. 'Helps me escape, y'know?' Jack doesn't know but he nods anyway. 'What's your name?'

'Jack. You?'

The boy doesn't respond. Instead he bends down and picks up a small chunk of rubble, weighing it in his hand. He shoots Jack a slow smile then hurls it over the fence. It clips the side of a zombie's head.

Jack's mouth goes dry. 'Why did you do that?'

'Why not?'

'One rock won't make any difference. There's hundreds of them.'

He shrugs, 'Maybe, but it feels good.' He picks up another piece of rubble, offers it to Jack. 'Try it.' When Jack hesitates, the boy sighs. 'It isn't about the rock, Jack. It's about the feeling of fighting back.'

'Like the way you fought that guy back there?' Jack wants to snatch the words back as soon as they slip out but the boy grins in response.

Jack takes the stone. It's heavier than he expected and the rough edges dig into his palm. He stares at the crowd of the dead, searching for a target. He chooses one that reminds him of his grade one English teacher, the one who always made him feel like an idiot, calling him to read aloud even though he knew Jack stumbled over simple words. The zombie's face is furrowed and dusted with a half-hearted attempt at a beard, its sandy mop of hair lank and greasy. The skin missing from its cheeks gives it a permanent, leering grin.

It might be a trick of his imagination but those empty eyes seem to swing towards him. His arm trembles.

He bites his lip until he can taste blood. They aren't human. Not any more. He has to remember that. He throws the rock. It slices through the air and strikes his target right between the eyes. The thing reels back, arms clawing at the air to stay upright, and is lost from sight as the dead jostle to take its place at the fence.

The boy was right. Jack does feel better. He turns to see the boy watching him carefully.

'Jova.' The boy holds out his hand for Jack to shake. His grip is surprisingly strong and the gesture feels very important and grown-up to Jack. Like they're making some kind of pact. 'My name is Jova.'

Ash

I gasp, sit up, fight to catch my breath, and realise I'm drenched, icy rivulets trickling down the back of my neck.

'Rise and shine, Pretty Boy.'

A bulky figure looms over me and I catch a flash of white teeth set against dark skin. I blink water out of my eyes, shake my head, try to assess what the hell I'm dealing with here. The water that drips off my chin and plops to the ground is tinged with pink. Blood. My blood. I run my tongue over my teeth, checking they're intact, then roll my shoulders. There's a distant ache at the back of my skull which must be from the blow that knocked me out last night.

'Man, I thought you'd never wake up.'

I try to place his accent. It's not as broad as Ginger's, but it's foreign for sure. American maybe?

'Where am I?' My voice sounds hoarse.

'Your new home.'

'How did I get here?'

'Blues brought you here last night. You were out cold.'

He's holding an empty bucket in one hand – my wake-up call – and his face looks like it's been carved out of wood, all hard planes and unforgiving angles. Mid-thirties, possibly forties. I picture sweeping his legs out from under him, snatching the bucket and dashing a blow to the side of his head.

'You can try it,' he says, reading my mind. 'But you'll regret it.'

He's definitely not one of the guys who manhandled me through tunnels that stank of shit and death after Lele, Ginger and I were dragged in front of that jeering crowd. I fought every step of the way, but ended up being pistol-whipped when I elbowed one of my captors in the jaw. After that, the rest is a blank.

My head is starting to clear – the big guy might have done me a favour by sloshing that water over me after all. I glance around. I'm in a large, square room, unremarkable except for an inept mural of stick figures with bulbous heads painted on one wall. The floor is covered with sleeping bags and neat piles of belongings.

There's a burst of laughter and a chubby-faced boy and a couple of women hustle into the room. All are barefoot, towels slung over their shoulders.

'Shit man, the water was cold again,' a woman wrapped in a faded grey towel says. She's tall, her limbs long and lean, but there's something about her that immediately reminds me of Lele. Maybe it's the close-cropped hair.

'I could've warmed you up, Noxi,' the boy grins. He's barely into his teens, his face angry with acne.

'Screw you, Danny.'

'You wish.'

She chucks the towel at him, leaving her naked but for a pair of boxer shorts. Her skin is smooth and unblemished and she doesn't look away when she catches me staring at her. 'Heita, new guy,' she says to me. 'Welcome to the newbie dorm. We hope you enjoy your stay. Please under no circumstances feed or talk to Danny.' She pulls a T-shirt over her head.

'Ag, throw another bucket over him, Americano,' the kid says to the big guy. 'He stinks, bru.'

'That's yourself you're smelling, Danny,' the girl – Noxi – says.

Americano sticks a cigarette in his mouth and lights it.

A girl in a headscarf and an oversized T-shirt clucks her tongue. 'Do you *have* to smoke in here, Americano?'

Americano shrugs. 'We've been through this, Nuush. If I don't smoke I get ornery.'

'Don't you mean horny, bru?' the kid cackles.

Noxi sighs. 'You're so effing lame, Danny.'

Americano's sharp – he hasn't missed the way I'm staring at the cigarette. 'Here.' He chucks me the pack and a box of matches. 'Knock yourself out.'

I can't bring myself to smile at him but I manage a nod. I light up, pull the smoke into my lungs, and wait for the last of the fog in my head to clear. Americano grips my shoulder as I stagger to my feet. My first instinct is to lash out at him, then I realise he's helping to steady me. I shrug off his hand and make my way over to the room's only window. The frame is scorched black, a parting gift from an old fire.

I rub off a layer of grime and grease and stare out at an expanse of flat, brown landscape, wide empty roadways cutting through it in all directions. The shell of an ancient passenger plane, its windows cracked, its wings sheared off, lies on its side a few hundred metres from an immense hangar. An orderly row of men and women jog into my line of sight and funnel past it. And in the far distance, next to what has to be the perimeter fence, a herd of sheep and cows is grazing.

Enough sheep and cows to feed an army.

I turn to look at Americano. 'We're in an airport?'

'You're a smart one aren't you, bud?'

'I want to talk to Jova.'

Noxi looks me up and down. 'Ha. Listen to him. He wants to talk to Jova.'

Danny pipes up: 'Who else do you wanna see? Coom? God, maybe?'

'Lucien, then. Tell him I need to speak to him.'

Noxi sniffs. 'We're not your bitches. If Jova wanted to talk to you then he would be talking to you.'

A skinny girl ducks into the room, out of breath. 'All hands on deck, Captain Morgan spotted on the gangway.'

Everyone immediately stiffens. Americano stubs out his cigarette and waves a hand through the air as if he's trying to dispel the smoke.

A moment later the door opens and a tall dreadlocked guy, a leather patch covering one eye, steps into the room. With a jolt I realise that I'm actually looking at a woman. Her size and build may be as substantial as a man's, but her features are feminine, not beautiful exactly, but striking.

Her eye sweeps the room. 'There'd better be a good reason why you aren't ready yet.'

'He's awake, Morgan,' Americano barks.

She stares pointedly at the empty bucket on the ground. Americano tries and fails to hide his smile. 'Yes, I can see that,' she says.

'He asked to see Jova,' Noxi scoffs.

She swings that one-eyed stare in my direction. 'He might just get his wish.'

62

'You serious?' Noxi says.

The woman ignores her, continues to pin me with that intense gaze. 'I'm Morgan. We'll leave the rest of the introductions until later. I heard you put up quite a fight last night. Can you walk?'

'Yeah.'

'Then come with me.'

She exits the room without checking if I'm going to follow her.

'Well, go on, dude,' Danny says. 'You don't want to keep Morgan waiting.'

I crush the cigarette under my boot, duck out of the room and jog to catch up to her. 'Where are we going?'

'You wanted to see Jova, didn't you?'

She strides down a wide, tiled corridor, and sweeps around a corner. We emerge into a glass-roofed area filled with rows and rows of dusty waiting-room chairs. The windows to my right are cracked and scored with bullet-holes, but beyond them I can still make out the carcasses of several planes stuck forever next to passenger boarding tunnels, their tyres sagging, the logos on their tails faded.

Morgan leads me past a series of gutted shops, a single rack of vuvuzelas the only stock remaining. She waves me towards a glass-fronted lounge and I peer inside, taking in the comfortable-looking pallets and long leather recliners. Neat piles of clothing and boots are placed along one wall.

'If your team passes the trials you will be assigned a dorm like this. Until then you sleep in the newbies' dorm .'

'Trials?'

'A test. Don't worry, if you're as good as Jova seems to think you are, you shouldn't have a problem.'

I snort. 'I won't be taking any trials. I'm not planning on sticking around.'

'We'll see.' She halts at a tinted glass door flanked by a pair of hefty khaki-clad guys who shoot sideways glances at me. Morgan nods at them and gestures for me to enter.

I step into an empty room that smells faintly of ancient cigarette smoke. The walls are a sterile white, reflecting the weak light of two paraffin lamps. The plastic seats look like they've been designed to be deliberately uncomfortable. I'm about to ask Morgan what the hell we're doing in here when I spot the diminutive figure sitting in the corner of the room. He stands up, the poor light glinting off his glasses. 'Jack,' he says.

The rage is immediate and irresistible. I lunge towards him, grab his neck and shove him back with such force the back of his head makes an audible *thunk* as it connects with the wall. Morgan melts out of the shadows and springs towards me, but Jova raises a hand and she stops dead. For someone about to be throttled, he's frustratingly calm.

His pulse flutters against my palm and I tighten my grip. He chokes for breath and his eyes widen and bulge, but I can't detect any fear in them.

I could kill him right now if I wanted to.

And I *do* want to.

Sick to my stomach, I release my hold, rubbing my palms on my jeans to wipe off the lingering warmth of his skin.

He coughs, rubs his throat, sits down. 'I guess I deserved that.' He motions for me to take the seat opposite him. For a moment I consider refusing, but what would be the point? Minutes pass as we regard one another, and it occurs to me that Jova might not know what to say.

Finally he smiles. 'You haven't changed at all.'

'What do you want?'

'Do you still smoke?' He digs in his pocket, pulls out a pack of cigarettes and chucks it on the table. He's never smoked a day in his life, has always hated the habit, and I know he sees my addiction as one of my character flaws. One of many. That pack is one of his tests.

'No.'

'You always were stubborn.'

If he thinks I'm going to take a trip down memory lane with him he has another think coming. Jova smiles and taps his chin. His trimmed nails are spotless. Hester used to say you can never trust a man with clean hands; they always have something to hide.

I cling to that.

'I have something for you.' He slips a hand into his jacket and pulls out two pieces of paper.

A coldness washes through me. I'd recognise their dog-eared corners anywhere. He unfolds Hester's letter – the last thing she gave me – and sets it down on the table. 'Lucien told me Hester passed away.' His expression is carefully blank. 'I'm sorry.'

'No, you're not.'

He shrugs. 'We had our differences in the end, Jack. She knew and you knew that I couldn't continue to trade with the Resurrectionists. But for many years she was like a mother to me.'

'Bullshit.' I can imagine his triumph when reading Hester's admission that she'd been wrong. I know the words off by heart: *The others are out there somewhere. You must find them; you must ask them to come back and help stop this. Please, tell them that I know now that they were right. And tell them that I am sorry.*

It wasn't supposed to be like this. When we left Cape Town, I hadn't truly expected to find Lucien and Jova. And here I am, stabbed in the back by my oldest friends and allies. Even Hester wouldn't have seen that coming.

I want to snatch it back from him, not just her letter but also her apology. Jova doesn't deserve it.

He places the other piece of paper on top of the letter. 'Not bad. She has quite an eye for detail.'

I look down at the sketch – one of Lele's early drawings of the four of us. The Mall Rats. Somehow she managed to capture the vulnerability behind Ginger's incessant wisecracks, the softness hidden underneath Saint's no-nonsense exterior. I kept this sketch because it's one of the few she drew herself into. The warped self-portrait of a skinny, plain girl with wide, frightened eyes told me more about her than anything she did or said.

He taps the sketch of Saint. 'This is the girl who died on the road, isn't it? I'm truly sorry about that, Jack.'

My hands twitch. But I know that if I lunge for him again, I won't be able to stop until the job is done. 'I don't want your apologies, Jova. Especially when you don't mean a single word of them.'

He shrugs, 'You're right, I'm not truly sorry about everything. I'm not sorry about bringing you and your friends here. But I *am* sorry that she is dead.' His voice drops. 'I could use someone of your calibre, someone I can trust.'

'No, Jova. You just want another pawn. Because whatever you're doing here, it's just one of your games.'

He leans back in his chair as if I've slapped him, deliberately letting me catch a glimpse of the vulnerable boy I met all those years ago in the soccer stadium. 'You of all people know that isn't true, Jack. I tried to make a difference—'

'You were the one who abandoned Cape Town.'

'And you're the one who came looking for me to help you save it.'

'My mistake.'

'Was it? Things must be very bad in Cape Town for you to leave Sasha behind. I can help you, Jack. What have you been doing for the last five years?' He taps Hester's letter. 'I have saved a city, Jack. I've done what we have always dreamed of doing for Cape Town.'

'And Jozi is saved, is it? At least the Resurrectionists didn't keep slaves.'

'For one thing, we don't belong to the Guardians. We aren't their breeding cattle. I have a plan, Jack.'

'Oh good. Because your last plan turned out so well, didn't it?'

His poker face slips for an instant. 'Cape Town wasn't ready to be saved then, Jack. I won't lie to you. I have unfinished business here. And when this city is free, Cape Town will be next.'

'And what is this amazing plan?'

He sighs and pinches the bridge of his nose. It's a familiar gesture, something I've seen him do a thousand times before. 'In time.' He scrunches up his nose, another familiar mannerism. 'You owed Hester a lot; I know now why you stayed with her. For a long time I couldn't puzzle it out. Why would you choose her over me? I should never have asked you to abandon Sasha like that, I should have known you wouldn't have been able to turn your back on your sister. But now you're here, Jack—'

'Stop calling me that!' I slam my hand on the table, aware of Morgan shifting behind me, a subtle threat. 'Where are my friends, Jova?'

'I'm not going to lie to you, the girl – the one with the red hair—'

'Ember.'

'Ember. She's in a bad way at the moment, but she will live. The others are safe.'

'You expect me to just take your word on that?'

'Yes. Because despite everything, Jack – *Ash* – I have never once lied to you.'

I hate to admit it but he's right. Jova is many things but he isn't a liar.

'I want to see them.'

'It's more complicated than that. I can't rock the boat. Not yet. Not until I'm ready to rock it. But soon, I promise.'

'I thought you were running this dump? I thought you were the big leader who saved a city?'

'You know that's not how these things work.' He leans forward, so close I can smell the mint lingering on his breath. 'Remember when we first met? I have the stone in my hand, and I'm just waiting for the right person to throw it for me.'

'Just words, Jova. And trite words at that.'

'Are they?'

'What about Lucien?'

'What about him?'

Jova's voice gives nothing away but I'm not an idiot. Lucien would have made a poor substitute for me all these years. He was more independent than I ever was, questioning Jova when it never occurred to me to do so.

I wouldn't be surprised to hear they had a bust-up.

A small treacherous part of me is secretly pleased that I wasn't replaced. But I'm not ready to examine this too closely.

As if he can sense my moment of weakness, Jova throws me one of his disarming smiles. 'You're a fighter. You always have been. This is where you belong.'

'Forget it. Because of you, because of *Lucien*, my closest friend is dead.'

'That was an accident. If I could put it right, I would. All I ask is that you stay for a while. Ember will need time to heal; she is in no state to travel. Give me a chance to show you what I'm doing here. If you and your friends wish to leave after that, then no one will stop you. You have my word on that.'

We stare at each for a long moment.

My silence is all the answer he needs.

He stands. 'Walk with me.'

I'm aware of Morgan ghosting our steps as we exit the room, turn right and weave through an ill-lit area, past long-dead security checkpoints and metal detectors, a smashed laptop and a dusty shoe still lying on a conveyor belt.

'Why choose to set up your base in an airport, Jova?'

A lopsided grin. 'Why not? Plenty of space, far enough away from the city to afford a level of privacy.'

Jova leads me down a long, winding walkway and out into another cavernous area, its walls and tiles soot-blackened and flecked with brown stains. Blood stains. I can't help but imagine the masses of people who must have flocked here during the first outbreak. Thousands, probably. A living time bomb.

One hatchling is all it takes.

I catch a whiff of cooking meat, and the sounds of clattering cutlery and laughter.

'You hungry, Jack?' Jova asks.

'No,' I lie.

He shrugs. We're heading towards a bank of old restaurants, the chairs and tables heaving with men and women. As we approach, there's a sudden hush, and every eye seems to be fixed on Jova. I study the soldiers' expressions, wanting to see hatred or fear, but finding only admiration and respect. I spot Americano, Noxi and that chubby kid – Danny – watching me. Danny's fork is frozen mid-air.

I'm put in mind of the Resurrectionists' mindless devotion to their leaders. But as much as I hate to admit it, this feels ... different.

Jova hesitates. 'I must leave you now. Morgan will show you where you can get cleaned up.'

He grins and I catch another glimpse of the boy I used to know. I want to believe that he is another tyrant, a clone of the Resurrectionists wrapped in different packaging. But I know him too well and I'd simply be lying to myself.

And I've been doing enough of that lately.

'Come on,' Morgan barks. I slow down to let her walk slightly ahead of me. There's something about her that's messing with my head and I think I know what it is. Her self-confidence and devil-may-care attitude reminds me of Saint.

'If you stare at me any harder your eyes might pop out,' she drawls without turning to look at me. 'And then you'll also be sporting the latest fashion trend this season; an eye patch. Go on, say it.'

'Say what?'

'The pirate joke. You might as well get it out of your system before you're officially initiated. Trust me, I've heard them all.'

When I don't respond, she sighs and shakes her head as if I've disappointed her. I wonder if she's noticed my own ocular issues. Most people pick up on it immediately, but having different-coloured eyes is hardly in the same league as having only one. We pass yet more shops, all but one stripped of its wares. A bookstore is stuck in time, its shelves stocked floor to ceiling.

Morgan gives me a long look as if expecting me to laugh. 'The library. It doesn't get used very often.'

She doesn't say another word as we duck down a series

of back corridors, halting outside a door marked 'Staff Bathrooms'.

'Wait here.' She disappears around a corner.

I could run. Right now.

But I don't.

Morgan reappears and hands me a towel and a bundle of clothes: the heavy combat pants, charcoal T-shirt and lace-up boots are worlds apart from my usual gear.

She gestures towards the bathroom door. 'What are you waiting for? I'm not coming in to scrub your back.'

The bathroom, a gloomy space lit by a couple of oil lamps, is clean and basic. I yank off my clothes, step into the shower and let the cold water wash over me, banishing the last traces of the headache. The water around my feet runs dark with a mixture of dust and dried blood. I dry off, pull on the combat pants and pad over to the chipped mirrors, deciding to use of one of the plastic razors on the shelves above the sinks. A droplet of blood wells on my jaw as I nick my skin with the old blade. I slip another blade into my back pocket. Even a pathetic weapon is better than none.

I run a hand through my fringe, shoving it away from my eyes, trying to stop the wave of sorrow crashing into me. Saint would say my hair is getting too long; she always preferred it shorter. After watching in horror as Hester carelessly hacked at it with a pair of blunt scissors, she took it upon herself to start cutting it. I can't stand the fact that my hair will just keep on growing while she lies on the side of a road in the middle of nowhere.

There will be a time when I can mourn her, but now isn't it. Not when Lele, Ginger and Ember are still out there. Am I willing to play along with Jova, trust that he'll stay true to his word and eventually let all of us return to Cape Town? My only alternative is to escape, try and make my way back to that Sandtown hellhole, hope that I can find my friends. And then what? If Jova is telling the truth about Ember, then we won't be able to leave immediately anyway.

Before I pull the shirt over my head I look in the mirror and study the scab that jags across my collarbone and down towards my chest. I've always been a quick healer, but the wound has knitted together incredibly fast. A memory nags at the edge of my thoughts, a half-remembered glimpse of the wound when it was fresh. I saw something, or thought I saw something. But what? I file this away to chew over later.

Morgan's nowhere to be seen when I leave the bathroom. Instead there's a note on the floor that reads: "Lesson one – Find your way back to the dorm", a small sketch of a skull and crossbones scrawled beneath the words.

I retrace my steps. The airport is gargantuan, but I've never had a problem with my sense of direction. In any case, I can hear the Americano's muffled drawl and Noxi's husky voice from way down the corridor. Feeling like an outsider, I hesitate. But screw that. If Jova wants me to play his game, then I'll play it. For now.

Silence falls the second I walk into the room.

'Is it true?' Noxi asks.

'Is what true?'

'That you and Jova are old friends.'

'So what?'

'But how do you know him?' Danny blurts, talking over Noxi.

'And you're seriously from Cape Town?' A short, pretty girl with a snub nose asks. I recognise her as the one who warned the group of Morgan's approach.

'Give the boy some space,' Americano says. 'Here. Got you

some food.' He hands me a fat roast-lamb sandwich wrapped in a napkin. Bread – when was the last time I had bread? 'Go on, eat. And I think it's about time you got to know who we are. Care to do the honours, Noxi?'

Noxi grins at Americano. 'Well, you've met Americano.' She points to the cute girl. 'And that there is Sumaiya, or Pockets as she is more fondly known. Watch your belongings around her.' Pockets blows me a kiss and waggles her fingers at me. 'Danny's our medic-in-training.'

Danny shoots me a one-fingered salute and grins. 'More like a glorified bandager.'

'He's got a vocabulary that would make an Outcast blush, but we do love him.'

'We just don't feed him after midnight,' Pockets says.

'Or let him near any sharp objects,' the girl in the headscarf adds.

'Ah, and this is the lovely Nuush. I doubt you will ever meet a better shot. This girl can put a bullet in a juju's eye from a mile away.' Pockets and Nuush share a secret smile. I'm beginning to figure out everyone's roles here. Danny's the joker, Americano's the tough one, Pockets and Nuush are clearly a couple, and Noxi … judging by the way her eyes keep lingering on me, she's obviously not the shy one of the group.

Interesting names. Ginger would love them.

'Well?' Noxi looks at me expectantly. 'Who the hell are you?'

I chew the last bite of my sandwich slowly, buying myself time to think.

'My name is Jack.'

It's not Ash who Jova wants, after all.

Saint

Saint has lost all sense of time. How long has she been lying here?

Hours? Days? Weeks?

It's as if she's just another piece of the wreckage scattered around her: her skin is as rusty as the wheel rims, her bones as dented as the truck's crushed carapace. It would be so easy to lie here forever until she's nothing but a stain on the tarmac.

She doesn't feel any pain, although she has an idea that at some point her back was broken. The memories of how she ended up in this position are vague and out of order, like pages of a manuscript scattered to the wind. At first she attempted to snatch at them, not ready to let go of the full story. *Her* story.

But then the darkness trickled in and her grip started weakening until all that was left were nonsensical scraps with no beginning or end.

And if she just lets go of those last meaningless pieces, if she forgets and gives into the darkness's seduction then she could be like the others, the ones tickling her subconscious. She could be like Ripley. She could be like the Rotters. She could be at peace.

But Ntombi, the stubborn part of her that refuses to forget, won't let her submit. Not yet.

The darkness allows her to see the threads that connect everyone and everything, some weak, some erratic like guttering flames and others thrumming with life. She knows she could gather the threads, draw the Rotters towards her. If she gives into the darkness completely, she could control them.

And some of the threads are familiar. If she concentrates hard, she can sense her friends. Lele and Ash's strands are the brightest; Ginger and Ember's threads fainter but no less there.

Saint, Ntombi prods. *We have to go to them. We have to go to them* now.

Answering Ntombi only encourages her. Saint closes her eyes, pulls down the shutter in her mind.

Time passes.

The hyena is back. It's lying next her; she can feel the warmth of its body. She senses that it's hungry, frightened. Alone.

The animal sniffs her face, reminding her of the sensation of tears on her cheeks. She tries to remember what sadness feels like, but can't. The hyena's meaty thread is different to that of the Rotters, but just as vital.

She wills herself back to Gaborone, to the time when everything was perfect and happy.

The blue of the sky above her snaps away, but instead of her childhood bedroom, she's in an unfamiliar city,

75

among the Rotters; she can feel the dry brush of their dead skin.

The world shifts, the ground bucks violently beneath her feet, and the scenery changes. She recognises the enclave where she spent most of her life. Cape Town. The high wooden fence, patched with metal, old tyres and car parts. An eye stares at her through a knothole. The eye blinks, and when it opens again it is filled with blood.

And then she's back in her childhood kitchen, sitting at the table across from her twin brother, Atang. Street sounds trickle through the open window, riding the breeze that sends the brightly coloured curtains fluttering. They no longer sound real to her; they're a tired song left on repeat.

She asks the question that Ntombi has been blasting into her mind ever since the crash. <why couldn't I stay dead? why am I like this?>

Atang doesn't open his mouth, yet she can hear his voice. <answers later. you must go>

<where?>

<here>

And then she's standing on a rocky precipice, looking down at a valley filled with writhing broken bodies, a red sky above her vomiting gouts of blood down onto the suffering masses below. She turns, sees a signpost next to her, but the words on it are indistinct. She steps closer to it—

Ntombi screams and Saint blinks, finds herself back in her chair, facing her twin. Her brother tilts his seven-year-old head to the side. She knows that he can sense Ntombi hidden within her, that he disapproves of her holding onto this piece of her past. The false sounds of her home town, the laughter and car horns abruptly cease, replaced by a distant roaring sound.

The roaring gets louder, more insistent. Atang is slipping away from her, the colours in the room fade.

She's back on the road. The roar still with her.

Ntombi flexes in her mind. *Get up.*

No.

Get up, Saint. Get. The. Hell. Up.

Why should I?

Because I need you. GET UP.

Will you shut up if I do?

Yes.

Saint rolls onto her stomach. Uses her weak arms to lever herself onto her hands and knees. Staggers to her feet. The hyena (*Bambi, his name is Bambi*) whines. He circles her, blunt muzzle nudging at her boots.

She sees the silhouette of a motorbike in the distance. Heading her way. She doesn't run, doesn't feel the need to. She only waits and watches as the bike draws near, skids to a halt, cuts out. Ntombi feeds her the biker's name.

Lucien.

She can't read his expression; his face is hidden behind dark glasses and a bandanna's tied around his mouth. She reaches for his thread, studies the turmoil within him.

Fear, surprise, resignation, anger ... and shame.

Saint stoops to pick up the hyena. The creature doesn't struggle.

Lucien won't stop her, she knows this; he's seen what he came to see, confirmed his fears and suspicions. He doesn't have the courage to confront her and see his future written in her eyes.

She turns and walks away from him, her legs shaky at first, but steadily growing in strength. She can't follow her friends. She knows what that will mean. She's being tugged somewhere

77

else. To the place Atang showed her. Doesn't allow Ntombi to resist it. She knows where she has to go. Knows that it's where she will find the answers she is looking for.

Saint is going to hell.

Tommy

'Here,' Olivia says, handing Tommy a bowl of mealie porridge. 'Get him to eat this. You will both need your strength today.'

Tommy passes the bowl to the giant, who starts listlessly spooning the porridge into his mouth. Since he was brought to their quarters yesterday evening, the giant hasn't spoken a word. He's like a sluggish doll: he moves when he's told to move, eats when he's told to eat. The giant's orange hair is matted and dreadlocked in places, and there's a frayed hole in his jeans where the denim was cut to accommodate the bandage swathing his damaged right leg. Tommy thinks he's almost as scruffy and filthy as that faker in the Archies.

How on earth is he expected to drag this great lump of a man around with him when he goes foraging? Because that, unfortunately, is what he's been ordered to do.

Tommy raced home from the market yesterday evening to find Olivia waiting for him, arms crossed, a grim expression on her face. Assuming that someone had seen him sneaking through the Archies and done a Benni on him, he steeled himself for a lecture (and readied himself to repeat the lie he'd told his supervisor about the loss of his jeans) but this wasn't the reason for her seriousness. Tommy had been summoned to his handler's quarters, an almost unprecedented occurrence. Sick with anticipation and dread – had Simo seen him the marketplace after all? – Tommy allowed Olivia to brush his hair, nodding as she reminded him to be polite. He didn't need reminding. Simo's father – Mister Lugosi – scared the crap out of him.

He hurried down the stairs to the lower floors, trying not to let the crystal chandeliers, deep carpeting and the soft lighting intimidate him. He hesitated outside Simo's family's unit, summoning up the courage to announce his presence. He suspected Simo was looking for an excuse to fire him. He'd hardly been the most productive runner so far. He felt very small when a butler ushered him through the door and into the suite's main area. Apart from the books scattered around the room, it still had the feel of the hotel suite it once was, the heavy curtains drawn to block out the sun. Simo lounged on the couch, playing with a Game Boy that must have cost twice Tommy's sponsorship. He barely acknowledged Tommy, only curling his lip at the football shirt that Jacob had given Tommy.

'Ah, Tommy,' Mister Lugosi harrumphed, striding through the archway that connected the suite to the one next door. 'How are you finding your running duties?'

'Fine, thank you, sir.' Tommy thought about mentioning his dream of taking the trials, but didn't dare. It would only give Simo an excuse to snigger at him. Mister Lugosi glided over to one of the plastic-wrapped chairs, but didn't invite

Tommy to sit. In his grey silk suit and tie, he looked as if he'd just returned from a meeting.

'Dad,' Simo said. 'Tell him that if he doesn't get something lekker soon then we're going to sell him to the honey wagon crew to pick up the poop.'

Tommy stared down at his shoes, trying to hide his blazing cheeks.

'Simo,' Mister Lugosi warned.

'But *Daaaaad*. Tell him I want another Transformer!'

'Enough, Simo. Leave us.'

Glaring at Tommy, Simo chucked his Game Boy on the floor and flounced out of the room, slamming the door on the way out.

Mister Lugosi steepled his hands. 'I have some news, Tommy. We have purchased another runner. An Outsider.'

Tommy was relieved that he hadn't been summoned here for a dressing-down after all, but couldn't fathom what this had to do with him. Mr Lugosi had several high-level runners for his own personal use, as did his older children and top-tier wives, so what difference did one more make?

'Your performance so far has been ... acceptable, Tommy, and Simo says you are more than up to the task.'

'What task?' Tommy blurted. 'I mean ... what task, sir?'

'This Outsider will need to be shown the ropes. Simo suggested it would be a good test for you.'

'*What?*'

Mister Lugosi pursed his lips. 'Do you have a problem with this, Tommy?' Tommy did have a problem – a big one.

'Why me, sir?'

'Two of my high-level runners are leaving this week to take the trials, and the others cannot be spared.'

'But ... shouldn't he go to runner camp first?'

'I don't think it is necessary. He is mature, and he has obviously encountered his fair share of the dead – if the report that he has come all the way from Cape Town is correct.'

Cape Town! So the rumours were true.

'But … what if he decides to run? How can I stop him?'

'The Outsider has been informed that if he does attempt to abscond, then the penalty will be severe.'

Yeah, Tommy thought, but for who? If the Outsider did make a break for it, then presumably Tommy would also get it in the neck. Still, he knew he didn't have a choice.

'He will be moving in to your quarters as soon as the clinic has given him a full bill of health. If he proves to be … valuable, then perhaps he will be assigned his own room.'

Tommy wasn't able to hide his look of horror.

'Are you clear on this, Tommy?'

Tommy nodded. An awkward silence stretched, and Tommy didn't know if he should just leave or wait to be dismissed.

Mister Lugosi's expression softened. 'How is your … how is Olivia, Tommy?'

'She's fine.'

Mister Lugosi tapped his front tooth with a fingernail. 'Tell me … does she have a significant other?'

'A what?'

A flash of irritation. 'Is there a man on the horizon?'

'No.'

'I see. And Nomsa's father? Where is he?'

'I … Olivia doesn't like me to talk about it.'

'I have heard rumours. That he was among the first of the runners to abscond.'

'Senyaka would never have run,' Tommy said, biting his lip when he realised he sounded rude. 'He was taken by the Outcasts.'

Mr Lugosi pursed his lips in distaste. Tommy didn't blame him. The Outcasts, after all, were the city's bogeymen, monstrous figures who hid in the shadows, stealing Sandtown's resources, preying on the runners who strayed too far from the Tri-Hotels area. There were rumours that it was better to be turned into one of the dead than be taken alive by them. 'Lefties and Outcasts,' was a popular game among the city's children, and there was even a rhyme about them: 'If they catch you, if they meet you, then it's certain they will eat you.'

But truthfully, no one knew what had *actually* happened to Senyaka. He was one of the first Lefties Jova recruited after he and his crew had slaughtered the Morts and freed the city from their hold over the citizens, but the details of Senyaka's disappearance were sketchy: one day he left to forage for supplies and never returned. The only other runner who'd been with him that day refused to mention Senyaka's whereabouts – he kept babbling about monsters, evil spirits. Days later he'd been caught in Sandtown's most recent cholera outbreak, another casualty of the epidemics that occasionally raged through the city. And to be honest, Tommy couldn't say that he missed Senyaka. He'd never actually lived with Tommy and Olivia in their quarters in Sandtown, although he was a regular visitor. Tommy still remembers blocking his ears to the noises he and Olivia made in the night. He was a difficult man. A hard man. Rarely smiled and only occasionally spoke to Tommy. Still, the day Olivia received the news of Senyaka's disappearance was the only time he'd ever seen her cry.

After that, Mister Lugosi dismissed Tommy with a curt nod and he rushed back upstairs to break the bad news to Olivia. Hours later there'd been a knock on the door, and a couple of blues had deposited the giant on their doorstep.

There's less than an hour before they're due to be at the kombi and Tommy's stomach is writhing with snakes.

'We are not the enemy,' Olivia says again to the giant. Tommy can only marvel at her patience. 'You can trust us.'

She takes the empty porridge bowl out of the giant's hands, reaches out and smoothes his hair back from his forehead. He doesn't react; she may as well have touched a block of wood.

Baby Nomsa gurgles and crawls forward. She laughs, fascinated by the giant's mass of ginger curls.

'Can you at least tell me your name?'

Nothing. Tommy recalls the girl with the short hair shouting something at the giant when she was dragged away. *Ginger*, that's it. But he can't let on that he knows this – Olivia will flip if she discovers he was loitering in the marketplace last night.

'I know you are hurting. I know you are broken, but if you do not do as you are told, then it is Tommy who will be punished. It is we who will feel the brunt of it.'

This seems to do the trick. Something shifts in his eyes.

'Friends,' he says. 'Where are my friends?' His voice sounds unused, broken. And Tommy can detect an accent he's only heard once or twice before in Sandtown. Tommy realises he must be talking about the girl with the shorn head and the tall guy he saw on the stage. He glances at Olivia. He has to speak up. He hopes she's got too much on her mind to berate him too harshly.

'Um ... You mean that tall guy with black hair?' Olivia stares at him, and Tommy shrugs at her apologetically.

The giant jerks his head up. 'Ash. His name's Ash.'

'He went to join the Army of the Left. Or at least I think

that's what happened to him. And ... I think the girl – the one with short hair?'

Olivia's still watching Tommy carefully.

The giant nods. 'Lele.'

'She was bought by Mister Coom.' Olivia winces, but thankfully the giant doesn't notice. 'He controls Sandtown's fuel supply.'

'What about Ember?'

'Ember?'

The giant looks straight into Tommy's eyes. They're bloodshot, alive with pain. 'She's a bit taller than you. She's beautiful, has wicked red hair.' His breath hitches. 'She's impossible to forget.'

'Sorry,' Tommy says. 'I didn't see anyone like that.'

'I will do what I can to find out where she has gone,' Olivia says. 'I have friends I can ask.'

The giant fidgets. 'You think she's okay? I mean ... we ... we were in an accident.' His eyes fill with tears. Tommy's hit with a mix of pity and irritation. How can someone so large be so weak?

'I'm sure she's fine,' Olivia says, using the soothing voice Tommy remembers from when he was small and his nightmares woke him. 'We would have heard otherwise. Now, what is your name?'

'Ginger.'

Olivia smiles. 'I like that name.' She takes his hand. 'Please listen to me, Ginger. Tommy means the world to me. If you try to escape when you and he go out today, he will be punished. I am begging you, please don't. Will you promise me that you won't run?'

Ginger brushes away the tears absent-mindedly. 'Yeah. I promise.'

Tommy hopes he means it. There's no way he'll be able to stop him if he does decide to flee.

'Thank you,' Olivia says. 'Now you must both go.'

Tommy's about to step out of the door when Olivia calls him back. She takes him in her arms and he breathes in the familiar scent of soap and the oil she uses in her hair – her only luxury. 'Be safe,' she whispers.

Despite his injured leg, Ginger manages to keep up as Tommy heads down the stairwell and through the hotel lobby. Tommy supposes it's because Ginger's legs are so impossibly long; each stride he takes matches two of his. As they head towards the service tunnels that lead to Sandtown proper, Tommy hears himself babbling; for some reason he can't stop talking.

'So what we have to do is forage for stuff that our handlers – that's Simo and his dad – can trade. They're seriously rich. You need to get enough stuff to eventually pay off your sponsorship. Then you'll be free to take the trials, maybe even join the Army of the Left.'

Tommy has no idea if Ginger is taking any of this in. He doesn't even seem to be curious about the people they're passing, many of whom stop and stare. Even in a settlement as large as Sandtown, a new face is something to gawk at.

'What's Cape Town like?'

Ginger acts as if he hasn't heard him. Tommy sighs. It's going to be a long day. He decides against taking a short cut to the parking lot. No way is it a good idea to drag the giant through the Archies. They emerge into the sunlight, trek past the high perimeter wall, the moans of the dead filling Tommy's head, and down towards the parking lot. Ginger's forehead is beaded with sweat, and he appears to be leaning more of his weight on his crutch. Tommy prays that his injured leg will stop the giant from doing anything stupid – if he does decide to run, he hopefully won't get far.

They reach the kombi with a few minutes to spare, and Tommy's heart sinks as he sees Mooki leaning against it, a finger excavating his nose. Tommy knows it's pointless to hope that Mooki won't make a scene. He'll just have to grin and bear it.

Mooki gawps, his expression morphing from surprise to scorn in seconds. 'Jess! Petrus! Come check this out!'

Petrus – a newbie runner with unfortunate skin and perpetually greasy hair – has never given Tommy any trouble before, but it's clear by the way he swaggers up to join Mooki and Jess that he's thrown his lot in with them.

'Who's your new friend, Tommy?' Mooki grins nastily.

'What's it to you?'

'Oooh, look, Piggy's trying to be brave. It doesn't suit you, Fatso,' Jess sneers. Petrus laughs way too hard at this and Tommy does his best to shoot him a withering look.

'Is this one of the Outsiders from Cape Town?' Jess asks.

'None of your business.'

'Shut up, Piggy,' Mooki says. He looks up at Ginger. 'Hey. Is it true you're from Cape Town?'

Tommy wills Ginger to speak up, but it looks as if he's locked himself inside his head again.

'Hello?' Jess says. 'Why isn't he talking to us, Piggy?'

Tommy tries to think of a witty comeback along the lines of 'because he's got good taste', but Mooki speaks before he gets the chance.

'Because he's a freak, of course. Piggy and the cripple. Two retards together.'

'Aw. How sweet,' Jess snickers.

'Hey!' Ayanda, storms over to them. 'Enough of that, Mooki. Get on the bus. *Now*.'

Mooki, Jess and Petrus climb on, sniggering together.

Ayanda looks dubiously at Ginger. 'You going to be okay today, Tommy?'

'Yeah. I'll be fine.'

'Let me know if you have any more trouble with Mooki.'

Tommy nods, but he knows he won't say anything, just like he's never told Olivia about Mooki's taunts. He doesn't want to be labelled a Benni – a grass – and what could Ayanda do about it anyway? No, if he wants to have any chance of joining the AOL, then he has to learn to fight his own battles.

'Come on,' Tommy says to Ginger, heading straight for the back of the kombi, where Jacob is already sitting in his usual corner seat, mumbling to himself as usual. Tommy nods at him, but gets no reaction. If only Mooki and his gang would ignore him as well. Tommy has to scrunch up to the window to allow Ginger enough room to sit down.

Mashele guns the engine and they start the twisty ride towards the parking lot gates. Tommy forces himself to look at the dead gathered around the edges of the settlement. He has to get used to them. If he joins the AOL then he'll have to face them on a daily basis; he can't afford to be squeamish. Still, it's not easy. His parents – his real parents – must be out here somewhere, maybe in this very throng. Olivia says that he and his family came from overseas, somewhere called Scotland, that his mom and dad were missionaries who had come thousands of miles to South Africa to teach people about religion or something. Like countless others, they were stranded here after the dead took over the city, and Tommy had been left at the entrance of the Sandton City, a giant shopping mall in the enclave that became known by its inhabitants as Sandtown after the dead rose. His left-handedness saved him from infection. Olivia says his parents were good people, but how would she know? She never met them. And the only connection he had to his real mom and dad – a passport and a note explaining who he was and where he was from – were destroyed in one of Sandtown's fires.

Lost in his own thoughts, Tommy is only aware that the kombi has stopped when Mashele claps his hands for attention. 'Listen up. The AOL hasn't had a chance to do a proper sweep of this area yet, so we don't know for sure what we're going to find.'

'Aw, what?' This from Mooki, of course. 'What about the Outcasts?'

Mashele sighs. 'You know they rarely venture this close to Sandtown, Mooki.'

'Whatever.'

'Please, everyone, be vigilant. Stay in groups and don't take any chances. I have a whistle for each of you here. Blow into them if you have any problems.'

'Oh, like that's going to help,' Mooki mutters.

Tommy follows Ginger off the kombi, which is parked in a wide residential street, metres in front of a fallen plane tree. Mooki and the others are already scrambling over its trunk and Tommy leads Ginger to the side where there are fewer branches to navigate.

The others are all heading towards the shell of a strip mall in the distance. Tommy makes out a cracked Woolworths sign, the ragged remains of a petrol station and what looks to be an ancient gaming arcade. Tommy knows he has to hurry if there's any chance of finding anything valuable after the others have taken their pick, but it doesn't look promising.

Even from here, he can see that at some stage the mall was ravaged by fire.

Tommy peers down a narrow side street to his left, and a faded, albeit still colourful sign catches his eye: 'God's Little Lighthouse Primary School and Care Facility'.

'Hey, Piggy!' Petrus yells. 'The mall's this way, dumbass.' Tommy ignores him. He's certain Mooki, Jess and their new sidekick are planning to steal whatever he manages to forage, and he'll have a better chance of reaching the kombi before they can scalp him if he searches this area. And who knows what treasures might be hidden in the school? At the very least, he might be able to source some books. Maybe he'll get lucky and the maintenance shed will contain something of use.

'Come on,' he says to Ginger. The giant does as he's told, wordlessly following Tommy as they approach the school's high permacrete walls. Tommy peers through the padlocked gate, makes out a courtyard and play area that's surprisingly free of weeds and the plastic bags that ghost through the city.

He uses his crowbar to ping open the padlock, and hurries towards the building's entrance. He spends a few minutes trying to pick the lock on the security gate barring the front door, but it's sealed with rust. The windows at the front are all protected by burglar bars – was life before the dead came so hectic that even the schools had to be barred like prisons? Ginger sticks to his heels like a loyal old dog as he slips around the side of the building.

'Awesome,' Tommy mutters, spotting a narrow unshielded window, the remains of its glass spiking up from the ledge like vicious teeth. He can knock that away easily. He reckons he'll just about fit through it, but there's no way Ginger will manage to climb up there on that leg.

'Ginger ... If I go inside, will you run?' Ginger shakes his head. Tommy has no choice but to trust him. 'I'll try and get something that you can take back, too.'

Ginger nods.

'Can you boost me up?'

Ginger nods again and makes a lattice with his hands. Tommy steps into it, almost losing his balance as Ginger boosts him up. He grabs hold of the ledge, knocks out the last remaining shards of glass with his elbow and peers inside. The drop down to the floor below isn't too bad. He'll make it. He heaves himself through, slides into gloom, catching his weight with his hands and rolling into a ball, just like he was taught at runner camp. He winces as his spine connects with the floor, but he avoids knocking his head. He scrambles to his feet, ears straining for any sign of life (or, more importantly, death). Outside, he could hear the distant whispers of the mob outside Sandtown along with the usual daytime sounds of birds and insects chittering, but all he can hear in here is the sound of his breathing. Fortunately, there's enough light filtering in from the broken window for him to see fairly clearly once his eyes adjust. There are no doors on the stalls, and the sinks and toilets are tiny – a bathroom made for midgets. Weirdly, it smells faintly of cleaning products rather than the mould he was expecting.

He steps into a corridor lined with identical doors. The air is stale, but nowhere near as rank as that of most of the houses he's explored. As usual, his imagination kicks in, and he's hit with an image of hundreds of dead students crammed into the classrooms, moaning in unison. He shakes his head to clear it.

He tries the first door, marked 'Staff Room'. Sunlight filters in from grimy windows, bathing mismatched furniture in light. A yellowing sign on the notice board reads: 'Please wash up your mugs! Thandi is NOT your skivvy! Thanks! ☺' The room is remarkably dust-free and Tommy spots several large bottles filled with slightly brown water next to the kitchenette. How can that be? Shouldn't it have evaporated by now? Tommy isn't certain. And on a shelf above the sink, there are several cans of apricots. Score of note! Trying not to think about the water, Tommy shoves the cans into his backpack, then creeps back into the corridor. Most of the doors are locked, but the one at the end of the corridor opens easily. He peers into a classroom stuck in time, the little chairs and desks still arranged in neat rows, backpacks hanging forever on pegs and colourful childish drawings stuck on the walls. Tommy feels a wash of melancholy. If the dead hadn't taken over, then he would probably have gone to a school like this one. Then he spots the bookshelf and his mood lifts. The books are all carefully wrapped in thick plastic covering, so most are undamaged. He has to choose carefully – he can't take them all. It's agonising. Finally he picks out *The Goblet Club*, *Charlotte's Web*, and *Charlie and the Chocolate Factory*. What a haul! Then he remembers that he can always pass more out of the window for Ginger to carry. For the first time he's glad he was forced to take the giant along with him.

He opens a desk at random – it's empty – then turns his attention to the backpacks, feeling, as usual, like a thief. He tips them up, wincing as a nest of small brown mice plops out of one, along with a Tupperware box black with dried mould. He pauses. Did he just hear something? A creaking sound?

He keeps absolutely still.

No, just his imagination. In his limited experience, all abandoned buildings have a life of their own. He digs in the third bag, feels his fingers encountering something hard and plastic. Unbelievable! A Transformer toy! Tommy recognises it as the one called (rather stupidly in his opinion) Optimus

Prime. Simo had described it in patronising detail when Tommy had first started working for him. He can hardly believe his good fortune. This will wipe the smirk off Simo's face!

He makes short work of digging through the other bags, but by now his backpack is full to bursting. Should he offload this stuff to Ginger first and come back?

He hurries out of the classroom, intent on heading to the bathroom, stopping dead as he hears a thump coming from the floor above him. Followed by what sounds horribly like a muffled voice.

And this time, he's certain it isn't his imagination.

He should really get out of here, but something compels him to walk towards the staircase. He can't be a coward all his life, can he?

Heart juddering, he climbs the stairs and creeps past empty classrooms on slow-motion legs. It's definitely a voice. A woman's voice. Barely daring to breathe, Tommy reaches the end of the corridor. He steels himself and peers inside the last doorway.

Six or seven small perfectly still figures are sitting at desks in the centre of the room. In front of them, a scrawny white woman with wispy grey hair is scrawling the words 'Kindness Equals Godliness' on the blackboard.

'Kindness is a rare commodity, children, and ...' She turns, her voice halting as she catches sight of Tommy; the chalk falling out of her fingers. Tommy gulps. She's as alive as he is. But ... but what is she doing here? Doesn't she know about Sandtown? The woman recovers, and Tommy's stunned to see that she's smiling. She claps her hands. 'Children! We have a visitor.'

One by one, the figures turn their heads. Tommy hears himself making a stupid peeping sound. He knows that if they've been dead for a long time then there's nothing he has to worry about – it's the freshly infected that are the dangerous kind. And judging by their sunken eyes and biltong skin, these kids have been dead for a very long time. Oddly, their clothes look brand new, and he can't detect the musty odour he associates with the dead.

The teacher's smile doesn't waver. Most of her teeth are missing. 'Aren't you going to say anything, young man?' she asks.

'Hello,' he says. 'Um ...'

She shakes her head. 'Cat got your tongue?' One of the children throws its head back and moans and the teacher waggles her finger at it. 'Now, Adam, it's rude to laugh at strangers.'

Tommy finds his voice. 'Listen to me. Um ... you don't have to stay here. There are other survivors. You can come with me, you'll be safe.' Bringing a Leftie back to Sandtown would be a huge triumph.

The teacher clucks her tongue. 'And leave the children?'

'But ... they're *dead*.'

The smile snaps off and she slams her palm on the desk in front of her. 'I will not have that sort of language in the classroom!'

Tommy readies himself to flee if he has to. 'Really, missus. They *are* dead ... I mean, just look at them.'

A student with the remains of a pair of pigtails drooping from the back of its neck moans loudly, and for a second, Tommy thinks he can detect understanding in its eyes. It looks almost ... sad. As if Tommy had just called it a dumbass or something. He's pretty sure it's how he must look every time Mooki calls him Piggy.

'Don't listen, children. Remember, sticks and stones can break your bones but words will never hurt you.'

Tommy almost laughs. Olivia's said this to him before, but it's far more apt for these kids. They're way beyond being hurt by sticks, stones or even the cruellest words imaginable.

The teacher clucks her tongue. 'Young man, if you aren't going to join our lesson, then you must return to your own classroom.'

'Right. Um … I'll just be going then.'

The woman turns back to the board as if Tommy doesn't exist for her any more. 'Children, it is almost time for break. But first, we must finish today's lesson.'

The children moan in unison again and Tommy's hit with a dizzying sense of unreality that makes him feel nauseous.

He whirls around, hears his feet thumping on the floor as he runs away, moving on automatic pilot. What should he do? Should he run back and tell Mashele about her? But … although clearly not all there mentally, she seemed happy. What right does he have to rip her away from the school?

And those kids … those *dead* kids. The dead are just things, empty vessels, everyone knows that. But the door to that classroom was open and they weren't restrained in any way. They could have left at any time. Why else would they have stayed unless they wanted to?

Tommy's heard the rumours that Jova's got some master plan to eradicate the dead.

Because the dead are monsters. Aren't they? *Aren't they?*

But the children in that classroom didn't act like monsters.

They acted like they knew what was going on. Like they understood every word that teacher was saying to them.

But how can that be?

He stumbles down the stairs, almost tripping over his feet and for a disorientating moment he can't recall the direction of the bathroom. He finally locates it, chucks his backpack out of the window, clambers onto the ledge, and heaves himself through head first. He rolls onto the ground only slightly winded.

He looks around for Ginger, but can't see him anywhere. Tommy retrieves his bag and hares around the side of the building. The playground is deserted. Out of breath and sick with fear, he hurries out to the road. There's no sign of him.

'Ginger?' he shouts, hearing the panic in his voice.

What the hell is he going to do now?

The giant can't have gone far, but to be honest Tommy has no idea how long he's been in that school. He can't deal with this now. It's too much. He slumps down on the pavement; he'll rest for a few minutes. Catch his breath and get his thoughts together, then sound the alarm.

'Told you he came this way.'

Tommy looks up to see Mooki, Jess and Petrus walking towards him. He's been so lost in his thoughts he hasn't noticed them approach. *Again*. How can he not have learnt his lesson?

'That mall was a dead loss,' Jess says. 'You got anything, Piggy?'

Tommy scrambles to his feet. Touches the whistle around his neck. 'Get back or I'll call Mashele.'

'Get back or I'll call Mashele,' Petrus mocks, putting on a high-pitched voice.

'I will. I mean it.'

'Don't talk to us like that.' Jess smiles, darts up to Tommy and slaps him hard across his face. The pain is so sudden and shocking that instead of gasping, Tommy laughs. Jess blinks in surprise, then yanks the whistle from his neck, snapping the string.

'Hand it over, Piggy,' Mooki says, sounding almost bored. 'Hey, where's your retarded friend?'

'I don't know.'

'O. M. G. Has he run?'

'I don't know.' Tommy turns his head and glances at the gate. Will he have time to run back into the schoolyard? And then what? He certainly won't have time to climb through the bathroom window. No, he'll have to stand his ground and fight. He's not letting the Optimus Prime toy out of his grasp. No way. They'll have to pry it out of his cold, dead hands. He's been through too much to lose it now.

'Grab his backpack, Petrus,' Mooki says.

'Nice,' Tommy says. His mouth is gummy. 'Three against one. You're such a bastard, Mooki.' Slowly, he ekes the strap of his backpack off his shoulder, lets it fall into his hand.

Mooki hoots. 'Listen to Piggy, trying to be brave. Forget it, Petrus, I'll show you how it's done.'

Mooki lunges for the bag, but Tommy steps back and swings it as hard as he can, aiming for Mooki's crotch. Thanks to the combined weight of the cans and the books, it hits its target hard.

Mooki squeals and drops to his knees, but Tommy knows he can't stop there. He spins in a circle, forcing Jess to jump back, and whaps it into Petrus's stomach. Petrus doubles over, his breath escaping in a whoof.

Mooki's crying. Tommy can't believe it – Mooki's actually crying! 'I'll get you for that, Fatty,' he blubbers, snot pouring down his face. 'You're gonna be sorry.'

'You're not going to let him get away with that, are you?' Jess sneers.

Mooki is still blubbering. 'It hurts, Jess.'

Without taking her eyes off Tommy, Jess digs in her bag. 'Here,' Jess says to Mooki. Tommy catches a glint of metal. On no … she's handed him a knife! Mooki looks down at it, and then, he matches her smile with his.

Tommy glances wildly around him. 'Don't do this, Mooki. I beat you fair and square.'

'You didn't beat nothing, Piggy. Petrus, hold him down.'

Petrus hesitates. 'But … but we'll get into trouble, Mooki.'

'No we won't. It'll be his word against ours. We can say that retarded Ginger did it.'

Petrus glances at Jess, who nods.

'Oy!' Tommy looks up, sees the giant hobbling towards them. 'Let him go!'

For a fleeting second, Mooki looks unsure.

'Do it!' Jess hisses.

Mooki springs, and Tommy has just enough time to use the bag as a shield, hears the ting of the knife connecting with one of the cans.

It happens fast. Moving far quicker than Tommy would have thought possible for someone of his size, Ginger grabs Jess and Petrus around their necks and pulls them towards each other. There's a dull clunk as their heads connect and they stumble apart, dazed. Despite the horror of the situation, Tommy lets out a burp of laughter.

Mooki howls and jabs at Tommy, but the giant blocks his knife-hand, twists it and the knife clatters to the floor. He sweeps his good leg under Mooki's, and Mooki falls heavily, catching the side of his head on the edge of the pavement.

Mooki shudders, and then is still.

Jess screams and points at Tommy. 'You killed him! You killed Mooki!'

Tommy feels his guts dropping into his boots. He's vaguely

aware that another figure – Jacob – is running towards them, moving with a slightly sidelong gait. 'But I didn't—'

Jess backs up. 'You killed him, Tommy. You and your ... *monster* killed Mooki. They're going to hang you for this. You're going to *die*, Tommy.'

She spins and sprints towards the main road, Petrus following close behind her. Tommy hears the reedy sound of their whistles being blown.

Now what? What is he going to do? If Jess gets there first and tells Mashele that he and Ginger killed Mooki, then—

He feels someone grabbing at his arm, and Jacob's face looms into his. 'Quickly. Both of you. Come with me.'

'But—'

Jacob grasps Tommy's shoulders and stares into his eyes. 'You don't have a choice, Tommy. It's your word against theirs. You have to run.'

'But you can tell them what happened! You can!'

'They won't listen to me. I'm an Outsider.'

'It was self-defence! It wasn't me!'

'It's your word against theirs.'

Tommy has to make a choice. He knows that Mooki's handler will stop at nothing to punish him. Injuring a Leftie, especially one who's been sponsored, is pretty much the worst offence anyone can commit. Jacob is already running in the opposite direction to the main road. He glances behind him, beckons and ducks down a side street. Without checking to see if the giant is lumbering after them, Tommy picks up his bag and hares after him.

Lele

I dreamt about Saint again last night, one of those hyper-real nightmares that took me right back to the aftermath of the crash. I walked on deadened legs to where her body was lying on the side of the highway, the light far brighter than it was that horrible morning, a hadeda cawing at double volume, the stench of spilled diesel rolling over me. Ginger, Lucien, Ember and Ash stood watching me silently – a shadowy troupe standing unnaturally still as if they were judging me. And this time, when Saint opened her eyes, they were clear and lucid. She groaned, sat up, rolled her eyes at me and said: 'What the hell are you staring at, Zombie Bait? You going to help me up, or what?'

The dream was so real that when I jerked awake, heart in my throat, skin clammy, I half-expected to see her in the room with me, griping about the kak we were in.

I wish I knew for sure that there's some part of her that's still *her*.

Still … part of me is almost jealous of her. Her troubles are over; mine are just beginning. If I don't do what Coom wants, Ember might die. She's not like Ash, Saint or me. She's a Leftie. She may be immune to Rotter attack, but she doesn't have the silvery tendrils squirming through her veins that will keep her body alive and turn her into a Guardian if she succumbs to her injuries – if becoming a Guardian can be termed *living*. If I manage to escape, what will happen to her? Or Ginger? And I can't depend on Ash racing here and whisking me away as if I'm a damsel in distress.

I need a plan, but all I can come up with is a vague notion of lulling Coom into a false sense of security, getting him to trust me, and then … what? Could I kill him if I had to? I'm certain that he's as self-serving and twisted as the Resurrectionists, but I don't think I have that in me.

And if I *did* find it in me, wouldn't that make me as sick as him?

For the first time in ages I find myself itching to sketch. My old fallback for dealing with stress. I grab the notepad that's placed next to the long-defunct phone on the desk in the corner of the room, and root around in the drawers for a pen. There's only one, an old ballpoint, but it's dried-up and useless. I scribble it on the desk, feeling a savage glee as its tip scratches the varnish. The familiar pressure is building in my chest, but crying isn't going to help anyone. I need to control myself, remember Hester's old lessons about dealing with my anger.

There's a hesitant knock on the door and Busi bustles in. She glances at the deep score marks in the desk, then shoots me a nervous smile. I realise I'm actually pleased to see her.

'Good morning, Lele,' she says. 'Cezanne has invited you to have tea with her.'

'Who the hell is Cezanne?'

'Mr Coom's head wife.'

Oh brilliant. 'Well, she can wait. Tell Coom I want to see Ember.'

'But—'

'I'm not even going to consider his gross proposal until I see my friend. That clear?' Busi winces. 'Sorry, Busi. I know none of this is your fault.'

'It's fine.'

'It's not fine. Seriously, I shouldn't take it out on you.'

She relaxes. 'I will see that he gets your message. Would you like me to bring you some breakfast? There are fresh eggs today.'

There's no chance I'll manage to eat anything with this knot in my gut. 'No thanks. I'll get something later.'

She digs in the wardrobe and places a pair of jeans and a long-sleeved T-shirt on the bed. 'I think these might be more your style.'

'Thanks. Busi, are you from Johannesburg? I mean, originally?'

'Ja. I was born here.' She hesitates. 'Lele, what's Cape Town like?'

I snort. 'How much time have you got?'

She takes me seriously. 'Not much, I have to get the bed sheets to the laundry and then it's my turn to clean the staff quarters.'

'Well, the short version is that it's different, but just as screwed up as this place.' There's a reason we left Cape Town, a very good reason. But who knew we'd end up in an even crappier situation than the one we were running from? 'Busi, you can leave here any time you like, right?'

'Ja. But the job here ... it's a good job. It means that my mother and sister get a bay in the Tri-Hotels area rather than in Sandtown, where we used to live.'

'You mean the mall?' I'm almost tempted to tell her about my mall – the Mall Rats' mall – the only building the Guardians left standing when Cape Town was razed at the start of the war.

'Ja. Sandtown was where many of the survivors flocked after the dead came,' she says. 'It used to be called Sandton City, but when a few survivors started calling it Sandtown, the name stuck.'

'And I'm guessing the Tri-Hotels place isn't as kak as that mall, right?'

'Ja. It's not as crowded, there's less chance of disease, fire. It's where the amaKlevas live, though I shouldn't call them that. The ones who have money, influence.'

'I thought Jova was all about equality?'

Busi shrugs. 'He says things will change when he sets us free.'

'And how is he planning on doing that?' But how would she know? Lucien doesn't even know.

She sighs. 'We'll find out soon, I hope.'

'Why doesn't everyone just rise up against Coom? I mean, I haven't seen much of Sandtown, but it seems to me that most of the people seem to be living in squalor, while Coom has this whole Montecasino place to himself.'

'If it wasn't for Mr Coom there wouldn't be running water or electricity. I know what he wants from you is terrible, Lele, but—'

'You're really defending him?'

A shrug.

I wonder if she's frightened I'll grass her up if she disses him or if she really believes this. 'Busi, is the clinic in Sandtown really that bad?' She shifts uneasily. 'I need to see it. I need to see my friend.'

'I will see what I can do.' With another hesitant smile, she scurries out. The clothes she's laid out are indeed more my style. I drag them on, then slump on the bed and wait to hear Coom's reaction.

One Ear parks between a kombi and a large cylindrical truck, and holds out a hand to help Busi down from the back of the cart. Who knew he was such a gentleman? She takes it and colour bleeds into her cheeks. Has she got a thing for him? Surely not, but then again, on more than one occasion I've caught her shooting sidelong glances at him. Talk about bad taste in men, but who am I to judge? Still, it's the last thing I should care about right now and I'm relieved she asked to come with us when Coom gave his permission for me to visit Ember. The long drive through the tunnels hasn't been so oppressive with her along.

A kombi screeches down the slope on the far side of the parking lot and jerks to a stop fifty metres or so away from us. The driver jumps out, hauls open the side door, and barks something into his radio. I can't make out what he's saying, but he's clearly distressed.

'What's going on?' I ask One Ear.

'None of our business,' he grumps. 'Come on.'

I hang back for a few seconds, watching as a pretty girl with a tear-stained face climbs out of the kombi, a shell-shocked pudgy teenage boy close on her heels. He attempts to put his arm around her, but she knocks it away.

'Lele!'

I jog to catch up with Busi and One Ear, who are waiting for me inside a concrete stairwell that reeks of urine and old dagga smoke.

'We really going this way?' Busi asks.

'Short cut,' One Ear says, heading down the stairs, Busi and I close on his heels. He nods at the guard sitting slumped on a chair outside a metal door, and she sighs, heaves herself to her feet and waddles over to unlock it.

'Stay close to me,' One Ear orders. 'This section can be dangerous.'

We step straight into chaos, and I almost gag at the stench – an unholy mixture of sewage, body odour and rotting meat. A river of raggedy people jostle past us; most look as if they have some purpose, others seem to drift aimlessly, faces blank. The noise is intense, a cacophony of raised voices, yelps and catcalls in a multitude of languages.

One Ear grabs my arm. 'Move it.'

'Where are we?'

'The Archies. A tunnel system that leads up into Sandtown.'

'It stinks like crap.'

'You'll get used to it.'

There's an aura of danger and desperation about this place, and I stay as close to his side as I can without actually touching him. Busi follows behind us. Hawkers lurk in the gloom at the base of the tunnel's curved, dripping sides, coughing into their fists and calling out their wares. I could easily melt into the crowd, give One Ear and Busi the slip, but this tunnel network is just as labyrinthine as the one we puttered through from Montecasino, and the thought of being lost down here makes me break out into a cold sweat. A gaunt-faced woman coiled on a filthy sheet and breastfeeding a squalling infant stares at me with hollow-eyed resignation.

'People *live* down here?' I say to Busi over my shoulder.

'Ja. There's not enough space for everyone to live in Sandtown.'

We pass a queue of children carrying buckets and other plastic containers, waiting for their turn at a single tap stuck to the wall, and a scabby-faced boy peels away from the line and tugs on my sleeve. 'Clean your shoes, ma'am? Polish and spit? I'll do a good job, you can count on it, lady.'

One Ear turns to glare at him and he scuttles away.

'Shame, poor kid.'

One Ear grunts. 'He knows the score. More than likely he was just getting close enough to see if you have anything worth stealing.'

One Ear ducks down a slightly less populous tunnel, and another bored guard waves us up a narrow set of concrete stairs, this one slow-moving and crammed with bodies. Just as I think I'm getting a handle of the stench, a new smell joins the rest – the thick, hairy stink of goat hide – and my stomach rolls over again.

We emerge into what has to be the heart of the mall. There's electricity on this floor, but the bare bulbs hanging from the ceiling pop and hiss and seem to deepen the darkness in the corners rather than dispel the murk. The reek of goat is stronger now, smothering the other charming odours. And then I see why. There are animals everywhere, most tied to the exteriors of old shop fronts which have obviously been turned into residences, tatty sheets dividing them into small makeshift rooms. A clutch of chickens trapped in a rusting cage squawk and squabble outside the open door of what was once, judging by the cracked signage, a cellphone store. I cover my mouth as we skirt a row of green portable toilets with a queue meandering in front of each one. But despite the filth, there's a marked difference from the dangerous atmosphere that infected the tunnels. It's just as crowded here, but many of the people around me – most of whom dart interested, but not threatening, glances in my direction – seem to be laughing or bantering with each other. I have to admire their resilience. If I was forced to live here, I think I'd go crazy.

There's a flurry of activity, and the crowd surges forward, almost knocking me off my feet. I look over my shoulder. For several seconds I fight against the tide, keeping my elbows close to my body to avoid being bumped, and then the throng thins. I look over my shoulder. Most of the crowd is funnelling through a pair of double doors of what was once a supermarket.

'What's going on over there, Busi?'

'Runners' food delivery most likely. Probably vegetables and fruit. They're difficult to grow here, although there is a potato and madumbi farm on the first floor.'

'Seriously? But there are so many people! How can they feed them all? How can anyone possibly survive like this?'

'They won't. Not much longer. It would only take the water being cut off, and that would be it.'

'And Coom controls all that?'

'His maintenance guys do, ja.'

One Ear strides ahead, the men and women around him almost unconsciously stepping out of his path. Busi's looking edgy, she keeps glancing at One Ear as if there's something she needs to tell him but can't quite find the words. I hustle to catch up to him.

'Is this really the only settlement in Joburg?'

'Ja. The others died out years ago. Disease, lack of resources. Most were over even before Jova destroyed the Morts.'

'Morts?'

'The Credos. The Inageza. The robed ones.'

'You mean the Guardians?'

He gives me a strange look, then gestures towards a pair of immobile escalators that disappear down into darkness.

'What's down there?'

'The clinic.'

'Seriously?'

Busi tugs on his sleeve. 'Sihle. Um ... Do you need me? I just thought ... Do you mind if I ...' she drops her eyes.

'You want to go check in on your family?'

She nods.

'Go ahead. Meet us back here as soon as you can.'

'Thanks.' She smiles gratefully and squeezes my arm. 'I hope your friend is okay, Lele.'

I follow One Ear down the escalators and into a wide, tiled area that thankfully isn't as gloomy as it looked from above. The stale air is undercut with a faint tinge of disinfectant, but despite the obvious lack of ventilation, it's nowhere near as putrid as the atmosphere above. Most of the people down here are elderly; all wear the resigned expressions of those who are used to waiting for long periods.

My eye is drawn to an old movie poster on the wall – *Avatar*. One of Ginger's old favourites.

'Are we ... Is this where the cinemas used to be?'

One Ear ignores me. He shoves through a queue of people waiting patiently in front of a booth that must once have sold popcorn and cold drinks, its shelves now displaying a meagre selection of bottles and herbs, and barks something at the tired-eyed woman behind the counter. She gestures at a pair of black doors on the other side of the space.

'Come on,' One Ear calls to me. We push through the doors and into a long, dark corridor lit by a couple of bare light bulbs. The stench of disinfectant is stronger now, and I wince as a muffled howl escapes from behind a closed door. The handwritten sign on the wall next to it (which, horribly, has a bloody fingerprint on one of its curled corners) indicates that this is the maternity ward. One Ear hesitates outside a pair of doors marked 'Trauma Ward'. 'Your friend is in here.'

'You're not coming with me?'

He drops his gaze, which isn't like him. 'No.'

I step inside, forced to breathe through my mouth to stop myself from gagging. The disinfectant smell can't hide the lingering stench of blood, vomit and sickly sweat. It's obvious that this 'ward' was once a mid-sized cinema. The blank screen is still in place, but the seats have been ripped out, replaced with narrow cots and mattresses slotted head to tail, all of which contain a body. There's barely any space between the patients, and no attempt to give any of the men and women lying here any privacy. I look away as a woman wearing a stained white tunic bends and starts unwrapping a crusty bandage hiding an elderly man's right eye. There's an occasional groan, but most of the men and women are silent, draped in sheets as if they're one remove from being carted away to the morgue.

A brisk, middle-aged woman wearing an apron and plastic gloves bustles up the side aisle towards me. 'Ja?'

'Um ... I'm here to see my friend.'

She clucks her tongue in exasperation. 'Visitors aren't allowed in this ward. You'll have to wait until your friend is transferred to Recovery.'

She turns away.

'Wait! Please. I must see her. Her name's Ember. She would have been brought here a few days ago. She's got red hair and—'

The woman hesitates. 'The Outsider?'

'Yes!'

She sighs. 'This way. But five minutes only.'

I follow her down the aisle, stepping over piles of towels and bedpans covered with discoloured cloths.

'Shawna?' The woman in the tunic waves to get our attention.

'Ja? What is it?' The middle-aged woman pauses.

'Mr Masood. He's gone.'

Shawna bends her head and murmurs a prayer in a language I don't recognise. 'Thank you, Lungi. Please prepare his body for burning.'

I shudder. At least they burn their dead here. Unlike Cape Town where corpses are ferried out to the Deadlands for their second shot at life.

An elderly woman lying wrapped in a sheet to my left looks up at me and reaches out a veined hand. 'Hurts,' she whispers.

'Now, now, Ms van der Merwe,' Shawna says briskly. 'You must be patient. I'll be with you as soon as I can.'

I hang back; now I'm here, I'm not sure I want to see Ember after all. Not if she's like these others, most of whom look as if they're barely clinging to life.

'Quickly!' Shawna snaps at me.

We weave past gurneys shoved higgledy-piggledy in the flat area directly in front of the screen. Shawna gestures towards a bed in a darkened area beneath an exit sign. 'She's there.'

At first I assume she's made a mistake. The figure lying on the bed appears to be frail and ancient, the opposite of the well-built, energetic girl I remember. I step forward cautiously.

Oh crap. It *is* her. She's lying on her side, eyes closed, mouth slack, her knees drawn up to her chest. Even her hair has lost its lustre, the thick red curls now dry and brittle. Shawna frowns and taps the drip attached to the back of Ember's hand.

I swallow, steel myself to ask the question I've been dreading. 'Is she going to be okay?'

'She's in a coma. A suspected haematoma on the brain.'

'A what?'

'She has had a head injury. Unless we can get the CAT scan working again, there's no way to be sure. If there is bleeding on the brain ... well, it is possible that she will not recover.'

'But ... but you think she will, right? There is hope?'

Shawna sighs, her efficient front slipping to reveal exhaustion and resignation. 'Look around you. We have too many patients to give them each the care they need. Our equipment dies every day – we simply don't have the expertise to fix it.' She scrubs a hand over her face. 'And until we can produce antibiotics we have to depend on natural medicine. Sometimes it works. Sometimes it doesn't. With her immune system compromised ... let's just say she's vulnerable.'

'Then she must be moved.'

'Where to? There is nowhere else unless you want to pay the Tri-Hotels rates. And who can afford that? Now, you will make your own way out? I have others to see.'

'Thank you.'

She gives me a curt nod and hurries away.

I touch Ember's hand, filled with regret for how I treated her when we first met. I was jealous of her, accused her of flirting with Ash. How could I have been so stupid? And now I'm her only hope. And if it means I have to marry Coom, well ... I'll do whatever it takes. If I don't, she'll die.

I bend down to whisper in her ear. 'Ember. I'm going to look after you. I'm going to get you out of here. Hold on.' I gently kiss her forehead – her skin feels too hot – then hurry to the aisle, scrubbing at my face to wipe away the tears that won't stop coming. One Ear is waiting for me in the corridor, but I push past him without speaking. Tears continue to roll down my face, and I'm only able to get them under control once we reach the top of the escalators.

I'm barely aware of the people milling around us. All I can think about is Ember.

Busi heads towards us. 'Lele, how is your friend?'

'Not good. She has to be moved out of there. Immediately.'

'I'm sorry.'

'Will you tell Coom when we get back?'

She nods. 'Of course.'

'Tell him I'll do whatever the hell he wants, okay?' Another sob snatches my breath away.

'I will,' she says, taking my hand. 'Really, I'm so sorry, Lele.'

'Let's go,' I snap at One Ear. 'The faster we get back, the faster Ember can be moved.'

'Hey! You! Wait!' The crowd parts, and One Ear grips the gun at his side. A large woman glides towards us. She's beautiful, her skin glowing even in the sickly light, her eyes huge and soulful.

'Stay back,' One Ear warns.

She barely acknowledges him, fixes those eyes on me. 'You are one of the ones from Cape Town?'

'Yes.'

'You know an Outsider named Ginger?'

'Yes! Where is he?' I look around, half-expecting to see him come barrelling through the crowd.

One Ear takes another step forward.

'It's okay,' I say to him.

'He has run,' the woman says, eyes brimming. 'He has my son with him.'

'What do you mean *run*?'

'They are saying things. That Ginger and Tommy – my son – attacked one of the other runners, a boy.'

'Ginger? No ways. Ginger wouldn't attack anyone.' I can hear the doubt in my voice. The Ginger who emerged after

112

the crash wasn't the wise-cracking, relentlessly cheerful guy I knew before. But despite this I just can't see Ginger attacking someone unless his back was against the wall.

'Please. I need to know – what type of person is he? Is he dangerous?'

'If your son's with Ginger then I can promise you this. He couldn't be with a better person. He's ... he's one of the kindest people I know.' Her eyes fill with relief. 'And if he did attack anyone, he would have had a good reason. The last person you need to worry about is Ginger.'

'Thank you, sisi. Thank you.'

Then she turns away and melts into the crowd.

————

I pace up and down, stalk into the bathroom, fiddle with the taps. Where the hell is Busi? Every second counts. I can't bear the thought of Ember remaining in that stinking hole a minute longer.

Finally I hear her tell-tale hesitant knock. I race into the bedroom. 'Well? What did Coom say?'

'He will call for you when he is ready.'

'I can't wait that long!'

'I'm sorry, Lele. I tried my best. Look ... why don't you go and see Cezanne now?'

'Cezanne?'

'His wife.'

I'd forgotten all about this morning's invitation. 'What can she do?'

'At least you will be doing something. She is not without influence, Lele. She might be able to help.'

What have I got to lose? It has to be better than lurking in my luxurious prison cell and driving myself crazy with worry.

I pull on my boots and follow Busi into the corridor. For once One Ear isn't at his post outside my door.

'Where's Sihle?'

'He'll catch up with us later. He has to report to his supervisor, sign off on our trip to Sandtown.'

'So I'm being let off the leash, am I? Isn't he worried I'll try and make a run for it?' She looks at me anxiously. 'Don't worry. I won't. Ember needs me.'

As we exit the hotel and cross the square, I think about quizzing her on her feelings for One Ear, but decide against it. Shame, she's nervy enough as it is. I don't want to make her even more uncomfortable.

I'm becoming used to the fake city's oppressive atmosphere, but today Montecasino's phony sky seems to be lower, the alleyways narrower, the muzak cornier and the dusty props and ornaments even more ridiculous. A shriek of laughter peals towards us as we stroll past the slot machines. Most of their lights are dead as usual, but I spy a couple of rows that are chinking and blinking, a cluster of Coom's runners gathered around them, slapping each other on the back and downing glasses of amber liquid. I catch a whiff of cigar smoke that instantly reminds me of the foul cheroots Lucien used to smoke when we were on the road.

'They've just returned from a raid,' Busi says. 'They're letting off steam.'

'Why is their job so dangerous? The Rotters – the dead, I mean – won't attack them if they're all left-handed.'

'It is not the Dead who are dangerous. It's the Outcasts they have to watch out for.'

'And they are?'

'A group of renegades. They are ruthless, vicious. You don't want to be taken alive by them.'

'Why not?'

'They *do* things to those they capture,' Busi whispers.

'Like what?'

'Just after Jova set us free, they used to slip into Sandtown, steal children – the left-handed and others to ...'

'To what?' I'm trying to imagine what could be worse than what Coom has in store for me, but it's a struggle.

'Muti,' Busi says. 'They ... they used them for muti and other medicines to try to make themselves stronger.'

'Seriously?'

'I'm deadly serious. Those who have seen them say they're monstrous, with claws and razor teeth, that they fight as if they are possessed.'

Sounds like crap to me, but I'm not about to argue with Busi. She's the only friend I've got here.

I mentally send that vile doctor daggers as we hurry past the clinic, down a sloping alleyway and into a part of the fake city I haven't yet encountered. A stream of laughter filters out of a huge glass-fronted activity area. It's stuffed with brightly-coloured toys, a climbing frame and trilling arcade games, around which toddlers and children are whooping and laughing and hitting each other with balloons on sticks.

'That's a lot of kids,' I say to Busi. 'Coom's been busy, hasn't he?'

'They are not all Coom's.'

'Don't tell me – they're all Lefties, aren't they?'

'Correct.'

As we step into the room I notice a cluster of women talking and laughing next to a Punch and Judy booth. Coom's wives. Two of them are heavily pregnant, but without exception they're immaculately groomed, complete with hair extensions, thick make-up, painted nails and towering platform heels. A woman in a revealing red sundress says something in a low voice, and they all squeal with laughter, although how anyone could keep a smile on her face after being slobbered over by Coom the Slug is beyond me.

The wife in red catches sight of me, murmurs something to the others, and I'm treated to a series of lipsticked smiles that actually look genuine. I guess I was expecting them to resent me or something, but maybe the more wives there are, the less time they have to spend with Coom.

'Lele!' The older, short-haired woman who was watching me with interest in the dining room approaches. 'I'm Cezanne. How kind of you to take up my invitation.' I search her face for any sign that she's being sarcastic, but can't see any. 'You may leave us,' she says to Busi. Busi nods, shoots me a tepid smile and disappears.

'Let's go somewhere more private, Lele,' Cezanne says, hooking an arm through mine as if we're old friends, and I try not to sneeze as her strong perfume hits my nostrils. 'We have a lot to talk about.'

She leads me through an archway, past a pair of leering stone cherubs capering in the centre of a fountain and into a cobblestoned square. A stuffed crane nailed to a balcony peers down at a round table draped in a crisp white tablecloth.

'Please, sit,' she says, treating me to a broad smile that reaches her eyes.

The second we sit down an obsequious waiter bustles over with a teapot and a plate of delicate cakes. My traitorous stomach rumbles, but I decide to watch my manners. For now.

Cezanne pours the tea and hands me a pot of honey. 'I was sorry to hear about your friend, Lele. I believe you have requested that she be transferred to the clinic here?'

News travels fast. 'Yeah. Do you think that's going to happen?'

'Yes.'

'But only if Coom gets what he wants, right?'

Cezanne takes a sip of her tea, folds her hands on her lap. The smile snaps off, a shrewd, serious expression taking its place. 'I know that his ... *offer*, isn't to your liking, Lele.'

'That's an understatement. I don't know how you can stand it,' I blurt. 'Putting up with a fat pig like that. Letting him walk all over you.' The anger is building up, but I have to remember Ember and not lose my cool entirely. If Busi is correct, this woman could be useful.

'Steven wasn't always this way, Lele. Before Jova came, he was the one who kept order in Sandtown. Without him, many would have perished.'

'But what about the Guardians?'

'The Guardians?'

'The Morts. The robed ones. Didn't they keep everyone in line?' They certainly did in Cape Town. They may have brought supplies from the agricultural enclaves to feed us and made sure the Rotters didn't break through the fence and attack us, but we paid a high price for their protection. They ensured that technology and medical care in the enclave was kept to a minimum so that there would be a constant supply of the dead to swell the Rotters' ranks in the Deadlands. Weapons were outlawed, in case we turned on them, and they must have been delighted when the Resurrectionist cult started doing their dirty work for them, punishing anyone who didn't treat the Guardians and the Rotters like gods.

'The Guardians, as you call them, kept us living on the breadline. Providing just enough resources to keep us subsisting, with no end in sight. Steven and others like him –

Sindiwe, for example – kept the gangs from stealing the food for themselves, ensured that nobody went without. Steven used his expertise to keep the water and electricity supplies alive. But after Jova came and he was granted this place in which to live, he changed.'

'But he's using his power to bribe or blackmail women into sleeping with him. How can you put up with that?' Cezanne winces, her cool demeanour slipping. *Good.* 'Were you married to Coom – to Steven – back then? Before the dead came?'

A pause. 'Yes.'

'Cezanne?' A young woman dressed in waiter's garb approaches nervously. 'I am sorry to interrupt, Doctor,' she says. 'But it's Khaya. He has a temperature again. I am worried and could not find you at the clinic.'

'I will be right there,' Cezanne says.

'Thank you.' The woman scuttles away.

'You're a doctor?'

'Yes.'

Now I'm totally thrown. Clearly Cezanne is a super-bright, capable woman, and it makes even less sense that she would sit back and let Coom carry on with this madness.

She reaches over and places a hand on mine. I let her. 'I will take very good care of your friend, Lele.'

'Can you save her?'

'Trust me, Lele. Can you do that?'

'I don't even know you.'

'The important thing is to get your friend here.'

'That clinic back in Sandtown … it was filled with the dead and the dying. You're a doctor. How can you just sit back and let that happen?'

'I bring as many children here as I can. It is one small victory. But it will not always be like this—'

'Yeah, yeah. I know. As soon as Jova sets us free blah blah blah. You'd think he was some sort of god.'

She smiles sardonically. 'Please. Trust me. Tell Steven that you will agree to what he wants only after your friend makes a full recovery.'

'And then what?'

'I enjoyed our chat. Thank you for taking the time. Now, I must go and see to my patient.' She stands up, lightly touches my shoulder, and glides away.

I sit back, replaying our conversation. I can't fathom Cezanne at all. I try and imagine my stepmother – a woman I'd initially thought was so brittle and unfeeling I'd nicknamed her the Mantis – putting up with a husband like Coom. No chance. The Mantis would have kicked his ass and thrown him to the Rotters the second he mentioned his desire to take another wife. I pop one of the cakes in my mouth and wrap the others in a napkin. Busi might like them.

'Lele!' And here she comes, twitchy and breathless as usual. 'Mr Coom will see you now.'

I'm expecting Busi to lead me back into the hotel, but instead she heads past the kids' play area and through a pair of huge wooden doors that lead outside and into a wide, circular driveway. The shell of a burnt-out hotel looms behind a high wrought-iron fence, and behind a reinforced steel gate, the Rotters' moans increase in volume as if they can sense Busi's presence.

'Where are we going?'

'To the bird park.'

'The *what*?'

She grins and I have to hustle to catch up with her as she hurries across the driveway and down towards a long, low building punctuated by boarded-up windows, a pair of strong wooden doors in its centre.

She bangs her fist on the wood and it's opened by the thuggish bodyguard who was skulking behind Coom's chair last night in the dining room. 'He's in the aviary,' he grunts, stepping back to let us pass.

Holy crap. I was wondering where Montecasino sourced its fresh meat, fruit and vegetables and now I know. A narrow path snakes through a wide grassy area flanked by animal enclosures and cages filled with chickens, guinea fowl and geese. To my left, a herd of tethered goats nip at the grass around a small dam peppered with ducks. A row of bee hives sit in front of a small orchard, the trees pregnant with apricots. If it weren't for the background Rotter choir, it would almost be idyllic.

'So where's Coom?' I ask Busi.

She points to the end of the pathway, and I spot his bulk lounging on a wooden bench next to a cage alive with colourful birds.

'I'll wait here,' Busi whispers.

I take a deep breath, straighten my back and approach him.

'Ah, Lele,' he says, glancing up at me. 'Please, join me.'

'I prefer to stand.'

'As you wish.'

I realise there's a baby bird cupped in his left hand, its little beak opening and closing. What the hell? 'I am concerned that this one is not getting enough nutrition,' he says.

He actually *does* look genuinely concerned. Unbelievable. Sandtown's population is riddled with disease and forced to live in revolting conditions, and he's worried about the fate of a bird. The disgust on my face doesn't appear to concern him the slightest. 'Have you made your decision, Lele?'

'I'll do it. But only if my friend is brought here and cared for. If she lives – then we have a deal.'

'You are bargaining with me?'

'Yeah.'

'Fine.' He picks up a syringe lying next to him on the bench, dunks its tip into a bowl and allows a drop of brown liquid to drip into the bird's mouth.

If I don't get out of here immediately, I'm not sure I'll be able to restrain myself. I dump the napkin and cakes on the floor – I've been clenching my hands so tightly they're nothing but mush – and turn to leave.

'Lele?' he calls after me.

'What?'

'If you run, there will be consequences. Am I clear?'

'If my friend dies, then I don't give a crap about your consequences, is *that* clear?'

We stare at each other, and one of his chins seems to wobble in indignation. He drops his eyes, focusing his attention once more on the bird. 'You may go.'

I stalk straight past Busi as I exit, and she scurries up to my side. 'Everything okay, Lele?'

'No. Of course it isn't. Do I have to have dinner with the fat pig again tonight?'

'Shhh, Lele,' she says, nodding at Coom's thug, who's still standing to attention in front of the gates. 'He'll hear you.'

'I don't care.'

I glare at the bodyguard as he hefts the gate open for us, but he doesn't spare me a glance.

'Mr Coom is meeting with Sindiwe and Jova tonight,' Busi says. 'So you won't have to eat with him. Shall I bring you some food up to your room?'

'Yeah. That would be cool. Busi … is there somewhere

I can get a pen? Some crayons, maybe?' Maybe sketching something will help the time go faster while I wait for them to bring Ember here.

'Of course. Is there anything else you need?'

'A time machine so I can travel back and stop myself from getting into this mess?'

She sighs. 'Sorry, Lele. But how about some anti-Coom bug spray?'

I stop dead. 'Busi, did you just make a joke?'

She giggles, cups her hand to her mouth. Then, almost instantly, her good mood vanishes.

'What is it?'

I follow her gaze to where a couple of black-clad guys are leaning against the huge carved doors that lead into the phony city. I recognise them from the dining hall – two of Coom's runners. Although the light is fading, they're both wearing sunglasses; hand-rolled cigarettes loll in their fingers. Ginger would crack up if he saw them, probably call them asswipe wannabe Ninjas or something.

'Heita, Busi,' the stockier of the two calls. 'You come to me tonight, okay?'

Busi drops her head. Nods. She moves as if to scuttle past them, but I grab her elbow.

'Come to you for what?' I ask.

The other runner, a lanky guy with overlapping teeth hoots. 'What do you think?'

I don't know Busi well, but it's obvious from the way she's refusing to look at the men that's she's deeply uncomfortable. 'And do you *want* to go with this jerk, Busi?'

'It's fine, Lele,' she whispers.

'It's not fine.' I shoot daggers at the stocky guy. 'Busi is with me tonight. I need her.'

122

'Need her for what?'

'What do you think?'

Stocky grinds his cigarette under his heel and smirks. 'Don't be late this time, Busi. We're going to have a real good party.'

'She's not going anywhere with you.'

'*Lele*,' Busi hisses.

Stocky snorts. Looks me up and down and grimaces as if I smell bad. 'You may be one of Coom's whores, but you have no authority over me. And Busi likes to party, don't you, Busi?'

He reaches out to touch Busi's cheek and I grab his hand, push his fingers back, step forward and knee him as hard as I can in the groin. He makes an 'ug' sound, then falls to his knees.

I don't wait for the lanky runner to attack first, I swing around, planning on elbowing him in the throat, but he blocks me, and my face explodes as he rams a fist into my cheek. He's not going to get away with that. I drop my head, pretend to stagger back, then hook my right leg under his and twist. He falls back heavily and I slam my boot down in his gut. He lets out an 'Oof!' and I raise my foot to do it again.

'Lele! Stop!' Busi yells, but I bat her away when she tries to pull me back. Everything I've been through, all the anger, the fear, the worry about Ember has coalesced into this. If I can't make Coom pay, if I can't get the hell out of here, then—

'You're dead.'

I freeze, turn around slowly. Stocky has managed to pull the gun out of its holster and is pointing it right at my head, his face still distorted with pain.

'Go on then,' I say, stunned at how calm I sound. 'How are you going to explain to Coom that you've shot one of his *whores*?'

Stocky blinks. 'What are you, some sort of psycho?'

The adrenaline surge is receding now, but I still don't feel a trace of fear. 'Something like that.'

'What's going on here?' One Ear strides towards us and Stocky shoves the gun back in the holster. One Ear takes in the two guys on the ground, then peers at my face. 'Well?'

'Let's go,' I say to him. 'I'm finished here.'

I grab Busi's hand and yank her through the entrance, walking as fast as I can.

'Hey!' One Ear shouts after us.

Busi's looking at me warily. 'Why didn't you say you could do that?'

'Do what?'

'Fight like that.'

'I'm rusty. Anyway, anyone can learn how to do that. It's no biggie.'

That lanky guy really whacked me. I open and close my jaw. He didn't hit me hard enough to crack my cheekbone, but it's throbbing like crazy. One Ear grabs my shoulder and spins me around.

'What was that all about back there?'

Busi catches my eye shakes her head slightly.

'Nothing. They were rude to us, that's all.'

One Ear isn't stupid. He stares at me, then at Busi. 'That all?' She nods. 'And you,' he says to me. 'You did that to them?'

'Yeah.'

'Alone?'

'No, me and my secret team of ninja assassins. What do you think? Will they cause any trouble?'

'Not if they know what's good for them.'

We walk the rest of the way back to the hotel in silence. The second I'm in my room I flump down on the bed.

Busi flutters at the door. 'I must go get your food.'

'Busi – wait.'

She turns, obviously reluctant to hear what I'm going to say. 'How long has this been going on?'

She shrugs. 'Not long. Really, Lele ... it doesn't matter.'

'It matters a lot.'

'Mr Coom's runners ... they can do what they like. They have certain privileges.'

'Yeah? Not any more they don't. They touch you again I will kill them.' And I realise I mean it. 'Busi ... are you and Sihle ... you know?'

Busi stares at her hands. 'No, Lele.'

'Is he married?'

'Sihle isn't married. Not as far as I know.'

'So what's stopping you and him getting together?'

She shrugs, clearly mortified. And who the hell am I to dispense relationship advice, anyway? Ash and I were hardly the world's most successful couple and Thabo, my only other boyfriend, doesn't count. We only shared one kiss before he ... I shiver. I don't want to think of him as he is now. It will only lead to more dangerous thoughts about Saint. 'I'm just making conversation, Busi. Forget I said anything.'

She nods and slips out of the room.

I gingerly touch my face. It's still tender but the pain isn't anything I can't handle. I've survived much worse. I stretch out, crack my knuckles and flex my fingers. The rush I felt when I floored those guys hasn't entirely gone. Maybe Stocky was right about me. Maybe I am some sort of psycho. I can't deny that I enjoyed every second of beating the crap out of them, which isn't normal, is it? Am I losing it? Have I always been like this? I shut my eyes, replay the scene over and over. Would I have done anything differently? No.

The door swings open. 'Lele,' Lucien says, striding into the room as if he owns it. 'You're a mess.'

'Where's Busi?'

'I gave her the evening off. She told me what happened.'

'If those guys touch Busi again then—'

'Do not worry, they will not.' He holds up a bottle of whiskey. 'I brought something to ease the pain.'

'Seriously? What's this, a social call?'

A chuckle. 'Something like that, *oui*. I wanted to see how you are.'

'Busi's going to think it's weird when there's no sign of a bruise on my face tomorrow. She saw how hard one of those jerks whacked me.'

Lucien slides nearer to me, reaches out, cups my jaw and gently turns it to one side. 'It is not too bad. The skin is not broken.' His finger slides down my cheek and I push him away.

'Don't touch me.'

I snatch the bottle out of his hand and take a sip. It burns, makes me gag, takes me straight back to that awful night on that grounded cruise ship, the last time I tasted alcohol. When I managed to drink myself into oblivion. A mistake. Saint and I had only just escaped with our lives back then, but right now I *want* the oblivion.

'What will happen to those guys?'

A shrug. 'Nothing. They will not want Coom to know what has happened. And they will not want to admit that they were bested by a girl.'

'Ah. Nice to hear that sexism is alive and well here along with all the other crap.' I take another glug, pass the bottle back to Lucien. 'They should be punished for what they've done, for treating Busi like that.' I sit up. It feels weird being so close to him.

'I agree. But they will not be doing anything like that again, Lele. You have my word.'

'Yeah, cos your word means so much, doesn't it, Lucien?'

He smiles ruefully. 'I deserved that.' He hands me the bottle and I take another throat-burning glug.

'Lucien, tell me. Which city do you think is more screwed up? Here or Cape Town?'

'They are both troubled in their own way. But when Jova is—'

'Gah. If I hear about Jova and his magical army and brilliant plan one more time I'm going to puke. He's a just a guy, Lucien. Not some sort of god.'

He's suddenly serious '*Oui*. You are right. And a flawed one as well. Like all of us.' He sighs. 'Maybe things will always be this way. Maybe it is impossible to ever find peace.'

He shifts his position. He's sitting far too close to me. I don't move away; decide not to question why I don't.

'Lucien. I saw Ember. She needs medical care. Urgently. If I don't help her then she could die. Looks like you were right. Looks like I have no choice but to accept that fat pig's proposal.'

'I am sorry, Lele. But maybe you are safer here.'

'*What?* What does that mean?'

'Calm down. I am sorry. I did not mean that.' He scrubs a hand over his face. 'The things that are happening ... but I will not bore you with that.'

Another swig. This one goes down easier. All I've eaten all day is a single tiny cake, and I of all people should know how dangerous it is to drink on an empty stomach. 'Have you seen Ash?'

Lucien freezes, the mention of his name chilling the atmosphere between us. 'He is doing well, Lele.'

'What do you mean "well"? Has he bought into Jova's Army of the Left crap already?'

No answer. I take that as a yes.

'Does he know about Coom? About what's going to happen to me?' If Ash knew what Coom had in store for me, he would stop at nothing to get me out of here, wouldn't he?

'I do not know.'

I knock back another mouthful, and the room tips. Whoa. 'I heard that Ginger's run off, Lucien. What will happen to him?'

'If he stays away from Sandtown, he will be fine. Ginger is the last person you need to worry about now.'

He takes off his jacket, throws it onto the floor.

'Making yourself at home?'

'*Oui*.' He smiles at me, holding my gaze and something sparks between us. 'You have a problem with this?'

My eyes drop to the tattoos that cover his arms. I remember the one on his back – a stunningly intricate design that he told me was Jova's handiwork. A tattoo in the shape of a hand. A *left* hand. Back then I wanted to meet Jova, thought that anyone who could create such an amazing work of art must be someone worth knowing. 'Lele. I am going to help you.'

'Help me what? Get even drunker? You're doing a good job of that already.'

'*Non*.' Lucien is suddenly serious. 'Get out of this situation. I am going to talk to Jova again.'

He moves his fingertips up my arm. I let him. A tingling sensation dances down into my belly, melding with the swirling alcohol.

'You're really going to help me?'

His face is close to mine. Too close.

'*Oui*,' he says. And then he pushes me down onto the bed.

Jack

Jack races along the metal roof, his feet beating time with the thumps of the long-dead commuters trapped below him in the train's bowels.

Despite the danger, a part of him loves these scouting missions. Jova says they're like quests in the old video games he used to play, and Jack clings to this fantasy as he leaps the short distance between the carriages. But all too soon, he runs out of roof. There's a good hundred metres of open track between him and the safety of the next train rotting on the tracks. If his feet touch the ground, he could be fair game.

He's in uncharted territory, far away from the familiar routes he and Jova have mapped out over the roofs in the devastated heart of the city. If Hester finds out he's come this far into no-man's-land, he'll be in deep kak. But with the sun starting to rise, warming his chilled muscles, he feels invincible. Untouchable. Free.

And the risk will be worth it when he sees the look on Jova's face. Jack figured it out when he borrowed one of Jova's fantasy books – *The Hobbit* – and noticed the front page had been torn out. Pressed into the page before it, like catching a glimpse of a ghost, was the imprint of a scrawled message. It felt wrong rubbing dirt into the indentations, but it allowed him to decipher the message: *31 December 2009. Happy birthday Jova, love Nana x*.

Thanks to Jova's fanatical need to document everything around them, to write down their 'new history', Jack knows that tomorrow is the last day of December – and Jova's birthday.

He scurries towards the houses hiding behind the station's sagging fence. He doesn't have time to do a thorough recce, and picks the first one that looks relatively unscathed. The fact that he hasn't seen any Rotters since leaving the train tracks emboldens him.

He scales the fence, trying not to look too closely at the mummified remains of a dog lying in the weeds in the garden. The back door is locked, but there's just enough room for him to squeeze his skinny body between the warped burglar bars of the open kitchen window. He clambers up, unstraps his rifle and pushes it carefully through the opening, hearing it clatter safely onto the floor. He slips his feet through first, twisting and wriggling like a snake until he manages to force his hips through the bars. For a horrifying moment his head seems to get stuck and he imagines himself trapped like that dog, starving to death until he's nothing but a collection of leathery skin and bones. But then he's free and he rolls as he hits the ground, sending a plastic dog bowl skittering across the linoleum. He retrieves the gun, then counts to ten, senses on high alert for any movement.

A loaf of bread on the counter has been reduced to a mound of black mould. Childish finger paintings are tacked to the fridge with magnets shaped like kittens. A rain spider whispers across the wall, disappearing behind a World Cup 2010 calendar hanging next to the fridge.

He tiptoes through the house, searching for a bookcase, aware that he hasn't got long. He left a note saying he was off to collect the water ration, but if he's gone for more than a couple of hours, Hester might decide to send out a search party, and then he'll be for it.

Just when he's about to give up, he finds what he's looking for in the master bedroom. He searches through the titles piled on the shelves, most of which appear to be self-help manuals or religious books. Then, half-hidden behind a giant Bible, he finds it. A battered paperback, one of the pulpy sci-fi classics Jova can't get enough of. *The Day of the Triffids*. Jack's certain Jova hasn't read this one; he'd remember that weird title.

He quickly checks under the mattress, where Jova told him most people tend to hide their shameful secrets, yelping in triumph when he pulls out a copy of Big 'n Busty. It will come in handy as a bribe, especially when supplies run low again and the older resistance members decide to keep the best food for themselves.

A muffled groan sounds from behind him and he spins, his rifle in his hands before he even has to think about it. His instinct for self-preservation has been finely honed over the months of fighting, hiding and running. As Jova's always saying, hesitation can mean the difference between life and living death.

He squeezes the trigger and the figure in the doorway crumples to the floor.

He approaches cautiously – Rotters can be hard to kill – but this one isn't even twitching. The figure is small – a child. A girl. His mouth goes dry and panic claws at his throat. He takes in the long dark hair and what's left of the delicate bone structure.

Sasha. She looks like Sasha.

The girl's body is so well preserved that for a horrible moment Jack thinks that he's killed a living, breathing human.

He shudders with relief as he spots a hint of decay on her right arm. But that doesn't change the fact that even if she had been human, he would have shot her anyway. He pulled the trigger without thinking – a reflex.

Mouth bitter with bile, he throws the rifle away from him. It goes off as it lands, hitting the leg of the side table, and a family portrait crashes to the floor.

Forgetting to retrieve Jova's birthday book, Jack runs.

He leaves the gun where it lies.

Ash

Never underestimate the power of a teenage boy with a marker pen.

I have to admire Danny's handiwork. The once-bare wooden target dummies have been transformed into cartoonish Rotter facsimiles; one of them even sports a stuffed bra and a mop-head for a wig.

Morgan has to raise her voice to be heard over the grunts of the graduates training behind us. Each gust of wind whips sand in our faces, bringing with it the stink of their sweat. I'm starting to think they deliberately put the newbie sparring area downwind of the main training grounds for this very reason. 'Nothing I can teach you will prepare you for your first encounter with one of the newly infected, or as we like to call them, newborns.'

Newborns. What sort of a crazy name is that? Ginger would crack up if he heard the AOL's nickname for hatchlings. Morgan catches my look of derision, but carries on speaking regardless: 'Forget what you might have seen of the jujus during runner camp. Newborns are fast and deadly and believe it or not, they can infect Lefties like you. If you have the balls to get into melee range, the safest way to dispatch them is to shoot them right here,' Morgan touches a finger to the centre of her upper lip, just below her nose. 'Take out the cerebral cortex. Contrary to what you might have been told, a head shot won't always kill a newborn.'

Danny raises his hand. 'Cereal what?'

Pockets groans. 'Great. Ladies and gentlemen, may I present our medic.'

'It's like, the brain, right?'

Morgan ignores the interruption, points to a box containing a motley collection of pistols and rifles. 'You know the drill.'

I hang back and watch as the others whoop and race to the box. Americano picks out a Glock, weighs it expertly in his left hand and grunts in approval. It's obvious he knows how to handle it. Danny's a different story. He's chosen a .38 special, and he's holding it sideways like a gangsta in one of Ginger's movies. Nuush, Noxi and Pockets all grab rifles, mock-squabbling over their choices. I still can't shake the feeling that they're all just playing at being soldiers, that the endless training is just a ploy to keep them busy.

Morgan nods at me. 'Care to join us?'

'I don't do guns.'

'Are you, like, one of those pacifics?' Danny asks.

Pockets whacks him on the back of the head. 'Pacifist, dumbass.'

'Bitch, please, not the hair.'

'You might change your mind when you come face-to-face with a newborn, Jack,' Morgan says.

'I've fought them before. And without a gun.' Even to my

ears it sounds arrogant, but I'm tired of being told things I already know.

'Do you think these lessons are beneath you?'

I shrug. 'Anything you can do with a gun I can do without one.'

Noxi whistles. 'So not only is he Jova's BFF, he fights newborns with his bare hands.' Her tone is mocking but she softens the blow with one of her dazzling smiles.

'Why don't you demonstrate these skills of yours to the rest of your team?' Morgan says, deadpan.

'Fine.' I choose the target with the fake breasts and move towards it.

'Not the dummy, Jack.'

Morgan strips off her jacket. Her T-shirt is skin-tight; I can make out the ridge of muscles on her belly and the shape of her breasts.

'Here we go,' Danny mutters.

'You serious?' I say.

'Let's go.'

I size her up. She outweighs Saint by a good few kilos but that'll slow her down. Her arms are well muscled, but my reach is longer – she won't touch me.

I bounce on the balls of my feet, feeling the crunch of loose tarmac beneath my boots. Morgan rolls her shoulders. I'm not stupid enough to think her impaired vision will give me any great advantage; she wouldn't be here if it did, but I'll make use of her compromised depth perception if I have to.

I expect her to make the first move, but she just smiles and beckons me closer.

Fine.

I decide to come in fast, test her reflexes, I feint to her left and lurch to her right at the last minute, but my kick to her kidneys never lands. Surprisingly light on her feet, Morgan spins and I just manage to dodge out of range of her left hook. I regain my balance and come in again. She shifts her weight on her left leg and it's all the warning I need to catch her wrist as she swings. I don't expect her right uppercut and it hits me like a truck. Darkness threatens at the edge of my sight; I really hope that cracking sound wasn't one of my teeth.

She doesn't give me a chance to recover and it's all I can do to block the assault, searching for an opening. I knock her fist aside and bring my knee up into her gut. It's not a move Hester would be proud of but I need the space. If she puts me on the defensive then she'll keep me there.

My knee feels like it hits stone; she grunts, but absorbs the impact. I'm starting to believe that 'cyborg pirate from the future' rumour Danny's started.

I need to change tactics and decide to give her an opening. She takes it. I let her land the hit and it knocks the air out of my lungs. But I'm finally within her reach. I clock a solid hit to her jaw and follow it up with a jab to her kidneys. But before I can set up my next kick, she catches me under my knee and tries to unbalance me. Using our combined momentum, I launch myself into the air and ram my other knee into the side of her head.

'That's some *Matrix* shit right there,' Americano says.

I regain my feet, just in time to see Morgan doing the same.

'Oh man, Jack, I'd run the hell away if I were you,' Danny chimes in.

'Nah, he's got this,' Noxi says.

I'm not so sure.

Morgan comes in for the kill. A flurry of fists pushes me back. I stumble and before I know what's happening I'm flat on my back, trying to suck in a lungful of air and blinking at the stars flashing in my vision. A heavy weight sits on my stomach; she's straddling me.

She leans forward and whispers, 'I don't need a gun either.' Then she climbs off and shrugs into her jacket.

Americano holds out a hand and hauls me to my feet. 'Don't worry, Pretty Boy. You aren't the first mouthy bastard to get floored by the Captain.'

Morgan pretends not to hear. She looks straight at me and says, 'The dead aren't our only enemy. The Outcasts have been known to carry guns. Hold onto that sentimentality of yours; I hope it's powerful enough to stop a bullet.'

Nuush offers me her rifle. 'Take it. We won't laugh at you for having bad aim.'

Danny snorts. 'Of course we will.'

'Yeah, the guy has to have one flaw, right?' Pockets says.

Morgan sighs. 'Well, I can't have you unarmed. Is there anything you *will* fight with?'

I shrug. 'Got any pangas lying around?'

Noxi snorts. 'You effing *serious*?'

The sun is setting as I make my way back to the dorm, my new panga knife strapped to my back. Every inch of me aches; I haven't been floored that comprehensively since Saint and I used to train back in Hester's hideout. I should be awash with humiliation, but all I'm feeling is a grudging respect. Morgan won her victory fair and square. In fact – even though I don't want to admit it – I'm actually feeling more like myself than I have since we left Cape Town. I don't want to dwell on why this is. I don't want to admit that Jova's right, that maybe I *do* belong here.

Because I don't. I belong with my friends. This is just a way station. After the trials, I'm out of here.

The others are clustered in a corner having a heated discussion when I shoulder open the door. I dump my stuff on my sleeping bag, intent on cramming in a few hours at the library.

Americano whistles, 'Hey, Jack. Over here.'

'What?'

'So, you've had your ass handed to you by Morgan, which means you're ready for the next step in your initiation'.

'Initiation?'

Danny nods gravely. 'It's tradition.'

'You can't be a part of the gang until you pass it,' Pockets adds.

I open my mouth to say that I won't be sticking around to be part of any gang, but something stops me. I sigh. 'What do I have to do?'

Noxi grins and holds up a pair of hair clippers.

'No ways.'

'You chicken?' Noxi asks with one of her slow smiles. She waves me to a chair obviously brought in for the purpose. I sit down heavily. 'Don't worry,' she whispers. 'I'll be gentle.'

The clippers buzz into life and I watch as locks of black hair cover the floor around my feet. The feel of the blade on my scalp isn't unpleasant. Nor is the soft press of Noxi's body as she moves around me.

'What if the batteries cut out and he's left with clown hair?' Nuush stage-whispers.

'Then we can call him Tufty,' Pockets giggles.

'Just be glad we're only shaving your head.' Danny points at his crotch and grins.

Noxi tilts my head to the side, her belly pressing against my arm. 'Have you even been through puberty, Danny?'

'Ja. It was kak. Morgan had to give me the talk.'

Americano laughs and bats at the cloud of smoke drifting around his head.

'All done,' Noxi says, but she doesn't move away. Nuush hands me a jagged piece of mirror. I hardly recognise myself. Without the fringe that flops over my left eye, my face looks ... naked. Raw.

'Not bad,' Americano grunts.

Noxi leans in close, her breath hot on the back of my neck. I meet her eyes in the mirror, 'It suits you. You look more ... real. Sets off those demon eyes.'

The door bursts open, and I don't have to turn my head to know it's Morgan – everyone is suddenly on their feet.

'Relax.' Morgan sets a bottle on the floor at my feet. She inspects my new haircut and smirks. 'Welcome to the team, Jack.' She slips out and the atmosphere lightens again.

Americano lifts up the bottle, twisting it to show us the label. A pirate, one leg raised and resting on a barrel, grins back at us. 'Captain Morgan, Spiced Gold rum.'

'Well, what do you know,' Danny says. 'The cyborg *does* have a sense of humour.'

We pass the bottle around, and my first sip burns a trail to the pit of my stomach. Pockets and Nuush are the only ones who don't take a hit. I take another gulp and Noxi smiles slyly at me. 'Drink up, Pretty Boy. We're going to have some fun tonight.'

Pockets giggles. 'What kind of fun, Noxi?'

Noxi holds my gaze. 'What would *you* like to do, Jack?'

I drop my eyes, feeling heat rushing to my cheeks. The bottle swings its way back to me, and I take another couple of hits, then pass it to Americano.

'Hey, Americano,' I say, hearing my words blurring slightly. 'What's your story?'

'He was a soccer player, way back when,' Danny says. 'Came out for the World Cup and then ... *bam*. It all went to kak and he got stuck in Mzanzi for good.'

'Uh-uh,' Americano says. 'You know that's not true, Danny. I was a coach. A trainer, for the United States soccer team.'

So he's like Ginger, a foreigner, stuck in South Africa when the Rotters took over the world. 'You get homesick?' I ask. Noxi sits down next to me, her thigh pressing against mine.

Americano shrugs. 'Used to. Try not to think about home any more. Won't do any good.'

'You're older than the others. How come you're a newbie? Shouldn't you have been part of the first wave of graduates?'

'It's a long, boring story, bud.' He offers me his pack of cigarettes.

'I got time.'

He sighs, holds up his hands. 'I'm ambidextrous. But I favour my right hand. Didn't even know I was immune until my wife—'

'You've got a wife?'

'Yeah.'

'And three kids,' Danny pipes in. 'Americano's been a busy boy.'

'Thanks for that, Danny. Anyway, I was helping fix the electrics on the second floor, fell off the step-ladder. Broke my right arm. Soraya – my wife – pointed out that I was managing very well with my left, *too* well, so I decided to test it out.'

'Walked straight outside Sandtown,' Pockets says. 'Right into juju central. This oke has got balls of steel.'

Americano shrugs. 'Sold myself to the highest bidder, got

my family into the Tri-Hotels area, paid off my sponsorship, and the rest is history.'

'I'm also ambidextrous,' I lie. It's easier than explaining the actual reason why I'm immune to Rotter attack. I try to imagine how that conversation would go: *Well, see guys, I have a stunted twin back in Cape Town who the Guardians experimented on at the beginning of the war and for some reason this makes me immune to Rotter attack.* I don't think so. And it will only make me think of Sasha.

Americano barks a laugh, holds up his left palm for a slap. 'Cool, man.' He hands me another cigarette. 'Your turn, bud.'

'Yeah,' Nuush says. 'We're dying to know your story, Jack.'

I light up and inhale, careful to blow the smoke away from Nuush's face. 'It's a long one.'

Americano shrugs. 'We've got all night.'

He passes me the bottle of rum and I take another stinging gulp. I start to tell them a paraphrased story of the journey to Jozi, but once I start I just can't stop and soon I'm spilling my guts out. At some point Noxi drapes herself across my lap, one hand raised to stroke my new hair. I lift the bottle to her lips without having to be asked. I have just enough sense left to keep a few cards close to my chest, like Sasha and my own brand of non-Lefty immunity. And there are some things I don't – *can't* – talk about, like Saint.

Pockets is the first one to speak. 'Zombie scarecrows. What the actual hell?'

'Crazy tree amazons,' Danny grins. 'I am so going there one day.'

'I'd say you were lying,' Noxi pries the cigarette from my hand and takes a long slow drag, 'but I don't reckon you can lie to save your life.'

'Trust me, I really wish I *was* making this up.'

'And Jova?' Americano asks.

'What about him?'

'How did you guys meet?'

There's too much to say about what happened with Jova, so I spin out in a few anecdotes about foraging for supplies together and fighting with the crew from the Last Resistance, but I keep it as short as I can.

Americano's watching me intently. 'If you and Jova were so tight back in the day, why didn't you leave Cape Town with him?'

I shrug. 'I had other responsibilities.' I don't want to go there in my mind right now. The room is starting to spin. I need to get some fresh air, clear my head. If I don't, I might be tempted to reveal too much. I gently shift Noxi off my lap, stagger to my feet. 'I'll be right back.'

'Where you going?' Noxi asks.

'Fresh air.' She moves as if to follow me, but I gesture for her to stay put. 'I won't be long.'

'You'd better not be,' she says with another one of her smiles. 'Or I'll come and find you.'

Danny thrusts the nearly empty bottle of rum into my hands, 'Take this, bru. It's dangerous to go alone.'

The alcohol has hit me hard, the floor undulates, and I'm forced to trail my hand along the wall to steady myself as I weave my way down towards the lower level, heading for the bathrooms. Maybe I'll feel better if I splash some cold water on my face. It's almost pitch black in some areas of the airport, and I bang my shin on a luggage trolley as I navigate through the long-defunct security gates.

As I swing around the conduit that leads to the canteen, the sound of angry voices echoes towards me.

Trying to soften my footsteps, I creep forward, sticking to the shadows. I can make out two figures standing in front of the old Wimpy and I hustle closer to them, using the darkness cast by the pillars on this side of the space to cloak me. I recognise one of them as Morgan – I'm already becoming familiar with the way she holds her body, straight-backed and confident.

'Please calm down,' she's saying. 'There's nothing I—'

'For the last time, where is Jova?'

It's Lucien, his French accent thick with anger. I shake my head, trying to clear it.

Saint.

It's Lucien's fault Saint is dead.

My grip tightens on the neck of the bottle; the urge to throw it at his head is enormous. With an effort, I control myself. I might learn something valuable by listening, and I'm hardly in a state to take him on.

'I've told you, Lucien. He's not here.'

'Where is he?'

'He mentioned something about travelling to the south of the city.'

'When will he be back?'

'I don't know. Lucien, there's no reason for you to lose your—'

'Ha! There are many reasons why I should lose my temper, Morgan. More than you could possibly know. *Merde!*' Lucien slams his fist down onto a table and then jabs a finger in her face. 'When you see him, you tell him that I will not do what he wants. I have told him what he wants to know and that is as far as I am prepared to go. You tell him that he has used me as his dog for the last time. You tell him that I am gone, that I am leaving Jozi for good. That I will no longer be part of this ... this ... *madness!*'

Lucien turns on his heel and storms off.

'Lucien!' Morgan calls after him, an uncharacteristic anxious note in her voice. 'Lucien, wait!' She jogs after him and I surprise myself by feeling ... what? Jealous? Why would the fact that Morgan's chasing after Lucien make me feel jealous?

I lean back against the nearest pillar and knock back another glug of rum. Bad idea. I need to get my head straight, not muddy it further.

I should go after them, catch up to them. Confront Lucien once and for all. Make him pay for what he's done to Saint.

Yeah. I peel away from the pillar, stumbling as the floor tilts again. A pair of arms snake around my chest. 'Found you,' Noxi whispers in my ear. 'I've been looking for you everywhere.'

I almost shrug her off, but then she kisses the side of my neck, a feather-light brush of her lips. I turn to face her, bend to kiss her back but she pushes against my chest.

'First things first. That girl, Lele. The one from Cape Town.'

'What about her?'

'Is she your girlfriend?'

'I don't know,' I say without thinking. Lele and I broke up, but ... there was something still there, wasn't there? I screwed up. All my fault. I can't even see Lele's face in my head any more.

'You don't know?'

There are two Noxis bobbing in front of me now.

She sighs. 'Come on. I know just what you need.'

'Where we going?'

She walks away from me, her hips swaying with each step. I know what she wants, and I know that I'm following her partly because she reminds me of Lele. I don't even notice where we're going until we're right outside it. The bookshop.

'Why here?' I slur.

'Why not?'

She takes my hand and leads me down a aisle towards the back of the store. She bends down, there's the hiss of a match and a candle flickers into life. There's a blanket laid out on the floor.

'Noxi,' I say, 'I'm drunk, I don't know if ...'

My voice trails away as she tugs her shirt over her head. She gives me one of her trademark slow smiles and says, 'I hope you're as good with that panga as you say you are.'

Saint

Saint can walk for hours without getting tired, leaving an endless trail of her footprints in the red dust. The steady throb at the back of her mind leads her away from the highway and into a world of dry dirt, thorn trees and bones. The fastest route to her destination is through the heart of the desert, but Bambi's need for water means that she is unable to stray too far from the river.

The hyena is the only weak spot in her new reality.

She should leave him behind. She knows this.

But every time she tries, Ntombi stops her. So she carries Bambi in her arms when his strength falters and waits for him when he darts off into the scrub. She can feel his driving need to hunt and she knows the second when his jaws snap around a rodent's throat; she can distantly feel its panic, and then – somehow worse – its acceptance.

And now, weaving among the twitchy strands of rodents and the spiky threads of scorpions, she senses the spark of human life.

Although it takes her away from her path, she follows it. She reaches a sagging farmhouse ringed with fences. The water pump next to the dam sighs and groans as the wind picks up.

The Rotters left this place long ago, made their way to the city where the pull of life was stronger. Their bleached bones laced with shrivelled white strands are all that's left of them. She reaches down and touches a skeletal hand, curled up like a spider.

The gate is locked, but she picks up a stone and breaks the rusted chains.

Then she feels it.

She was wrong. One of the Rotters *is* still here, its grey thread smothered by the brighter one. It's distressed, trapped. Locked in a wooden structure not far from where she's standing. Saint knows that it was once a woman. A *good* woman, but her captivity isn't the source of its distress. There's something else.

What are we doing here? Ntombi grumps. She's been quiet for a while. Her continual efforts to stop Saint becoming seduced by the darkness exhaust her.

Something I need to do.

What?

Saint ignores her, walks past dying mealies and on towards the farmhouse. Bambi shoots off, chasing chickens. She lets him, although their terror disturbs her. He has to eat. She skirts a tree heavy with rotting fruit. A cloud of midges floats around her; she brushes away a hornet that darts for her face. Ntombi whoops as Saint spots a row of beehives. She loved honey, back then.

She steps through the door into a kitchen and heads down a dark passageway.

The man is lying in his own filth. Saint is aware of the smell around her, but feels no disgust. If it weren't for the faint pulse of his thread, she'd think he were dead. Skin pulled tight over sunken bones, jaundiced eyes. His head jerks, there's a moment of panic, and then a calmness. 'Andisa. You came.' He sucks in a rattling breath between brown and broken teeth.

There's a bond between the trapped Rotter and this man. Love. A bond of love. Saint can't quite grasp this, but Ntombi sends her a flash of Ripley laughing, showing off her crooked teeth, pulling her into a hug, both of them dancing to one of Ginger's cheesy movie soundtracks. Snap to another image of Ripley. She's lying on Saint's old mattress back in Hester's hideout in Cape Town, an arm flung carelessly over her forehead, her lips moving in her sleep. Saint had known she and Ripley would be together the second they met; had known it from the way Ripley held her gaze when they were introduced. Although back then she wasn't Ripley, Ginger hadn't yet given them all their nicknames. She was ... Saint fumbles for Ripley's real name.

Shemina, Ntombi feeds it to her. *And you were Ntombi, not Saint.*

How many months had they had together before Ripley was taken from her? Saint can't remember this, either. She doesn't want to think about this any more. She can no longer feel pain but the memory of it is bad enough.

Tough. It's part of you. It's what we were.

Sensing a weakness, Ntombi shoots her images of the friends she's left behind, something she frequently does, imploring her to search out their threads again. Ginger's flares blue, heavy with anguish. Ash's thrums with colour and life. Ember's is weaker, a soft yellow glow. And Lele's ... Lele's is now entwined with another, quieter strand. Saint doesn't know what this means. Tries not to care.

Saint shakes off Ntombi's grip and turns her attention back to the man. He doesn't have long left. But he is content. She can sense the moment when the fluttering flame of the man's life gutters out.

He's gone.

Yes.

Sad.

Is it?

Saint leaves the farmhouse, walks behind it to a large reinforced shed. Pulls back the bolts and opens the door. The Rotter – (*Andisa*, Ntombi whispers) – stumbles into the light. Saint knows that the woman will instinctively feel the lure of the body on the bed, will want to consume it. But, like Saint has, she will resist it.

Saint watches as she staggers towards the gate, drawn by the lure of life in the city miles from here.

Atang calls to her. Ntombi sighs. *Not now. We're busy.*

I'll be quick.

Saint allows herself to drift to her childhood kitchen. Atang looks up at her expectantly.

<why aren't you moving? you must hurry now>

<I will>

He sends her another jolting vision of that valley and its twitching, blood-soaked inhabitants.

Ntombi shudders, flexes her muscles, and the vision fades.

Three's a crowd. Ntombi mutters. *Feed the hyena, Saint. He's not fast enough to catch the chickens.*

Feed him with what?

There must be some food somewhere.

Saint returns to the farmhouse, searches the kitchen, finds thin strings of meat drying in the pantry. They're tough and wizened but she's seen the hyena eat worse.

It's time to leave. Atang is right. She walks past the beehives, ignoring Ntombi's pang of longing, pushes through the gate, drawing the hyena away from the chickens. Then she senses something else. A thread like a fluttering heartbeat. Different from Bambi's and those of the other animals she's sensed so far.

A horse!

The animal trots towards her, shaking its head. Before the darkness Saint would have run from it. Her old self wasn't keen on animals. It stops several metres from her, snorts.

Bambi grumbles in his chest and the horse drops its head and skitters away. Saint tries to send it a wash of calm, but fails. Ntombi feeds her a recollection of something Ash said years ago: The world and everything in it are just molecules, bonded together. He tried to explain DNA to her, but she wasn't able to follow that at all. She has to attach herself to the horse in the same way she connected herself to Bambi.

She reaches out, touches its strong but jittery thread. It's lonely. Not a human loneliness, but a longing to be part of something bigger. *One is not enough*, is the closest translation Ntombi can come up with for this feeling. And this is what she attaches herself to.

It stops, snorts again and swings around and approaches cautiously. She feels its thread binding with hers. She tugs, trying to dampen Bambi's instinctive urge to snap at it.

It's close enough to touch. She strokes its neck, feeling its heat radiating into her palm. Its coat is softer than Bambi's.

We should take it with us, Ntombi says.

Why?

It needs us. Just like our friends need us.

Ntombi bombards her with another barrage of images of Ash, Ginger and Lele. Laughing round a campfire in the

Deadlands. Haring through the mall, gathering up goods to sell in the new arrivals market. Sitting with Hester in the hideout, sharing a pot of rooibos. It hurts. And this time, the pain is real.

Stop doing that, Ntombi.

No.

Then I have no choice.

As Ntombi keens in her mind, Saint mentally takes a pair of shears and cauterises the strands belonging to her friends.

Tommy

Tommy's fighting to keep the despair at bay, but it's a losing battle. It wasn't so bad when they were forced to keep moving; eventually all he could think about was how much the soles of his feet were throbbing. But now the day's light is waning and anything could be hiding in the sinister pools of shadow cast by the buildings around them.

Anything at all.

'Tommy!' Jacob calls, gesturing at a massive building on the opposite side of the road. 'We can stay there tonight.'

Jacob can't be serious. It looks old and forbidding, haunted even, and Tommy can hear moans emanating from behind the building's thick walls – it must be stuffed with the dead. The sign above the entrance reads: 'New Hope Hospital Casualty', only the word 'no' has been sprayed over the word 'new'. No Hope. *Awesome*.

'Why there, Jacob?' After all, they've passed countless apartment blocks, and they're standing just metres in front of a mansion nestled within an overgrown garden. Jacob turns to look at him and Tommy's relieved to see that his eyes look ... normal. They haven't always been so. Jacob seems to have moments of lucidity – like when he insisted Tommy run from the Mooki situation – but with no warning he'll switch to incoherent rambling, frantically digging his nails into his palms as if he has no other outlet for his energy.

'If they bring the dogs to follow our scent, they could track us down. The best place to hide is in the dead. Yes.' Jacob nods his head violently. 'Yes, yes. Hide in the dead. The dogs can't sniff us then, see?'

Dogs? This is news to Tommy. Far as he knows none of the runner teams use dogs – they're discouraged in Sandtown as they use up too many resources. But perhaps Jacob knows something he doesn't. After all, it's not the first time Jacob has run from Sandtown. 'There won't be any of those fresh dead ones in there, will there?'

'You mean hatchlings?' Ginger says, making Tommy jump. It's the first time Ginger's spoken since they decided to run. 'That's what we call them where I'm from.' The giant's face is haggard with exhaustion and pain. Tommy has no idea how he's even managed to keep going for as long as he has.

'Hatchlings,' Jacob says with a humourless smile. 'Hatchlings. Ha!'

'It's unlikely they'll be any hatchlings,' Ginger says to Tommy. 'The ones in there must have been trapped inside when it happened, been like that for ten years.'

Tommy shudders, glances at Ginger. Can he depend on him to take charge? He doesn't know. Physically, Ginger's a wreck, but he looks like he might have snapped out of his fugue. But then again, Tommy's not sure he even cares any more. All he feels like doing is curling into a ball and praying for it all to be over. How could he have got himself into such a mess? He almost hopes that the runners or the Army of the Left find them.

Throughout the day, throughout the relentless running and hiding, and once, a horrible crawl through a tunnel full of rat-ridden, rusted cars, Tommy's mind hasn't stopped whirring. He should've turned back hours ago. He shouldn't have run. He should have stayed and explained what had happened: that Mooki and Jess and Petrus were trying to steal from him when the situation turned nasty. He shouldn't have let the panic overwhelm him. Jess will have wasted no time dripping poison in the supervisors' ears. Will they believe her? He doesn't know.

If it weren't for stupid Simo's dad insisting that Tommy take Ginger foraging, none of this would have happened. He smothers another burble of resentment. He knows he's being unjust – if it weren't for Ginger he could have been the one lying prone and bleeding in the gutter, but he can't help but feel that it's all so *unfair*.

'Come on!' Jacob whoops and scuttles between the cars concertinaed across the road.

'We'd better follow him,' Ginger says, setting off after Jacob.

Tommy hesitates, then reluctantly follows. He hangs back as Jacob skirts the rusting hulk of an ambulance, weaves past broken signs proclaiming 'Quarantine, do not enter', and bangs his fists against the double glass doors. The glass is covered in a reflective film that distorts their reflections. A heavy chain is looped through the door handles.

'Maybe we should find somewhere else,' Tommy tries lamely. 'It's locked up tight.'

'Hand me your crowbar,' Ginger says.

Tommy hesitates then does as he's told. Ginger slots the crowbar through the padlock's arm, twists and it pops open.

'You might want to stand back,' Ginger says.

'Why?'

'You'll see.'

Ginger hauls the door open and a chorus of moans rushes out to greet them. Tommy hears himself yelp as a deluge of the dead stumbles out, jostling and lurching against each other. Tommy covers his mouth with his hand as the stench of their skin – that old-paper and damp-carpet reek – washes over him. He wants to look away, but he can't. Horribly, most look to be in good condition – some could almost be … alive. Is this because they haven't been exposed to sunlight for so many years? Even their clothes look relatively clean. A figure that was clearly once a nurse brushes past him, the sun glinting off a heavy gold necklace around her neck. Eyes sunken in their sockets seem to assess him and find him wanting. The nurse reels away, joining a pack hovering around the ambulance.

'It's like a Rotter convention,' Ginger says.

'That's what you call the dead? Rotters?' Tommy asks.

'Yeah.'

Tommy has to admit it's a better word for them than jujus or zombies or the countless other monikers he's heard people using.

'Let's go in,' Ginger says. Tommy hesitates. Ginger moves to place a hand on his shoulder, but Tommy flinches away. 'It'll be okay, Tommy,' Ginger says, closing the doors behind them. But now the lock is broken, a child could wander in here. The dead on this floor may have fled, albeit leaving their stench behind, but Tommy can hear the shuffle-clod of countless footsteps on the floor above them, the ghostly sound of muffled moaning.

'Will you look at that,' Ginger murmurs. He hobbles past a counter on which still sits a computer monitor, zigzags through a forest of upended plastic chairs and hurries towards a snack machine. He kicks out the glass in the front panel and hauls out three cans of Coke.

'Super!' Jacob claps his hands. 'I *told* you this was a good idea.'

Tommy barely tastes his, chugging it back in one go. He was so thirsty! He burps loudly, instantly feeling more energised and less like he wants to curl into a ball.

Ginger leads the way down a dim corridor packed with empty hospital gurneys, the signs on the walls pointing the way to 'X-Ray' and 'Maternity'. He pauses outside a room containing several cots and Tommy pushes past him to peer inside it. The sheets, blankets and pillows are dusted with greenish mould, but the lingering stench of the dead isn't as strong in here.

'Shouldn't we find somewhere more secure?' Tommy asks, although his feet are screaming at him to take his weight off them.

Ginger groans and drops onto one of the beds. 'You can, mate. I can't walk another step.'

Tommy perches on the edge of one of the cots. The room is windowless, and when the last of the light fades it will be pitch black in here. He shudders. Still, he supposes it's as safe as anywhere. His stomach groans, reminding him that he hasn't eaten all day, and he remembers the cans in his bag. He reluctantly jettisoned the books when it became clear they were in for a long walk – the strain of their weight on his shoulder was too much – but he kept the tinned fruit and, for some reason, the Transformer toy.

'Nice one,' Ginger says. 'You got a can opener by any chance?'

Tommy slumps. 'No.'

Jacob has tipped his backpack upside down and is rummaging through a barrage of dog-eared paperbacks, crumpled paper and empty styrofoam cups. He yips in delight as he extracts a plastic packet.

'What you got there?' Ginger asks.

Jacob grins, showing off his mossy teeth. 'Biltong. Chicken. Mmmm. Finger-lickin' good.' Jacob pulls out several strips, passes the bag to Ginger who does the same before handing it to Tommy.

Tommy's mouth fills with water. He bends a strip in half and shoves it in his mouth. It's way too salty but he's so hungry he couldn't care less. 'Where did you get it from, Jacob?'

'My handler. I took it when she wasn't looking. She's a butcher. Not a good butcher, oh no ...' his voice trails away. 'I'm not going back. I can't go back. No, no, no, no, no. I can't go back now.' His voice has become a whisper.

'Don't worry,' Ginger says. 'You won't have to go back.'

'I won't?'

'No.'

'Good. Good good. My dad used to say that. Jacob, always be a good boy. A good boy, he'd say.'

'Did he?' Tommy tries to keep his voice bright, but he can feel the tears encroaching. 'Do you know where we are, Jacob?'

'We're in hospital.'

'I know that. But where in the city are we?'

Jacob ignores him. He's pulling strips of dried flesh apart, examining them and popping them into his mouth. Then he stands up abruptly.

'Where are you going, Jacob?'

'I have business to conduct in the bathroom,' he says in a haughty voice.

Despite everything, Tommy can't help catching Ginger's eye and they share a grin.

'That fella's not right in his head,' Ginger says. His face is regaining some colour. He sighs. 'I'm sorry, Tommy. I lost my temper. I shouldn't have done that to that kid.'

'It's okay.' It's not okay, far from it, but Tommy feels the resentment fading. 'How's your leg?'

'Let's see, shall we?' He rolls up his jeans. 'Phew. Thought the stitches might've ripped, but they're cool.'

Tommy winces. Ginger's leg is a bloom of multi-coloured bruises, a line of thick black stitches sealing what must have been a nasty gaping wound. He can't believe the giant managed to make it this far with such a terrible injury. He must have been in agony. And here he is, blaming him for saving his life!

'Um ... Thanks for what you did back there, Ginger. For saving me from Mooki.'

'Wish I'd been there when they first showed up.'

'Where were you?'

'Over the road. Jacob asked me to help him break into one of the houses.'

'Do you think ... do you think Mooki's ...'

'Dead? Nah. He was still breathing.' Tommy can't tell if Ginger's lying or not.

'We shouldn't have run,' Tommy says in a small voice. 'I shouldn't have listened to Jacob.'

'I don't know much about the rules where you're from, mate, but Jacob was trying to help you. Those others ... they really had it in for you.'

'I guess.'

'Look, I know you have to get back to your mum. I'll say it was all me, take the blame.'

'But it wasn't your fault, was it? It was Mooki's fault. He would have stabbed me. You saved me.'

'Yeah. But you're just a kid and—'

'I'm *not* just a kid.'

'It's all right, Tommy. I'm not having a go at you. Look. I reckon we stay the night here, then I'll take you back, all right? Take the blame.'

'You'd do that?'

'Course. They can't do much worse to me than they've already done, can they? I'll have a word with Lucien. Make him listen. We'll sort it out.'

'You know *Lucien*?' Tommy can hardly believe it. Maybe things will be alright after all.

'Yeah. Wish I could say that I didn't.'

'How come you know him?'

'Long story.' The giant flinches as he slings his leg up onto the cot.

'Ginger … *is* it true that you're from Cape Town?'

'Yeah.'

'What's it like there?'

'You really want to hear?'

Tommy nods.

'Okay. I'm warning you, though. It's not pretty.'

As Ginger speaks, Tommy soon forgets about his aching feet and empty belly. Ginger's almost as good at telling a story as Olivia, and Tommy finds himself becoming lost in Ginger's words; he can almost picture the Cape Town city enclave with its towering fence, the hustle and bustle of the new arrivals markets and the bizarre (and not a little creepy) Resurrectionists, who worship the dead. He finds himself wishing he could meet all the exotic characters Ginger describes, like the Mall Rats and the people they encountered on their journey to Joburg, and he's particularly taken with Ginger's account of his pet hyena, Bambi. The giant talks and talks, and barely seems to be aware as tears roll down his cheeks. Tommy doesn't dare interrupt, even when Jacob slips back into the room, a piece of toilet paper stuck to his foot.

Finally, Ginger yawns and absent-mindedly brushes away the tears that have run into his beard. 'Part two tomorrow, yeah?'

'Ginger?' Tommy asks. 'You're not going to go all weird on me again, are you?'

'What do you mean, weird?'

'Like all spacey? Like you were before.'

Ginger sighs. 'Nah, mate. I'm not going to do that. Had to snap out of it sometime, didn't I?'

Jacob giggles for no reason that Tommy can fathom. 'Jacob ... why did you help me? I mean ... I'm nothing to you.'

'Everyone is someone to someone,' Jacob says. 'Everybody needs somebody.' He sighs. 'Even when you're dead.'

'Where are you from, Jacob?' Gingers asks.

'Out there,' Jacob says.

'Aren't you from the Eastern Cape?' Tommy asks, remembering the rumours he'd heard from the other newbies.

'No, no, no not me.'

'Oh. I thought that's where Lucien found you.'

'No, no. That isn't where ...' Another sigh, this one a real lung-basher. 'I've been to hell, Tommy. They took us there.'

'Who did?'

'The army. Survivors. *People*.' He looks into the far distance. 'Long is the way, and hard, that out of hell leads up to light.'

'What do you mean "hell"?'

'Long is the way, Tommy,' Jacob says. 'Can't take me back. It's too far.'

'You don't have to go back to Sandtown, Jacob.'

'Not there!' Jacobs says scornfully. 'Don't you understand anything?'

'Steady on, Jacob,' Ginger says.

Jacob's eyes lose their fanatical gleam. 'Sorry. Sorry, Tommy. I get confused. My mind, it plays tricks on me, you see.'

'What did you used to do? Before the dead came, I mean.'

'Lecturer. English.'

Tommy can't quite imagine Jacob teaching anyone anything. He shudders, struck with another image of that schoolteacher in the classroom. Something nips at the edge of his mind. Something important ... But he can't quite grasp it.

Jacob shuffles over to the cot in the far corner of the room, lies down, his back to them and rolls himself into the blanket. 'Good night, my friends,' Jacob sighs. 'This horror will grow mild, this darkness light.'

Ginger passes another piece of chicken biltong to Tommy. 'We should get some sleep. It's a long walk back tomorrow. You have even a vague idea where we are?'

'No. I just hope we're nowhere near Outcast territory.'

'Near whattame territory?'

'Outcast.'

'I'm still none the wiser, mate.'

'The Outcasts – they're monsters,' Tommy says. 'They killed Senyaka.'

'Who's that?'

'Olivia's husband. Boyfriend, whatever. They ... people say that they do terrible things to the runners they capture. That they ...' Tommy doesn't even want to think about it, never mind say it. 'That they *do* things to their bodies.'

'What kind of things?'

'Make muti out of them, *eat* them even.'

Ginger scoffs. 'Come on, Tommy. You don't believe that, do you?'

'It's what I've heard.'

'Well, then. We'd better not run into them, yeah? Now, seriously, get some sleep.'

Tommy lies back on the bed, stares up at the ceiling, listens to the thump-shuffle of the dead on the floor above. There's no way he's ever going to be able to sleep with that racket going on.

But seconds later, he's out like a light.

Tommy wakes with a jolt, his bladder aching. He sits up, opens his mouth to call for Olivia, but then the heavy knowledge of where he is hits him. The room's darkness is impenetrable, but he can hear Ginger snoring softly next to him.

The last thing he wants to do is leave the room, but if he doesn't relieve himself soon he's going to wet himself.

He scrabbles in his backpack for his torch and clicks it on. Careful not to shine it in Ginger's eyes, he tiptoes to the door and slips out into the corridor. He's surprised to see the weak light of early morning shining through the waiting room's windows; he could have sworn it was the middle of the night. Trying to block out the soft thunder of the dead – the *Rotters* – trapped on the floor above, Tommy decides to head left, away from the waiting room. No one will care if he pees right where he is, but it doesn't feel right.

He creeps around a corner, and finally finds a sign for a bathroom. There won't be any water in here, but that can't be helped. Using his torch to prop the door open, he hurries towards the urinal.

With the ache in his bladder dealt with, he zips up and

wanders over to the mirror. The light is poor, but his eyes look lost in his face, ringed with dark circles.

A thump.

A low moan.

It's coming from behind him – in one of the stalls.

A chill trickles down his spine. There's a Rotter in here with him.

He could easily make it to the door in a matter of seconds, but something makes him hesitate. The moan comes again. A solitary, mournful sound. And it can only be coming from the disabled stall at the end of the row which is blocked by a cleaning trolley. He creeps towards it, his heart now somewhere in his throat, tensing as the moans intensify.

Imagine, Tommy thinks, being trapped inside a toilet stall for over a decade. He could easily walk away and leave it to rot for another ten years, but it just feels wrong. Nerves ready to snap, Tommy squeaks around the trolley and gives it an almighty shove. The door slams open, almost hitting him in the face, and a small figure hobbles out, so close to him that he could easily touch it. It turns back and moans, as if it's saying 'thank you' – reminding Tommy of the weirdly human behaviour of those dead schoolchildren – then lurches towards the door and lunges into the corridor.

There's no sign of it when he leaves the bathroom. He bypasses the room in which he spent the night, intending to grab another can of cooldrink from the vending machine, stopping dead as a small figure peels out of the shadow cast by the open door. It steps into the light.

It has to be the same one.

Now that he can see it clearly, Tommy reckons it was probably a few years younger than he is when it died. Just a kid, really. A boy. And, like the others he saw who were trapped in here, it's in remarkably good condition. In fact, its SpongeBob T-shirt and black jeans – complete with a red key-chain looping from its belt – are cleaner than Tommy's own gear. A shock of blond hair tops a face that Tommy thinks might once have been cute. Its sunken eyes seem to be looking straight at him and Tommy's stunned at the lack of disgust he feels. The Rotter moans and paws the air around its head.

Is it trying to tell him something?

'Hi,' Tommy whispers. 'I'm Tommy.' The Rotter cocks its head on one side as if it's listening. 'What's your name?'

What *is* he doing? It's not as if the Rotter can understand a word he's saying, is it? But still it shows no sign of lurching away.

'Wait here,' he says to it.

Tommy runs back into the room, digs through his backpack and grabs the Transformer toy. He doesn't stop to question what he's doing.

When he makes his way back into the waiting area, the Rotter is still there.

'Check this out,' Tommy says. He brandishes the Transformer, and attempts to twist its parts into whatever vehicle it's supposed to be. The Rotter watches him silently for a few minutes, then huffs as if it's finding Tommy's efforts amusing.

'Stupid toy,' Tommy mutters. He holds it out to the Rotter. 'Here. You can have it.'

The Rotter cocks its head again, and this time Tommy's certain it's looking straight at him. Tommy steps nearer, within touching distance, and places the toy in the thing's hands. The Rotter makes a grab for it, but it fumbles through its fingers and drops to the floor. It throws its head back and moans again.

'It's okay.' Tommy says. 'It's cool. Let's try again.' Keeping his eyes glued to the Rotter's, he bends to pick it up, and this time, the Rotter manages to grasp it, holding it clumsily in folded arms.

'Aren't you going to say thank you?'

It moans once more, then turns and shuffles towards the glass doors.

The *open* glass doors.

That's not right. Ginger closed them last night, didn't he?

'Where's Jacob?' Ginger says behind him, making Tommy start. He turns, sees Ginger scrubbing a hand through his matted curls, stifling a yawn.

'What do you mean, Ginger?'

'He's not in his bed.'

'He must have gone outside.'

There's a loud bang as a door slams, followed by the squeak of running feet. Jacob jogs towards them down the corridor on the opposite side of the reception desk, out of breath but with a triumphant grin splitting his face in two. He's clutching a crowbar in his hand.

'Where've you been?' Ginger asks.

'You'll see!'

And then Tommy gets it. The thundering sound is weak at first, but it quickly increases in volume, followed by a deafening tide of moans.

'You'd better get behind the counter,' Jacob yells. 'There are a lot of them!'

'What the hell are you doing, Jacob?' Ginger shouts, joining Tommy behind the reception desk as the first glut of shambling dead lurches into view.

'What does it look like? I'm setting them free!'

A couple bounce against the walls, spin around as if

disorientated, but most seem to head straight for the sunlight. Unlike the child Rotter, none appear to show any sign of what Tommy can only term 'life'. A couple are missing limbs, but apart from this (and Tommy can't tell if these injuries were sustained before or after they were infected) they look fairly intact. Several are dressed in stained green scrubs. A couple even sport face masks – doctors who were infected mid-surgery?

They funnel out of the doors, first a flood – the moaning reaching a terrifying pitch; Tommy can barely hear himself think above it – and then a trickle. Tommy remembers his runner camp supervisor telling the class that the dead tend to congregate around survivor settlements. If there are any runners in the area, (or even worse, Outcasts), they'd be stupid not to investigate the source of the cacophony.

'Hadn't we better get out of here?' Tommy asks.

The Rotters have congregated in the parking lot, but thankfully several start trailing away.

'It won't be long till that lot bugger off,' Ginger says. 'And in any case, we'd better decide where we're going to go.'

Tommy feels a cold hand squeezing his heart. Has Ginger decided against returning to Sandtown? Tommy needs him – if he returns alone, then it's just his word against Mooki's and Jess's. The fact that he's run will be taken as proof of his guilt.

Ginger thumps Tommy's shoulder playfully. 'Don't look so worried, mate. I'm still going to take you back home. I meant I reckon we should try to find a map. The last thing we want to do is ramble round in circles.' He taps his knee. 'Not with this gammy leg.'

Limp with relief, Tommy sinks onto one of the waiting room chairs, takes the can of fizzy drink that Ginger hands to him. Jacob is standing by the window, watching the dead, rubbing his hands together as if he's washing them in imaginary water.

'Ginger, I don't think it's a good idea for Jacob to come back with us.'

'What do you mean?'

'It's the third time he's run. The handlers and amaKlevas will want to make an example of him.'

'How?'

'That's for his handler to decide. Um … he'll probably be lashed.' Tommy is fairly certain that this is the least Jacob will have to face. It's rare for a Leftie, even a runaway, to be punished harshly – they are valuable commodities after all – but with three strikes against his name, coupled with his unpredictable behaviour, it's likely Jacob will face far worse than public humiliation.

Ginger sighs. 'I tell you, Tommy, I don't know this city. I don't know its people. But from what I've seen so far, Sandtown is like something out of *Mad Max*. Selling people like slaves? I mean, what is this, the eighteenth century? We have to help him, mate. Escort him to the edge of the city before we take you back to Sandtown. Poor bugger went out of his way to help us, didn't he?'

Tommy bites his lip to stop himself whining *I don't want to!* He makes himself nod and murmurs, 'I guess.'

Jacob skips up to them. 'They're free now, Tommy. You see that? After all those years.'

'I see that, Jacob,' Tommy says, smiling weakly.

'Jacob, listen,' Ginger says. 'We're really grateful for everything you've done for us, and we'd like to help get you out of the city, but after that, I've got to take Tommy home. Back to his mum.'

Jacob nods. 'Yes. You are right. A boy needs his mother.' Jacob straightens his back. 'You must go now. Take Tommy back. I will be fine.' Somehow it's worse that Jacob's eyes are focussed, his voice sane and reasonable.

'No,' Tommy says. 'We'll help you, Jacob.'

Tommy waits for Jacob to say something freaky, but he simply says, 'Thank you.'

They trail outside. It's still early, but the sun beats down on Tommy's scalp. Today's trek is going to be even more arduous than yesterday's.

The Rotters are dispersing now, but one seems to be hanging back. It turns and moans and Tommy can't help but smile when he sees the toy clutched in its arms.

'Look!' Tommy calls to Ginger.

'What?'

'That Rotter. I know him.'

Ginger shakes his head. 'Come on, Tommy, you're not going to go soft on me as well, are you?' Ginger turns his attention to Jacob. 'So what do you reckon, Jacob? You know the quickest route out of the city?' Ginger motions towards the cars crunched nose to tail on the road parallel to the hospital entrance. 'We should see if there's a map book in one of them.'

But Jacob is standing stock-still, his head cocked. 'Uh-oh,' he says.

'What is it?'

Jacob shields his eyes, peers towards the ambulance. Tommy hears the toe-curling sound of metal scraping against metal and a stooped, grotesque figure emerges, dragging a huge knife against the side of the ambulance. It's head is a skull, its teeth filed to sharp points, porcupine quills jut in a crown around its head. Its body is smeared with a white glutinous substance.

Tommy's legs buckle, his throat closes up.

There's a clang from behind him and he whirls, sees two more figures creeping out from behind the shattered corpse of a kombi. If anything, these are more monstrous. One is draped in the hide of a leopard, the big cat's eyes atop its head flashing in the sunlight. The other, whose head is hooded in what looks to be elephant hide, has hands too big for its body, and claws the size of sharks' teeth. Both are holding automatic weapons, and even Tommy can tell they know how to use them.

'No no no no,' Jacob babbles.

'Tommy,' Ginger says. 'Get behind me.' Every muscle in Tommy's body starts to shake. He's felt fear before, of course he has, but this isn't fear – this is pure terror. Icicles of panic slice into his belly.

Leopard man barks something in Zulu and Skull Face lets out a cruel screech of laughter.

Ginger brandishes his crutch, but it's less than useless against those guns. Jacob falls to his knees, caves his hands over his head. 'I'm ready,' he whispers.

'Get up,' Leopard Man motions with his gun.

'What do you want with us?' Ginger asks, and Tommy's amazed at how steady his voice sounds.

'You'll see. But speak again, boogooman, and you'll be sixed.'

Tommy now knows that fear has a smell. A raw, feral odour that reminds him of the stink of the dead. It feels like they've been in the back of the vehicle – an old police van by the looks of it – for hours. It's moving at a snail's pace, but every time it lurches over an obstruction or pothole Tommy's spine bangs painfully against its side. The heat encases him like a sweaty glove; the windows are covered in metal sheeting and there's no airflow. Tommy's unrelenting terror is now mingled with shame; he lost control of his bladder when the Outcasts pushed them into the back of the van and his wet pants chafe his thighs.

He can see the outlines of the Outcasts' heads through the mesh that seals the driver's cab from the back, but the roar of the engine smothers their voices.

'It'll be okay, Tommy,' Ginger murmurs, and Tommy clings to the surety in his voice. 'Jacob? You doing okay?'

Tommy had expected Jacob to lose it completely when they were forced at gunpoint down a side street and into the back of the van. But he was subdued and compliant, and Tommy hasn't heard a peep out of him since their hands were tied roughly behind their backs. His head is bowed so Tommy can't see his face.

'I am doing fine, thank you, Ginger,' Jacob says as if they're all on an outing rather than facing imminent death.

'What do you think will happen to us?' Tommy whispers.

'You have nothing to fear, Tommy,' Jacob says. 'We will be fine.'

'How do you know that?'

'Because I have seen the worst that men can do,' Jacob says, sounding deadly serious and completely sane. 'These are not the worst of men.'

'I hope you're wrong about the Outcasts, Tommy,' Ginger says and now Tommy can hear a hint of fear in his voice. 'Those had better just be rumours.'

'There are worse things than death,' Jacob says. 'Much, much worse.'

Like being eaten alive, Tommy thinks, swallowing back bile. Like being turned into muti. He's heard that the sorcerers who believe in the power of human body parts prefer to cut the … bits off while their victims are still alive. *Goodbye, Olivia*, he mouths to himself. *I love you.*

The truck thumps over another obstacle and Tommy realises he can hear the mournful cry of Rotter moans. Then the engine cuts out.

He needs to be brave. When they do whatever it is they're going to do to him, he won't cry. He won't.

The back door swings open. 'Move,' Leopard Man barks. Tommy climbs out of the vehicle on jelly-legs, blinking in the bright sunlight. They're in a large dusty area, penned in by high wooden fences. And … did he just hear laughter in the distance? It almost sounds like children's laughter. That can't be right, can it?

'Are you going to eat us?' Tommy asks.

A roar of laughter. 'And spoil our appetite?' Judging by the voice, Tommy realises that Skull Face is actually a woman, although her body is as flat-chested and muscular as that of a man's. She pulls the mask off her head, shakes out sweat-soaked short, black hair. Her eyes are a brilliant blue. 'Yessus, it's a relief to take that thing off. I been sweating like pig. So, aren't you going to tell us your names?'

Ginger – who looks as relieved as Tommy that they're not about to be made into Outcast sandwiches – steps forward. 'I'm Ginger. This here's Tommy and the old guy is Jacob. Look, do what you like to me, but let the kid go. He's no threat to you.'

Skull Face looks him up and down. 'Funny accent, man. Where are you from?'

'London originally. Then Cape Town.'

'Cape Town?'

'Yeah. You hard of hearing?'

Skull Face cackles. 'I'm Kathleen. Kat for short.'

'What is this place?' Ginger asks.

But Tommy has spotted a faded sign: 'Johannesburg Zoo'. What can they be doing here?

'Kat!' a deep voice calls. 'What you got there?' A tall figure pushes through a gate and walks towards them, sunlight lashing off the mirrored sunglasses shielding his eyes.

'Not sure yet, bru,' Kathleen says. 'Looks like some kind of giant, an old chommie and a kid.'

'Ha!' The man is smiling and Tommy realises this is why he hasn't recognised him immediately. The Senyaka Tommy knew rarely smiled.

'Heita, Tommy,' Senyaka says. 'Welcome to the zoo.'

Part Two
Welcome To Hell

Lele

I open my bedroom door and peer into the corridor. One Ear is in his usual position, sitting on his plastic foldaway chair, a book open on his lap. It looks like another of the crime novels he favours, this one titled *Wake Up Dead*. *Ha ha*, I can almost hear Saint saying. How *apt*.

'You're up early, Lele,' he says.

'I know. I've got something for you, Sihle. A gift.'

He stares at me as if I've just spoken in a foreign language. 'A gift?'

'It's your birthday, isn't it?'

It's not often that he looks thrown. 'How did you know?'

'Little bird told me.' I hand him the portrait of Busi I've been working on for days. I'm proud of it. I think I've managed to capture the *real* Busi – the sweet but tougher-than-she-looks character who's hidden somewhere beneath the facade of subservience and nerviness.

I watch him carefully, trying to read his expression. It's as guarded as usual, but I'm sure his eyes soften slightly.

'This is good.' He folds it carefully and slides it into his pocket.

'So what are you going to do today, Sihle?'

'Do?'

'Aren't you going to take the day off? Maybe spend some time with your family and friends in Sandtown?' I still don't know anything about his personal life – or if he even *has* any family or friends. He refuses to talk about his life before the Rotters came, and occasionally his eyes take on that guarded, faraway look Ash's used to get whenever his past was mentioned.

As usual he dodges the question. 'No. What about you?'

'Dunno. Usual, I guess. I'd like to draw you before I go down and check on Ember. Will you let me?'

'No.'

'Please?'

'Why would you want to draw this face?'

'I'm bored.'

This is true. As the days have slipped into weeks, I've let myself slide into a routine of sorts. I spend each morning at the clinic, but there's only so much I can do there. Ember still hasn't shown any signs of snapping out of her coma, but her colour is improving and Cezanne seems to be pleased with her progress. Busi has sourced several books for me, and I read to Ember every day, although I haven't a clue if she's capable of hearing me. I'm currently working through *A Thousand and One Nights*. The story of a princess who spins out a series of tales, leaving each one hanging in order to keep the murderous sultan from lopping off her head, mirrors my situation so perfectly it gives me the chills. I don't think Coom is going to kill me any time soon, but what he does have planned is somehow worse.

'Sihle, have you heard from Lucien?' I keep my voice light. I've been biding my time, waiting to ask this. I haven't seen Lucien since that night, although he hasn't been too far out of my thoughts. Why hasn't he been back to see me? Does he regret what happened between us? I don't even know if *I* regret it. But One Ear must have known he spent the night with me.

Another subject we don't discuss.

One Ear mirrors my careful tone with his. 'I have not seen him, Lele.'

Has he gone on another one of his countrywide journeys? Scouring the land for more Lefties to bolster Sandtown's runner population? I'm shocked at the number of times I allow what happened between us to replay over and over in my head. It's not as if I was cheating on Ash – we broke up ages ago – but surely I should feel *some* residue of guilt. But the only guilt I feel is that I've been dwelling on that night rather than more important issues – like the fact that I have no idea what's happened to Ginger. Like the fact that Ember hasn't woken up.

A door slams at the end of the corridor, followed by quick-moving muffled footsteps. 'Lele!' Busi rounds the corner and hares towards us. 'Lele! It's Ember!'

'What about her?' Oh no. Please no. Please let her be okay. I search Busi's face for any indication of what might have happened, but she's out of breath and can't yet get the words out.

'She's opened her eyes!'

Without bothering to go back into my room to put my boots on, I fly towards the stairwell, taking the stairs three at a time. I can hear Busi and One Ear thumping after me, but I don't slow down. I skid into the lobby, race down the stairs that lead towards the hotel's basement and the gym that's been converted into Cezanne's mini-clinic.

Cezanne is sitting perched on Ember's bed when I shove through the doors. 'Ember!'

'Lele.' It's clear that she's still weak, but her eyes are fairly bright. I throw my arms around her. She's thin, *too* thin. It's almost like hugging a skeleton. I can feel the tears soaking my cheeks. 'Why are you crying, Lele?'

'I'm just so happy you're awake.'

'Lele ... Cezanne said we were in an accident.'

I glance at Cezanne and she nods in encouragement.

'You don't remember it?'

'I remember camping by the side of the highway and someone shooting at us. That's all.' Her voice wobbles, grows weaker. 'The others ... are they okay? Where's Ginger?'

'The others are fine,' I lie. She's in no condition to deal with the truth just yet. 'We'll talk about everything when you're stronger.'

'And we're really in Joburg?'

'We really are.'

Her eyelids flutter. 'Good. Ginger said he couldn't ... wait ... to ...'

Her eyes close and her breathing evens out.

'Don't panic,' Cezanne says. 'She will be extremely weak for a long time. And Lele, even though she has woken up, she is not out of the woods yet.'

'But she'll be okay, won't she?'

'There are no guarantees, Lele. From the little I can glean so far, she has not suffered any mental impairment. I'm amazed that she remembers as much as she does. I would have expected some memory loss. She is strong.'

'How much did you tell her?'

'Just that she was in an accident en route to Johannesburg.'

'So she doesn't know about Coom?'

'No. I thought it best not to go into too much detail at this stage.'

Good. I don't want her to know anything about that particular situation. Knowing Ember, she'll be wracked with guilt if she discovers I've agreed to marry the slug to ensure her wellbeing, and that won't help her recovery. 'So what happens now?'

'Now we wait. I will monitor her closely. But it could be a while before she is strong enough to be moved.'

'Can I stay with her?'

'She needs peace and quiet. Why don't you come back later?'

'Have you told Coom that she's woken up?'

'No, Lele.' She squeezes my hand. 'But it will not be long before the news reaches him. You must be prepared.'

I suppress a shudder. Ember has woken up – that's the most important thing. But my legs are numb as I leave the clinic and make my way back to my room, and I can't shift the feeling that everything around me is now draped in shadow.

'Lele,' Busi catches up to me. 'This is good news, nè? Cezanne says that she will live?'

'Yeah. Of course it's good news. I think I'm going to have a bath, Busi. Is that cool?' Some days I spend hours in the bath, holding my breath under the water. Maybe I do it to tempt fate, on the off chance that Lucien will arrive unexpectedly like he did on the first day I was here.

She's watching me carefully. 'Of course. Are you alright?'

I slap a smile on my face. 'Why don't you and Sihle go and celebrate his birthday? Go and hang out in the bird park or something.'

Busi blushes. 'I don't know ...'

'Go and ask him. I bet he'll jump at the chance.'

'But I can't leave you, Lele.'

'Go on. Really, I feel like being by myself.'

I wave her away and slog into the bathroom. I sit on the edge of the bath and turn the hot tap to full blast, stare into the mirror as the steam balloons in the glass and hides my face. What the hell is wrong with me? Ember has woken up. How can I be so selfish?

The water scalds my skin as I slide in, but I don't care.

Self-pity won't help anyone, Lele, the Saint voice whispers. I block it out and duck below the water, shutting out the world.

My fingertips are still wrinkled from staying in the bath too long. I pick up yesterday's jeans that I left lying on the floor by the side of the bed, and pull them on.

There's a tap on the door and Busi appears.

'Hey. Did you and Sihle have a nice time?'

She looks away. 'Lele ... Mr Coom wants to see you in his rooms.'

So this is it. 'Right now?'

'Ja.' Busi glances dubiously at my jeans and baggy T-shirt. It's obvious she doesn't think this is appropriate attire to wear in his presence. Good. I *hope* I look like crap.

I'm sick to my stomach with dread; maybe talking will stop me from doing what I really feel like doing – which is screaming or punching something really hard.

'So,' I say. 'How did it go? Between you and Sihle, I mean.'

She shrugs. 'I'm not sure ... We were together for about half an hour, and then he left. Lele ... do you think he likes me?'

'Are you kidding? He'd be crazy not to. No offence to him, but you're way out of his league.'

'It's just … I've heard things about him.'

'Go on.'

'One of Coom's new domestics, Cindy, says her boyfriend knew him way back when. Before the dead. She said he worked for a loan shark in Lenasia, that he *did* things to people who didn't pay up in time. Hurt them.'

'What, like an enforcer or something?'

Busi nods.

I've never been to Coom's private quarters on the first floor, and while I know I can't put this off forever, I slacken my pace as we head down the stairs. 'She knows this for sure?'

'So she says.'

I can't say I'm that surprised. 'Listen, I can't tell you what to do, Busi, but we've all got a past, okay? Stuff we're ashamed of. It's how we act now that counts.'

Oooh, listen to Little Miss Grown-up, the Saint voice scoffs.

'I s'pose,' she sighs.

We're here. Busi leads me down an identical corridor to the one on my floor and smiles tentatively at the hulk lounging outside one of the doors.

'Go straight in,' the guard drones without returning Busi's smile. 'He's expecting you.'

'Here goes,' I say.

A clone of the guard outside the door waves me inside. I'm expecting to walk into a plush palatial area, but Coom's rooms are actually fairly low-key. A couple of leather couches, a bookshelf piled with what look to be technical manuals and a depressed pot plant. Coom's sitting at a gargantuan desk, his back to the window, papers stacked around him and a pair of reading glasses perched on his bulbous nose. He sighs and gestures at the guard to leave us alone.

He looks tired, less pompous than I've ever seen him. I'm struck by how many sides he seems to have. The self-important windbag I met that first night; the old fusspot stressing over his birds and now here's studious Coom. But when all is said and done he's just a man. An obese, old-looking man wearing what basically amounts to a dress.

'How lovely to see you, Lele.' He glances at my jeans. 'Nice of you to dress for the occasion.'

'Cut the crap, Coom. What do you want?'

He taps a laptop computer lying underneath a pile of papers. 'It is incredible how much we depended on these things. Maybe one day we will have the wherewithal to fire up the internet again.'

'I'd settle for being free, thanks.'

He takes off his glasses, rubs his eyes. 'So. I believe your friend is awake.'

'Yeah. But she's still not a hundred percent.'

'Cezanne will take good care of her.'

'Is she the one who told you about Ember?'

He shakes his head. 'No. Sihle passed the news on to me.'

I can't hide my dismay. I'd stupidly thought One Ear was on my side. But I guess Coom would have found out soon enough. 'Coom … Steven … Do you really believe surrounding yourself with Lefties will keep you safe? I mean, it's really just an excuse for you to sleep with loads of different women, isn't it?'

'Don't be naive, Lele. Men and women have been making exchanges like these for centuries.'

'Doesn't make it right.'

'Right and wrong are philosophical constructs, Lele. As are good and evil. Empty words that mean nothing. Most of us inhabit the grey areas between the two. There is always a compromise to be made.'

'And it doesn't bother you that I find you repulsive? That the thought of you touching me makes me want to puke?'

He twitches. 'My wives are all extremely happy and content. In time, I hope you will come to regard me differently.'

'Fat chance. You told me once that you're not a monster. I agree. You're far worse. Those Rotters out there have more integrity than you.'

'Really? I could have sat back and let Sandtown wither and die. Instead, I expend a great deal of time and energy in ensuring the city is supplied with water and fuel.'

'Blah blah blah. You been into Sandtown lately, Coom? Right inside it? Into the heart of it? Where the people are dying in the clinic, the children queuing for hours just for water?'

He smiles. 'Yes, yes. I get that you have a fine social conscience. Now, let us move on to why you're here. Do we have a deal?'

'Yeah, we have a deal. Only ... I want you to promise me something.'

'And what is that?'

'Ember. When she's fit, you have to allow her to leave.'

He sits back in his chair. 'That decision is not just up to me. It is also up to Jova. He might want her to join his little *army*.'

'Doesn't sound like you're one of Jova's fans, Coom.'

A slow smile that doesn't reach his eyes. 'He's just a child. A child who likes to play soldiers. A child who is unable to keep even those closest to him loyal.'

'What do you mean by that?'

'Oh, just something that came my way via the grapevine. Apparently that sidekick of his, the big one, tattooed, Congolese, I forget his name—'

'Lucien?' Coom knows very well what his name is.

'Is that it? Well, Jova and Lucien have had some sort of tiff, and Lucien has left the playpen. Apparently for good.'

'Where's he gone?' I fight to keep my voice steady. He's already caught me off guard once and there's no way I'm going to let him know how much this news has rattled me.

'Oh, nobody knows. Hasn't been seen for weeks.'

How could Lucien leave me like this? I know we only had one night together, but still. He said he'd try and help me, and a part of me – a large part – has been holding onto this.

'My dear,' Coom says smoothly. 'Are you quite alright?'

I mentally take a deep breath. 'Of course. So seeing as you're so powerful, you must know about Jova's plan to free the city, right? He must have told you what it is, surely.'

He shifts in his chair. 'I know some of it,' he says stiffly.

'What will happen to you when the city is free, Coom?'

'The people will always need leaders.'

'And you think they'll just follow you? After you've basically kept them living in squalor like animals?'

'I have kept them safe. I have made sure that they have fuel, and want for nothing. They need guidance, Lele. People are sheep, they *want* to be told what to do. They will always need people like me to lead them.'

I think about the Resurrectionists back in Cape Town and the people who joined their ranks, blithely worshipping the Rotters and Guardians. But not all of us followed the herd.

'But what about the people who fight back?'

'They never last long.'

'And the Outcasts? They're fighting back, aren't they?'

He purses his lips. Another sore spot. Good. 'I have arranged for you to have your medical examination.'

Way to change the subject. 'How romantic.'

He chuckles. 'You and I are going to get along just fine, Lele. Cezanne says that it would probably be best if she conducted it. Especially as I know you have issues with some of my other medical practitioners. You are to go to her rooms immediately.'

I don't wait to be dismissed. Ugh. The thought of him touching me really does make me squirm. The only way I'll get through it is to get so drunk I pass out.

I pull my T-shirt over my head, shivering as the fan whips around, its breeze chilling my skin. Cezanne stands with her back to me, fiddling in the sink. She barely said a word as she conducted the examination, and I'm starting to suspect that she might have discovered my secret. She must know that I'm not left-handed. I've been trying to keep up the charade – at least when Coom or any of the runners are around – but she's sharper than the others. Why else is she behaving so strangely?

I need to know. 'Cezanne? Is there something wrong?'

Her back stiffens.

Crap. She *must* know. But how? The examination had been thorough – uncomfortably thorough – although I know she tried to be as gentle as she could. But the tendrils are deep in my veins, aren't they? Perhaps she saw signs of them in the blood she took.

'Cezanne?' I say again.

She sighs, then turns to face me. 'Lele,' she says, her voice as expressionless as her eyes. 'You're pregnant.'

Jack

17 January 2012

'We must embrace our saviours! And we must embrace the resurrected, the reborn, who gather around our walls!' The lunatic has to shout to be heard over the chaos of the food market, but none of the hawkers or traders waiting for the food cart spare him more than a passing glance. Jack's getting tired of these dead-lovers in their smelly woollen robes. There seem to be more and more of them clogging up the enclave's streets every day.

Jova pauses, stares up at the lunatic, grabs one of the flyers piled at his feet. It's Lucien's turn to help Hester unload her black-market stock at the new arrivals market, so it's just the two of them today, and despite Jova's insistence that they trudge all the way to the edge of the enclave, Jack feels a guilty pleasure at having his friend all to himself.

Jack glances at Jova, rolls his eyes as the freak spouts more nonsense. 'I can't believe anyone buys into this kak.'

Jova folds the flyer into a neat square and pockets it. 'Never underestimate the power of fear, Jack.'

Jack snorts, 'But worshipping the dead? Even fear isn't enough to make people do something that crazy.'

Jova doesn't respond.

A hush falls over the marketplace. It's the moment Jova's been waiting for. The huge wooden gate set in the enclave's fence creaks open, catching on the uneven ground and revealing a tantalising glimpse of the world outside. A sweat-lathered black horse, its eyes rolling behind blinkers, pulls the morning food wagon through it. A hooded figure sits motionless at the front of the cart, reins clasped in hands hidden by the long sleeves of its brown robe. It doesn't even acknowledge the men and women who start unloading the wagon's contents.

Jack can't see its eyes but he gets the distinct feeling that it's staring at him – through him. He shudders. He wishes Jova would get over his morbid fascination with the Guardians. He's sick of coming here every other morning.

'Don't you ever wonder what they want in return? Why they keep us here?' Jova asks, without taking his eyes off the robed figure. 'You believe people won't buy into this new cult but you need to wise up, Jack. The Guardians are the only things standing between us and the dead. And the dead are never going to go away.'

'Whatever, Jova,' Jack mumbles. It's not the first time he's heard this or something like it.

The wagon unloaded, the robed figure gives a barely discernible flick of the reins and the horse lunges forward, scattering the crowd that's edging towards the baskets of mealies and potatoes brought here from the Agriculturals.

Jova turns and he and Jack make their way towards the path that leads back to Little Brazzaville and Hester's shack.

'I'm starved,' Jack says. 'I hope Hester's—'

Another dead-lover steps into their path, his bulky body draped in a robe that reeks of dirty sheep. Jack attempts to bypass him, but the fanatic grabs his sleeve.

'Hey!' Jack yells, trying to snatch his jacket out of the man's grip. 'Hey!' Then he catches a glimpse of the man's face, half-hidden beneath his hood. It can't be. But it is. 'Dumisa?'

Jack can't believe he's looking at the same guy who used to slice through Rotters with his machete, a savage grin on his face, displaying such fearlessness that he and Jova had dubbed him The Terminator. Dumisa had been a legend among the men and women who had fought in the Last Wave, refusing to back down, leading onslaught after onslaught right up until the end; right up until the resistance had no choice but to give up the fight and join the other survivors in the enclave. But the giant of a man that Jack remembers is now a shivering wreck, hunching to hide his size, his once-powerful muscles reduced to flab.

'Jack,' Dumisa hisses and Jack almost gags as he's hit with a gust of putrid breath. 'Jack. You must repent, Jack. We must all repent for what we have done. It's time to be reborn, Jack. Resurrected.'

'Get away from him!' Jova yells. Jack has never heard Jova sound so incensed, out of control.

Dumisa drops his grip on Jack's arm and turns away. 'It's pointless to fight it,' he murmurs. 'It's the only answer.'

Jack looks into Jova's eyes and sees an emotion there he's never seen before.

Fear.

'Jova? What is it?'

'I'll tell you what it is, Jack,' Jova says, whipping the flyer out of his pocket and stomping it into the mud. 'It's the beginning of the end.'

Ash

'Jack?'

I groan and glance at the window. The sky has just begun to lighten, washing the room in a blueish haze. It's barely even dawn. 'Go back to sleep, Danny.'

'I can't.'

He's sitting on the edge of his sleeping bag, hugging his knees. Gone is all trace of his cocky persona. He's just a frightened kid.

Careful not to wake Noxi, I reach over her for my cigarettes. She murmurs in her sleep and snuggles closer to me.

'Can I have one of those?' Danny asks.

'No ways. Pockets and Nuush will kill me.'

Instead of one of his usual trying-to-be-witty retorts, all I get is a sigh and a muttered, 'Whatever.'

'So what's up?'

He clears his throat. 'I've ... I've never seen one of the dead up close.'

'Eh? I thought you had to be a runner to get into the AOL?'

'You do. And I was one, but I'm... Look. I haven't told the other guys this but my mom's rich, not like amaKleva rich, but okayish, so she helped me pay off my sponsorship early. I went out into the city a few times so I know I'm immune but ... I only ever saw the jujus from a distance. And ... I've heard things about the trials.' He drops his chin, refusing to meet my eyes. 'I'm scared, Jack.'

'I was scared the first time I saw a Rotter up-close.'

'Seriously?'

'Yeah, of course.'

'What happened?'

'I threw a stone at its head.'

He laughs, but it's forced. 'How old were you?'

I shrug. 'Eight.'

'Oh, great. Now I *really* feel better.'

'Look, Danny, I'm not going to lie. The first time you're face to face with one of them it isn't easy.' I sigh and drag my fingers through my hair; it's been weeks, but the habit's ingrained and I still get a jolt when my hand meets stubble. 'You just have to learn not to let the fear take over.'

'What about newborns?'

I still can't get over the AOL's ridiculous moniker for hatchlings. 'What about them?'

'At the trials. Do you think ... do you'll think we'll have to fight them?'

'Course not. Jova isn't an idiot. He's not going to put us in danger like that.'

'Really?' He doesn't sound convinced.

'Really. Anyway, newborns aren't so tough.'

'Please tell me you didn't kill your first newborn when you were eight? That's just messed up ... and way too much for my ego to handle right now.'

'I didn't have much choice. Newborns don't care how old you are. But even if there *are* newborns in the trials, you have something I didn't have the first time I killed one.'

'And what's that?'

'A team who's got your back.' I'm making myself cringe here; cheerleading isn't my thing. 'All I had was Jova, and you've seen the size of him, right?'

Finally a genuine smile. 'Remind me to never turn to you for a pep talk in the future, okay?'

'Fine with me. Disturb Americano's sleep next time.'

He huffs. 'Like you get much sleep anyway, bru. At least Pockets and Nuush are ... what's the word ... discrete. You and Noxi do realise we all have to live in this room, right?'

Noxi stirs. 'I heard that, you little pervert.' She yawns, stretches, nestles against my chest. 'Morning, Demon Eyes.' She slaps my cheek when I bend to kiss her. 'Keep your morning breath to yourself, thanks.' She crawls out of the sleeping bag, claps her hands. 'Rise and shine, chommies. Today is the big day.'

It usually takes a good few minutes to coax everyone out of their sleeping bags, but even Nuush is awake and on her feet within seconds. The group is oddly quiet as we gather up our belongings and head to the showers. Noxi and Pockets make a half-hearted attempt at their usual pseudo-bitchiness but their banter falls flat.

Danny isn't the only one fighting a losing battle with his nerves.

As usual, Noxi slips into my shower. She shivers, sidles closer, snatches the soap out of my hands and works it into a lather. She smiles slyly while she watches me watch the water streaming down the long lines of her body. 'So,' she says. 'We've got a few hours of free time to "mentally prepare ourselves" for the trials. I've got a few ideas about how we can do that.'

'I was going to head to the library,' I say without thinking and immediately regretting it.

She stiffens. 'Oh, there's an effing surprise.'

I move to pull her against me, trying to diffuse the situation, but she slaps me away. 'What do you even do there?'

'Well ... there are these square things with pages and—'

'Ha effing ha. You know who I heard also likes the library?' She turns her back on me.

'Jova?'

'Morgan.'

I blink water out of my eyes. 'What's that supposed to mean?'

'It means that you should go and enjoy your books, Jack.' She yanks the shower curtain back with such force that half of it rips off the rail, snatches up a towel and storms towards the door. 'And try not to get a paper cut.'

I must have read the same paragraph three times over and none of the words are making any sense. I randomly grabbed the book out of the fantasy section, and judging by the cover art (a beefy dwarf hatcheting a many-headed lizard creature) it's a generic Dungeons & Dragons novel. The kind of fun pulp I used to secretly devour back in Hester's hideout, the kind of book that finally hooked me onto reading after Jova had tried and failed for months to get me interested in his mini-library.

My latest argument with Noxi is stuck on repeat in my head, spiced with an added layer of guilt. I should have chased after her, pulled her back into the shower and said I'd like nothing better than to spend the day with her. I should have told her that I have zero interest in Morgan.

The increasing tension between us reminds me painfully of how it went down with Lele in the end. Noxi has been getting snappier over the last few days, angry when I ask her what's wrong and even angrier when I don't. My instinct is to shut her out, which mirrors too closely how I treated Lele all those weeks ago.

Guilt piled on guilt. Because the Noxi situation isn't just a reminder of Lele. It's also opened the door to other shameful thoughts. Like how easily I've let myself slide into life at the base. Letting the days and their rigid training schedules flow by, hanging out with Americano, shooting the shit with Danny, Pockets and Nuush and fooling around with Noxi. Doing nothing about finding out exactly what's happened to Ember, Ginger and Lele. Some days, I don't even think about them. Or Saint. Or even Sasha. It's easier not to. Sticking my head in the sand has always been my greatest skill.

The clump of approaching footsteps snaps me out of my fugue. I look up expecting to see Morgan maybe clutching one of the trashy romances she reads without a trace of embarrassment. I find myself sitting straighter, chest filling with anticipation. But I'm not ready to inspect this feeling either, or admit there was some truth in Noxi's accusations.

But it's not Morgan, it's Jova.

'Heita, Jack,' he says. 'I thought I'd find you here.' His lips twitch as he glances at the book in my hand. 'Having fun?'

I don't reply immediately. We haven't spoken in depth since our first face-off, although I've seen him around the training grounds occasionally. I manage a stiff 'Haven't seen you for a while.'

'Been busy.'

'Doing what?'

'Stuff. Feel like a walk?'

I shrug, chuck the book on a shelf, and follow him out into the walkway, the air busy with the clatter of the canteen crew clearing up after breakfast.

Jova heads towards the old domestic departures section, nodding at the graduates who stream past us, all of whom stare at him with that same mixture of awe and admiration. He doesn't speak as we trek up through security, but the silence between us isn't awkward. Jova doesn't do awkward silences, just like he doesn't do small talk.

We walk through the departure gate opposite the ruins of the tourist shop containing that lonely rack of vuvuzelas, along a passenger tunnel, down a metal staircase and out onto the runway. It's early, but I know that my shirt will soon be plastered to my back with sweat. I hope there will be another thunderstorm later to cool us down. As we pass between the planes either side of us – their 1Time and Kulula logos scratched and peeling, their bodies and oblong windows smothered in a thick layer of bird guano – I'm hit with the memory of Ginger, Saint, Lele and me crawling through the carcass of the crashed plane which lay sprawled across the N2 on our route out of Cape Town. The first step on our big adventure. The adventure that eventually led to at least one Mall Rat's death.

Yet another wave of guilt.

Jova doesn't speak until we've left the planes far behind and are heading towards the control tower. 'So,' he says. 'Heard you're fitting in well.' I flinch at this. Is he goading me? But his tone is neutral. 'Also heard you got yourself a girlfriend. Fast work.' In the old days, Lucien and I used to tease Jova about his apparent lack of interest in girls (or boys), especially as Lucien had a different girlfriend every week, and I did okay.

But these days, judging by the admiring glances being shot our way by the graduates jogging across the runway, he could have anyone he wanted, boy or girl. Power, the ultimate aphrodisiac. I wonder if Noxi would have been so interested in me if I were just another grunt and not Jova's old friend. I wonder if Jova's ever tempted to take advantage of his new status.

I shrug, playing it cool. 'The guys here aren't so bad.'

'We've got some good people here. Dedicated. Loyal.'

I bristle slightly. 'Unlike me, you mean?'

'I didn't say that.'

Why do I care if Jova thinks I'm loyal or not?

Another thought I don't want to examine too closely.

There's a hive of activity around one of the freight hangars in the far distance and I can hear the occasional pop of gunfire from the shooting range. Before I allowed myself to get sucked into daily life here, I asked around, trying to see what I could uncover about Jova's mysterious plan. I didn't make much headway. Not even the graduates who only deigned to talk to me because of my connection to Jova appeared to know exactly what it was they were being so rigorously trained for. I've heard rumours that Jova's instructed several teams of AOL runners and mechanics to scour the city for as many buses and trucks as they can find, but for what?

'What are you doing here, Jova? Jumping jacks and hand-to-hand combat isn't going to work against the Rotters. You of all people should know that. And I can't see any sign that you're fixing up fighter planes, which would be the only effective way to wipe them out.'

He shrugs. 'Thought about it. It's the jet fuel that's the main issue. It's corrupted. We've got diesel to run the generators and other vehicles, of course, but that's it.'

'Can't you make more?'

'We don't have the time to refine it. Sandtown can't keep running like it is forever. Sooner or later the infrastructure will break down completely.' He sighs.

'Do you regret wiping out the Guardians, Jova?'

He jerks his head up. 'No.'

'Remember when you used to be so obsessed with them? Dragging me and Lucien out to the edge of the enclave to watch them bringing in the supplies?'

A slight smile. 'I'm still obsessed with them. They're the key to all this. The ones who hold the answers to why we're here. Why some of us are immune.'

'What did it feel like killing them?'

'I don't know.'

'But you wiped them out, didn't you?'

'No. Lucien and the Lefties I gathered did that.' Typical Jova, avoiding getting his hands dirty. He always was the puppet master. He grimaces. 'We weren't always successful. Many lives were lost. Other settlements didn't fare as well as Sandtown.'

'And when you finally saw that they were nothing more than infected teenagers, what did you think?' When we were kids, Jova, Lucien and I spent hours speculating about what the Guardians might look like under the robes that covered their faces and bodies, grossing each other out with images of tentacled aliens, multi-eyed monsters or gore-soaked vampires. It was somehow worse to discover that the robed creatures everyone in the enclave feared or revered were actually human (at least on the outside).

'I wasn't surprised. But tell me, Jack. Or Ash, if you prefer?'

'Jack's fine,' I say stiffly.

He nods as if something has clicked into place. 'Tell me, why is it that the Guardians use the bodies of teenagers to harbour that particular strand of the infection? Lucien says you found this out in Cape Town.'

'Apparently they're the only ones who can handle the transformation. Something to do with hormones, I guess. Everyone else just becomes a Rotter.'

Another careful nod.

An old yellow schoolbus chugs across the runway, the driver skidding to a stop in front of the freight hangars.

'What's with the buses? Are you planning to use them to ferry the people out of the city? Use the AOL to protect them? That's seriously risky, Jova. One hatchling and it's all over.'

A shrug.

'So what is it? You found a nuke hidden somewhere? On one of your mysterious trips?'

'Something like that.'

He removes his spectacles, scrubs at his eyes. Without them he looks younger, vulnerable and exhausted. He slips them back on. 'I have made the people a promise. I won't go back on it.' The sunlight hits his glasses, turning his eyes into flat, sinister spheres. 'One way or another, we shall win. And you know I'll find a way, right, Jack?'

'You've done a pretty good job of organising this lot.'

'Thank you. It hasn't been easy.'

'So what's going to happen at these trials?'

'Wouldn't want to spoil the surprise for you. And I'd like to thank you for keeping your side of the bargain, Jack. For staying until the trials.'

'They haven't started yet. I might still do a runner.'

He smiles. 'I will keep my end of the bargain. I promised that I'd take you to see your friends. And I will.'

My heart leaps. 'When?'

'Jova!' We both turn to see a graduate sprinting towards us, holding her cap to her head with one hand. 'Sorry to interrupt, Jova. But we've just received a message from Coom. It sounds urgent.'

Jova sighs. Holds out his hand for me to shake. 'We'll finish this later. Good luck.'

'Will I need luck?' I call after him.

'We all need luck, Jack.'

———

Morgan leads us through the international arrivals area, a section of the airport that's been abandoned fully to the rats and creeping black mould. Much of it is hidden in inky shadow; it's almost fully dark outside and there's no electric lighting in here. Morgan's powerful torch beam sweeps over a pair of glass doors spiderwebbed with bullet holes, tiles soiled with soot and dust, and a towering pile of old suitcases, luggage trolleys and chairs blocking the entrance to a restaurant. Someone's last desperate attempt to keep the Rotters out.

We follow her out to a service road with an ambulance parked at an angle across it, and stare up at the hulking grey building in front of us. The gaps between its pillars are sealed with wood, plastic sheeting, wire mesh and barbed wire, but it's clear that in a past life it was once a multi-storey car park.

'Oh, crap, bru. You hear that?' Danny mutters. His eyes are wide, and he keeps jamming his fingernails into his palms.

Rotter moans. Faint, but still eerily audible. I check to see how the others are doing. Nuush and Pockets are standing close to each other, shoulders touching, faces grim, Americano is toying with an unlit cigarette, and when I try to catch Noxi's eye, she pointedly ignores me.

'This is it?' Americano asks.

Morgan nods.

'What are we going to do here?'

She ignores him, eyes us in turn. 'You all got your weapons?'

'You sure you'll be able to handle that panga, Jack?' Noxi sneers. 'Haven't had much practise with it lately, have you?'

Danny glances at Noxi and then at me in confusion, opens his mouth as if he's about to make one of his pithy comments, then clamps it shut. Morgan frowns slightly. 'This way.'

She leads us across the road and towards a featureless grey door. The dusty, piss-stinking stairwell behind it is lit with flickering oil lamps. I count six flights and then Morgan pushes through and into a huge, dark area, the paltry light from the stairwell allowing us all a glimpse of a gloomy graveyard of abandoned cars, and the shifting silhouettes of what can only be Rotters knocking about among them.

'Oh, shit,' Danny whispers. 'Jujus.'

Their moans echo around us, making even me shiver.

'So what do we have to do?' Pockets asks.

'It's simple,' Morgan says. 'Make your way down to the ground floor.'

'Easy,' Danny says, making for the stairwell.

'Not that way, Danny,' Morgan says, a slight smile in her voice.

'That's not too bad,' Nuush says. 'What's the catch?'

'I'll be timing you. See if you can break the record.'

'And what's the record?' Americano asks.

'Fifteen minutes.'

'Easy.'

'Who wants the torch?'

'We only get one?' Danny whines.

'You okay to take it, Jack?' Americano asks and Noxi rolls her eyes.

'Sure.' I wait for Morgan to pass me the weighty flashlight

she's been using to guide us here, but instead she hands me a small wind-up torch.

'Good luck,' she says. She closes the door, leaving us in the shifting darkness.

I have to thump the flashlight against the palm of my hand a few times before it flickers into life. I swing it around. The beam is too weak to penetrate more than three or four metres in front of us.

'All right,' Nuush says, her voice shaking slightly. 'Let's get this shit done.'

Americano grunts. 'What's the plan?'

'We should try and find the exit,' I say.

'Wow, what an effing genius,' Noxi mutters.

I shine the torch upwards, catching an exit sign pointing directly ahead. 'This way.'

Danny sticks close to my side as we weave our way through a maze of cars and kombis. A raggedy figure staggers out in front of us and I hear him mumbling. 'Shit, shit, shit,' Danny mutters.

I nudge it away with my boot. 'Don't panic, Danny,' I murmur. 'Be cool.'

There's a clack as someone readies her weapon. 'I could always shoot 'em for you, Dan Dan,' Pockets says.

'Don't do that,' Danny says.

'I thought they freaked you out?'

'They do. It just doesn't seem right. They're not doing anything to us. And it must suck being trapped in here for eternity.'

'Yeah,' Americano says. 'With nothing but each other and wannabe grunts like us for company.'

We switch left, head down a slight slope and there's a chorus of muttered swearing when we see what's in front of us. A small bus is skewed sideways, blocking the exit, razor wire and thick metal mesh sealing the narrow gaps between it and the concrete pillars and roof. I shine the torch across its windows, and Danny yelps as the light catches the glint of several pairs of sunken eyes belonging to Rotter-shaped silhouettes.

There have to be six or seven Rotters inside the space, including a couple crammed together on the back seats like lovers. They're in pretty poor condition. The light slides over yellow bone peeking through ragged flesh and rotting clothing.

'So this is the catch,' Nuush says miserably. 'I'm guessing the only way out of here is to crawl through juju central.'

The side door is welded shut, but one of the windows is free of glass. It's our only way through.

'I'll hang back with you,' I murmur to Danny. 'We can go in together.'

He breathes in. 'Nah. I gotta do this on my own, Jack.'

'I'll go first,' Pockets says. 'Americano. Boost me up. Jack, give me some light.'

I hold the torch to the window as Pockets bumps fists with Nuush, steps into Americano's laced hands, and slinks easily through the aperture. Using the butt of her rifle, she nudges a Rotter out of the aisle between the seats.

'You cool, Pockets?' Nuush asks.

'Ja. But yessus, it stinks in here, guys.' She scrambles across the next row of seats, hauls herself through the window opposite and slides out safely into the gloom beyond.

Nuush is next, then Noxi, who pointedly ignores my offer of a leg-up.

'Danny?' Americano says. 'You okay, bud?'

Danny nods, takes a deep breath, knocks fists with both of us, and climbs up into the bus. 'Hey, Jack!' he calls. 'It's not so bad after all! These things stink, but nowhere near as bad as Americano's socks after a round of push-ups.'

'I'll remember that, Danny,' Americano grunts, giving me a boost into the bus's depths. I lean out of the window, grasp his forearm and steady him while he heaves himself up. He barely manages to squeeze through the window's frame.

The bus's long-dead passengers don't even turn their heads in my direction as I slip through and out to where the others are waiting.

'Come on, granddad,' Danny calls to Americano. His voice wobbles slightly, but he's sounding way more like his usual cocky self.

Americano squeezes himself out of the window, lands heavily. 'Goddammit. How many floors are there?'

'I counted six,' Pockets says.

'We got to do this six times? How long did that take us?'

'Five minutes.'

'This is going to take way too long. Any ideas?'

'What about the elevators?' Danny says.

'They're out of order, dumbass.' Pocket sighs.

'Oh, duh, really? I *mean*, let's just climb down the elevator shaft, straight down to the bottom. No zombies, no fuss.'

Nuush sniffs. 'Isn't that cheating?'

'Nah, it's just clever use of game mechanics.'

I almost miss the terrified Danny. 'This isn't a game.'

'I'm with Danny on this,' Pockets says. 'I really don't want to go through all of that again.'

Americano shrugs. 'S'pose it's worth a try.'

We hustle down a short slope to the fifth floor, and I light the way towards a bank of lifts set into a concrete bunker.

'How are we going to pry the doors open?' Noxi asks.

'Leave it to me,' Pockets says. 'Jack, hand me your torch.'

She slips off into the gloom, leaving us with the doleful sound of the Rotters for company. I glance at Noxi, but all I can see of her face is the faint sparkle of her eyes.

There's a tinkle of breaking glass, a grunt, the clunk of a car door or boot opening, and then a cry of triumph.

Pockets sprints back to us, brandishing a crowbar and wedges the edge of it into the crack between the lift doors. 'All yours Americano.'

Arm muscles bulging, he pulls back on the crowbar's handle and the doors open with a metallic screech.

'Someone's thought of this before,' Nuush says. 'That was way too easy.'

I stand as close to the edge as I dare, Americano gripping my forearm to steady me, and shine the torch down, trying to illuminate the bottom of the shaft. It's a dead loss. The beam is too insipid to cut through more than a couple of metres of the hole's flat darkness, although there is some good news – there's a narrow metal maintenance ladder bolted to its brick sides. I target the beam upwards and Danny breathes a sigh of relief at the sight of the lift stuck above us.

'Well, looks like we're in luck,' he says. 'The elevator is above us so we can make it all the way down.'

'Unless it falls on our heads,' Pockets mutters.

'Okay,' I say. 'Americano and I will go down first and if it's safe we'll call up to you.'

Noxi snorts. 'Hear that girls? The *men* are going to conquer the big bad elevator for us.'

Danny looks at me and then at Noxi. 'Did something happen between you two?'

Americano shoulders his rifle. 'We don't have time for this. You can sort your issues out when we're out of here.'

'I'll go first,' Danny says. 'I'm the best climber. And it was my idea.' Before I can stop him, Danny drops to a crouch, swings his leg over the edge, reaches for the ladder, and twists his body onto it. 'Easy!' He starts scampering down it.

'Steady, Danny,' I say. 'It could be rusty.'

'I'm cool.'

I tuck the torch into my belt and follow suit. The ladder's rungs are cold and flaked with rust and the lift shaft stinks of decaying concrete and something else – a dank, dry odour that makes me sneeze.

There's a clunk above my head, and I look up to see someone else climbing down. Noxi.

'Wait till we're down,' I call up. 'It might not be safe.'

She mutters something that sounds like 'screw you'.

'Jack!' Danny shouts. 'Can you pass me the torch? Wanna see what I'm getting myself into down here.'

I move as far down the ladder as I can without braining him, ease the torch out of my belt and lean down.

'Can't get it. Wait, let me move up a bit.' He shifts his position, hanging on with one hand as he reaches up towards me.

'Careful, Danny.'

'It's easy, no worries—'

There's a rasp as his foot slips, his hand meets empty space as he flails for balance, and before I can make a grab for him, he's gone.

A second later: the sickening thud of his body hitting the ground.

'Danny!' I roar.

'What the hell is going on?' Noxi yells.

'Danny! Are you okay?' My heart freezes as I wait for a reply.

I can hear the others panicking above me, their shouts echoing around the small space.

'Uh,' Danny calls. 'Busted my arm.' His voice is twisted with pain, but at least he's alive.

'Hold on. Don't move.' I scoot down the ladder as fast as I can. When I judge I can't be too far from the bottom, I twist and shine the torch downwards.

Danny's flat on his back, his right arm lying limply at his side, a jagged piece of bone jutting through the skin. And ... he's lying on what looks to be the remains of several Rotter bodies, scraps of fabric still clinging to their desiccated bones, calcified white tendrils curled around them.

I jump the last metre, fighting to regain my balance as I land on the uneven surface.

'Hold on, Danny,' Noxi yells. 'I'm coming.'

I crunch over to him, hearing the crump of Noxi landing next to me. She shoves me out of the way and drops to her knees next to him. She glances at his fractured arm and hisses through her teeth. 'Oh, Danny!'

I jam the torch into a gap in the slimy walls so that my hands are free to deal with Danny. 'Americano!' I yell. 'You and the others find another way down. Get help. We need a medic asap!'

'Is Danny okay?' Nuush calls back.

'He'll be fine!' I say, more for Danny's benefit than hers.

Danny gives me a weak smile.

I force myself to grin back at him. It doesn't look like he's losing a lot of blood, but even in the torch's weak light I can see that he's getting paler by the second. His eyes widen, 'Did you feel something move, Jack? I just felt something move.'

I stare down at the bones beneath our feet.

Oh no. Oh shit, no.

The white tendrils wrapped around the bones aren't entirely dead. And it happens fast. Too fast. The strands woven around the rib cage closest to him twitch and jerk and slick towards him, spiking into the wound. He opens his mouth to scream, but he doesn't get a chance.

'Jack?' Noxi gasps. 'Jack ... what ...'

'Noxi!' I roar, grabbing her by her elbow and hauling her to her feet. 'Get back up that ladder right now!' I've seen this too many times before. The sudden deadening of the eyes even while the rest of the body is still alive and functioning. But Noxi is immobile with shock.

'It'll be okay, Danny,' she whispers. 'Everything will be fine, we'll—'

His head snaps in her direction and then, moving with that alien hatchling speed, he twists, coiling his body onto his hands and knees. He scrabbles across the bones, clawed hands reaching for her.

'Danny!' Noxi croaks.

I snatch the Glock out of the holster on her hip, disengage the safety and fire, putting a bullet straight through his upper lip.

One moment he's moving; the next ... nothing.

My ears ringing from the gunshot, I let the gun fall out of my fingers. Noxi stands frozen next to me, sucking air deep into her lungs with shuddering gasps. Then, she screams and lunges for me, trying to scratch at my face. I grab her wrists, pull her towards me, wrap my arms around her, feeling her whole body shaking with the force of her grief.

I look over her shoulder, down at the figure lying crumpled and broken on the bones. I will myself to believe I'm looking at a hatchling, but all I can see is a dead teenage boy.

With Danny's blood still fresh on my hands, I flee to the only place where I can think, and sink to the floor in my usual spot in the fantasy section.

He was a just a kid.

And I shot him.

None of the others could look me in the eye as the medics removed his body. Nuush and Pockets stood silently, their arms around each other, tears sliding down their cheeks. Americano turned away, his skin ashen, unaware that he was crushing the unlit cigarette he held in his fingers. Noxi had shoved herself away from me the second the lift doors were pried open. She'd fled into the arrivals area. I haven't seen her since.

Only Morgan spoke to me: 'You did the only thing you could have done, Jack.'

True as those words were, they meant nothing.

And Danny's death has brought with it a fresh floodtide of guilt and remorse. I can no longer bury thoughts of Saint and the knowledge that her death is my fault, my responsibility.

I was the one who insisted we leave Cape Town, heading off on a secret mission to find Jova and Lucien. I was the one who insisted we carry on to Joburg after Saint discovered the reason why Ginger and Ember were immune to Rotter attack. Saint wanted to return to Cape Town, spread the news, let the ANZ know that anyone who was left-handed would be able to leave the enclave, and that we no longer had to depend on the Guardians for our survival. If I hadn't been so arrogant, so selfish, if I'd listened to her, to Lele, then she would still be alive.

It's all my fault. I can't even blame Lucien any more.

And there's Ember. I didn't even ask Jova how she was when I saw him this morning. I was too obsessed with what was going on between me and Noxi.

Morgan's right. I didn't have a choice but to shoot Danny, but that doesn't make it any easier. And as much as I hate myself for it, it isn't just Danny's death or the memories it's dredged up that are messing with my head.

That white stuff. The tendrils that slicked into the wound in Danny's leg. Seeing them scratched away at something else I've been trying to keep buried: I'm not like the others; I'm not left-handed.

And then there's Sasha ... Sasha who has never grown up. My twin. The Guardians did something to her at the beginning of the war, something that keeps her locked inside her seven-year-old body. Something that's connected to my immunity to Rotter infection.

I pick up my knife, testing its sharpness on the pad of my thumb. A part of me still doesn't believe it, thinks all I'll end up with is a gashed hand. But another part ... *knows*, and has always known.

The cut has to be deep, I've collected hundreds of injuries over the years – injuries that all healed alarmingly fast – but I've never been seriously wounded until the crash, when I saw, or thought I saw, something glinting deep in the wound on my collarbone. Before I can change my mind I slash my left palm, almost glad of the instant flare of pain. Blood wells and I pull off my shirt and wrap it around my hand. I count to five in my head, then ten and when I hit twenty-five I pull the shirt away.

My hand is sticky with blood, but it doesn't hide the silver tendrils writhing deep in the wound. Tendrils that look horribly similar to the white strands that keeps the Rotters animated.

The nausea comes thick and fast, but I swallow it back and force myself to take a closer look, breathing in deeply to calm myself. The strands are finer than the white ones that infected

Danny. They're so delicate they'd almost be beautiful if it wasn't for the fact that they're *inside me*.

'Jack?' Morgan steps around the bookshelf. Her eye is shining with anger. 'Why weren't you at the burning? I thought Danny was your friend.'

Her gaze flicks to the shirt around my hand. 'You hurt?'

She drops to her knees beside me. Moves as if to take my hand, but I jerk it away from her. 'Don't.'

Her eye strays to the panga. 'Did you do this to yourself? Are you doing this because you're feeling guilty?'

'No, nothing like that. Don't worry.'

'You didn't kill him, Jack. He was infected—'

'Save it.'

A sigh. 'Listen. I think it's a good idea for you to stay in here tonight. The others ... It's going to take time, Jack. Jova says that even Noxi will come around eventually. You saved her life.'

'Oh, Jova says that, does he? Well, that's okay, then. If it wasn't for him and his stupid war games, Danny would still be alive.'

'You know that's not true. He says he wants to take you to see your friends tomorrow. Says you've more than proved your worth. He wants you to stick with him for the next few days.'

Despite the guilt, the pain the horror, I can't suppress a small swell of pride. I try to hate myself for it, but I can't.

She reaches for my hand again and this time I don't fight her. 'I need to take a look at this, Jack.'

'I'm not *right*, Morgan.'

She starts to unwrap the shirt, I feel giddy, dizzy ... almost drunk. 'I'm not like the others. I'm not left-handed, Morgan.'

For a long moment she stares down at my palm. 'Jack. Does Jova know about this?'

'No. Yes. Probably. Jova knows everything.' I swallow hard. 'I'm a monster.' I sound like a child.

She slowly and purposefully rewraps my hand in the shirt. 'Listen to me very carefully, Jack. You are not a monster. Not even the dead out there are monsters.' She smiles at me and it isn't the amused twitch I'm used to seeing on her face, but the real deal. And it puts Noxi's dazzling grin to shame.

Without thinking, I grab her shoulders, pull her towards me and then I'm kissing her.

For a split second she kisses me back. And then she twists away and whacks me across the face. Hard. 'What the *hell* do you think you're doing?' For a second I'm certain she's going to slap me again. She sighs. 'Get that hand cleaned up. Get some sleep.' She stands up. 'You're not a monster, Jack. But you are definitely an asshole.'

Saint

Ntombi's humming again: *dum de dum de horse with no name de de dum de de dum de de dum ...*

Do you have to?

Yes, I do. Why not?

Saint knows she shouldn't goad her, not now that Ntombi's more content, almost completely resigned to her new reality. Saint has allowed her to drift into a false sense of security about the darkness, and it helps that Ntombi doesn't flex her presence with quite so much force as she used to. Whole hours can pass without her nagging: *What about Ash, what about Lele, what about Ginger, what about Ember, what about ...*

Part of Ntombi's contentment has to do with Horse. Horse still longs to be complete; he's not whole without others of his kind, but as Saint becomes more practised at joining her thread to his, he is beginning to accept her, and even Bambi, as part of his existence. Once or twice, Ntombi's managed to convince her to sit on Horse's back. Ntombi loves being lulled by the rhythm of his rolling gait. But Saint prefers the feel of the ground beneath her feet and more often than not she walks next to Horse, Bambi nipping at her boots and exploring the scrub around them. Because of the animals' need to eat she's forced to take a meandering path, sticking close to rivers, streams and the dead towns.

Saint has told Ntombi that Horse cannot stay with them forever, and as they walk she stretches out, looking for similar threads to his. Occasionally she senses them, but they are always too far away. She's not prepared to detour too far off their route. But one day soon, she'll set him free.

Intermittently, she picks up on the threads of living people. Bright twanging strands. They keep their distance; they have no interest in her. They're nomadic, avoiding the cities and the Rotters. They're at home in their environment, more at home than they were before the darkness.

When they reach the banks of a small dam, Saint sends Horse off to graze. Bambi shoots off, following the trail of a rabbit.

Atang is waiting for her, like he always is. Sometimes when she arrives in the kitchen, he has laid out one of the board games they used to play when they were children. Checkers, backgammon and snakes and ladders. He always lets her win.

Today there's a pack of cards on the table between them. They play hearts while she asks questions; questions fed to her by Ntombi. Sometimes Atang answers them; sometimes he avoids them.

<am I the same as Ripley now?>

<not yet. first you must eradicate the other>

<Ntombi?>

<yes>

Saint feels Ntombi bristling in her mind, decides to change the line of questioning. <where is the real Atang?>

<I am the real Atang>
<is he still in Botswana?>
<I am here, with you, now>
<where is Ripley? I can't sense her>
<in time>
<why are the Rotters so hungry?>
<they want life>
<why did you take it away from them?>
<we had no choice>
<who's we?>

Atang shows her an image she can't read: a swirl of unrecognisable colours surrounding an impenetrable nothingness. He tried this once before, and Ntombi translated it as an alien being, with black, slitted eyes and a bulbous, grey head. Atang found this amusing, although Saint knows that he – and the darkness – are not capable of any emotion she can understand. Atang can only use words and images that already exist in Saint's mind and most of what he shows her doesn't translate. The closest correlation to what Ntombi calls the 'spaghetti infection', the white strands that keep the Rotters' faint threads pulsating, is a snapshot from an old cartoon Saint has kept deep in her subconscious. A figure touching a glassy surface; the surface rippling and pulling the figure through and into a mirror world.

<why did you come here, Atang?>
<dying>
<you were dying?>
<no, *you* were going to die>

An image of a frozen world; a dark sky. Thousands of people trudging through thigh-high snow, laden down with possessions, many of them falling and not getting up again. Saint can't tell if the devastation is a result of a cataclysmic

213

natural disaster or if it has been caused by some kind of nuclear bomb or other human-made device. She isn't sure if she *wants* to know.

<you saved us?>

<yes>

Saint waits for Ntombi to jump in and ask how turning millions of people into the living dead can be construed as saving anyone, but she's distracted by something in the real world and stays silent.

<and this place?> she bats him back the image of the blood-filled valley, the snapshot Ntombi calls hell.

The kitchen door explodes and Ntombi bursts through it. She's never found the strength to join Saint in person here before.

Saint! Come!

What is it?

Bambi!

Saint stretches for Bambi's thread and feels a sudden burst of pain. She snaps back to reality, follows Bambi's weak thread. She finds him next to a sagging barbed-wire fence, a ring of spiked metal biting deep into his foreleg, his fur soaked with pumping blood. He keens and gnaws at it.

Saint bends, tries to fill his head with calm, but his panic is a bright, searing yellow leaking out of his eyes and staining the air around him. He nips at her, teeth slicing through her flesh, and she's surprised to see blood blossoming. She hadn't expected that. There's even a faraway sting of pain but instantly it starts to heal, her skin knitting together.

Hurry! Hurry, Saint!

She must work fast. He's losing too much blood.

It takes all of her strength to snap the trap open. Bambi

stops writing. He drops his head onto his ripped paws, his eyes eloquent with agony.

He's dying. The life force she associates with him is fading.

Ntombi screams at the back of her mind and the darkness ebbs closer, gathering as Bambi fades. She takes the animal into her arms, cradles him to her chest, studies his wound, the blood from her own injury mingling with his. She thinks back to the crash, her body lying broken on the road.

Do it.

DO IT, SAINT

Yes.

She strikes her wounded hand against the trap's teeth, breaking the skin again, and presses her palm to the hyena's leg. He twists in her arms and shudders as the strands trickle into him. She can feel his life force bloom, intensifying as it shifts and changes.

Ntombi's fear heightens, flooding Saint's mind with a blood red hue. It's distracting.

Stop it, Ntombi.

Saint knows why Ntombi's so afraid. She doesn't want Bambi to become like her, like *them*, trapped in a limbo existence. She can feel his unnatural pulse, the alien life in his veins.

He stops struggling.

Will he live?

Yes.

Will he be like you?

Like us?

Yes. Like us.

Yes.

Horse has picked up on Bambi's distress and is snorting and shivering on the far side of the dam, senses twanging, primed to flee. It takes all of Saint's concentration to calm him, washing the panic from his thread and tightening her grip on it. Then she picks Bambi up, nudges Horse over to a rock and asks him to allow her to climb on his back. Bambi wriggles weakly, twists his head to look up at her. There is an intelligence in those eyes that wasn't there before.

Saint freezes.

What is it?

She's aware of the tingle of an approaching thread. One she recognises.

Lucien?

Lucien.

What does he want?

Saint touches the hyena's head gently.

Well?

He doesn't know, Ntombi.

Tommy

Tommy's up early this morning. He downs a slug of water, crawls out of his sleeping bag and collects his backpack. Ginger's still fast asleep, but Jacob's place by the long-dead fire is empty, which is typical. Jacob doesn't seem to need more than a couple of hours sleep a night, and tends to spend most of his time in the small library in the zoo's conference centre. No one seems to mind that he doesn't help with the chores. Even Ma Beccah, the stout woman who coordinates the food rationing and cooking roster (and who scares the living daylights out of Tommy – she has a hairy chin and doesn't suffer fools) hasn't insisted that Jacob pull his weight. Everyone has a job to do here, be it cooking, tending the animals or teaching the children, and Tommy's never heard anyone complain about being assigned the crappiest jobs, such as shifting the animal dung or digging the outhouse trenches. (He still has the blisters from volunteering for that particular day's work.)

As he often does when he has free time, he walks up the hill towards the old polar bear enclosure. The cows low in the paddocks below, demanding to be milked, and a flock of tame guinea fowl dart and dance around his feet. Tommy steps carefully onto the viewing ledge (the wood is rotten, and the last thing he needs is a broken ankle) and peers down at the sun-bleached skeletons lying half-hidden behind algaed rocks. He can't look at the bears' bones without being flooded with a mixture of pity and sorrow, and he thinks he's finally figured out what draws him here. They remind him of the people who are trapped in Sandtown. If the Lefties didn't bring them food or water, then this is how everyone would end up.

And he's a long way from Sandtown now.

In his heart, all Tommy cares about is somehow getting home to Olivia and Baby Nomsa. But since he's been spending time with Ginger and the others in the zoo settlement, he feels as if his brain has been turned inside out. Even his big dream of taking the trials and joining the AOL seems stupid now. How can things have got so screwed up? How can the people have allowed men and women like Sindiwe, Coom and Simo's dad to live in luxury while they live in filth?

What he can't get over are the lies and rumours that have spread through Sandtown. The Outcasts may wear masks and creep through the city like wraiths, but they aren't monsters or murderers. They don't eat the runners they capture; they don't make muti out of body parts. Tommy's been amazed at the number of former Sandtown runners here, men and women who have chosen, out of their own free will, to remain. No, most of the Outcasts are just ordinary people, just like those who struggle daily to subsist in the Sandtown ghettos. It's the amaKlevas, the rich who lord it over everyone in their luxury hotel suites, who are the real bogeymen.

But still … it doesn't matter how many times Senyaka tells him that the Outcasts have no intention of harming what he calls 'the people' in Sandtown, and that their only goal is to destabilise Coom and the other amaKlevas' hold over the city, Tommy can't entirely rid himself of the notion that by being here, he's going against everything he's ever believed in.

And what about Jova's plan to wipe out the dead? He's tried talking to Senyaka about this, but has never received a straight answer, although he gets the impression that Senyaka doesn't entirely disapprove of Jova's mission. And that's another thing that keeps Tommy up at night. What if the dead – the Rotters – what if they *aren't* the enemy? He can't forget what he saw in that school, and he can't forget that Rotter he met in the creepy hospital – he's even mentally dubbed him Optimus Prime, after the toy he gave it.

'Sorry,' he whispers to the skeletons, before making his way back to the canteen to see if Ma Beccah has started the fire for the morning tea. People are stirring now, a couple of fathers lead a snake of small children to the little dam for their morning wash; an elderly woman helps an ancient man shuffle towards the outhouses. He waves at Bulelani who is wheeling a bundle of hay towards the ponies' enclosure. Tommy can hardly believe this friendly, soft-spoken man was one of the terrifying figures who captured them outside the hospital.

He hears a bark of laughter, spots Ginger giggling with Helen, a loud, cheerful woman of around Olivia's age who treats the pigs, sheep and cows in her care as if they're her children. She even shares her sleeping hut with several cats and allows Tommy to play with the latest batch of kittens. Cats are discouraged in Sandtown. They kill rats, and for most of the population, rat meat is the only protein they can get.

'Awright, Tommy?' Ginger calls. 'I'm off for a recce. You want to come?'

'What sort of recce?'

Ginger looks down at his tatty T-shirt. None of the clothes in the settlement fit him – he's taller than all of the men here. 'Need a couple of things. Thought there might be a chance some of the houses round here haven't been picked clean.'

'You mean go outside?'

'Yeah, course.'

Tommy hasn't been out of the settlement since they arrived. He'll be that little bit closer to Olivia outside the gates, and until he can return to her, it hurts to be reminded of this. 'Okay,' he says. 'Why not?'

Ginger musses his hair and Tommy mock-fights him off. Now that Ginger's leg is healed, he's been teaching Tommy a few fighting moves. Tommy's surprised himself at how much he enjoys these impromptu sessions, even if they do always result in one or two bruises the next day, and he thinks his stomach is shrinking; his jeans feel looser. Certainly his skin is clearing up from being out in the sun all day.

'Cool. Tell you what, later on we'll get on with your training, yeah?' Ginger grins at him. Tommy's been stunned at the change in Ginger's personality since they've been here. Gone is all trace of that shut-off monosyllabic behaviour. The settlement's inhabitants seem to have taken to Ginger too, especially the smaller children, who, given half a chance, follow him around like a pack of semi-feral dogs.

They pass through the first set of gates and head into the dirt parking lot. Kathleen (who Tommy still can't help but think of as Skull Face) is half-hidden in the open bonnet of a rusty bakkie. She says something to the weedy kid who's passing tools to her, and he sniggers. Tommy colours, even though he knows they're not laughing at him. He was wary of the few teenagers in the settlement when he first arrived, half-expecting them to make fun of him like Mooki and Jess did, but they've been friendly enough, albeit a bit distant, which he's put down to the fact that he's still a newbie here.

'Awright, Kat!' Ginger yells.

'Howzit, Ginger,' Kathleen shouts back. Tommy's pretty sure Kathleen's got a bit of thing for his friend, but it won't go anywhere, and not just because Kathleen is seriously scary. Ginger's heart belongs to the mysterious Ember, a girl who has taken on mythic proportions in Tommy's mind after hearing about her so often.

The Outcasts lounging by the gates grin at Ginger and mock-salute. That's the other thing Tommy can't get over. No one seems to care if you just leave – there's no one to report to and the settlement seems to run smoothly despite the lack of structure and fear that underpins Sandtown. Even Senyaka and Kathleen, the leaders of the settlement, live under the same conditions as everyone else.

There are fewer Rotters milling around outside the gates than in Sandtown, but there are enough to chill Tommy's bones. These are in a far worse state than the ones in the hospital, and Tommy tries to ignore the clutch in his chest as he and Ginger push through the throng.

'Let's head left,' Ginger says. 'There are a couple of streets that might be worth exploring. Senyaka said they've cleared out most the houses in the area, but you never know.'

The crowd of the dead thins, and Tommy shivers as a small Rotter breaks away from the group and lurches in his direction. Tommy's eye is drawn to a red keychain on its belt.

Hang on. Tommy can't believe it. 'It's Optimus!'

'Eh?' Ginger says.

The Rotter throws its head back and moans, almost, Tommy thinks, as if it's trying to laugh in recognition.

'Hey,' Tommy says to it. 'Hey.'

Unbelievably, it's still clutching the Transformer toy.

'Tommy,' Ginger says. 'What's going on?'

'It ... he was in that hospital. You know, where we stayed the night. He must have followed me here!'

'You serious, mate? That's impossible.'

'I'm certain, Ginger.'

'You sure it's the same one? I mean, they all look alike once they get to a certain stage of their ... rottenness.'

'It's definitely him. And look, he's not that rotten.' Optimus's clothes are slightly more dishevelled than they were, but Tommy thinks his face and limbs are as intact as they were back at No Hope. Has Optimus been hanging around here since he, Ginger and Jacob were brought to the zoo? And how did he find his way here? Tommy feels a touch of doubt. Is it possible for two Rotters to look so alike? Perhaps. But what are the chances of coming across two Rotters wearing identical SpongeBob T-shirts and clutching a Transformer toy?

Ginger sniffs. 'Come to think of it, he does look like a long-dead Justin Bieber, doesn't he?'

'Who?'

'Doesn't matter. What's it doing?'

'He wants me to play with him.'

Ginger shoots him a dubious glance. 'No offence, Tommy, but Jacob's supposed to be the nutter around here.'

'Tommy! Ginger!' Tommy turns to see Senyaka jogging towards them and he tries to quash the mixture of awe and discomfort he always feels whenever he's in Senyaka's presence. He admires and respects him, sure, and he supposes Senyaka's the closest thing he's ever had to a stepfather, but

222

he just can't read him. There's a secretive, guarded side to Senyaka that makes Tommy uneasy. Senyaka didn't act that surprised to hear that he had a daughter back in Sandtown, which must mean that the Outcasts have spies in the city. But what else is he hiding?

'Kathleen said she saw you guys heading this way,' Senyaka grins. 'What are you doing out here? Not planning on leaving us, are you?'

'Not just yet,' Ginger says. He taps his knee. 'But now this is kosher I'll be on my way soon. Got to find my friends.'

'You can't!' Tommy blurts. It's the first he's heard of Ginger's plan to leave the settlement; he hasn't realised how much he depends on him.

'I got no choice, Tommy. Much as I like the set-up here – and the people – I have to put my friends first. The offer of speaking to Lucien still stands. You didn't do anything wrong. I'll back you up.'

'It might be too late for that,' Senyaka says. 'Tommy has been gone for weeks now. They might assume he has changed his loyalties. And what if they interrogate him about where he's been?'

'I won't say anything!'

'You might not have a choice, Tommy.'

'So what you going to do, Senyaka?' Ginger pipes in. 'Keep him here forever? He has to get back to his mum, doesn't he?'

Senyaka nods. 'Of course he does. And he will. And soon, you have my word. But first ... we need your help.'

'What kind of help?'

'According to my intel, Coom's runners are planning an extensive recce to the Eastgate mall now that they've cleared that section of the highway. We must take advantage of this. We might not get another chance.'

Tommy shivers. A raid. But now he knows for sure Senyaka has spies in Sandtown's midst.

'So what do you need from us?' Ginger asks.

'They travel in well-organised groups. We need something to draw them away from their vehicles, get them out in the open.' Senyaka eyes Ginger. 'You have run from Sandtown. And forgive me for saying so, but you are extremely distinctive. They'll want to bring you back if they can.'

Tommy fidgets, makes himself speak. 'But why would Coom's runners care about us? We ran from Sandtown, not Coom.'

'Sindiwe would have asked Coom to instruct his runners to keep an eye out for you. No doubt she's offered a reward to whoever brings you back.'

'That's one way to get back to the city,' Ginger says, half-seriously.

Tommy shivers. A reward. For him! But he still doesn't understand exactly what it is that Senyaka is planning.

Ginger runs a hand through his hair. 'I think I get you. You want me to lure them somewhere? So you can ambush them?'

'Yes.'

'And then what?'

'You're going to shoot them, aren't you, Senyaka?' Tommy says in a small voice.

'Not if they surrender quietly, Tommy. The other Outsider has already agreed to join us.'

Ginger shakes his head. 'Jacob? Seriously, you don't want him going along. Jacob's cool and everything, but he's not right in the head.'

'They'll be keeping an eye out for three of you. If Jacob wishes to join, I am not going to stop him.'

'Whoa. Hold on, you're not suggesting that Tommy ... No way. That's not on. He's just a kid.'

'I'll do it!' Tommy feels his mouth dropping open stupidly. Did he really just say that? Is he so desperate to prove to Senyaka that he's a man?

'No way. It's too dangerous, Tommy.'

'It's up to Tommy to decide,' Senyaka says. 'I will not try to influence him in any way. It will be dangerous, and I completely understand if he chooses to remain behind.'

'I'm going.' Tommy feels a flush of pride as Senyaka nods at him in approval.

'I give you my word that ...' Senyaka's expression darkens and he places a hand on the knife stuck in his belt. Tommy realises Senyaka's staring straight at Optimus, who's swaying slightly just metres from where they're standing. Tommy's been so caught up in the tension, he's almost forgotten about him. 'That is not right. That one seems to be able to sense us.'

'Tommy thinks it followed him from that No Hope Hospital place where Kat, Bulelani and Koebus picked us up,' Ginger says.

'That's impossible.'

'That's what I said,' Ginger grins. 'But the kid's got a point. This Rotter isn't like the others. Seems to be a bit more alert.'

'Don't get too close to it, Tommy. You may be a Leftie, but it can still infect you.'

'Seriously?' Ginger looks dubious. 'But we're immune.'

'I've heard of it happening,' Senyaka says, without taking his eyes off Optimus. 'One of our team, Lulu – a good woman, dependable – was injured in a raid, shot in the arm. As she fled from the scene, she brushed up against one of those things. The infection they carry squirmed its way into the

225

wound ... The others were lucky to get away with their lives when she turned.'

'Blimey,' Ginger says. 'Lucky we're not injured, then.'

Tommy shudders. But Optimus would never knowingly infect him, would he?

'I'll be careful, Senyaka,' Tommy says, desperate to placate him. Senyaka still looks as if he's a hair's breadth away from lopping Optimus's head from his shoulders. Thankfully, as if Optimus can read Senyaka's mind, he turns and stumbles back into the throng gathered next to the fence.

Senyaka frowns. 'You must have imagined it's the same one, Tommy. Those things are not capable of communicating with us. Now, shall we return? We have much to plan.'

Tommy hangs back as Ginger and Senyaka make for the main gate. The mass of the dead shifts, and Tommy glimpses the blue of Optimus's SpongeBob T-shirt among them. He waves, and he's almost certain that Optimus attempts to wave back at him before he disappears amid the dead rambling aimlessly around him.

Ginger sighs and mock-punches Tommy's shoulder. 'You have to eat something, Tommy.'

'I can't.'

'You need your strength. Did you get any sleep at all last night?'

Tommy shakes his head.

'Can't say I blame you. Not exactly the Ritz, is it?' Ginger wrinkles his nose, scuffs his boot over the floor of the old service station convenience store in which they've spent the night. The cracked tiles are peppered with rat droppings, and when Tommy swept his torch around its dark interior last night, seemingly hundreds of pin-prick eyes shone back at him. The rodents kept out of sight, but even if he could have calmed his mind enough to drop off, Tommy's certain that the sound of their night-time squabbles would have kept him awake. 'Listen. You don't have to do this. It's not too late to back out, Tommy. No one's going to think badly of you.'

'I know.'

It's not just the danger – the fear of being captured, or worse – that's making Tommy's empty stomach churn. Despite all he's seen at the zoo settlement, he still can't squash the feeling that he's being traitorous. That he's going against Olivia and everyone he knows in Sandtown – betraying them somehow.

He couldn't even enjoy the journey here; the novelty of travelling on the back of a motorbike had been marred by anxiety. They were forced to find alternative routes when the corpses of cars and trucks had blocked the route, and every time Bulelani slowed, Tommy was hit with the urge to jump off the back of the bike and shout that he'd changed his mind. But each time he swallowed the words. How could he back out now? What would Senyaka think of him?

'What about you, Ginger? Are you scared?'

'Course I am, mate. I'd be stupid if I wasn't.' He nods to where Jacob is curled up in his sleeping bag. 'We'd better wake Sleeping Beauty here.'

Ginger shakes Jacob's shoulder, and he stretches and grins up at them. 'For once I didn't dream,' he says. 'What a perfect night!'

'I'm happy for you, mate,' Ginger says. 'But it's time to get going.'

Jacob scrambles to his feet, runs his hands through his dusty hair. 'I'm ready.'

'Listen, Jacob,' Ginger says. 'This is going to be dangerous. Dunno quite how to say this ... but are you going to be able to keep a lid on the crazy?'

Jacob grins. 'No great mind has ever existed without a touch of madness.'

'Awesome,' Ginger mutters, rolling his eyes at Tommy. 'We'd better hope Senyaka knows what he's doing.' Ginger looks up as the door bursts open. 'Speak of the devil.'

Senyaka stalks towards them. 'It's time to get into position.'

Ginger ruffles Tommy's hair. 'You sure, Tommy?'

'Yeah,' he says, although he can't seem to swallow. He picks up his bag and clenches his fists to stop his hands from shaking. Senyaka leads them out into the sunlight, across the road and towards the parking lot.

The mall where the ambush is to take place towers in front of them. When Senyaka brought them here last night for a recce, Tommy was astounded by its size, a giant concrete monolith that – at least from the outside – appeared to be almost untouched by ten years of neglect. He wasn't certain, but it looked as if it was even bigger than Sandtown.

They didn't venture too far inside its dim, stinking interior, but Tommy shuddered as the ghostly moans of the dead drifted towards them. Despite spending the night in that hospital, despite Optimus, he couldn't entirely conquer the primal dread he felt at the thought of how many Rotters could be lurking in the murky depths of the mall's sinister shops.

'Are there any survivors around here?' Tommy asked Senyaka, when he found his voice.

'Not as far as we know,' Senyaka said.

'So why are the dead in here?'

Senyaka shrugged. 'They could be all that remains of a settlement that was hit by infection. Or perhaps it is just habit? Perhaps they are drawn here. Who knows why they do what they do?'

Tommy breathed a sigh of relief when Senyaka led them outside again.

'We'll be waiting up there,' Senyaka said, gesturing at the roof on the far side of the building. 'We need you to draw them towards us.'

'Why there?' Ginger asked.

'There aren't that many vehicles in the parking lot in that area – nowhere for them to hide.'

'And you really won't shoot them if you don't have to?'

'Really, Tommy,' Senyaka said. 'If they surrender, then they will not be hurt. You have my word.' He led them to the rusty shell of a bakkie in the middle of the parking lot. 'Hunker down here. When you hear the engines, start running towards the mall. Remember, they will be reluctant to shoot – there is a reward out for you. They'll want to capture you alive.' Senyaka must have seen Tommy's pained expression, because he clapped a hand on his shoulder and said, 'We won't let that happen.'

'How will you know when they're on their way?'

Senyaka grinned and tapped the side of his nose. 'I have my sources.'

It sounded so easy last night. And now it's time. There's no going back from here.

'Are your guys in position?' Ginger asks.

'Of course. When we get close enough I'll ask them to—' Senyaka's radio crackles. 'Senyaka. They're …' Bulelani's voice is lost in static, and Tommy prays that he imagined the panicked note in it.

'Say again, Bulelani,' Senyaka says. 'Over.'

'… en route. Repeat. They're en route. Ahead of schedule. Take cover. Suggest we abort. Over.'

There's a growl of an approaching engine and Tommy swings around. He can't figure out where it's coming from. 'Shall we head back to the store?'

'No time. Head for the mall.' Senyaka takes off running. '*Move!*'

Tommy doesn't need to be told twice. He sets off after Senyaka, doing his best to keep up. He can hear Ginger and Jacob following behind, the grumble of the engine – a motorbike, he's sure – increasing in volume. There's no way that they'll make it inside the mall before it reaches them. Senyaka puts on a burst of speed, dodging and weaving and flying towards the entrance of an underground parking lot, and then Tommy feels something yanking him back with such force his feet go out from under him and he lands heavily on the tarmac, his head smacking against the side of the car next to him.

Dazed, he twists around and sees that the strap of his backpack has looped around a side mirror. Ginger and Jacob come thumping up next to him.

'Go!' Tommy shouts at them.

'No way,' Ginger says, helping him to his feet. A motorbike screams across the parking lot from the right, and there's a crack as Senyaka gets off a shot. The driver and passenger riding pillion duck and the bike swerves, but it's clear the bullet hasn't found its target. And now it's heading straight for them.

Jacob is looking around anxiously, bouncing on his heels and muttering. 'Uh-oh.' He points towards the main road, and Tommy turns to see a long line of vehicles approaching slowly: several motorbikes, two buses, a bakkie, a van, a yellow army vehicle and three fuel trucks. One by one, the bikes peel away, cutting straight across the embankment towards them. 'We'd better run!'

230

But it's too late. The bike is on them. It skids to a halt and the passenger leaps off, already pointing a gun at Ginger's head.

'On your knees,' the passenger barks.

The driver joins him in seconds. Like the guy with the gun, she's dressed all in black, her eyes obscured by mirrored sunglasses.

'You got us,' Ginger says. 'We'll come quietly.'

'Where's the other one?' the woman snaps.

'What other one?' Ginger asks innocently.

'There were four of you. The one who shot at us.'

'Must have been your imagination.'

'Don't toy with me.' She grabs the radio at her belt. 'We've got three here. At least one other in the mall. Need back-up, over.' She steps closer. 'You the group who ran from Sandtown?'

'No, no, no, not us,' Jacob babbles. 'Not us. We didn't run. You can't take me, I'm not going back there!' His voice increases in pitch. 'I won't go!' he screams.

The passenger swings the gun in Jacob's direction and Tommy's about to yell at him not to shoot when the windscreen of the car next to them explodes. 'Down!' the driver screams.

Another shot.

'Move it!' Senyaka shouts at the top of his lungs.

Ginger grabs Tommy's arm and then they're off running. Tommy can only pray that Jacob has the sense to follow. Tommy's now so flooded with adrenaline that the terror washes away, and he can see everything with crystal clarity. He hears shouts behind him, the crack of more gunshots, and he glances over his shoulder, relieved to see that Jacob is just metres behind them. Ginger hauls Tommy into the dark mouth of the parking garage, almost pulling his arm out of his socket in the process, drags him past the remains of a ticket machine and towards a door next to a bank of lifts where Senyaka is waiting.

'Go!' Senyaka snaps, opening the door and shoving Tommy into a black stairwell.

'What about you?'

Senyaka thrusts his walkie-talkie into Ginger's hands. 'Going to try and meet up with the ambush. Hurry!'

'Jacob, come on!' Ginger roars. Jacob staggers, clutching at his back as if he has a stitch, and finally reaches them.

Tommy fumbles in his bag for his torch, almost drops it, then manages to make his hands work and clicks it on. He scrambles up the stairs, Ginger and Jacob panting behind him, shoves against the first door he comes to and falls out into the mall's fusty interior, Ginger on his heels.

'Not good,' Ginger mutters. 'Where's Jacob?'

'Wasn't he behind you?'

'Yeah, he must have—'

'Uh,' Jacob groans, collapsing through the door.

'Jacob!' Tommy yelps, running to his side. Jacob holds his hand up to his face. It's dripping with black blood. 'Uh-oh,' he says.

Ginger skids towards them. 'We got to move it, try and find a back way out of here.'

'Jacob's hurt. Shot, I think,' Tommy can hear the sob in his voice, but he's so deep in shock he can't yet feel anything other than numbing disbelief that this is actually happening.

Ginger yanks his T-shirt over his head. 'Press this to the wound. I need to block that door. Give me your torch.' Tommy hands it over and Ginger sweeps the beam around. He grabs a shopping trolley, flips it over and jams it under the handle.

'It'll be okay, Jacob,' Tommy whispers. It's too dark to

see the wound, but he presses the bundled shirt to Jacob's back.

'That won't hold them for long,' Ginger says.

'Should we hide?'

'Nah. We don't want to get trapped in here, end up as sitting ducks. There must be another exit. Help me lift Jacob up.'

Together they manage to get Jacob upright, and as the beam of the torch Ginger's trying to hold in the crook of his arm hits Jacob's face, Tommy almost screams. His face is soaked with sweat, his skin a dull grey. Tommy hopes this is just a trick of the light. Jacob groans as Ginger hooks an arm under his shoulders, Tommy following suit on the other side.

'Shhhh, Jacob. It's cool, mate. We'll get you out of here,' Ginger says.

'Keep going,' Jacob whimpers. 'Leave me.'

'That's not going to happen, mate.'

There's a thump from behind the door. He hears a woman's voice yelling: 'They came this way! Shoot to kill. They're armed.'

'Come on,' Ginger hisses. 'They'll burst through at any minute.'

Tommy knows that there's no way they'll be able to move fast enough to outpace the runners, not with Jacob slowing them down. But they have to try.

They limp along the passageway, feet slurping over mouldy tiles, and Tommy feels a slow warmth trickling over his arm from Jacob's waist. Even with Ginger shouldering most of Jacob's weight, it's slow going. A figure suddenly looms in front of him and Tommy yelps. But it's just a Rotter, and mindful of Senyaka's revelation that the dead can infect Lefties after all, Ginger nudges it out of the way with his boot. The torch's beam only illuminates a short stretch in front of them, and

Ginger instructs them to take turnings at random. The mall appears to be an endless warren of connecting passageways and criss-crossing aisles, and Tommy prays they're not going in circles.

The Rotters' moans are increasing in volume, but beneath them, Tommy can hear the sound of multiple voices, the slap of running feet. He jumps as the faint pop pop pop pop of sustained gunfire in the distance. Senyaka and the Outcasts must be engaging the runners from their vantage point outside, but that won't help them in here.

'Faster!' Ginger whispers, his breathing laboured. They stumble down a narrow corridor and out into a smallish quad, feet crunching over broken glass.

'Can you take Jacob's full weight, Tommy?' Ginger asks.

'I'll try.' Jacob slumps the second Ginger steps away, and Tommy staggers, arm muscles straining to hold him up. Jacob's eyes are shut, and his breathing is shallow.

Ginger sweeps his torch around, the light bobbing over several Rotters who are lurking next to a pair of frozen escalators, then races over to the exit doors at the far side of the area. Tommy can see that it's hopeless. They're sealed with a metal roll-down gate. 'Dammit,' Ginger mutters, kicking at the gate and making a clanking sound that's way too loud for Tommy's liking. 'Trapped.'

He shines the beam above them. The escalators end at a small food court sporting McDonalds and Wimpy signs; the only possible exit is a narrow glass door on the right-hand side that's bleeding meagre daylight and looks like it leads to an outside balcony. 'We should head up there,' Ginger whispers. 'We can try and hold them off.'

'With what?'

'We'll have to improvise.'

Jacob sags, and Tommy's unable to hold him up any longer. He tries to ease him to the floor as carefully as he can. The thud of running feet sounds way too close now, and Tommy can make out the faint glow of a flashlight from the corridor.

'C'mon,' Ginger says, moving to heft Jacob back onto his feet. He and Tommy carefully push the Rotters out of the way as they reach the base of the escalators.

'Wait,' Jacob whispers. 'Tommy. Ginger.' He points up to the food court. 'Can't make it. When I say run, *run.*'

'We're not leaving you,' Tommy sobs.

'Damn straight we're not,' Ginger says. 'Now let's—'

'You have to.' Something glints in Jacob's hand. A shard of glass. He squeezes his fist around it.

'Jacob – what are you *doing*?' Tommy cries.

In the weak light Tommy sees that not only does Jacob look saner than he's ever seen him look before, but he's smiling. 'Thank you for being my friends,' he says in a clear, loud voice. He throws his body towards the nearest Rotter, grasping its arm with his torn hand. Tommy's never seen anyone get infected before – well, he *must* have seen people getting infected at the beginning, he just can't remember it – and it happens sickeningly fast. The white tendrils squirm out of the Rotter's skin and writhe straight into Jacob's body.

Jacob shudders and twists. He's facing away from the light so Tommy can't see his eyes. '*Run!*' Then he lets out a shriek that Tommy knows he'll be hearing in his nightmares for years to come.

Ginger heaves Tommy towards the escalators.

'No! We have to help Jacob!'

'He's past helping, mate! Now run!'

Ginger pushes him up the metal stairs, steadying him when he trips over the lip at the top, and yanks him towards the glass door. Tommy manages to catch a glimpse of the scene below, which is lit up by the multiple beams of the runners' flashlights. A hunched figure – Jacob? It must be, but Tommy doesn't want to believe it – roars towards six or seven men and women, its limbs moving unnaturally, inhumanly fast, swiping, biting and grabbing at them. They try to scatter but they don't get far.

Ginger's swearing under his breath – Tommy's never heard words like it – and he hauls open the glass door, pushes Tommy onto the balcony beyond it, spins around and slams the door shut, leaning his weight on it. Howls, screams of anguish and pain rocket up from below, the door doing little to block them out.

Tommy's teeth are chattering, his whole body is shaking. Is he going into shock? He must be.

Ginger reaches out a hand. 'Don't panic, Tommy, try and stay—'

A dark shape jerks out of the darkness behind the door and smashes against it, howling with fury and spraying the glass with spittle. It's one of the runners, his face a distorted mask of rage and hatred, his eyes blank, black holes. He leans back, slams his body into the door again and Tommy's certain that the glass is about to splinter into smithereens. But somehow it holds. The runner shudders, stumbles backwards and flits into the gloom beyond.

Ginger hauls the walkie-talkie out of his pocket. 'Senyaka. Don't come into the mall. Repeat. Do *not* come into the mall.'

'What's happening?' Senyaka crackles back.

'It's Jacob. He …' Ginger's voice cracks. 'The place is crawling with hatchlings. Stay out there. Repeat, stay away, over.'

A pause. 'Roger. You are safe?'

'Tommy and I are okay. Jacob … Yeah. For now anyway.'

236

Tommy turns away, slumps onto his haunches and buries his head in his knees, hands clamped to his ears. But it doesn't help. He can still hear the screams.

———

Tommy doesn't remember falling asleep – how could he have dropped off in the middle of all that? – but it's now fully dark, and he can no longer hear the howls of the infected. His neck is stiff and his thigh muscles ache from being in such an awkward position.

Ginger's silhouetted shape is crouched in front of the glass door.

'You awake, mate?' Ginger yawns.

'Yeah. Stiff though.' He clamps his mouth shut. What right has he got to complain? None. He's alive. Unlike Jacob ... 'How long will we have to stay up here?'

'It's been ages since I heard one of them things making a racket. We should be fine now. It doesn't take that long for their senses to dull and for them to turn into plain old Rotters. It's like they stop being so angry at being infected or something after a while.'

'Ginger?'

'Yeah?'

'What Jacob did ... do you ... do you think it hurt?' Tommy's glad it's too dark for Ginger to see his face.

'Don't think about that, Tommy. What he did was incredibly brave. He saved our lives.'

'Do you think he knows?'

'Knows what?'

'What he is now?' Tommy can't decide what's worse, knowing you're one of the walking dead, or feeling nothing and just *being*.

'Tommy, seriously. You can't allow yourself to think about it.' Ginger clambers up, stretches, holds out a hand and pulls Tommy to his feet. 'I think it's safe for us to get out of here.'

'You think they've gone?'

'Yeah.'

Ginger opens the door, sweeps the torch through the dim space beyond it. The beam catches a pair of gleaming eyes and Tommy yelps.

'It's cool,' Ginger says, 'It's just a Rotter.'

Tommy breathes a sigh of relief when he sees that Ginger's right. The creature that was slamming its body into the door has lost all trace of its furious energy. It slumps aimlessly away and doesn't even turn its head in their direction as he and Ginger step warily into the food court.

'I hope we can find our way out of here,' Ginger murmurs.

Tommy barely breathes as they hustle back down the escalators and charge through dark corridors, the torch's beam lighting the way. He tries not to look too closely at any of the Rotters they encounter. He doesn't want to see Jacob like that. He doesn't even want to see Coom's runners in their new living dead incarnations.

Senyaka's waiting for them when they finally make their way back into the parking lot. 'I'm proud of you, Tommy,' he says. 'You made it through.'

Tommy doesn't respond, just snatches the water bottle Senyaka hands to him and downs as much of it as he thinks his stomach can handle, then pours the rest over his head. He feels filthy, as if he could scrub his skin forever and never get clean.

'That wasn't right, mate,' Ginger says to Senyaka. 'What happened there. Jacob sacrificed himself. I told you it was a bad idea to bring him along.'

Senyaka nods seriously. 'He was a good man, and we will remember him.'

'And the runners? How many ...' Tommy lets his voice trail away. He doesn't really want to know how many have died today.

Senyaka slings an arm around Tommy's shoulders. 'Are you ready to go home?'

'Back to Olivia?' he blurts.

'No,' Senyaka says. 'But soon. I promise.' He nods at Ginger. 'You okay to handle one of the bikes?'

'Yeah.'

As Senyaka leads him away, Tommy looks back at the mall one last time. 'Thank you,' he whispers, knowing that even if Jacob could hear him, he wouldn't understand.

Lele

I climb onto the toilet lid – the only way I can get a full view of my body – and turn sideways. My stomach's still flat, although ... is my face slightly rounder? I seriously hope it's just my imagination.

I still don't believe it. It's ridiculous. Unthinkable. *Pregnant*. How can I be pregnant? No, Cezanne must have made a mistake. Lucien and I only did it once. What are the chances?

I can't help but think of all those girls back in the Agriculturals who couldn't wait to get pregnant to prove they were doing their bit for the Resurrectionists. I thought they were insane. It can't happen to me. I can't have a baby!

More than ever I long for Saint. She'd be able to rationalise this. Last night I even found myself wishing I could talk to the Mantis. On a couple of occasions, I've almost blurted it out to Busi and Ember. But Cezanne says that it's best for us to keep it quiet, and after finding out that One Ear keeps his good ear to the ground where I'm concerned, I'm not taking any chances. Who knows how Coom might react?

The door opens and Busi enters, her eyes glistening with shock or excitement or both.

Oh crap. Does she know? Has she heard? No. Impossible. What if something's happened to Ember? Cezanne did warn me that she could have a relapse at any time. 'What now?'

'Coom's runners. They've been hit hard. Attacked. Yesterday. The Outcasts almost wiped them out.'

'Seriously? How many are hurt?'

'It's worse than that. Only a couple managed to get away. The rest are ...' she shivers. 'The Outcasts used the newly infected to attack them.'

'Busi ... were those two guys I beat up among them?'

She twists her hands. 'Ja,' she says, 'Wessel and Eric didn't come back either.'

I'm not sure how to feel about this. I wanted them to be punished for abusing Busi, but I'm not sure even she would have wished such a horrible fate on them. The sardonic Saint voice pops into my head: *Karma's a bitch, Lele.* 'Coom must be freaking out.'

She nods. 'He's furious. Apparently the AOL were supposed to have escorted them but never showed up. Jova and some of his army guys have just arrived to talk to Coom. I saw them downstairs.'

My stomach twists. 'Is Lucien with them?'

She shakes her head. 'I don't think so, Lele. I just saw Jova, a scary-looking woman and another guy in the dining room.'

If Jova's here, could Ash be with him? No. He would have come straight to find me, wouldn't he? But I need to be sure.

'Let's go.'

'Where?'

'To see Jova, of course.'

'But we can't!'

'Oh yeah? Watch me.'

One Ear looks up from his book as I storm out of the room, but I don't even glance at him. I haven't yet confronted him about his backstabbing ways. I'm biding my time on that score. Busi's still unaccountably got the hots for him, and I don't want to burst her bubble just yet by revealing that her almost-boyfriend is a snake in the grass.

The hotel lobby is buzzing, Coom's internal security guards and harassed-looking waiters clogging the space, and I shove through them to get to the dining room. I can't see Coom or his bodyguards anywhere, but there's something familiar about the guy standing next to the buffet counter, conversing with a couple of khaki-clad people.

Is it him?

It must be. I'd recognise the set of his shoulders anywhere. Only … what's happened to his hair? 'Ash!'

He turns around, starts and for a few seconds we just stare at each other, neither of us knowing quite what to do.

'Lele!' he moves towards me and I run up to him and throw my arms around him. There's a beat of a couple of seconds and then he hugs me back. I lean back to check him out properly. His skin is darker and he looks fitter, leaner. And for some reason his shaved head suits him, sets off his eyes. I immediately wonder what he thinks of me. Have I changed? I flinch – of course I've changed. I'm pregnant. But that's not something I'll be telling him any time soon.

He steps back, breaking our embrace first. 'Lele,' he says, gesturing to the short, bespectacled guy behind him. 'This is Jova.'

I recall seeing Jova when I was on the stage, but up close he's even weedier than I remember. He's practically my height, maybe a few kilograms heavier, his arms and legs almost as skinny as Busi's. *This* is the person who inspires so much respect? I almost laugh.

He smiles at me, his eyes flicking over my face as if he's mentally totting up my defects. 'I have heard a lot about you, Lele.'

'Not nearly as much as I've heard about you, I bet.'

Ash nods at a tall, dreadlocked woman standing motionless behind Jova. 'And this is Morgan.'

She removes her sunglasses to reveal that she's wearing a patch over her left eye, which somehow doesn't make her look ridiculous. She nods at me brusquely. No way would I want to mess with her. Her forearms are corded with muscle, and that eye doesn't look like it misses anything.

'You two must have much to discuss,' Jova says. 'We will leave you two alone, Jack.'

Jack. Ash's real name.

Jova and the tall woman move towards the door. The woman hesitates before she follows Jova out into the lobby and for a second our eyes lock. Then she glances at Ash, and I get it. She has feelings for him.

I file this away for later, unable to quell a spike of jealousy. How can I feel jealous? Ash is as free as I am, isn't he? We broke up. And he isn't the one who's got someone else's baby growing in his stomach, is he?

As soon as they've gone, an awkwardness slides between us. There are so many big things to say I don't know where to start. We both start talking at once.

'Have you seen—'

'How's Ember?'

Ash smiles and the uneasy atmosphere evaporates.

'Ember's much stronger,' I say. 'She's still weak, but

Cezanne – her doctor – says she can start exercising soon. She'd love to see you.'

'Good.'

'Ash … Have you heard anything about Ginger?'

He scowls. 'Apparently he's joined the Outcasts.'

'He's *what*?'

'The survivors we've just debriefed say they saw a huge guy with orange hair at the scene of the ambush. Sound familiar?'

'But I thought the Outcasts were like, crazy muti-guzzling freaks or something?'

Ash shrugs. 'Who knows? I can't believe he's joined the enemy.'

'The *enemy*? Whoa, Ash. Whose enemy?'

He blinks, but doesn't answer. There's a flash of what could be guilt in his eyes, but then it's gone.

'Ash, why haven't you come to see me until today?' And even now, I think bitterly, *I* was the one who came to *him*. 'Jova must have told you where I was.'

'He said you were safe.' He glances pointedly at the dining room's leather seats and plush furnishings.

A flare of anger. 'Appearances can be deceptive, Ash. Why didn't you get the hell out of wherever you've been – this Army of the Left camp or wherever – and come and find us?' But I already know the answer to this. I saw it in the way that Ash looked at Jova. He hero-worships him, just like pretty much everyone I've met so far, with the exception of Coom. Weirdly, this almost makes me think kindly of Coom.

'It wasn't that simple, Lele. The AOL base is miles from here. And Jova says it won't be long before—'

I snort. 'Come *on*. You're too smart for this, Ash. *Jova says*. All he is is a kid who's playing soldiers.' I wince, realising I've just used almost the exact words Coom used to describe Jova.

Ash's shoulders stiffen. 'Say what you like about him, Lele. But I know him. He cares about the future. The long-term future.'

'Have you been into Sandtown, Ash? People are dying there. The place is run by a handful of greedy assholes, and top of the heap is your new BFF, Jova. He's letting them get away with it.'

'It's the people who are letting them get away with it, Lele. The *people*. Just like they did in Cape Town. Do you think anyone would be able to stop them if they rose up against their oppressors? There are too many even for the AOL to control.'

I'm not about to concede that he has a point. 'Tell me, Ash, what is this amazing plan "to set us all free" I keep hearing about?'

He goes to flick his hair out of his eyes, an old gesture he can no longer accomplish because he no longer *has* any hair. It's almost comical. 'I don't know all the details.'

'If you're so close to him, why hasn't he told you?'

A sigh. 'I think he's planning on moving the inhabitants to a safer location, and then destroying the Rotters. Then, maybe, we can move back.'

'*We?* What about Cape Town? What about home?'

'Cape Town will be next.'

'Right. Awesome plan. Really sounds like it's going to work.'

He doesn't respond; his eyes take on a guarded look.

'Look, didn't they try that at the beginning of the war, Ash? That's one of the reasons the infection spread so quickly. You blast the Rotters to bits, there's more of that white spaghetti stuff around.'

'Jova knows what he's doing.'

'Sounds like you're in love with him.'

'Don't be childish, Lele.'

'Childish? It's clear whose side you're on, Ash. Or should I say, Jack. Five minutes with your old pal Jova and you forget about your other friends. What about me? What about Ember, who nearly died? What about Ginger, who's out there somewhere? And what about Saint?'

'Lele ...' he warns.

It's time to do something I should have done ages ago. 'Ash. Does Jova know what you are?'

'What do you mean?' He looks down at his hands, clenches his left fist.

'You know what I mean, Ash. He must know you aren't left-handed, but that you're immune to Rotter attack.'

'He knows I have a twin, of course. He knows that a few of us from Cape Town all have twins who are ... special. That somehow the fact that they don't seem to age has something to do with our immunity.'

'But *why*, Ash?'

'What do you mean?'

'Why is Sasha like she is? Uncommunicative, shut-in. Why doesn't Jobe grow like a normal kid?'

'You know why, Lele. The Guardians. They did something to them during the war.'

'Not just them. The Guardians also took *us*, Jack. *Us*. Infected us with something, another strain of the virus that runs through the Rotters. It means that when we die ... we'll live. Become Guardians.' I wait to see if the implications of what this means for Saint hit him.

'Bullshit, Lele. If the Guardians ever took me I'd remember that happening. And when I found Sasha in the enclave she—'

'Didn't you think it was strange when the injuries you sustained during the crash healed so quickly?'

A jolt. So he does know. 'How did you find all this out?'

246

I look down at my feet. 'Thabo showed me. After the fight at the mall. Just after he changed into a Guardian.' I hold up my left hand, revealing the faint white scar on my palm where Thabo had sliced it with a piece of glass, deep enough to show me the silvery infection squirming under my skin. His face shuts down. 'You've known this all along? Since *Thabo*? And you never said a word?'

'I don't want to fight, Ash. What's done is done. It was wrong of me not to tell you. Even Lucien said that he was reluctant to tell Jova when he discovered that—'

'*Lucien* knows about this?'

'Yeah. Have you seen him?'

'No. What do you care about Lucien?'

'I heard a rumour he got tired of playing soldiers with you guys.'

'No. And we're not playing, Lele. Just so you know, it's not a game. What we're doing, it's dangerous. People are ...' his voice dies and his face shuts down completely. But I can't let him cut me off and block me out again. Like he did all those weeks ago.

'Just so you know, while you've been *playing* emo soldiers I've had deep crap to deal with here.'

'You don't get it, Lele. This whole thing ... it's bigger than us.'

'"It's bigger than us." Are those your words, Ash, or Jova's? And what about Sasha? Your sister? If you stay here sorting out this city's problems, how long is it going to be before you get home to her?' This is pure emotional blackmail, but I don't feel a trace of guilt.

'I'm doing this for Sasha, Lele.'

I've had enough. 'You know what, Ash? If you want to bond and hang out with your new best buddy, go ahead. But don't

247

pretend you're doing this for your sister. You're not. You're doing this for yourself.'

'Lele, that's not true.'

'Okay. Then get me out of here. Get Ember out of here. Use your amazing influence with Jova. Do you know what is going to happen to me? Do you know that Jova sold me to that fat pig, Coom? And do you know why? So that I'll become his wife, Ash. You get that? You understand *that*? You hearing me?' Again, no reaction. 'What's happened to you?'

Silence. *Awesome*.

That's it. I can't stand it any longer. I turn away from him, hare through the dining room and into the lobby. He doesn't call after me or try to stop me. Jova and the woman with the eye patch are hanging out near to the hotel's entrance, a few feet from One Ear and a knot of internal guards who are gossiping.

I storm up to Jova, jab him in the chest. He barely flinches. 'Where's Lucien, Jova?'

He raises an eyebrow. 'He's out on one of his recces.' He's lying. I know he's lying. I lean in close, ignoring the pirate woman who is watching me carefully. 'There's no difference between you and Coom, Jova. *None*. I would rather have the Resurrectionists than you any day.'

I push past him and run outside, One Ear moving to grab my arm. I shake him off. 'Leave me *alone*.'

No one tries to stop me as I run through the fake city, making a beeline for the exit.

It's getting dark when One Ear comes to fetch me from the bird park, the sky grumbling and the air electric with the promise of a storm. I'm finished, cried out. There's not a jot of emotion left inside me. I haven't even been to see Ember today.

'Lele,' One Ear says, his voice softer than usual. 'Mr Coom wants to see you.'

Excellent. It's not as if the day could get any worse, is it? 'Have they gone? Ash, Jova and the rest of the Army of the Losers, I mean?'

'Yes.'

So I really am alone. I guess in my deepest heart there was a small sliver of hope that Ash would decide to stay and fight in my corner. Fat chance. My eyes are sore and puffy and I'm pretty sure I must look like crap. Good – hopefully this will put Coom off.

'I have something for you.'

'Oh yeah? Hope it's something that'll put me out of my misery.' He hands me an envelope. 'What's this?'

No answer.

I rip it open, pull out a flimsy piece of paper. The handwriting on it is messy and difficult to decipher, but I get the gist:

Lele,

I am sorry, but I must go. I can no longer stay in Jozi.

I would have taken you with me if it were possible.

Watch out for Jova. Do not trust him. And do not trust Ash.

It is safer to trust no one.

I have faith in you. You are strong.

A bientôt, xx

Awesome. Left in the lurch by another guy. And as for the stuff about not trusting Jova, I'm already way ahead of Lucien on that score.

'Where did you get this?' I ask One Ear.

'The woman with Jova.'

'*Pirate Chick* gave you this?'

A snort. 'Ja.'

What the hell is *that* about? Are she and Lucien friends? Maybe more than friends? Do I even care any more? I'm on my own. That much is clear.

'How come you didn't just take this to Coom?'

'What do you mean?'

I sigh. 'I know you told him Ember woke up.'

'Of course I did. He asked me how she was and I told him the truth.'

'Is that all you've told him?'

He frowns, looks genuinely confused. 'What are you implying?'

'Oh, just forget it.'

We walk back to the hotel in silence. A peal of kids' laughter from the activity centre mocks me. The smell of braaing meat in the courtyard turns my stomach. I'm hit with an overwhelming flood of homesickness for Cape Town, for my brother, even for the Mantis and Dad.

Coom is sitting alone at his table in the dining room. The runners' table is empty; the wives and Coom's advisers are eating in silence. I look around for Cezanne, but I can't see her anywhere. Perhaps she's with the children back in the activity centre. Hardly anyone looks up as I walk slowly towards him. I almost gag at the sight of the bloody meat on his plate.

'Sit,' he says. I wonder which side of Coom I'll be facing this evening. My bet is on pompous bastard.

None of the waiters rush up to sweep a plate in front of me. I don't care. I'm not hungry. 'What is it, Coom?' If he says tonight is the night, I'm not sure I'll be able to restrain myself from lashing out at him. Even if the thug behind his chair beats the crap out of me for it, it might be worth it.

'I know,' he says matter-of-factly.

'Know what? That I think you're a great fat slug who should be squashed?'

His eyes drop to my belly.

Crap.

Cezanne. She must have told him. How could she? Still … maybe this means I won't have to marry him after all.

'Is it true?'

'Yeah. Guess this messes with your plans, doesn't it?'

'Who's the father?' His eyes flick to One Ear, who's standing to attention at the dining room's entrance.

'You're kidding, right? As *if*. It's not Sihle.'

'Who, then?'

I almost blurt out the truth, then stop myself just in time. Lucien may have deserted me like everyone else, but Coom doesn't deserve the truth. 'One of your runners.'

'Who?'

I scramble to remember the name of a runner wiped out by the Outcasts – someone who won't be able to refute my story. 'Um … Wessel.'

'Wessel? He wouldn't dare!'

I shrug. 'Looks like you should have kept a closer eye on your staff.'

I try to catch One Ear's eye, but he's standing rigidly, looking into the far distance. At least he hasn't told Coom about Lucien, which is something, I suppose.

'I'm afraid this means our deal is off,' Coom says. 'Which is a pity as I paid a great deal for you.'

'Guess you'll just have to chalk it up as a bad investment.'

'Oh, I don't think so, my dear,' he says, piggy eyes sparkling. 'I always hedge my bets.'

And then I get it. Ember.

I lean my forehead against the window and stare down at a bunch of kids who are chasing a chicken around the courtyard. It's a beautiful day, the sky as flawless as the painted one inside Coom's mock city. I bang on the glass and wave, but the children don't look up. I'm beginning to feel like Rapunzel No Hair stuck in her luxury tower. But it's not funny, not even slightly. No one is coming to rescue me.

The guard who brought my breakfast tray refused to answer my questions about Ember, Busi or One Ear. I thought about grabbing his sidearm, but he wasn't alone – through the open door I caught sight of two or three others in the corridor. Coom's not taking any chances with me. But he can't keep me here forever, can he?

I turn away from the window, flump down on the bed and pull the pillow over my head.

The door unlocks. It can't be time for another meal. I look up to see Cezanne slipping into the room. She must be able to read the fury on my face, but she seems not to care.

She perches on the edge of the bed. 'How are you feeling?'

'How do you think I'm feeling? I thought you were my friend. Why did you tell him?'

'I had no choice.'

'Yeah, you did. And now I'm stuck in this room, a prisoner.'

'I thought the last thing you wanted was to become his wife, Lele.'

'Of course I don't want that. But what about Ember? He's set his sights on her.'

'You don't need to worry about Ember.'

'Oh yeah? How do you know?'

'I asked you to trust me once. Will you?'

'What do you think?'

She smiles, glances at my belly. 'Any nausea? Tiredness?'

'What do you care?'

She sighs. She looks exhausted, the lines around her mouth deeply creviced. I'm still angry with her, but I'm getting sick of playing the petulant victim and despite her recent betrayal, she's one of the few people around here who's been decent to me.

'Cezanne ... really, how do you put up with what Coom's doing? Doesn't it make you sick to your stomach?'

Another deep, indrawn breath. She stands up and wanders to the window. 'I was pregnant once. I had a child. A boy.' She says this in a soft voice, a voice so quiet I have to strain to hear her.

I don't know what to say to this, apart from 'so?', which would be too callous, even for me.

'Do you remember much about the beginning of the end, Lele? When the dead and the infected first rose? I imagine the horror, confusion and panic was much the same in Cape Town as it was here.'

'No. I remember hardly anything.' The biggest blank spot is when the Guardians took me and my twin brother away, but Cezanne doesn't need to know that.

'I was working in a government hospital back then, Lele. New Hope, it was called. Ironic really. I was used to seeing humanity's brutality on a daily basis. Gunshot wounds, victims of domestic violence and those suffering from poor medical care and neglect. When they brought the first of the infected into casualty, I was right there. I was on the front line as the infection raged through the city. Time seemed to stop; I worked until the authorities shut us down, quarantined the hospital. I was so overwhelmed by what I was dealing with that I didn't stop to think about Ryan, my son. Until it was too late. The infection hit the suburbs hard. My son's school ...'

'I'm sorry.'

'I didn't want to go on, but Steven convinced me. He said that I was needed, that there would be other children. But there never were.'

'So that's the *real* reason why he's so desperate to have so many children? So he won't lose another one?' A nasty thought starts to surface. 'Cezanne ... this wasn't your idea, was it? Coom marrying other women. Lefties, I mean?'

A long pause. 'I colluded with it, yes, Lele. I'll admit that. But he has taken it too far. Way too far.'

'What do you mean?' But I know what she means. How could I not?

'Power. It corrupts. Everyone knows this, but they still want it. Still crave it.' She turns to look at me. Her eyes are dry. 'Things are going to change, Lele. And soon. You must be prepared.'

'Prepared for what?'

She looks down at the children playing outside, then bends and kisses my cheek. 'Be strong,' she whispers, then she slides out of the room, shutting the door softly behind her.

Stunned, I flump back onto the bed. It would be so easy if Coom were just plain evil. Did the loss of his child push him over the edge? But thousands – millions – of people lost family members to the infection and didn't turn into power-greedy despots.

I curl myself into a ball, clutch my hands to my stomach, and shut my eyes.

Jack

11 February 2015

They should be screaming. The people around him should be screaming.

But all he can hear is a high-pitched ringing. It's almost musical, has no business providing the soundtrack to the horrendous scene in front of him. The Rotters move with that terrifying speed they always seem to muster when they get the scent of life in their maggoty nostrils. Jack can only watch, numb with horror, as they pour through the gaping wound in the enclave fence and fall on the small crowd of early-morning merchants.

A hand grips the still-smouldering sleeve of his jacket and jerks him around. Jack barely recognizes Jova beneath the mask of blood coating the left side of his face.

Jova shouts at Jack but the ringing sound eats his words. Jova points behind him. Jack follows his gaze, sees a crumpled figure lying half-buried in the tortured rubble of the fence.

Lucien.

Jack's hand tightens on the hilt of his panga, an early birthday present from Hester. For a moment he's torn between helping his friend and doing what he can to save innocent lives. It's not a hard decision.

All of this.

Is because of them.

He shakes off Jova's hand and then he's running, kicking up mud and muck as he sprints towards the Rotter horde. Everything seems unreal without sound, but he can feel the solid thunk of his panga slicing into a Rotter's throat and that's all that matters. He's fighting a losing battle; for every Rotter he manages to fell, another soon takes its place. And he knows from experience that the fresh ones will be able to sense him.

He's beginning to tire, and not only from the exertion. The ringing is still trilling in his ears, but it's joined with a slow, steady throbbing in his lower back. His eyes catch on details that somehow seem worse than the carnage around him. A child's shoe stuck in the mud. A fine leather wallet stuffed with credits abandoned on a market stall counter.

Where are the Guardians? Why haven't they arrived yet to stop the dead in their tracks before it's too late? The irony isn't lost on him: he's praying that the very things they were trying to destroy with their homemade fertiliser bomb – the bomb none of them really thought would work, but had worked too well – will rock up and put a stop to this.

The Guardians must be close by. It's nearing the time in the morning when they arrive with their supply wagons. And if they don't come soon, the entire enclave will succumb to infection within hours.

His heart freezes.

Sasha.

He can't let anything happen to Sasha.

He's only just found her again – his sister stuck in time, his stunted twin. He'd resigned himself to the belief that she had joined the ranks of the dead. But she was in the enclave all along, in a home for others like her. Lucien discovered her. And when Jack first arrived on the doorstep of Mandela House, and Naomi, the bright, capable carer, took him to see her, Jack's life took on a fresh perspective. As if he'd been underwater for years and was suddenly able to breathe again. Even though she didn't – couldn't – speak, even though the Guardians had done something to keep her trapped forever in her seven-year-old body, he knew then that he could go on. And he knew then that he wouldn't stop until the Guardians, and their Rotter puppets, paid for what they'd done to her. To everyone.

Others are joining in the fight now, hacking away at the Rotters and hatchlings, faces raw with desperation. A Rotter stumbles into Jack's back and he doesn't have the strength to keep himself upright. He sinks to his knees, feeling warm mud and blood seeping through his jeans.

He closes his eyes, enters a dark silent world, and when he opens them he sees her. At first he thinks the girl is just another well-preserved Rotter, but she's standing stock-still, her chest heaving with each sobbing breath.

Jack staggers to his feet, yells at her to run, but he's too far away and there are too many of them.

The girl opens her mouth in a silent scream as the Rotters close in on her.

Jack tells himself he can't look away, tells himself that he needs to remember this moment, see it burned into his nightmares for the rest of his days. He deserves to remember it.

Hating himself, he drops his eyes, studies a discarded Resurrectionist amulet, the delicate chicken bones crushed into the mud.

When he finally looks up the girl is still standing, unharmed. And then it hits him. She's like him. She's like Jova and Lucien. Immune. He forces his legs to carry him towards her.

His astonishment has been so overwhelming that he hasn't realised the Rotters have stopped attacking. They stand as if frozen in place and then, as one, they throw back their heads and let out a long, drawn-out moan. He hears it as if from a great distance, the ringing in his ears giving over to a dull buzz.

The Guardians are here.

The girl trembles as the Rotters shuffle past her, making their way back through the ruptured fence.

Jack gently takes the girl's wrists and pulls her into his arms. 'It's okay. You're okay.' She stares up at him, wide eyes glazed with shock. There's a small yellow flower tucked into the bandana holding her unruly hair back from her face.

He has to get her away from here. He has to get her to Hester.

'What's your name?' His voice sounds far away, like an echo.

The girls swallows hard, choking back tears. 'Ntombi. My name is Ntombi.'

Ash

I don't even bother picking out a book. What would be the point? The words would only blur in front of me. Instead I sit in my corner in the dark and wind the torch, the one Morgan gave me during the trials. I wind it until my wrist aches.

I'll stay here all night if I have to. There's no way in hell I can return to the dorm. And not just because I'm not wanted there. Exhausted as I am, I won't be able to sleep.

Lele's words stung, just like she knew they would. And in response, I defended Jova. When it came down to it, I defended him. I took his side, the old habits kicking in. There's too much history between us; too many stories, too many experiences. I blindly followed him back then, just like I'm following him now.

Lele hates me. Saint is gone. Ginger is doing God knows what with the Outcasts, and Ember is severely injured.

I didn't even make the effort to go and see her after Lele stormed off. Instead, I waited like a good little soldier for Morgan to come and fetch me.

Morgan: someone else I've disappointed. What the hell was I thinking trying to kiss her? I've barely thought about Noxi. And when I try, all I can see is ... Morgan.

And Lele. Lele who knew all along what we are. Freaks. Monsters. Outsiders.

I tried to empty my mind on the long drive back to the army base, attempting to lose myself in the roar and grumble of the bike's engine beneath me. I tried and failed to concentrate on the landscape, the unfamiliar hues, the flat brown and tan expanses, the half-hidden townhouse estates, their umber walls looking barely untouched after eleven years of abandonment.

It didn't help.

A rippling crack of thunder sounds, making me jump.

The only thing I have left to cling to is Jova's plan. I have to believe that all this shit is going to be worth it.

'When are you leaving?'

I start, look up to see Morgan's silhouette in front of me. How long has she been there? I click on the torch and shine it into her face. She doesn't blink and I drop it onto my lap. 'I'm not. Not yet.'

'Have you told Jova you're hanging around?'

'It's Jova. I don't have to tell him anything, remember? He sees it all.' I pick at the scab on my hand. Only there's no scab there now, is there? It's healed completely. 'Look, Morgan, about what happened after—'

'Forget it. You weren't thinking straight.'

'Wasn't I?'

'What about Noxi? Have you even tried to talk to her?'

'What for? She hates me. I don't blame her. I was the one who killed Danny.'

'You had no choice. This is a war, Jack. People die.'

'You sound like Jova.'

A shrug. It's too dim in here to make out her expression clearly. 'And here's some advice: the whole self-pity thing? It really doesn't suit you.'

It's so close to something Saint would have said that it almost makes me smile.

Almost.

'Morgan ... just what is Jova planning?'

'You really think he'd tell me?'

'He trusts you.'

'He doesn't trust anyone. Anyway, you can ask him yourself. He sent me to fetch you.' She grins, a flash of white teeth. 'What? Did you think I came here to sit in the dark with you?'

'Where is he?'

'I'll take you to him. But first, you have some unfinished business.'

Morgan hangs by the door and gestures impatiently for me to enter.

Noxi is bent over her sleeping bag, shoving her belongings into a rucksack. Americano is sitting cross-legged, leaning against the crap mural – the mural Danny painted when he first came to the base – smoking and staring into the distance.

Americano looks up and grunts when I step inside.

'What?' Noxi says to him. Then she turns, her mouth twitching in dismay.

Before she can speak, I say, 'I'm sorry, Noxi. I had no choice.'

Her shoulders slump and she shakes her head slightly. 'I don't blame you, okay, Jack? You did what you had to do, I get that. I just can't ... Her breath hitches. 'I can't be around you right now. I can't be *here* right now.' She slings her bag on her shoulder, makes for the door.

I move to grab her wrist, but she twists away from me. 'Where are you going?'

'Away. Back to Sandtown. I don't know. Somewhere.' She brushes past Morgan on the way out. 'He's all yours.'

I listen to her footsteps slapping down the corridor. Americano is watching me carefully, an inch of ash at the end of his cigarette threatening to topple onto his hand. I attempt to study him without looking directly at him, trying to gauge where the two of us stand.

'Where are Pockets and Nuush?' I ask finally. Their sleeping bags are empty.

'Canteen. Jack. Noxi ... She'll calm down. It's ... You didn't come to the burning. That got to her.'

There isn't a trace of reproach in his tone, but I feel the rebuke nonetheless. 'I couldn't face it. That was wrong of me.'

I make my way over to my sleeping bag, stripping off my shirt and pulling on a fresh one. There's no time for a shower; Jova will just have to take me as I am. I make the mistake of glancing at Danny's sleeping area. Someone has packed up his stuff, placed it in a neat pile.

Americano slides his cigarette pack across the tiles to me.

'I don't have time.' I manage a smile and kick the packet back to him.

'There's always time for a smoke.'

'Not when Jova's waiting.'

I start to head for the door. 'Jack.' Something in Americano's voice makes me pause. 'I'm here if you need me. That goes for Pockets and Nuush too.' He chucks me the pack, and this time I take one and throw it back.

'Thanks. That means a lot.'

I turn and follow Morgan. I hang back, let her walk ahead as she leads me through the Domestic Departures area, down

263

the now-familiar corridors and towards the sterile room where I first saw Jova all those weeks ago. Lightning flashes behind the dusty picture windows, momentarily illuminating the planes stuck forever on the runway. Morgan shoots me a small smile, then without a word, drifts away.

This time, there are no guards flanking the doors. I slip inside.

Jova's sitting in the same corner as he was when I nearly throttled him. 'Jack.' He gestures for me to sit opposite him, but I stay standing.

'Taking me to see Lele: that was the final test, wasn't it, Jova?'

A shrug, a small smile.

'What she said about Coom. About being sold to him; about marrying him. Is that true?'

'Yes. But it's irrelevant.'

'Why is it irrelevant?'

'Because things are moving, Jack. Moving fast.' A slight frown. 'Faster than I anticipated, but we can handle it. Your team. Can you trust them?'

'Yes.'

'Good. Can you trust me?'

I don't respond.

'I need you, Jack. You ready to come on one more adventure with me?'

'What kind of adventure?'

He leans forward, adjusts his glasses. His eyes are glinting with excitement like they used to do when he was brewing one of his plans. 'A recce tomorrow night. Bring your team. Those you can trust. And after that ...'

'What?'

He slams his fist on the table. 'Endgame, Jack.'

Again, I stay silent. The thunder thwacks again. Hard rain pads against the roof.

'Jack. What happened with Danny. You made the right choice. You made the only choice. You did what had to be done. What happened with Lele today – the things she said ... it can't have been easy to hear.'

'It wasn't.'

'Seeing old friends. Opening old wounds. You and I both know all about that, don't we?'

'I let her down. I let all of them down.'

'That's not true, and you know it, Jack. You made the right choice by staying here. You made the difficult choice. And I'm close, so close to finishing what we started all those years ago.' He sits back, fixes me with his eyes. 'I admire you for staying loyal to your friends, Jack. But your true loyalty has and always will be to the war we fight against the dead. As is mine.' He frowns. 'I need you, Jack. I thought Lucien was the one. I was wrong.'

And then, right then, I know what he wants of me.

He pulls out a box of cigarettes, slides it across the table. 'But first I need to know, Jack. Are you with me?'

I hesitate.

Thunder cracks once more, followed by a spark of lightning so bright it penetrates the room.

'This is it, Jack. The last push. Are you with me?'

I reach down and pick up the box. 'I always have been.'

Saint

It's time to say goodbye to Horse.

For the past hour Saint has sensed a glowing tapestry of interlaced threads that radiate the completeness that Horse has been missing. There's a herd nearby.

Ntombi is awash with grief. Saint leaves her to it, but doesn't slip away to Atang or allow more of the darkness to invade while Ntombi's guard is down. Instead she concentrates on sending Horse a powerful image of the herd's energy, pushing him towards it. He can sense it too, not as strongly as she can, but there's a glimmer of growing understanding. She knows Horse isn't young, but he will have enough years left to bond and bind himself to the others. *One is not enough.*

Go, Horse. She's been trying to send him images in the same way that Atang sends pictures and snapshots to her, but Horse doesn't see things in the same way that she does. He doesn't have the same points of reference. She knows that it would be easier if she let in more of the darkness. But she won't. Not yet.

She pushes one last time, transferring the feeling of completeness directly into him, and this times she feels a strong response. A burst of pure joy so bright that she almost laughs aloud. He crackles with fresh vigour, as if he's drawing life from the other horses.

Go.

He drops his head to Bambi, blows once through his nostrils, shakes his mane, and then he's off, galloping through the fynbos, tail high. He calls to the herd, and in the far distance, Saint hear the faint sound of answering whinnies.

I'll miss him, Ntombi says.

Me too. And Saint realises she means it. Let's go.

Bambi sticks close to her heels as they continue on their way. Their connection fizzes with energy. Sometimes she allows herself to slip into his head, where she can see, hear and smell through his heightened senses. Bambi lives through scent and sound; the threads he follows are on a different wavelength from those she knows. But his compulsion to hunt and his need to eat, drink and rest is waning, which also makes Ntombi sad.

Saint walks.

The pull of her destination is increasing, as if she's caught in a current, being washed along a river. Without Horse stopping to rest and feed, and now that Bambi is becoming like her, (*a monster, a freak,* a *Guardian,* Ntombi hisses) they can move faster. Ntombi has estimated that since they left the scene of the crash they must have travelled more than a thousand kilometres, but there's still a long way to go. Day or night; it's all the same to Saint. She moves back to the highway, able to sense Lucien's anxious presence humming in the vicinity, still searching for her. When her boots break she walks barefoot. Sometimes she slips off to spend time with Atang, leaving her body for Ntombi, and when she returns, the scenery is entirely different.

She walks through a dusty, deserted village, serenaded by a church bell rung by the wind, its cottages and shops home to rodents and spiders. The unreadable thread of a cobra twitches, makes her pause, but it has no interest in her. Bambi stiffens as the raw threads of feral dogs, and once a leopard, curl out to them. Like Lucien, the animals keep their distance. They walk through a mountain pass, ragged rocks spilling debris across their path.

Through an expanse of fynbos, spiky proteas snagging at her clothes.

She walks until she reaches a wide cemetery of broken vehicles. Army trucks, kombis, Land Rovers, buses alive with birds' nests, a helicopter lying on its side, its blades rusty and jagged.

And Lucien is getting nearer, has picked up her trail. She can sense the curiosity sparking out of him. He won't approach. He won't return here because he has been here. He has seen what happened here.

Then abruptly, his thread fades.

He's leaving.

Saint walks to a snaking dirt road that leads forever down into a valley.

Her valley.

We're nearly there.

Where?

Saint looks down at a sign lying half-hidden in curling weeds. 'Gamkaskloof. "Die Hel / The Hell" 50 km = 2 huur / 2 hours.'

That's *where we're supposed to go?*

Yes.

What is Die Hel?

A place.

Duh. Really? What will we find there?

Answers. We have to go down there to find them.

To hell?

To hell.

Ntombi shudders. *So let's go.*

Tommy

The bonfire in the centre of the circle pops and crackles, and Tommy watches the sparks twirling up into the night. Thanks to the bottle of mampoer and the fat dagga cigarettes being passed around the fire, several of the men and women are already laughing too loudly. The smell of spit-braaied lamb floats towards him, but just the thought of eating makes him want to gag.

It's as if Jacob never existed.

Sure, when they returned to the settlement after the Eastgate nightmare, Senyaka made a speech about Jacob's sacrifice, going on about how he'll be seen as a hero for generations, but to Tommy's ears the words sounded hollow. 'There are always sacrifices to be made in war,' Senyaka intoned, staring straight at Tommy as he spoke. 'We all make choices, and some of those choices are hard. Our brother Jacob's unselfishness will never be forgotten. Let us have a minute's silence to remember him.'

The atmosphere during that minute was grave and

respectful, but the second it was over, people drifted away and went straight back to work. Jacob may have been damaged – whatever he had encountered before he was brought to Sandtown had clearly scarred him badly – but he deserved more than a minute. Everyone deserves more than that.

Ginger passes the mampoer bottle to Bulelani without taking a sip and Tommy tries to catch his eye. Ginger hasn't said a word all evening. The aura of expectation that's crackling through the circle is as palpable as the heat raging from the roaring fire, but it doesn't appear to have infected Ginger. Now that Coom's prize runners have been all but wiped out, Tommy knows that Senyaka's planning something far more ambitious than the ambush that took Jacob's life. Tommy doesn't know the details, suspects not even Ginger is party to the plan, but he's certain that whatever it is, it's a game-changer.

Senyaka stands up and calls for silence. There's an instant hush. Not even the small children make a peep. 'I'm looking for volunteers for our next manoeuvre,' Senyaka says. 'We will be leaving tomorrow evening.'

'Where are you going?' Ma Beccah calls.

A pause. 'To Coom. We're going to hit the spider in its lair.'

A gasp breezes around the fire.

Ginger nudges Tommy and mutters, 'Isn't that where Lele is?'

Tommy nods. 'I think so.'

'How are you planning to do that?' Bulelani asks. 'Coom's place is a fortress.'

Senyaka grins humourlessly – and Tommy can't help but be reminded of the rictus of Kathleen's skull mask. 'You know the story of the Trojan horse?'

Ma Beccah laughs and claps her hands, but most of the other Outcasts look none the wiser.

'Be under no illusions that what we are planning is extremely risky. We may not come back from it. But if we are successful, this could be the start of the revolution. Coom's had his fat fingers gripped around the neck of this city for far too long.'

'Who cares about Sandtown? It's nothing to us,' a woman calls from the back. 'Let them rot!'

A weak cheer.

'And us? What about the rest of us?' Ma Beccah asks. 'No offence, Senyaka, but this sounds like madness to me. A suicide mission. How are we going to survive if something happens to you?'

Several of the older Outcasts nod in agreement.

'We will take only a core group. As I have said, this endeavour will be extremely dangerous, but the safety and well-being of this settlement is my first priority. There will be enough Lefties remaining to ensure that all of your needs are taken care of.'

Ma Beccah smiles with relief. 'Thank you, Senyaka.'

'Is anyone going to step forward?'

'Count me in!' Bulelani raises his hand.

'I'll come along,' Ginger calls.

Is it Tommy's imagination, or does Senyaka look uneasy? 'You've done enough, Ginger. I don't expect you to do more. Besides, I know you are still troubled by what happened to your friend.'

'Troubled is putting it mildly. I don't like your way of doing things, mate. I told you not to bring Jacob along on that ambush, but my friend is apparently staying at this Coom fella's place, and you're not going without me.'

Tommy's never heard Ginger sound so assertive.

Senyaka glances at Kat, who shrugs. 'Thank you,' he says stiffly to Ginger. 'We could use someone like you.'

'But after this, I'm gone. That clear?'

'Agreed.'

'I'll go!' Tommy squeaks and several of the adults in the crowd laugh. He stands up on shaky legs. No way is he going to be left behind. If Ginger's going, then he will too.

'Tommy,' Senyaka says, 'I applaud your bravery. But it's far too dangerous for you. You do not have the experience.'

'You asked for volunteers. I'm volunteering.'

'Tommy, mate,' Ginger says. 'It's not going to happen.'

'I agree. He could be a liability,' Kathleen adds.

'Let the boy go if he wants to,' a man calls. Tommy knows that many of the Lefties have families and loved ones in the zoo settlement. They'll be relieved if he takes the place of someone else.

Senyaka pauses and Tommy holds his breath, waiting for his answer. Then he shakes his head. 'I'm sorry, Tommy. But Ginger and Kat are right. I can't risk it.'

'I won't get in the way, I *promise*.'

'Soon as I find my friends, I'll come back for you, Tommy,' Ginger says. 'Then we'll go talk to Lucien and—'

'You keep saying that, Ginger, but it's been *weeks*. Coom's place isn't that far from Sandtown. If I came with you, we could go there straight afterwards.'

Ginger glances at Senyaka. 'Well? He's got a point.'

Senyaka sighs. 'I'm sorry, Tommy. I can't compromise the safety of my team.'

'Fine,' Tommy snaps, feeling angry tears pricking the back of his eyes. He stands up and hurries away from the fire so that Ginger and Senyaka won't see how upset he is.

'Tommy!' he hears Ginger calling. 'Wait!'

'Leave me alone.'

There's only a half-moon tonight and the path up to the

polar bear enclosure is swallowed by shadows. But he's walked this route so often he knows the exact location of the gnarly roots that might trip him up. Faint laughter drifts towards him from the bonfire. It sounds forced, as if everyone senses that after tomorrow things will change for good. He peers behind him to see if Ginger's followed him after all. He hasn't. Some friend.

Feeling like an outsider, he watches the fire flicker for a while, listens to the laughter mingling with the distant moan of the Rotters outside the fence. Is Optimus still with them? Tommy feels the urge to find out. He's beginning to think of Optimus as a friend of sorts. An ally.

As he walks down the hill, keeping to the shadows so that the group gathered around the fire won't spot him, that same niggling feeling he felt back at the hospital hits him again. An itch at the back of his mind that he can't quite reach to scratch. Something to do with Optimus ... no, not Optimus, but definitely the dead. Something that—

And then he gets it.

That teacher. The teacher he saw in the school.

She wasn't left-handed.

She was writing on the board using her right hand.

Tommy almost shouts. He swings around, intending to race back to the fire to tell Ginger what he's remembered. But then ... what if his memory's playing tricks? What if he's wrong? And even if he *is* right, will they even believe him? Senyaka and Ginger both dismissed Optimus's unusual behaviour as a fluke, and they're hardly likely to believe him when he tells them that there's a school full of sentient zombies in the Sandtown suburbs.

No. He'll find Optimus, then decide what to do from there.

He reaches the first set of gates that lead into the parking lot and peers around them. They're unguarded, but Tommy knows that there's no way he'll be able to sneak through the main gate without being questioned. He won't be stopped, of course, but he'll have to explain why he fancies a walk among the dead at this time of night. A car door slams. He can just about make out the shapes of two vehicles parked facing the main gates. A large, windowless van and an angular, mine-proof army vehicle with huge tyres and slitted windows, the one Senyaka called a Buffel, the vehicles they took from Coom's runners. So that's how they're intending to break into Coom's fortress! By pretending to be surviving runners. Smart. *Very* smart. But Tommy can't help but wonder – is this the real reason Senyaka planned the Eastgate ambush in the first place? In order to get hold of what he called his Trojan horse?

He's not doing anything wrong, but Tommy still ducks down into the shadows when he hears voices.

'All done?' he hears Kat calling from behind him.

'Ja,' a boy's voice shouts back. It's Moosa, Kat's teenage sidekick. 'Um. You sure about this, Kat? It's just ...'

She snorts. 'Senyaka's sure. That's what matters.'

'But it's madness.'

'True, true. But if it works, it's genius. Now come and have a drink.'

'You know I don't drink, Kat.'

'Ja, ja. Okay then, come and watch *me* have a drink.'

Tommy hears the crunch of footsteps and a burst of laughter, and waits until their voices fade.

The seed of a plan is beginning to form in his mind. Could he hide in one of the vehicles they're planning on taking to Coom's place? That way they'd have no choice but to take him along, and after it's all over, he and Ginger could slip away to Sandtown and Olivia. The air is still warm but he shivers. Does he dare? He weighs his longing to see Olivia up against facing Senyaka's wrath.

Homesickness wins.

He tiptoes towards the van and tries its side door. Locked. *Dammit.* He'll have to try the Buffel. It's so high off the ground he has to climb on the back ledge to reach the handle. The heavy back door opens with a clunk and a screech, and he holds his breath, waiting for someone to ask him what the hell he thinks he's doing.

Nothing. Just the Rotter moans and the muted sound of laughter from the fire. A soft snore echoes from the main gate. How's that for luck?

The Buffel's interior is way more cramped than it looks from the outside and the narrow slits in the metal panels sealing the windows aren't wide enough to let in any light. He's left his torch in his bag next to the fire, so he'll just have to do the best he can with the poor moonlight floating in from the back door. He crawls inside, detecting a trace of nervous sweat, probably all that's left of the runners who were last inside it. He can make out a row of seats, and ... *awesome*, a large storage locker underneath them. He unclips the bolts holding the locker's flap in place, and thrusts his arm inside it, feeling out its size. It's going to be tight, but he thinks he'll just about fit – something he wouldn't have managed just three weeks ago. And there's a small hole through which he can eke a finger to close it from the inside.

Is he really going to do this?

Yes.

He shuts the back door carefully, then gets down on his belly and rolls into the narrow space before he changes his mind.

A rumble, a roar, the ground beneath him starts vibrating, and Tommy clamps his mouth shut before the yelp escapes. He's soaked with sweat and his left arm tingles with pins and needles from being trapped under his body for so long – he must have fallen asleep on it just after he rolled into the locker.

'Senyaka,' he hears Ginger shouting over the engine racket. 'You seen Tommy? I wanted to say goodbye.'

Tommy listens hard but can't make out Senyaka's response.

The vibration increases as the truck starts moving. It bumps over something in the road and he bangs his elbow painfully on the metal. It's becoming harder to breathe, and the locker's sides seem to creep nearer to him. What if he can't get out? What if the flap jams and he's trapped here forever?

But he can't show himself now. He has to see it through.

It's the longest hour of Tommy's life. The nausea comes in greasy waves, and sweat dribbles into his eyes. Finally he can't stand it any longer and he begins to panic; he just has to hope that they've travelled too far to turn back. He bangs on the sides of the locker with his fist 'Hey!' he shouts 'Hey!'

He hears Ginger shouting something, and then the engine cuts out. The panel drops down and he looks up and into Ginger's confused eyes.

'Tommy?'

He rolls out, lies on his back on the floor, gulping air. Even the stale atmosphere of the Buffel's interior is a thousand times fresher than the rank odour inside that coffin-like space.

The door crashes open and he hears the thunk of someone leaping into the back. Senyaka grabs his arm and hauls him roughly to his feet. 'What do you think you're doing, Tommy?' Senyaka's grip is tight – too tight, Tommy will have a nasty bruise tomorrow – and his eyes blaze with anger. Then Tommy realises that Senyaka is covered in dried blood – animal blood, he hopes – and he's dressed in black combat gear, the same clothes as the runners who chased them through Eastgate mall.

Even Ginger is looking annoyed. He and Bulelani aren't as mucky as Senyaka, and Ginger's black shirt strains over his chest.

'Senyaka!' Kat calls from the van. 'What's happening?'

She jumps out of the driver's seat of the van and heads towards them, barking a short, surprised laugh when she catches sight of Tommy. 'Yessus,' she says. 'We got a stowaway?' Like Senyaka, she's smeared with dried blood, a filthy bandage wrapped around one arm.

'We have to take him back,' Ginger says.

'We've come too far,' Senyaka says. 'We don't have the diesel for an extra trip.'

Kat shakes her head in wonder. 'You got to admit, the kid's got balls.'

Ginger fixes Tommy with serious eyes. 'Tommy, if you come with us, you got to promise to stay in the truck, yeah?'

Tommy nods. 'I promise.'

'*As'vaye*,' Bulelani says. 'We've wasted enough time as it is.'

The Buffel has slowed to a crawl, and the Rotter moans Tommy's been hearing for the last ten minutes are becoming steadily louder. It's taken most of the day to carve a route through the city and he can't understand why Kat just didn't ride with them in the Buffel. Why did Senyaka want to bring along another vehicle that's nowhere near as capable of traversing obstacles and roads eroded by water damage and years of neglect? He hasn't dared ask him. The last thing Tommy wants is to annoy him further.

'Are we here?' Tommy whispers.

Ginger tucks his hair under his cap. 'Your guess is as good as mine, Tommy.'

Tommy peers out of one of the window slits. He can't see much, not now that the sun has set, but behind a fence surrounded by a swaying mass of the dead, he can make out the outline of a towering building that has the look of a castle.

Leaving the engine idling, Senyaka heaves open the back door.

'This is it?' Ginger asks.

Senyaka nods, his cap shadowing his eyes. 'When we get inside, duck down, keep quiet. Let me do the talking. I'll only need you if things don't go to plan.'

'And what is the plan?' Ginger asks. 'I don't appreciate being kept in the dark, Senyaka.'

'It is best for you to have plausible deniability if something goes awry. But you will find out soon, I promise.'

'I need to get inside that place. My mate is in there somewhere. Don't think I'm going to be hanging around out here like a spare part.'

'As soon as Kat and I and ... the others are safely inside, we will call you. Right now I need you to stay here with Tommy.'

'What others?' Bulelani asks. 'Who else is with us?'

'Who goes there?' an unfamiliar voice calls.

Senyaka slams the door. Tommy strains to hear what he's saying over the grumble of the engine.

'Runners,' Senyaka says. 'We managed to escape. Let us in. Some of us need urgent medical help.'

A pause. 'Code?'

'Land Rover One.'

'How did you escape?'

'What does it matter? We've got injured people with us!'

'Wait ... I'll have to check with my supervisor.' There's a pause and then, 'We have a Buffel and a van at the gates, sir. Driver says they're runners who survived the last raid, over.' A beat. 'Understood, sir, over.'

'Come on, man,' Senyaka snaps. 'Have you any idea what we've been through?'

'Stay back. You have to wait until I receive further orders.'

Tommy feels sweat trickling down his sides. Ginger's hands are clasped in front of him and Bulelani's left knee is jiggling up and down. The minutes drag.

'I can vouch for them,' a woman's voice calls. Tommy does his best to get a glimpse of her, but she's standing way out of his line of sight.

'Ma'am. My orders are to—'

'Tumiso, is it?' she says. 'You're new here, aren't you?'

'Yes, ma'am.' He sounds respectful, deferential – almost afraid.

'I think I should know my husband's staff by now. They have been through enough and we need to get the injured inside.'

'If you're sure, ma'am.'

'You can trust me, Tumiso.'

Tommy hears Senyaka climbing back into the Buffel's cab, followed by the screech of a gate inching open.

'Slowly!' Tumiso yells. 'I've got to keep the dead back.'

Tommy looks out onto a courtyard, spots a fountain in its centre. Tall stone buildings frame the area. The rumble of the engine ceases.

'We'll take them through the main entrance,' he hears the woman saying.

'Roger, ma'am,' the guard replies.

Doors slam. 'They're in the back of the van,' Kathleen barks. 'Three of them. And be quick about it!'

Three bulky, unfamiliar figures in blue uniforms flick past Tommy's view.

'Quickly!' Kat snaps.

There's a grunt, and Tommy sees a stretcher being carried past the side of the Buffel by a couple of the men in blue. The figure on it is covered up to its chin in a blanket, face swathed in bandages. Another stretcher containing a similarly blanketed figure follows.

'But who's on the stretchers?' Tommy whispers to Ginger. 'I thought we were the only volunteers?'

'Your guess is a good as mine, Tommy.'

Bulelani is really looking anxious now. 'We have to trust Senyaka,' he says.

Tommy swings back to his vantage point, looks down as a third stretcher wobbles past him.

The similarly bandaged body on the stretcher looks smaller than the others. Way smaller. Childlike, even.

Oh no.

No.

Senyaka wouldn't ... he couldn't ...

Tommy leaps up, lunges for the door, almost makes it when Ginger hauls him back. 'No, Tommy. Stay put.'

'Ginger – I think I know what Senyaka is planning! We have to stop him!'

'Tommy, it's not safe. Those guys out there could be armed.'

'But you don't under—'

The door swings open and a blonde woman stares in at them in confusion. 'Who the hell are you? I thought there were only five—'

Tommy takes advantage of the distraction, flies forward, slips past the guard, feels her fingers brushing his collar, hears her crying 'Hey!'

'Tommy!' Ginger hollers after him.

Legs pumping, Tommy hares around the Buffel, dives towards a row of heavy wooden doors in front of him. Thankfully one of them is open and he slides through it, hears Ginger and the woman shouting at each other behind him.

What the—?

Where on earth is he? He pauses, stunned, stares in bewilderment at the interlocking cobbled streets, quaint colour-washed buildings around him and the perfectly blue sky above him. It must be some kind of theme park, but he doesn't have time to dither. There's no indication where Senyaka, Kat and the stretcher-bearers might have headed, and Tommy takes a right turn at random, darts down a dim alleyway framed by columned apartments, their porticos draped in plastic ivy.

A couple of women pushing a cleaning trolley around a corner start and stare at him, and he doubles back, decides to head left this time, passing what looks to be a massive children's playroom, full of flashing arcade games.

Then he hears it. A scream. A scream so naked with horror that it resonates in the pit of his stomach. A scream that takes him straight back to that morning at the mall when Jacob—'

'Tommy!' Ginger roars. 'Where are you?'

Tommy whirls, sees Ginger racing towards him.

The screams are increasing in volume, and oh no, oh crap, a hundred metres or so behind Ginger he sees Senyaka and Kat speeding towards the heavy wooden doors, chased by a trio of twitching, jerking, howling figures. Senyaka and Kat slip through at the last second, slamming the door behind them, the hatchlings hurling their bodies against it.

Tommy freezes. His legs don't want to work. He feels Ginger dragging him into the activity room, pushing him behind an game machine and clamping a hand over his mouth. 'Quiet.'

Tommy bites down on his tongue, barely dares to breathe, shuts his eyes, tries to block out the demented screams, praying that he and Ginger haven't been spotted. Gradually, the howls appear to fade, as if the hatchlings are moving away from the area in which they're hiding.

'We can't stay in here,' Ginger whispers.

'Should we head back to the doors?'

'Might be locked. We might not have time to mess about.'

Ginger edges forwards, peers out of the room. Turns and beckons Tommy to follow him. They slip across the alleyway, through an archway and into a small courtyard. A stone staircase to their left leads up to a balcony attached to a plasterboard hacienda and Ginger inclines his head towards it. 'You first,' he hisses. Tommy ducks his head and runs. He flies up the staircase, the hatchlings' screeches still ringing in his ears, Ginger hot on his heels.

'Ginger, will we—'

'*Shhhh!*' Ginger grabs the back of his jacket, pulls him down behind the balcony's balustrade. Tommy looks through the slats, sees a man in a white coat staggering into the courtyard below, clutching at his hair, saliva frothing at his snarling lips. The man writhes, twitches then tears back through the archway. Tommy bites his knuckles till they bleed.

'Did you know?' he whispers to Ginger. 'Did you know what Senyaka was planning?'

'Nah, mate. Of course not. It's smart, though.'

'*What?*' Tommy almost forgets to keep his voice down.

'Think about it. What he's done is effectively wipe out the whole settlement in one fell swoop – even the Lefties. No one's immune to hatchlings. A dirty bomb, Tommy. That's what this is.'

Tommy can't help but wonder if Senyaka came up with the idea of his 'dirty bomb' after what had happened at Eastgate. After Jacob had sacrificed himself to save them. It's monstrous. No, it's worse than that. It's *evil*. He must have rounded up the Rotters the night before, disguised them as burn victims, tied them to the stretchers and stashed them in the van, probably just before he gave his speech about Jacob.

'Ginger. I think one of the Rotters they brought in on the stretchers is Optimus.'

But Ginger's not listening. Moving at a crouch, he runs along the balcony, heading for a fire axe hidden behind glass on the wall next to the hacienda's phony window. 'Now that's what I'm talking about,' Tommy hears him mutter. He smashes the glass with his elbow, grabs the axe, weighs it in his hand.

Tommy watches as Ginger creeps further along the balcony, pulls open the single door at its far end, peers inside it.

'Tommy!' he hisses. 'Over here.'

Tommy joins him. The door opens onto a small dark space, some sort of storage area, empty but for a broken plastic chair.

'Listen,' Ginger says softly. 'This place will be swarming with hatchlings in no time, and there could well be too many to take on, even if I did have my chainsaw. I got to go get Lele. You hide in here, keep the door shut, yeah? I'll be back for you, I promise.'

'No, Ginger, you can't—'

'You'll be safe in here. Just don't leave, okay?'

'But I want to come with you!'

'I know, mate, but it'll be harder for me if I have to worry about you. You understand?'

Tommy nods reluctantly, allows Ginger to usher him inside.

'Be brave, Tommy. And don't leave this room, whatever happens.'

Ginger shuts the door, leaving Tommy in absolute darkness. He slides his back down the wall and wraps his arms around his knees.

Lele

Screaming. Someone's screaming.

I leap up, fly to the window, stare down into the courtyard. The air is hazed with fog or smoke and the putrid glow cast by the paraffin lamps outside the hotel's walls seems to muddy rather than illuminate the scene. All I can make out is a bunch of shadowy figures that appear to be grappling with each other in the centre of the square. One of them breaks away, moving fast – abnormally fast – and dashes into the relatively clear area directly below my window. It throws its head back, revealing features disfigured by madness and fury.

Oh, no.

It's a hatchling.

But how did it get into the complex?

The mist in the centre of the square partially dissolves, and I look down on the twitching figure of one of Coom's remaining runners lying on the cobblestones. He shudders, lurches to his feet, lets out a scream that I seem to feel somewhere in my gut rather than my ears, and zigzags away, heading in the direction of the fake city.

I have to get out of here. I have to get to Ember. If the hatchlings find a way into the hotel and down into the clinic, she's toast.

I bang on the door, thump my fists against it. 'Hey! *Hey!*' I try again, yelling at the top of my lungs. 'Let me out of here!'

A click of a lock. The door opens, Busi grabs my arm and hauls me into the corridor. 'Quick, Lele.'

'What the hell's happening?'

'The dead have found a way in and—'

'I have to get to the clinic, get to Ember!'

'She's not there, Lele. I checked. The clinic's empty.'

'So where is she then?'

'I don't know! Come, we have to get out of the hotel. There's a fire downstairs in the kitchen and it's spreading fast.'

Busi's already haring towards the stairwell door and I sprint after her. 'You think Coom's taken Ember?'

'I don't know!'

I spot a fire extinguisher in a corner of the hallway next to the lifts. I kick it out of its protective casing and slot in under my left arm. 'Busi, wait. We can't just run outside. There are hatchlings out there. Without any weapons we'll be screwed.'

'We can't stay here, Lele – this place is mostly run on gas and there's tons of spare fuel for the generators stored all over the place. It could blow at any time.'

Awesome. Face-off with hatchlings or burn to death. 'Fire exits?'

She shakes her head. 'Sealed up years ago, when Coom first moved here.'

Figures. And now his paranoia looks like it's about to bite him in the arse. 'Can we get up onto the roof of the hotel?'

We could end up trapped if the fire really does rage out of control, but it's better than being turned into one of those things.

'No – Sihle already thought of that. There's an attic space, but no outside area up there.'

'Crap. Where's Sihle now?'

The stairwell door bangs open and One Ear flies through it, his face slick with sweat, a gun in his hand. 'What's taking so long?'

'Sihle, have you seen Ember?'

'No. Come on, we have to be quick, it's getting bad down there.'

'I need to find her, check she isn't with Coom.'

'There's no time for that!'

But I'm not listening. I shove past him, gallop down the stairs. And now I can detect the first whiff of smoke, becoming stronger the lower I go.

I slam through the door that leads to Coom's corridor, sprint to his door. I bang my fist on it as hard as I can. 'Coom!'

'Lele!' Busi yells at me from the stairwell's door. 'We don't have time for this.'

The lock disengages, and Coom's head emerges. 'Where are my bodyguards? They were supposed to come back for—'

I shove past him. 'Ember? Ember, are you in here?'

'Why would she be in here?'

I yank open a door that leads into a massive bedroom, the truck-size bed draped in black satin sheets, backtrack, and haul open another that opens onto an empty bathroom. 'Where is she? What have you done with her?'

His chins wobble. 'I haven't done anything with her.'

One Ear and Busi barrel into the room.

'Sihle!' Coom roars. 'I demand to know what's happening here!'

'You don't get to demand anything any more, Coom,' I snap. 'Let's go, guys. She's not here.'

One Ear hesitates. 'You'd better come with us, sir.'

'But outside ... those things ...'

'There's a fire in the dining room,' Busi says. 'It's not safe to stay in the hotel.'

Coom hesitates. Frowns. 'The fuel in the basement ... the generators.'

'We know about that, sir,' One Ear says, somehow managing to remain respectful.

'But still ... isn't it better to stay in here?'

'Fine,' I say. 'Stay here and burn.'

Busi and One Ear are already heading out the door and I move to follow them.

'Wait,' Coom says. 'The smoke ... We should wet some towels, wrap them around our heads.' For the first time I get a glimpse of the man Coom once was before he was ruined by power and greed. Maybe not a nice man, or even a kind man, but a man who got things done.

He waddles into the bathroom, turns the bath taps to full blast, and I hand him towel after towel to soak.

We drape them over our heads, and One Ear leads the way down to the ground floor. Wisps of smoke curl up through the gap at the bottom of the door.

'Listen up,' One Ear says. 'I'm thinking the best place to head for is the bell tower across the square. There are no windows, and the doors are solid. Stay behind me and keep close. Mr Coom? You hearing me?'

'Yes.'

I look over my shoulder. Coom's eyes are free from fear, but full of calculation. I have no doubt that if he has to trample over us to save himself, he will.

I heft the fire extinguisher in one hand, testing its weight, and then One Ear opens the door.

The smoke is thicker than I was expecting and stings my eyes immediately. I drape the towel over my mouth and step into the lobby, Busi close behind me.

'Move!' One Ear roars.

'Sihle!' I yell as a figure rushes through the smoke towards us, a demented, ear-splitting shriek blasting out of its throat.

One Ear raises his gun and fires, the sound of the blast echoing painfully through my eardrums, and the hatchling jerks, twitches, but keeps on coming. One Ear fires again, but One Ear's eyes are streaming from the smoke by now and he can't get a clear shot – and then it leaps, barrels into One Ear and they both crash to the floor.

'Sihle!' Busi screams.

One Ear manages to kick the thrashing creature away from him, and I don't hesitate. I step back, swing the fire extinguisher, and putting every ounce of my weight and strength behind the blow, I smash it down onto its head. It raises its arm to claw at me, but I hit it again, and again, ignoring the sinister sound of crunching bone.

I drop the extinguisher and whirl to see Busi leaning over One Ear, coughing and crying and trying to haul him to his feet.

'He's hurt badly, Lele!'

The smoke is rising and as it clears momentarily I can see gouts of black blood from a jagged gash in his forearm staining the marble tiles beneath him. He groans, his eyelids flutter, and then they snap open to reveal a flat, black nothingness.

'Back up, Busi!' I yell. But Busi's still keening and coughing, her eyes fixed to his. 'Busi! Get back into the stairwell.'

I shove her towards it. She snaps into life, stumbles to the door and yanks on the handle. 'It won't open!'

'Where's Coom?'

I've forgotten all about him. Bastard. He must be leaning his weight against the door. 'Coom! Let us in!'

One Ear howls, a terrible sound laced with fear and agony. I look over my shoulder. He's coming fast. I spin, zigzag forward, trying to draw him away from Busi. He hesitates, scrapes his fingernails over his face as if he's trying to fight the infection, but he won't be able to control it much longer.

Throat and lungs now on fire, I yell at Busi to keep trying to force the door open. One Ear lunges for me and I sidestep, my boot knocking against something on the tiles. I glance down. The gun. I pick it up.

There isn't another way.

I've never used a gun before, and I pray that there isn't a safety or something. Busi is screaming at me to stop, not to do it, that it's Sihle, but she must see the way his eyes have changed, the way his body language is twisted, as if he's made of rage.

Calm down, Lele, the Saint voice whispers. *Take your time*.

But I don't have time. He's less than a metre from me when I raise my hand, amazed that my fingers aren't shaking, blink once, and aim. One Ear stops, staggers, but keeps on coming. I fire again, and this time, he falls.

Busi, I have to get to Busi. She's doubled over, hacking and sobbing and she looks to be one step away from collapsing onto the tiles. I grab her elbow, yank her around One Ear's twitching body and towards the door, the smoke searing my lungs, my eyes raw.

'Lele!' Busi shrieks as a shadowy frenzied shape lunges towards us, head thrown back, arms reaching for us.

I lift the gun again, pull the trigger, but there's nothing but a shallow click.

For a second I forget about the smoke scorching my throat as I watch in disbelief as the hatchling drops to its knees, its head toppling off its neck. And behind it, striding through the smoke, there's another figure – a figure I'd recognise anywhere, a figure with a crazy corona of orange hair and an axe in his hands.

'Ginger!'

'Lele!' he shouts. 'Bloody hell, thought I'd never find you.'

But there's no time for a reunion. 'Come on! Help me with Busi!'

We wrap her arms around her waist and hare towards the exit, somehow managing to avoid tripping over the bodies littering the steps that lead up into the hotel.

'Ginger,' I shout, my sandpapered lungs heaving. 'The bell tower. Cross the square.'

A hatchling darts out of the coiling smoke towards us, and Ginger strides forward, swinging his axe without breaking stride and dispatching it instantly. Busi stumbles, but somehow I manage to hold her up.

Ginger joins us again, helping to shoulder most of Busi's weight. Ahead of us, the door to the bell tower opens and one of Coom's waiters waves us forwards. 'Hurry!'

'Nearly there, mate,' Ginger huffs.

'Help me! Help!' The voice is so filled with anguish and panic it carries above the roars and screams around us.

Coom.

I stop dead.

It comes again. *'Please!'*

I can't let him burn. I know it's insane, but something inside me won't let that happen.

'Ginger! Give me your axe. Take Busi.'

'What?'

'Take her!'

Before he can stop me I snatch the axe out of his hand, whirl, and hare back to the hotel, dodging and weaving around the prone bodies scattered on the cobblestones.

And then I see him, his large silhouette weaving in the hotel's open doorway, a hatchling heading straight for him.

'Coom! Get back!'

I race forward and then there's a roar, a boom, and it's as if all the air has been sucked out of the world. I throw my arms over my face as flames boil out of the door, consuming the hatchling heading for Coom. Another gout of flame shoots out and someone grabs me around the waist and pulls me back, but not before I feel the hair on my arms singeing.

'What the hell, Lele?'

Ginger half-carries, half-drags me away from the heat blazing out of the hotel.

I can't stop coughing; my lungs feel like they've been blowtorched, the skin on my face is too tight, as if it's two sizes too small.

'Oh bloody hell,' Ginger mutters. I look up.

There have to be five or six of them and they're coming fast.

Tommy

Something slams into the storage room's door with such force it shudders. Tommy yelps and backs up against the wall.

He hears a screech, a man shouting 'Help me!'

What should he do? There's nothing in the room he can use as a weapon except for that flimsy plastic chair. Another scream, this one naked with pure fear. He can't let what happened to Jacob happen to whoever's out there. He *has* to help him.

Tommy counts to three, and picks up the chair. He opens the door a crack, the handle is snatched out of his hand and he feels himself being hauled out of the room, landing heavily on his hands and knees. He turns to see a flash of a black jacket before the door slams.

A snarl. He looks up.

There's a hatchling directly in front of him, and even through his terror Tommy realises that the distorted features are familiar. It's the blonde woman who tried to stop him as he leapt out of the Buffel.

Tommy jumps up, grabs the chair and chucks it at her. She lunges for him, but her trousers catch on the chair leg, and she stumbles, buying Tommy some time. He leaps past her, flies along the balcony and almost falls down the stairs, an electric jolt of adrenaline speeding his heart.

He turns, sees that she – *it* – is gaining on him, flailing down the stairs, black eyes fixed on his. He backs up, looks around desperately, trying to decide which way to run.

Too late.

The hatchling snarls and jerks towards him. He darts to his right but it's quick, way too quick, and he dives forward as it reaches for him, landing heavily on his stomach. He rolls onto his back, kicks out blindly with his legs, feels them connect.

A low moan echoes through the space.

The hatchling stops suddenly, mid-swipe. It shakes its head, and almost looks confused, as if it's just remembered something it's forgotten.

Another figure lurches into view. A small figure, the blue of its T-shirt visible beneath a swathe of bandages drooping off its limbs like a mummy's.

'Optimus!'

Optimus sways, raises a hand and opens his mouth in a facsimile of a smile.

Moving with a horrible crablike gait, the hatchling shambles away, disappearing into a darkened area behind the stone staircase.

Tommy scrambles to his feet. 'Optimus! You saved me! I can't believe that—'

'Tommy! Step away from it!'

Tommy whips his head around, sees Senyaka standing behind him. He's aiming his rifle right at Optimus's head.

'No!' Tommy screams, jumping in front of Optimus. 'You can't shoot him!'

Senyaka hesitates. 'Tommy ... step away.'

'No!'

'We've got to move it, Senyaka,' Kat shouts from beyond the archway. Tommy hears the crack crack crack of gunshots. 'There are more coming!'

'*Tommy!*' Senyaka roars.

'Promise you won't hurt him!'

Senyaka reluctantly lowers the weapon. 'Now *move*!'

Tommy reaches out a hand to Optimus, but Senyaka hauls him away, drags him towards the archway. Tommy twists, sees Optimus lurching behind them.

'How could you *do* that, Senyaka?' Tommy sobs. 'Bring the dead in here? Bring Optimus here?'

'Later,' Senyaka growls. 'I've got to get you back to the truck.'

'Where's Ginger?'

'Come on!' Kat yells. She's waiting for them next to the wooden entrance doors, rifle on her shoulder, Bulelani next to her, sweeping his automatic weapon in every direction. Tommy looks desperately for a sign that Optimus is still following, but he's nowhere to be seen. A series of furious screams reverberates towards them and Senyaka practically throws Tommy through the door. Bulelani and Kat heave it shut.

'Get in the truck,' Senyaka snaps to Tommy. 'I told you to stay put.'

'Screw you!' Tommy yells. 'Screw you, Senyaka! How could you *do* that?' Tommy's words are barely understandable, he's sobbing so hard, but he's past caring what Senyaka thinks of him. 'And what about Ginger? He's still in there. We have to go get him.'

Tommy spins, making for the door, but Senyaka wrenches him back.

'Oh, great,' Kat mutters. She shoulders her weapon again.

Tommy feels Senyaka loosening his grip, and turns to see what's happening behind him.

Dark figures drift in the shadows, and Tommy hears the click of weapons being cocked.

'Hello, Senyaka.' Tommy knows that voice, but can't immediately place it. 'Sorry we're late.'

And then he steps into the light.

It's Jova.

Lele

'Get behind me,' Ginger roars. But there's no way that even Ginger and his superhuman axe-wielding skills are going to be up to the job, there are just too many, and more seem to be darting and twisting through the smoke towards us. The crazed rage that's blasting out of them is as tangible as the heat radiating from the inferno consuming the hotel.

Ginger bellows and runs forward, his axe lifted above his head, ready to swing at the nearest hatchling, but he doesn't get a chance.

There's a pop-crack and it stops dead, just metres from us, before staggering and collapsing onto the cobblestones.

'What the hell?' Ginger looks around in wonder as the ghostly shapes of the others meet a similar fate, some dropping mid-leap, others managing a few staggered steps before crumpling to the ground.

A sudden gust of wind thins the smoke slightly, and several figures stride towards us, guns cradled in their arms, the tallest of them quickening his pace.

I'd know that loping walk anywhere.

'Ash!' Ginger yells. He runs up to him and enfolds him a bear hug, rifle and all. 'What the bleeding hell you done to your hair?'

The Ash I remember hated guns. He's changed more than I thought.

'Hey, Ginger,' Ash says, clapping him on the back. Is it my imagination, or does he hold back a little?

A giant of a guy with huge, white teeth barks a laugh. 'What's this, Jack?' he says in a lilting accent. 'I thought you liked girls?'

Ash steps back. He glances briefly at the woman with the eye patch – Morgan – then looks over at me. He moves as if he's about to approach, but then hesitates as more gun-wielding figures hustle towards us – a lean fellow with eyes as hard as One Ear's and a chunky white woman who looks as if she could give Pirate Chick a run for her money.

And bringing up the rear, a small bespectacled guy: Jova.

Jova's eyes flick towards me. 'Where's Coom?'

I point to the hotel, ducking as another of the windows on the first floor explodes. 'In there.'

'Senyaka,' Jova says to the guy with the penetrating eyes. 'I thought you had this under control. Coom was supposed to be taken alive.'

Ginger's looking from Jova to Senyaka in confusion.

'You're Jova, right?' Ginger asks. Jova glances at him and nods impatiently. 'Ash's old mate and the fella who runs Sandtown?'

Another impatient nod.

'And you guys were working together all this time? You and Senyaka?'

'In a sense.'

'I see,' Ginger says. He looks thoughtful for a second and then he strides up to Senyaka and punches him in the face. Senyaka's a big man, but the blow sends him flying. He reels over, knocking into the woman behind him.

Ginger turns to face Jova, 'And you're next, mate!'

Ash grabs his arm. 'Ginger, you don't understand—'

'Yeah I do, mate,' Ginger shrugs him off.

There's the sound of running footsteps and a girl in a headscarf, her rifle banging against her back, flies towards us. 'There is a bunch of people in an enclosure near the main entrance,' she pants. 'Chick called Cezanne said there's tons of kids there too.'

She must mean the bird park. Cezanne must have moved the children there. But ... she would only have had time to do that if she knew beforehand that Coom's place was about to be awash with hatchlings, wouldn't she?

'Hey!' I shout at the girl. My voice is ragged from the smoke, but even Senyaka and Jova turn to look at me. 'You see a redhead with them? She might have been in a wheelchair.'

The girl nods. 'Ja.'

'Lele?' Ginger asks. 'Do you mean *Ember*?'

I manage a nod. Then, dizzy with relief and exhaustion, I sink to my haunches and drop my head onto my arms.

'Lele?' I hear Ash saying. 'Lele? Are you okay?'

I ignore him and let the darkness take me.

I sit in my quiet corner, half-hidden behind a plane tree in the bird park's old cafe, and watch the others go about their business. Busi's nowhere to be seen – I haven't had a chance to talk to her since she and the other survivors were escorted out of the bell tower to safety last night. She can't have joined Jova's troops who are herding the last of the Rotters out of the city, although Ginger's new sidekick, a shy, earnest boy called Tommy, who Ginger said kept him sane during the last turbulent weeks, insisted on accompanying them. Perhaps she's already left on one of the vehicles that have started transporting Coom's remaining staff and wives back to Sandtown. According to Ginger, Jova and Senyaka left hours ago to start the process of reorganising the city now that Coom, the monster, the slug, is dead. Preparing 'the people' as Jova calls them, for his big announcement; the unveiling of his amazing plan to save the world.

The fire only died out this morning, and I haven't yet managed to muster the energy to inspect the damage. When we leave this place, I'll never return. The memories I'll be carrying will be bad enough without adding another vile mental image to the list.

Ember waves at me and gestures for me to join her and Ginger who are sitting close together on a bench next to the dam. I smile back weakly and shake my head. Ginger can't seem to stop staring at her, or touching her hair and face. I haven't heard his full story yet, and I wonder if I ever will. There's a serious edge to him that wasn't there before, as if he's aged ten years overnight. Maybe we've all grown up or changed.

I've never felt so worn out, not even during my gruelling training sessions with Hester and the other Mall Rats. Not even during the long journey from Cape Town. The tendrils lurking inside me must be working flat out to fix my scorched lungs. Each breath seems to be coming easier and my throat no longer feels like it's been sliced open with rusty razor blades.

Oh, *crap*.

I'm pregnant. It hasn't occurred to me to wonder – or I've

been blocking it from my mind – what the silvery strands might be doing to the baby.

Will it have the same affliction?

And is this a bad thing? If it weren't for the Guardians infecting me and my brother Jobe all those years ago, I would be needing some serious medical treatment right now, a new pair of lungs for a start. Saint's eyes wouldn't have opened after the crash. Is being alive all that counts? Surviving whatever the odds and whatever the price?

For the first time the reality of my situation really starts to hit home. I can't block it out of my mind any longer; I can't deny it.

Pregnant.

I finally have to accept it.

'Lele?' Cezanne approaches me cautiously. I don't blame her for being wary. She must be able to see the hatred in my eyes. Because that's what it is, hatred. I wonder if this is what Lucien was talking about all those weeks ago when he first came to my room. He said, 'I've seen the evil that people can do,' or something like it. And if I ever see him again, I'll be able to tell him that I have, too.

'How are you feeling, Lele?' she asks, as if nothing's happened. As if her husband hasn't just died. As if scores of innocent people haven't just been infected.

'How could you do it, Cezanne? How could you have let this happen? You're a *doctor*.'

'Believe me, Lele. I didn't know that Senyaka was planning to bring the dead into the city.'

'Lies,' I spit. 'Why else move the children out here? Why else move Ember?'

Her hands are shaking. 'I thought Senyaka and the Outcasts were going to sneak in and kidnap Coom. That is all. I moved the children and Ember because I knew Coom's remaining guards would fight back.'

I can't read her well enough to figure out if she's telling the truth or not.

'And how could I have known there would be a fire in the hotel, Lele? But I heard what you did. That you tried to save Steven. Thank you for that.'

I snort in derision. 'I have admit it was smart, though, Cezanne. You and Jova using the Outcasts. That way if it all went wrong you could both plead innocence. Deny any culpability. Shame about all the people who got hurt along the way.'

'There are always casualties in any worthwhile battle, Lele.'

'That's what Coom would say. Now please, get out of my sight.'

'Lele—'

'Seriously. Get away from me.' I can't – won't – hold the anger back any longer.

As if she senses this, Cezanne hesitates, then walks away.

'Mate, over here!' Ginger's face lights up. I turn to see Ash striding down the path towards him and Ember. Ginger may have forgiven Ash and Jova for all that happened last night, but I haven't.

For the first time in weeks we're all together in the same place. Ash, Ginger, Ember and me. The old Mall Rats crew back together. *Almost* all of us. More than ever, Saint's absence is a gaping hole, like a missing front tooth. No, more like a missing limb.

Ash looks over at me, eyes shielded behind large sunglasses.

But I know him. He's hiding more than just his eyes. And the time for secrets is over.

Ginger helps Ember climb onto the bus and turns to me.

'You sure you want to wait for the next one, Lele?'

'I'm sure.' I have unfinished business here, but he doesn't need to know that.

As we waited for the buses to be readied for the drive to Sandtown, I did my best to hide my true feelings, keeping my false smile in place until my cheekbones ached. Only Ember seemed to sense that something was up with me, but I hope she just put it down to the trauma I went through the night before. Fortunately I wasn't called upon to say much; Ginger and Ash's new army buddy, Americano, a hulk of a man, had taken centre stage. Cracking jokes and trading war stories while Ember looked on fondly and Nuush and the weirdly named Pockets convulsed with giggles. Every so often Ginger would bring Tommy into the conversation and the boy would blush with such ferocity I half-expected him to explode. I wish Saint were here to see Ginger in his element, shedding most, but not all, of the heaviness I picked up from him earlier. And Saint would have sensed what I had sensed. That something is eating Ash up from the inside.

'Well, I guess we'll catch up with you there then, Lele.' Ginger looks over my shoulder. 'Oy! Tommy! Get a move on!'

Tommy runs up, smiles shyly at me. 'Um … it was nice to meet you, Lele,' he stammers.

'You too, Tommy.'

'Come on, Tommy,' Ginger grins. 'Your mum's waiting.' Tommy jumps onto the bus, blushing again as Ginger musses his hair.

'Yo, Ginger!' Americano yells, waving a half-empty rum bottle at him. 'You owe me a drink, remember!'

'Sure, mate. First one back to Sandtown is buying!'

Americano roars with laughter and staggers off to join Pockets and Nuush who are loading the last of Coom's tinned goods and luxuries into the back of a Buffel truck.

The bus chugs away and I head back into the bird park to find Ash. He's sitting with Morgan on Coom's bench, next to the now-empty aviary. The birds, like the animals, have been set free to roam. I wonder if Coom's baby bird survived. I hope it did.

Morgan spots me first, and gives me a curt nod.

Ash looks up, twitches when he sees me. 'Lele. I thought you were travelling back with Ginger.'

'I'm taking the next bus.'

There's a moment of such awkwardness I'm surprised the air doesn't freeze and splinter.

Morgan straightens her shoulders. 'I'll see you later, Jack. Better make sure Americano doesn't drink away all of Coom's booze.'

She shoots me a tight smile and Ash and I watch her walk away in silence.

He clears his throat. 'What's up, Lele?'

'You tell me.'

'What do you mean?'

'You're hiding something.'

That telltale slip of the eyes to the left. 'I didn't know the details of Senyaka's plan, if that's what you mean. Jova didn't even know hatchlings were involved. First thing I knew about it was when Jova asked me and my team to join him on a recce.'

My team. The Mall Rats were supposed to be his team. 'That's not what I mean. But nice to know you're willing to follow wherever Jova leads without question, Ash.'

He flinches. Ha. A strike.

'No, Ash. There's something else. When we left Cape Town I knew all along you were hiding something from us. I knew then, and I know now. What is it?'

'I wasn't the only one who was hiding something, Lele.'

And you're not the only one now, the Saint voice says.

'So what is it? What are you hiding? And I know you have feelings for Pirate Chick, so it's not that.'

Another start. 'Lele—'

'Don't worry, I'm not jealous. Once I would have been, but no more. How does Jova get you to do so much, Ash? What power does he have over you?'

'He doesn't have any power. I just want what he wants. For us to be free.'

He gets up from the bench. 'We need to get moving. The last bus will be leaving soon.' He steps away, his back to me. 'You coming?'

I open my mouth to retort, but instead I find myself saying, 'I'm pregnant.'

He flinches. 'What?'

'You heard me. I'm pregnant.'

He turns around slowly. 'Is it mine?'

'No. How could it be yours?'

'Coom's?

'No!'

'Then whose?'

I almost tell him about Lucien, then change my mind. 'It doesn't matter.'

'I … I don't know what to say.' He swipes a hand through his nonexistent hair. His hands are shaking. 'Are you … um … how are you feeling?'

'How do you think I'm feeling?' My chest hitches, but I

won't let myself cry. I *won't*. 'The world is screwed up beyond belief, Ash. The last thing I want to do is bring a child into the middle of all this crap. I feel … I dunno, scared.'

The silence drags. What else is there to say?

He takes my hand, squeezes it. His eyes are faraway, unreadable. 'It's going to be fine, Lele.'

And then he walks away.

Tommy

There's chaos in the Hilton's lobby. People are shoving and shouting, some are weeping, and others are pleading with the AOL troops Jova's sent over to clear the amaKlevas out of the bottom floors.

When the news about Coom's death and Jova's proposed restructuring of the city's resources spread through Sandtown, there was a call to throw the amaKlevas out of the city to join the ranks of the dead. Tommy knows that Jova's working hard to prevent this from happening, but he suspects that it's only Jova's promise to reveal his plan this evening that's keeping a lid on the situation. For now, until the redistribution of space and wealth is sorted out, the amaKlevas and their families will be joining everyone else in the bowels of Sandtown. It will give them an idea of how the other half live, but Tommy knows they won't have an easy time of it.

Tommy spies Mister Lugosi, Simo and an agitated woman who must be Simo's mother hovering next to the old reception desk. Uncharacteristically sweaty and dishevelled,

Mister Lugosi is gesticulating wildly at the soldier in front of him.

'You can't do this. Do you know who I am?' Mister Lugosi's voice rises over the hubbub.

The soldier remains unmoved. 'One bag each, and let's go.'

Simo starts sobbing. Tommy almost feels sorry for him, but a part of him regrets that he'll never get the chance to tell Simo he gave his Optimus Prime toy to one of the dead. The look on Simo's face would have been priceless.

He slips past unnoticed and runs up the stairs towards the runners' and workers' floors. He pauses outside his old room, knocks on the door.

Olivia appears, gasps in delight and sweeps him into her arms. 'Thank goodness you are safe.' Still clutching his shoulders, she leans back to assess him. 'You have lost weight, Tommy. But you look good. Strong.'

'Olivia. Senyaka. He's—'

'I know.'

Senyaka appears behind her in the doorway, Baby Nomsa clinging happily to his hip, and Tommy battles to hide his dismay. The bruise on Senyaka's cheekbone where Ginger punched him has bloomed into a deep purple. How did Senyaka get back here so quickly? He must have taken one of the first vehicles that ferried the Montecasino Lefties to the city.

Glowing with happiness, Olivia squeezes Tommy's hand and draws him into the room. Tommy can feel the weight of Senyaka's gaze on him. 'Now, Tommy, tell me the truth. Did Senyaka take good care of you?' She beams at Senyaka. Tommy's never seen her looking so ... *whole*.

He feels about a million years old. How can he tell her that Senyaka deliberately brought the dead into Montecasino to infect the living? It's possible she'll find out eventually, but he doesn't want to be the one to tell her. He's tired of everyone saying that war isn't a game, that you need to make sacrifices and hard choices to win. But that isn't an excuse. No one has the right to make that sort of decision. No one has the right to play god. 'Yes,' he lies. 'Senyaka kept me safe.'

Olivia looks deep into his eyes. 'You are telling me the truth, Tommy?'

'Leave the boy alone,' Senyaka says. 'He's a hero. He fought like a man.'

'He fought?'

'Yes,' Senyaka says. 'He acquitted himself well. You would have been very proud of him, Olivia.' Tommy finally looks into Senyaka's eyes, and catches a glimmer of what can only be relief.

Differing emotions flash across Olivia's face. Tommy knows she wants to believe Senyaka. And despite the hell he unleashed in Coom's city, didn't he keep the zoo settlement safe? Didn't he prove that it is possible for everyone to live on an equal basis?

Why does everything have to be so complicated? Far as Tommy can see, there's no such thing as good and evil. Good men do evil things all the time, don't they?

Olivia strokes Tommy's cheek. 'Tommy, after Jova has told us his plans and freed the city, Senyaka wants us to return to the Outcast settlement.'

'Do you know what his plan is, Senyaka?' Tommy asks.

Senyaka shakes his head. 'I do not know the details. But he is certain that it will work, and as we have seen, he can be trusted to do what is right.'

'But he's still planning on destroying the dead, isn't he?'

'Of course,' Senyaka says.

Tommy feels as if he's just swallowed a stone.

'Tommy?' Olivia looks at him questioningly. 'What is the matter?'

'Listen, Olivia,' he says, trying to smile and failing miserably. 'I'll be back now-now. I have to go and do something.'

'What is there to do?' Senyaka asks. 'We need to be at the square in a few hours for the announcement.'

'I know. I won't be long.' Tommy kisses Olivia's cheek and runs out, pretending not to hear her calling after him.

He flies down the stairs and through the now-empty lobby, and makes his way down to the entrance of the Archies. It's slow going – most of Sandtown's untouchables have chosen to start the celebration early – but he shoves his way determinedly through the swaying drunks who are lurching and singing and vomiting noisily into the drains. There's going to be chaos tonight when Jova reveals his plan if this lot are anything to go by.

He jostles his way into the stairwell and into the parking lot where he used to catch the runners' kombi. A crowd of workers is huddled around the honey wagons, passing a bottle around and cawing at the top of their voices, and Tommy spies Ayanda, his old supervisor, among them. Praying he won't be spotted, he starts the long hike up the curving conduit that leads to the main gate. He's amazed he's not gasping for breath – all those weeks of hard work and training in the zoo settlement have definitely paid off. Or it could be the desperation he's feeling, the now-familiar tingle of adrenaline rushing through his veins.

The blue at the gate is leaning against the wall, humming to himself and sipping from a bottle. He straightens when Tommy runs up to him. Tommy breathes a sigh of relief. It's Molemo, his old neighbour.

'Toooooommmmy!' Molemo calls. 'Tom-*my*. Looking good, my man. You come to check in on your old friend?'

'Hey, Molemo.'

Molemo staggers slightly and his voice is slurred. Despite being on duty, he's more than half-drunk, which, before Coom and the amaKlevas were dethroned, would have been a lashing offence. 'Proud of you, Tommy. Heard you helped Jova. And ... you really with the Outcasts?'

'Something like that.'

Molemo nods with exaggerated care. 'Never believed what they said about you, Tommy. No way did you hurt that kid.'

Mooki. Tommy realises he hasn't even thought about Mooki's fate in all the excitement. 'He's okay, right? Mooki, I mean.'

Molemo flaps a hand. 'Ja, ja. Bump on the head. Probably knocked some sense into him. Little bastard anyway.' Molemo hiccups. 'So what can I do for you?'

'I need to go out there.'

'What for?' Molemo leans into him and Tommy's hit with a blast of stale pineapple-beer breath.

'*Please*, Molemo. It's important.'

Molemo sways again. 'How can I say no to a hero?'

Tommy helps Molemo shift the gate open just far enough to allow him to squeeze through. He takes a deep breath and steps out into the throng of the dead. There are thousands of them, surging as if they're all being pulled by the same invisible string. How on earth is he going to find Optimus in this lot? Tommy didn't see him when he tagged along with Jova's intimidating troops to sweep the remaining dead out of Montecasino. He must have already been ousted by the time Tommy caught up with them. In any case, it's a long shot that Optimus would have followed Tommy here. How would he even know where he was? For all Tommy knows, he's returned to the outskirts of the zoo settlement or to that hospital. This was a stupid idea. It's just ... he thought they had a bond. That somehow, Optimus would sense where he was, do his best to be near to him, like a dog that instinctively found its way home after being left on the side of the highway.

'Optimus?' he calls, now feeling really ridiculous. It's hopeless.

But he'll find Optimus eventually, Tommy vows. They're friends, and you can't break that thread, can you?

He turns away, bangs on the gate to be let back in.

'Tommy!' Molemo slurs, clapping him on the shoulder. 'You going to be on the stage tonight with Jova? For the anna ... announce ... When Jova tells us his plan?'

'I don't know.'

'Ja. Gonna be good. Buses, see?'

'What?'

'Buses. You know my sister's boy? Shafiek? Went to the AOL. Says there're buses. Lots of buses. To take the people away when they bomb the dead. Ja. Wipe 'em all out. Then we're all free. Even the non-Lefties.'

What does this mean for Optimus? But Tommy knows what this means. He needs to speak to Jova. He has to make him listen. Tell him about the teacher, tell him about Optimus. Because the dead – he can no longer bear to call them Rotters – aren't as soulless and inhuman as everyone thinks. Tommy knows this in his heart. If that teacher is actually right-handed and not naturally immune, then this must mean that the dead can be ... tamed? Is that the right word? Tommy isn't sure. And Optimus saved him at Montecasino. He knows he did. If it wasn't for Optimus, Tommy would have been torn to pieces.

'I'll catch you later, Molemo,' Tommy shouts, already sprinting back down to the parking lot.

This time, he doesn't bother to keep a low profile as he jogs towards the door that leads into the Archies. Time's running out.

'Piggy!' a familiar voice yells.

Dammit. Tommy thinks about legging it into the Archies, losing himself in the crowd, but he finds himself stopping, turning to face Mooki and Jess, who are approaching rapidly. He waits for the old sense of dread to come. The twang of trepidation.

He feels nothing.

Jess looks him up and down. 'You think you're hot stuff, don't you?'

'I don't have time for this, Jess.'

'Make time, Piggy,' Mooki sneers. 'Where's your retard now? You're on your own, and you're going to pay for what you did to me.'

Tommy clears his mind, allows time to slow. When Mooki throws the punch, Tommy steps into it, just like Ginger taught him, catches his fist, bends it back and kicks him in the gut. Mooki drops, making a sound like a wounded buffalo.

Tommy looks straight at Jess. 'Well? You want to be next?'

'You wouldn't hit a girl,' she hisses, then spits right in his face.

Tommy wipes the spittle off his cheek. 'You're not worth it,' he says. 'You're nothing. You're less than nothing, just a bundle of spite packed inside a person who thinks she's hotter than she actually is.'

Whoa. Where did that come from?

Jess's face wobbles. 'You can't talk to me like that.'

'Guess what,' Tommy says. 'I just did.'

He steps around Mooki, shoves past Jess and hurries towards the Archies. He doesn't feel triumphant; all he cares about is telling Jova what he knows. He's heard that Jova has set up his base in the heart of Sandtown, rather than taking occupation of one of the hotels vacated by the amaKlevas, and he heads in the direction of the marketplace, ignoring the grunts of irritation as he elbows through the crowd. He shoves his way up the stairwell that leads up to the first floor and pushes towards the queue of people clamouring around the entrance of the old Woolworths store.

Ducking his head, he barrels through the throng, twisting away from hands attempting to slow his progress, ignoring the shouts of protest and irritation.

Tommy fishes for the name of the woman with the eye patch who's standing straight-backed in the entrance. Then he gets it. *Morgan*. A fellow who keeps scratching his hair as if he's riddled with lice is weaving in front of her, yelling, 'But I need to see Jova! My mama – she needs a clean room. I must state my case.'

Tommy manages to dodge past the lice-ridden man and grab Morgan's attention. 'I need to talk to Jova.'

'Join the club,' she says.

'Please. Don't you remember me? I was at Coom's place, I'm—'

Then Tommy spots a cloud of ginger hair in the shop behind her.

'Ginger!' he shouts.

Ginger peers over the clamouring crowd, breaking into a broad smile when he spots him. 'Tommy! You seen your mum?'

'Yes. Ginger, I need to speak to Jova. It's really important.'

'Steady on, mate.'

'*Please*, Ginger.'

Ginger assesses him. 'Come on.'

The woman in the eye patch ushers Tommy into the store, shaking her head at the others who attempt to slip in after him. Ginger leads him towards a desk at the end of an empty aisle, around which Jova and a few of his soldiers are sitting. Tommy recognises Ash, one of Ginger's Mall Rats, the guy with the cool mismatched eyes and stiff body language.

'Jova, Ash,' Ginger says. 'Tommy here wants a word.'

Jova looks up and Tommy breathes in deeply, feeling his heart skip.

'What is it?' Jova says. He smiles at Tommy, but there's a hint of impatience to it. Close up, Jova's eyes radiate an intimidating, intense intelligence.

Tommy will have to be quick, state his case clearly and succinctly.

'Um, I know you're busy, Jova. I … it's just …' One of the soldiers behind Jova's desk rolls her eyes. 'Jova. The dead. The Rotters. You can't destroy them!' he blurts. 'They're not … they're not entirely … well, *dead*!'

The woman snorts, but Jova remains impassive. 'Explain.'

Tommy wills himself to calm down. Thankfully, the more he speaks, the easier it becomes, and Jova appears to be listening closely as Tommy runs through what he knows, telling him about the teacher, the kids in the classroom, and how Optimus saved him from the hatchling in Montecasino.

When his words dry up, Jova nods, turns to Ginger. 'Ginger? You've seen this?'

'Yeah. Not quite sure what it means, but he's right about the little Rotter – the one he calls Optimus. There was definitely something different about that one. Why didn't you tell me about this before, Tommy? About him saving you, like?'

Tommy shrugs. Truth is, meeting Lele and Ash and the mythical Ember, as well as rubbing shoulders with real AOL soldiers had overwhelmed him.

'So where is this Rotter now?' Jova asks.

'I don't know,' Tommy says miserably.

'So there's no proof?'

'There's the teacher.'

'You don't know for sure she was right-handed though, mate,' Ginger says gently. 'You could have been mistaken.'

'But shouldn't we check it out?'

Jova smiles. 'Tommy, is it?' Tommy nods, tries to swallow. 'I applaud your compassion. It's truly something. But you must understand, while it is possible that the dead may harbour some traces of humanity, there are thousands of them. They are not all like your Optimus Prime, are they?'

'Not to mention the newly infected,' Ash adds.

Tommy makes himself speak up. 'But Optimus – he helped me. He saved me! I know he did. I was there.' Tears are building up, but he can't bear the thought of crying in front of Jova and he smothers the sob. 'It might take time, but what if we could find a way to live with them?'

'Tommy, time is what we don't have,' Jova's eyes seem to pierce his soul. 'And Ash is right. You were in Montecasino; you saw the devastation just one of the newly infected can wreak. They cannot be reasoned with; they cannot be stopped. Do you want to take that chance? The chance that you were mistaken about this ... Optimus and risk your loved ones being infected?'

Of course Tommy knows what hatchlings can do. How could he not? He's seen it first-hand, up close. Was right there when Jacob sacrificed himself. But ... he knows in his heart that Jova is wrong. That there *is* a spark of humanity left in the dead. Or at least in one of the dead. But is it worth the risk? What if Optimus is just an anomaly? The only one who's managed to hold onto his humanity? And Ginger's right. He *might* have been mistaken about that teacher. He thinks about Olivia and Baby Nomsa. Imagines putting them at risk. He can't.

'Tommy,' Jova says. 'There will always be a place for you in the AOL. You have proved your worth. We would be proud to have you.'

How often has Tommy dreamt of this very conversation? A hundred times? A thousand? So why now does it make him feel so hollow?

'Thank you, sir,' Tommy manages to murmur, shaking Jova's outstretched hand. 'I won't take up any more of your time.'

Tommy turns away. Barely feels the sharp elbows of the jostling people outside the doors. He walks on leaden legs towards the sunlight. The preparations for the evening's celebration are underway, and Tommy should really be getting back to Olivia.

'Tommy. Hold up, mate!' he hears Ginger shouting.

He waits for Ginger to catch up to him. 'Sorry about that, Tommy, but you saw what those hatchlings can do.'

'I know.'

'I'm sure your Rotter mate will be fine.'

'Will he, though? We don't even know what Jova's planning.'

'It won't be long till we find out, will it? Tommy ... I been thinking. I know how much you want to join Jova's army and all, and I know you have your family here, but after this is all over, me and the other Mall Rats will be heading back to Cape Town. Would you like to come with us?'

'*Me?* Why?'

'Thought you might like to see it for yourself. Be there when we liberate that city too.'

Tommy doesn't know what to say at first, feels his mouth dropping open stupidly. But now that Olivia has Senyaka back … It's not that he thinks he'd be a spare wheel, but she has someone to look out for her now, even if that someone isn't exactly who Tommy would have chosen for her. And imagine, travelling through the country like Ginger and the others did in his stories. It would be a real adventure.

'Yeah, Ginger. I'd like that.'

'Awesome.'

Tommy feels as if his heart has been ripped out and replaced with shattered glass, but he makes himself smile up at Ginger.

He's made his choice. There's nothing he can do for Optimus now.

Saint

Parts of the road that leads into the valley have fallen away, leaving steep, crumbling sides that drop down into yawning chasms. At one stage Saint has to gather Bambi into her arms, press her back against the side of a cliff to traverse around a pothole that could swallow a car. She walks around a barricade made of razor wire, past angry signs reading, 'No Entry Quarantine', 'Dangerous Road, use at own risk!' and 'Danger Gevaar Ingozi Trespassers WILL be shot'.

Saint reaches out for other signs of life but can sense only the grey threads of a few Rotters, lost and lonely at the base of the valley. No animals. The occasional black thread of what she has come to recognise as a snake. Even they don't like this place.

Ntombi shivers inside her.

As day slips into night, she walks past the skeletons of motorbikes. She passes a torrent of bones; all that remains of countless bodies thrown over the side of the mountain, their skulls crushed.

The road creeps and curves.

As she – *they*, she's not alone, after all, Ntombi is alert and with her every step of the way – reach the end of the road, a cold stillness creeps into their bones. Bambi can sense it and whines. Saint reaches down, touches his head, calms him.

The Rotters moan, the wind hisses.

They pass the shell of a burned-out house, the tattered skins of tents and the cracked bodies of portable toilets. Bones in the grass.

She pulls the threads of the Rotters that are down here towards her.

What are you doing?

I want to see what they did here.

Saint probes the Rotters' last memories, burnt into their minds like photographs. People screaming as men in black uniforms cut them open, looking for signs of the infection. Rotters burnt alive to see how long they will survive. Rotters tied down and drenched in water that won't stop coming.

What were they doing here? Ntombi sobs.

Experiments. They were looking for answers. Trying to discover what the Rotters are.

Why here?

But Saint can see why. It's remote, cut off, but self-sufficient, with water and food, an old community that had managed to exist for decades without help from the outside world. They thought they'd be safe here, that they could do what they wanted undisturbed.

Ntombi flexes again, ripples of disgust bubbling through her.

The atmosphere of pain and suffering hangs heavy over the place, a heady yellow glow. Army trucks. Barricades. Blood. Desperation. The images come quick and fast.

Stop it now, Saint. I don't want to see any more.

Saint breaks the threads between her and the Rotters. She sits cross-legged in the grass. Bambi crawls into her lap. She travels to Atang. Today there is no board game waiting for her. Today he looks serious. Ntombi slips in behind her.

<why are we here?> Saint asks.

<so you can see what they are capable of>

<I've always known people are capable of cruelty>

<it is worse than that>

<then why save them in the first place?>

<because we could>

He sends her another image. An image of a group of robed figures. There's a word for what they are, one that she can feel Ntombi searching for. *Environmentalists*. The ones the Resurrectionists in Cape Town call the Guardians, ones that are different from the Rotters, different from the darkness. Ones who wanted to stop the whole of the population becoming like the Rotters and tried to save as many as they could.

<why are some of us immune?>

<to see what you would do with the power. a test>

<what kind of test?>

<to see what you would do. to see how you would treat them>

<they attack us. we have to protect ourselves against them to survive>

<did you even try another way?>

<this test. how did we do?>

<you failed as we knew you would.>

<where is Ripley?>

<later>

<I need to know>

The lure of the darkness and the peace it promises is stronger than ever, and this time Atang allows her to detect a trace of silvery dancing threads. One of them, she knows, is Ripley's. Another reminder that if she jettisons Ntombi, she'll be at one with the darkness and all of this turmoil will be over. <why am I like this? Why am I not like the Rotters? Why do you want me?>

<you'll be the next wave. one of the survivors. evolution> And then, <look>

Ntombi gasps as Saint's mind is flooded with an image of hundreds and thousands of Rotters being herded to the edge of an immense pit. She hears a chorus of plaintive moans as men and women dressed in green uniforms use hoses attached to a cylindrical truck to pour liquid over them. There's a whoof as the liquid is set alight.

The image dies abruptly, replaced with that scene of the devastated, snow and ice-covered world, a raging blackened sky above it.

<what does this mean?> Saint asks.

But Ntombi understands. *If people destroy the Rotters, wipe them out, then we're all screwed. We have to tell them not to, Saint. We have to put it right.*

You saw what they did here, Ntombi. You saw what they did in Cape Town.

But what about our friends? What about Lele? What about Ember? What about Ash? What about Ginger?

What about them? If I let go, if I let go of *you*, I can be with Ripley.

No, you can't. It's too late for that. And you need me, Saint.

Do I?

Yes. Because I'm you.

Saint looks at her brother. As usual, she can't read his

323

face. Because he isn't really her brother after all. He's just the darkness.

Can we save them? Our friends?

Atang does not answer.

Can we save them? Saint asks, although she's not yet sure if she *wants* to save them. Still, she allows Ntombi to join her voice to hers to ask one last time.

CAN WE SAVE THEM?

And then Atang shows her a final image.

The high walls of the Cape Town City Enclave.

Home, Ntombi whispers.

It's burning.

Lele

I try to catch Busi's eye – we've ended up standing only a few metres from each other – but either she hasn't spotted me in the crowd or she's deliberately dodging my gaze.

The first thing I did when I arrived in Sandtown after the journey from Coom's place was try and track her down. I even enlisted Tommy's help, and Olivia, his mother, personally escorted me to Busi's sister's quarters. But Busi either wasn't there or wasn't answering. I can't really blame her for avoiding me – the thought of me must take her straight back to that terrible moment when I was forced to end Sihle's life. Maybe in time she'll forgive me; she must know in her heart I had no alternative.

Not that she'll have long to do so. As soon as Jova's announcement is over, I'm out of here. Back to Cape Town. Back to Jobe. Leaving all of this behind me.

The crowd shifts as if it's taking a collective breath and next to me, Ginger places a hand on Ember's shoulder. She shifts in the chair that Ginger sourced for her – she's getting stronger every day, but she can't stand for too long without becoming exhausted – and smiles up at him. I'm hit with a spark of envy. It's unlikely that that I'll ever get the chance to experience the special connection that Ginger and Ember share. Not now. How long before everyone knows? Before they *all* find out I'm pregnant?

Ash is the only one I've told, and I know why I blurted it out to him. I wanted to hurt him, lash out and make him pay for choosing Jova over me and Ginger and Ember. For insisting we leave Cape Town in the first place. For shutting me out. For just being *him*.

'Bloody hell, but it's hot,' Ginger gripes, wiping beads of sweat from his brow.

Most of the people here are blind drunk, only managing to stay upright because the throng is so tightly packed there's no room to fall. The relentless heat is starting to make me feel dizzy and sick. It doesn't help that for the past hour I've been subjected to the stench of sweat, sour breath and vomit from those who can't hold their drink.

'Jova!' A man slurs at the top of his voice. 'One zombie, one bullet! Amandla! Amandla!'

There's a sudden hush. It's impossible to see the stage over the crammed bodies, but Ember gets to her feet, and indicates that I should stand on her chair while Ginger puts an arm around her to steady her. A woman wearing a colourful headdress, who I assume must be Sindiwe, the only one of the amaKlevas prepared to bargain with Jova and the Outcasts, steps up on the stage. She's looking cowed, unsure of herself. There's a chorus of booing which instantly morphs into cheering as Jova joins her and Ash and Morgan take their places behind him. He pushes his glasses back on his nose and raises a hand for silence.

'Thank you. I know you are all waiting to hear what I have to say. I know you have been waiting many months for this. And I thank you for your patience.'

Another cheer, another chant: 'Jova! Jova! Jova!'

Jova waits patiently for it to die down.

'I will now tell you what is going to happen.'

'You're going to take us out of here!' a woman screeches. 'Then burn the dead!'

'No,' Jova says. 'I'm going to take the *dead* out of Jozi.'

There's a ripple of laughter and Sindiwe shakes her head. 'And tell us, Jova, how are you going to do that?'

'There is only one way.'

'And?'

'We need a Guardian. One of the robed protectors, those who have the ability to control the dead.'

A stunned second of pure silence. Then an instant eruption of roaring and shouting. Jova holds up a hand and the throng ripples into uneasy silence.

'We need a Guardian who will do what we want. Who will lead the dead away from our walls and take them to a place where they can be destroyed so that we can reclaim the city. I have a number of locations for this – the old mine dumps in the south, for example. We have collected and maintained hundreds of vehicles for this purpose.'

Sindiwe clears her throat. 'Jova ... this is madness. How do you mean to accomplish this? It was you, was it not, who wiped out the robed ones in the first place? It was you who convinced us that they were our enemies.' She says this waspishly but with the practised ease of a speaker who knows she will receive a warm response from her audience. She's not disappointed.

Once more, Jova calls for quiet. I reach over and take

327

Ginger's hand. I know his eyes are focussed, like mine, on Ash, who is standing in the shadow cast by that huge statue of Nelson Mandela.

'I will tell you,' Jova says. 'There is one among us who has volunteered to become a Guardian. One among us who is prepared to make the ultimate sacrifice for the greater good. Someone among us who has the power within him to exact the change we need to set us free, while remaining loyal to our cause.'

I realise I'm squeezing Ginger's hand so tightly my fingers are hurting. There's a low, sick throb starting deep in my belly. I know what's coming next, but I don't want to believe it.

'And who is this?' Sindiwe asks.

'Jack,' Jova says, pulling a pistol out of his belt. 'Please step forward.'

The scream rips out of my throat. 'No!' I jump off the chair and push through the packed bodies in front of me. No one tries to stop me. A path is cleared so that I can make my way to the front of the stage unimpeded, as if the absolute horror I'm feeling might be contagious. The crowd is now so silent I can hear the throb of my pulse in my ears. 'Ash!'

Ash steps closer to Jova. 'It's the only way, Lele. First here, then Cape Town. Don't you understand?'

'You mustn't do this, Ash!'

I can hear Ginger panting up behind me. 'Ash!' Ginger shouts. 'We've got to get back home. What about your sister? What about Sasha?'

The bland smile on Ash's face falters. 'My name is Jack,' he says.

'Please, Morgan,' I say to the only person I suspect may be able to stop this. 'Do something.'

Her expression doesn't shift a millimetre.

'You more than anyone know why I have to do this, Lele,' Ash says.

And it hits me. He means because I'm pregnant. Hadn't I said I was scared of bringing a child into a screwed-up world like this? 'Ash. Listen, I didn't mean it, the baby—'

'You know the truth more than any of us, Lele,' Ash says.

'What truth?' I hear myself croak. 'What are you talking about?'

'When you die, you will live.' Ash holds his hand out for the gun.

HUNGRY FOR MORE?

Enter the DEADLANDS, where life is a lottery...

'Fantastic! Teen-fighting Zombie-fun. **The Hunger Games** meets **The Walking Dead.**'

LAUREN BEUKES, author of THE SHINING GIRLS

'Riveting plotlines, nail-biting-tear-jerking-heart-pumping moments which seem to jump out at you every few chapters... Go buy yourself a copy – that's an order!'

GUARDIAN

'Enjoyably fresh pacey prose packed with cliffhangers.'

SFX

EVERYTHING'S BETTER WITH ZOMBIES -NOT

@herne13 @muchinlittle www.constablerobinson.com

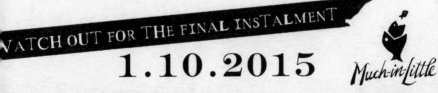

Much-in-Little